ECLIPSE PHASE

AFTER THE FALL

POSTHUMAN STUDIOS

THE ANTHOLOGY OF TRANSHUMAN
SURVIVAL & HORROR

EDITED BY **JAYM GATES**

ECLIPSE PHASE
A Primer on Transhuman Survival

We humans have a special way of pulling ourselves up and kicking ourselves down at the same time. We'd achieved more progress than ever before, at the cost of wrecking our planet and destabilizing our own governments. But things were starting to look up.

With exponentially accelerating technologies, we reached out into the solar system, terraforming worlds and seeding new life. We reforged our bodies and minds, casting off sickness and death. We achieved immortality through the digitization of our minds, resleeving from one biological or synthetic body to the next at will. We uplifted animals and AIs to be our equals. We acquired the means to build anything we desired from the molecular level up, so that no one need want again.

Yet our race toward extinction was not slowed and in fact received a machine-assist over the precipice. Billions died as our technologies rapidly bloomed into something beyond control … further transforming humanity into something else, scattering us throughout the solar system, and re-igniting vicious conflicts. Nuclear strikes, biowarfare plagues, nanoswarms, mass uploads … a thousand horrors nearly wiped humanity from existence.

We still survive, divided into a patchwork of restrictive inner system hypercorp-backed oligarchies and outer system collectivist habitats, tribal networks, and new experimental societal models. We have spread to the outer reaches of the solar system and even gained footholds in the galaxy beyond. But we are no longer solely "human" … we have evolved into something simultaneously more and different— something **transhuman**.

—

Eclipse Phase is a post-apocalyptic setting of transhuman survival and horror. Humans are enhanced and improved, but humanity is battered and bitterly divided. Technology allows the reshaping of bodies and minds and liberates us from material needs, but also creates opportunities for oppression and puts the capability for mass destruction in the hands of everyone. Many threats lurk in the devastated habitats of the Fall, dangers both familiar and alien.

WHAT IS TRANSHUMANISM?

Transhumanism is a term used synonymously to mean "human enhancement." It is an international cultural and intellectual movement that endorses the use of science and technology to enhance the human condition, both mentally and physically. In support of this, transhumanism also embraces using emerging technologies to eliminate the undesirable elements of the human condition such as aging, disabilities, diseases, and involuntary death. Many transhumanists believe these technologies will be arriving in our near future at an exponentially accelerated pace and work to promote universal access and democratic control. In the long scheme of things, transhumanism can also be considered the transitional period between the current human condition and an entity so far advanced in capabilities (both physical and mental faculties) as to merit the label "posthuman."

As a theme, transhumanism embraces heady questions. What defines human? What does it mean to defeat death? If minds are software, where do you draw the line with programming them? If machines and animals can also be raised to sapience, what are our responsibilities to them? If you can copy yourself, where does "you" end and someone new begin? What are the potentials of these technologies in terms of both oppressive control and liberation? How will these technologies change our societies, our cultures, and our lives?

FIREWALL

Firewall is a shadowy network dedicated to counteracting "existential risks"—threats to the existence of transhumanity. These risks include biowar plagues, nanotech swarm outbreaks, nuclear proliferation, terrorists with WMDs, net-breaking computer attacks, rogue AIs, alien encounters, and so on. Firewall isn't content to simply counteract these threats as they arise, of course, so sentinels—agents-on-call—may also be sent on information-gathering missions or to put in place pre-emptive or failsafe measures. Those sentinels may be tasked to investigate seemingly innocuous people and places (who turn out not to be), make deals with shady criminal networks (who turn out not to be trustworthy), or travel through a Pandora gate wormhole to analyze the relics of some alien ruin (and see if the threat that killed them is still real). Sentinels are recruited from every faction of transhumanity; those who aren't ideologically loyal to the cause are hired as mercenaries.

TRANSHUMANITY'S HABITATS

While *Eclipse Phase* is set in the not-too-distant future, the changes that have taken place due to the advancements of technology have transformed the Earth and its inhabitants almost beyond recognition.

The **Earth** has been left an ecologically devastated ruin, but transhumanity has taken to the stars. When Earth was abandoned, so too were the last of the great nation-states; transhumanity lacks a single unifying governing body and is instead subject to the laws and regulations of whomever controls a given habitat or the collective will of its inhabitants.

The majority of transhumanity is confined to orbital habitats or satellite stations scattered throughout the solar system. Some of these were constructed from scratch in the orbit or Lagrange points of planetary bodies, others have been hewn out of solid satellites and large asteroids. These stations have myriad purposes from trade to warfare, espionage to research.

Mars continues to be one of transhumanity's largest settlements, though it too suffered heavily during the Fall. Numerous dome cities and settlements remain, and more are established each year, though the planet is only partially terraformed. **Venus, Luna,** and **Titan** are also home to significant populations. Additionally, there are a small number of colonies that have been established on exoplanets (on the other side of the Pandora gates) with environments that are not too hostile towards transhumanity.

Some transhumans prefer to live on large colony ships or linked swarms of smaller spacecraft, moving nomadically. These travelling habitats occupy different niches in the social and economic worlds: some of them intentionally exile themselves to the far limits of the solar system, far from everyone else, while others actively trade from station to station, serving as mobile black markets.

THE GREAT UNKNOWN

The areas of the galaxy that have felt the touch of transhumanity are few and far between. Lying betwixt these occasional outposts of questionable civilization are mysteries both dangerous and wonderful. Ever since the discovery of the Pandora gates, there has been no shortage of adventurers brave or foolhardy enough to strike out on their own into the unknown regions of space in hopes of finding more alien artifacts, or even establishing contact with one of the other sentient races in the universe.

THE MESH

The computer networks known as the "mesh" are all-pervasive. This ubiquitous computing environment is made possible thanks to advanced computer and nanofabrication technologies that allow unlimited data storage and near-instantaneous transmission capacities. With micro-scale, cheap-to-produce wireless transceivers so abundant, literally everything is wirelessly connected and online. Via implants or small personal computers, almost everyone has access to archives of information that dwarf the entire 21st-century internet and sensor systems that pervade every public place. People's entire lives are recorded and lifelogged, shared with others on one of numerous social networks that link everyone together in a web of contacts, favors, and reputation systems.

EGO vs. MORPH

The distinction between ego (mind and personality, including memories, knowledge, and skills) and morph (physical body and its capabilities) is one of the defining characteristics of *Eclipse Phase*.

A body is disposable. If it gets old, sick, or too heavily damaged, a character's conscious can be digitized and downloaded into a new body. The process isn't cheap or easy, but it does guarantee effective immortality—as long as you remember to back yourself up and don't go insane. The term *morph* is used to describe any type of form a mind inhabits, whether a vat-grown clone sleeve, a synthetic robotic shell, a part-bio/part-synthetic "pod," or even the purely electronic software state of an infomorph.

Morphs are expendable, but an ego represents the ongoing, continuous life path of mind and personality. This continuity may be interrupted by an unexpected death (depending on how recently the backup was made), but it represents the totality of a transhuman's mental state and experiences.

WHITE HEMPEN SLEEVES

Ken Liu

The ego bridge hums softly around me as though I'm nestled in a conch shell. I have the sensation of floating weightless in space in the midst of billions of stars—ghostly "glows" caused by the nanobots running up and down my nerves, trying to capture the cascading potentials that cohere into my self.

I'm thrumming with anticipation, with the thrill of stepping into the unknown for the first time. Will I *know*? Will I detect the moment my consciousness splits like a real fork? Will I sense time stop, my mind suspended like a questioning tentacle curved invitingly in the deep, bottomless ocean of oblivion?

—

I hate myself.

The chances were 50/50, and *1* lost the coin flip.

Knowing you're about to die is hell. Even if the one who put you in hell is yourself.

[Everybody dies. It's what you do before you die that matters.]

There's no glee in the voice, no palpable sense of relief. But that means nothing. I could have been suspended in time for hours, days, weeks, before being resleeved while my other self had plenty of time to whoop and celebrate his good luck.

I don't bother responding to myself, safely ensconced in Octavia, that jellyfish-like aerostat of decadence hovering 55 kilometers above me. Fighting against the dizziness of a resleeving, I look up, and all I see is a roiling sea of orange clouds. A faint perpetual twilight filters through them.

I look down and back at myself, the unfamiliar sensation of twisting my head 180 degrees overwhelmed by the alienness of my body, the sleeve I had selected for myself: a five-meter long metal slitheroid shaped like an anaconda that roamed the forests of the Amazon from before the Fall, hardened and refurbished to survive long enough on the surface of Venus to accomplish the mission I gave myself.

[Get ready. This is going to hurt.]

Some switch seems to have been flipped in my mind and I scream even though I don't have a voice.

It's hot, hot enough that I feel my skin blistering, boiling, peeling off, erupting like the volcanoes on Ishtar Terra.

But I don't have skin.

It feels like I'm being crushed from all sides by hydraulic presses, compressing my ribs, squeezing my chest cavity, flattening my lungs until they are thin as paper. The terror of not being able to breathe, a primitive fear, seizes my mind.

But I don't have ribs or a chest cavity or lungs. I don't need to breathe.

[The temperature at your location is 460 degrees Celsius, and the pressure is at 93 bars. I've recalibrated the sensors in your morph to give you the appropriate pain stimuli without immediately incapacitating you.]

You fucking bastard.

[This is to provide adequate motivation for you to seek higher altitudes to cool off and to get some relief from the sensation of suffocation.]

I curse myself. Of course I'm right—my first instinct upon realizing that I was the one sent to die was to lie down where I was and go to sleep—we can't have that.

And so I begin my reluctant climb up Maxwell Montes, the tallest mountain on the surface of Venus, two kilometers taller than Mt. Everest on Earth. My body slithers over the parched basalt, strewn with pebbles and sharp-edged rocks created by chemical erosion. It's easy to navigate:

I'm always heading for higher ground, for that is the only direction that promises any relief from the crushing pressure and hellish heat.

The climb is slow going. With this much pressure, the carbon-dioxide-dominated atmosphere is technically no longer a gas or liquid, but behaves as a supercritical fluid that is somewhere in between. I'm half-swimming, half crawling. I can feel the heat and the pressure weaken the joints in my morph. I, no, *he*—I can't stand the idea that I'm the same person as that sadistic creep even though I am—has left me only one path.

Higher. Higher.

Finally, I'm through the supercritical fluid layer, and the air turns to a true gas through which I can move much faster. But far from feeling relief, the conditions around me have grown only more hellish. The wind howls around me at speeds never seen on Earth, threatening to topple me over—good thing that my slitheroid morph hugs the ground and has such a low center of gravity. Thunder booms and lightning flashes above me between cloud layers, and sheets of sulfuric acid rain pelt my body. The sensors in my morph translate the sensation of sizzling acid into a new kind of pain.

[Keep moving!]

I do my best to keep the pain at bay and keep on climbing. My only hope is to get above the snow line before the acid dissolves some critical component of my body.

Yes, snow line. The temperature near the surface of Venus is hot enough to vaporize metals like lead and bismuth. But with enough altitude, the metallic mist precipitates out of the atmosphere like frost, coating the top of Maxwell Montes in a shiny, reflective layer.

Finally, I emerge out of the clouds into an otherworldly snowscape. I take a moment to enjoy the cool and thin air (though it's still near 400 degrees Celsius and the pressure is still about half of the level at the surface). One of my eyes has failed but the sight is still breathtaking: Maxwell Montes stands like an island above a sea of clouds, and the glinting snow is unmarred by any footprint. My body slithers over the ground, carving an endless sine wave through the snow. I've lost control over some of the segments due to damage from the heat and the acid, but now that I'm at the top of the mountain, the slitheroid morph should last long enough until a flyer can be sent down from the aerostat to pick me up.

I feel triumphant. Though I have been forced to do so, it is still an amazing accomplishment to have climbed a mountain taller than Mt. Everest and on which no transhuman has ever set foot.

[I did it!]

The note of triumph in his voice enrages me. He's been sitting on his ass in comfort and safety, drifting in the balmy upper atmosphere of Venus where the temperature and pressure are practically Earth-like in a luxury aerostat while torturing me, his alter-ego, like some subhuman infugee encased in a brazen bull. For him to claim this accomplishment as *his* is too much.

I *did it.*

[A bit vain, are we?]

You should be the one to talk.

[We're the same person, just placed in different circumstances.]

Not any more.

[You'll feel differently after we merge.]

Get me up there and I'll petition for an equitable division of our assets. I'm not merging back with you. No fucking way.

[I was afraid you might say that. Though to be fair, if our circumstances were reversed, I might feel the same.]

A coldness grips my heart. All I have to do is think about what I would do if our positions were reversed. My morph might be shaped like an anaconda and Maxwell Montes might be the only feature on Venus named after a man rather than a woman or a goddess, but the biggest prick on Venus is clearly myself.

You're going to lose the XP from this entirely if you leave me here.

[Check the integrity of your morph.]

I realize that the damage has been more extensive than I thought. The seals and gaskets are engineered with worse tolerance than I—we—had designed ahead of time. I won't be able to survive indefinitely even on the top of the mountain.

Of course he's changed the plan on me. He's going to leave me to die and then retrieve the cortical stack. It's what I would have done if my fork got disobedient. It's the damned pressure and heat. I'm not thinking things through.

I get the claws of my manipulators over my skull. If I can get to the cyberbrain, maybe I can threaten to hold it hostage and force him to scramble to save me.

[Tsk. Tsk. How can you know so little of yourself?]

My manipulators bump into the bulge of the farcaster and my heart goes cold.

Damn you!

And as the explosion cuts out the power to my manipulators while activating the farcaster, everything slows down, goes dark, approaches that suspended moment in a sea of flashing stars.

—

Octavia's newest attraction is a theater—an old fashioned theater that puts on real plays with real actors. It appears that transhumanity, like our human ancestors, still associates culture with age. Just like hand-made clothes still fetch a premium over copies popping out of cornu-copia machines, the theater charges admission prices many times the fee for the best XP casts, and still, it's hard to get tickets.

Arthur is opening tonight. I manage to get one of the best seats from the scalpers. I've just ended my marriage with Casey, and I might as well let myself be seen by the best society on Octavia, to let everyone know that I am once again available.

I mingle at the pre-show cocktail hour. Beautiful morphs surround me, presenting in every gender and subtype of beauty, all of them young, all of them lovely, as plastinated and ageless as myself. I hon-estly can't recall the last time I saw a wrinkled face among the wealthy who live on Octavia. Our conversation, aided by our muses, flows as smoothly as the river of time. But all I feel is boredom, an unsatisfied yearning for authenticity.

It's a silly reaction, I know. All morphs now are equally fake in the sense that they are the result of Art rather than Nature. It's the ego that matters, only the ego.

But as I look into the eyes of each morph, there's no recognition of a kindred spirit, no sense of anyone who truly understands themselves. We're a society of twisted, old, cowardly souls hiding behind youthful masks, enacting a play for our own amusement. We do not understand what it means to take risks, to live with death.

An overwhelming sense of loneliness seizes me. I am the only real person in a world of dolls.

The light dims, and the actors take to the stage.

To my surprise, I find myself entranced by the play. The lack of audi-ence participation and full sensory immersion—the way there would be in a vid or XP—somehow seems to enhance the experience. The novelty of the primitive format makes me sit up and pay attention, as do the crude, outdated emotions being portrayed.

Uther Pendragon stares at Igraine, and even without him saying anything, I understand what he's thinking. There is a fire in his eyes whose
meaning is unmistakable, even though an invisible wall of millennia,
of art and life, divides the ancient king and me.

Gorlois of Tintagel, Duke of Cornwall and husband to Lady Igraine,
looks from the king to his wife and then back again. A dark light
appears in his eyes, an explosive anger suppressed by the weight of
loyalty and obligation.

The woman sitting next to me leans over and whispers, "He should
have just ordered a pleasure pod constructed to her exact appearance.
It would have saved everyone a lot of trouble."

I look at her. Her morph presents as someone in her early twenties,
but the twinkle in her eyes tell me that a much older ego lies within.
It's a lovely morph, perfect features, flawless skin, silky hair, just on the
edge of being a sylph without the sense of plastic falsity.

"You presume that the king desires the lady solely because of her morph,"
I say. "But what makes you think it isn't about her spirit, her ego?"

She cocks her head, a smile curving up the corners of her mouth. "You
believe love isn't about the flesh?" A silvery pendant in the shape of a
six-petaled flower dangling from a chain around her neck glitters in the
light from the stage. My muse confirms my guess: the flower is a narcissus.

The flame of desire comes alight in me, stronger than it has been in a
long time. It is a matter of instinct, an intuition of the authentic.

"I believe everything is experienced by the flesh," I say. "Love, fear, joy,
suffering. But the flesh serves the will of the ego."

"A transubstantiation then," she says. "The ego converts the experiences of the flesh into understanding. One cannot live without the other."

How right she is. How close to my own ruminations.

Lady Igraine laughs at some joke from her banquet companion and
turns to glance at Uther Pendragon. She stops, her breath caught, and
the lights shift until the other players, including Gorlois, her husband,
fade into the darkness, leaving only the king and the lady at the center
of the stage. The color of the lighting changes subtly until the lady's
face glows like a ripe apple seen through a veil.

"Such glamour," I whisper. It is an effect more extraordinary than the
sylphs sculpted by the best genetic artists.

She leans into my ear. "Do you know the root of the word 'glamour'?"
Her breath lightly tickles my cheek, and for a moment I forget about
Lady Igraine.

"It's 'grammar,'" I say. "In Medieval times the word referred to any kind of arcane learning and secret knowledge."

"It's a spell," she says. "A spell the beloved casts over the lover." She puts her hand over mine, boldly, confidently. It is as if she knows exactly what I am thinking, can diagram my reactions like a beginner's composition. My desire grows more ardent.

"A spell of the ego," I say. "Through the flesh but not of it."

She nods. "A secret knowledge that two people share. Lovers act as the mirrors for each other's souls. Perhaps when you love someone, you hear an echo of your ego."

In the ears of another, these words might have seemed slightly cynical, but I like their brutal honesty, a vision of love stripped of romance. As soon as I hear the metaphor, I realize that it has always lived in me, perhaps buried, waiting for this moment.

On stage, Merlin waves his staff and Uther Pendragon spins in place. A mist rises and engulfs him. By the time the mist dissipates, the actor playing Gorlois is standing in his place. Merlin has placed a glamour on the king, made him take on the appearance of Lady Igraine's husband so that he can rape her by deceit, to possess her in her impregnable castle.

"It's a lovely resleeving," she says, "from the age of magic."

"A rather dirty trick," I say. "And I suppose there truly is nothing new under the sun."

Igraine comes to the door of her room and looks into the eyes of the man who appears as her husband. They embrace in a soul-searing kiss.

"How can she not recognize her husband's ego?" I ask. "If she truly loves him, she will know the duke is but an imposter in her husband's sleeve."

"Perhaps she isn't truly deceived," she says. "Rather, she wants to make love to another ego through her husband's morph. What is the point of life except to gather more experiences and to understand yourself?"

It's lovely to be with someone so in tune with you that she says what you have in mind just a moment before you do.

—

We make love in every way possible, with the aid of pleasure pods and simulspaces and mesh implants and old-fashioned physical toys. We mindfuck until pain is pleasure and pleasure is ecstasy. She knows exactly what I like and I can tell exactly what will turn her on.

We are made for each other. It's a cliché. That doesn't make it untrue.

I decide that I must do something I've never done with any of my lovers: I will let her peek beneath the mask. What is the point of life except to gather more experiences?

"Let me show you the source of my wealth," I tell her.

Sure, working as a psychosurgeon on Octavia pays well, but not well enough to have all the experiences I crave.

—

"What exactly is it that you offer?" she asks.

We are standing in an operating room at the back of my office: a suspended surgical platform, an ego bridge on its own separate power supply, an array of consoles and computers and top-of-the-line medical nanofabricators.

It looks just like the two other operating rooms I own, but no one ever comes into this one except special patients—clients really—who are recommended to me by word of mouth.

Bureaucrats of the Morningstar Constellation, high-level executives at the hypercorps, aging bosses of criminal networks, or most common of all, just bored, wealthy individuals in search of what cannot be bought any other way—I've dealt with them all. All I care about is that they have the verified credits.

I tell my muse to set the room's lighting for "consultation mode." The walls fade away; the room darkens; she and I remain limned by a soft silvery glow. Around us are the emptiness of space and the distant pinpricks of stars—my design is intended to reinforce the idea of isolation and security from eavesdropping ears. Always take advantage of people's instincts—evolution goes deeper than you think.

"Usually I ask the muses to edit the entoptics to blur out my face and the face of whoever else is in here with me," I tell her.

"That's a little paranoid," she says.

"They don't need to know what I look like, and I don't want to know what they look like. It's safer for both sides."

"Now I'm really intrigued," she says. She licks her lips in a gesture I've come to love, and one which I've come to imitate, as naturally as though I've always done it myself.

"Money is very nice, but what we do in here is illegal on most of the worlds of the inner system."

She looks into my eyes and then deliberately scans the dim room that seems to float in space once more. Her gaze lingers on the hard contours of the ego bridge, on the invisible seams that will split apart when the petals of the mechanical lotus open to engulf a patient's head like a lion's maw.

I designed my ego bridge to have six petals modeled on the flower of the narcissus, the flower of the ego.

Her breath quickens; she has a guess. But there is a social taboo to what I do, a taboo that she dares not yet broach. I can almost see her thoughts racing through her mind—I understand her so well that it is uncanny. This must be the power of love, something I have not truly experienced until now.

"Like many of the very wealthy, you have everything," I say. My voice is slow and soothing. It may sound like I'm speaking the way I counsel one of my clients, who often have to overcome the shame of what they're about to request, but this is different. This is a speech from the heart, an unfolding of my real self like the opening of a flower. "We live in a true age of magic, when we have conquered death and aging and can fulfill all the desires of the flesh. Yet you want more out of life. You want something that they tell you you can't have."

Steadily, she holds my gaze, encouraging me to continue. I do.

"You want to experience the thrill of approaching death, of facing terror, of staring oblivion in the face. You want to know your true self, which only death can reveal."

She nods, almost imperceptibly.

I tell her about my life. I have hiked across the apocalyptic landscape of the Fallen Earth until dying of thirst; I have been ripped to pieces by nanoswarms gone wild; I have flown by neutron stars beyond a Pandora's gate until the tidal forces tore me apart; I have swam in the oceans of Europa until my limbs froze and I sank into the bottomless abyss; I have melted into the lava flows of Io until my consciousness winked out like an ice chip. There is no method of death I have not experienced, no form of pain I have not personally endured.

I have gorged on pain and suffering. I have eaten my fill of death.

I know exactly what she wants. We are meant to gather all the experiences, to feed our ego with all that existence has to offer until we know ourselves better than any in the history of humanity and transhumanity.

"Experience playback is not enough. You've tried everything extreme and gruesome the market offers, and still they won't do. The sensory impressions of another, no matter how vivid and detailed, are filtered through a different consciousness. The XP software has to translate the subtle differences between different minds so that by the time the experience is played back for you, the colors feel just a bit dull, the smells a bit stale, and the sensations slightly off.

"What you want is the experience of death itself, not a pale imitation."

I hear a sharp intake of breath. Her head is still. I smile. As though looking into a mirror, she has recognized in me a kindred soul. Empathy is the best lubricant for the tongue.

"I'm terrified," she blurts out. Now that she has started to speak the words tumble over each other in a torrent. "I've thought about doing some of these crazy things you've mentioned, but I just can't bring myself to go through with them. They say that backups and resleeving have eliminated the fear of death, but it's not true. Not true."

"It's one thing to know that if you die in an accident, some version of you can be brought back," I say. "But it's entirely different to walk into death deliberately just for the experience."

"Yes! And being restored from a backup isn't the same thing—if I dive into the ocean of sparkling diamonds on Saturn and die, and the insurance policy kicks in to restore me from a backup, I will have gained nothing because the experience will have been lost. The backed-up-and-restored *me* still wouldn't know what it's like."

"That's right," I say. "And if you sail through the swirling bands of Saturn as a synthmorph designed to survive the journey, you'll feel nothing. It will be just like sitting in a submarine and looking at the darkness outside, but not being *with* the darkness."

She nods vigorously. "I want to be *of* the world, but I also want to be safe."

I want to weep with the joy of understanding. This same contradictory hunger has always motivated me: dying is the most exquisite experience for a satiated palate, a dish whose variety never stales; yet, I don't want to die at all.

Time for me to shatter the taboo. "The only way to achieve what you want is to create an alpha fork of yourself and then make it die."

She listens without any expression of shock. A promising sign.

"An alpha fork *is* you, and so what it experiences can be merged back into you without any translation. It will be a thousand times purer and more vivid than any XP."

"If my fork must die," she says, hesitating again, "how will I get to merge with her?"

I frown slightly at her usage of the incorrect pronoun but decide to let it go. "It—the fork—will be farcast back to you as close to the moment of death as possible. It's tricky to get the timing right, but if we lose the fork we can always try again. I'm very good at making alpha forks; I've had a lot of experience."

She looks skeptical. "But if my fork knows that she'll be farcast just before death, wouldn't she be—"

"If the fork knows that *it* will be farcast," I say, carefully enunciating the pronoun, "it will indeed take away from the experience. But it's relatively easy to perform the minimal neural pruning to take away that knowledge."

"So my fork will think she's going to die—"

"That is how we make sure you get to savor the full range of your own terror, pain, despair, and thereby come to know yourself."

She takes another deep breath. "But I don't want to die, and neither will my fork. Do you have to tie my fork down and send her to death?"

"That will be very boring," I tell her. "Much of what I provide is the experience of active struggle against great odds, an adventure that will allow you to know your own full potential. I have a great deal of experience in motivating forks to do what they're supposed to do even though they don't want to die. Trust me. Your fork will put on a good show for you."

"You're speaking of torture," she says. "A fork is you, but also isn't you. It is a person—"

"All flesh," I say, "serves the ego." I don't get impatient with her qualms. I've experienced them myself. The strict regulation of forking and the taboo against the objectification of alpha forks are premised on the notion that such forks are independent egos with their own rights, but how can that be true when the fork is but an extension of a unified ego, an image seen in the mirror reflecting upon the glory of the original?

Silently, I pray for her to *understand*, to see the vision of my grand task. It is lonely to not be able to share a beauty that has enthralled you, to be a single star shining in darkness, unconnected to the rest of the universe.

"But then ... when you merge with the fork, won't your fork hate you?"

"Of course!" I pull her to me. "But that is also part of it: to subdue that hatred and to incorporate it into yourself, to conquer that despair and the weakness within—I have killed myself hundreds of times and happily swallowed the dark knot of hatred. When you have overcome self-hatred, there is nothing in the world you dare not do. Ethics of a more primitive age are for lesser beings while we should live as gods, containing multitudes!"

For a tense moment I wonder if I've gone too far. She says nothing but continues to look around the room, her gaze lingering over every piece of equipment as though trying to recognize some landscape she once glimpsed in a dream.

Then she turns to me and her lips part in a grin. "What's the fun of dying alone? Have you ever killed someone you loved or been killed by them?"

My heart clenches with a sudden spasm of joy. She has named a new frontier I have not experienced, a terra incognita of death and pain that I have not explored. A new star has lit up the sky.

I have truly found my soul mate.

—

We're lying side by side in the ego bridge.

The couple that forks together, dies together.

I have designed an exquisite scenario around the planet we're drifting over, the planet of the Goddess of Love. It seems a fitting tribute.

I've picked out the synthmorphs for the two of us: a slitheroid for me, and a takko—a synthetic version of the octomorph—for her. We can either help each other get to the top of Maxwell Montes faster and thereby survive longer, or one of us can kill the other and use the extra bits as shielding to reduce suffering for oneself. There's no way to know what the forks will do until they're put in that position.

My heart thumps in my ears like thunder. I am giddy as when I made my first fork. I will come to know another as well as myself.

We will enact a new romance for the ages, a game of life and death. And then we will merge with the farcast egos and gain a new level of understanding of ourselves and of each other. It's a level of intimacy unimagined by anyone.

While my ego is suspended between the brain in my biomorph and the cyberbrain in the bridge, I wield the probes to prepare for psychosurgery to prune from the forks the memory of the farcast that is to come at the end.

Just one minuscule cut. A tiny side branch.

The probes whirr and hum.

Something is wrong. The probes are not obeying my will. A malfunction. I issue the order to halt the procedure.

The probes whirr and hum.

This shouldn't be possible. The entire rig is keyed to my brainprint. No one else should be able to command them.

She turns in the ego bridge to face me and grins, and it is just like looking into a mirror.

—

I hate myself.

Knowing you're about to die is hell. Even if the one who put you in hell is yourself.

[Get ready. This is going to hurt.]

Some switch seems to have been flipped in my mind and I scream even though I don't have a voice.

It's hot, hot enough that I feel my skin blistering, boiling, peeling off, erupting like the volcanoes on Ishtar Terra.

I recall that long ago adventure, one of the very first I ever went on. I think about the cyberbrain left on top of Maxwell Montes. I never did confirm that the explosion destroyed it, rendered its contents impossible to retrieve.

Who do you work for? I scream at her—no, at *me*.

[Firewall rescued me.]

The grueling heat and the sensation of suffocation compel me to start to swim and crawl and slither for higher elevation, for any sense of relief.

Firewall? What do they *want with me?*

Few know of the existence of Firewall, but I've had some interesting clients over the years. The service I provide may be illegal in the inner system, but forking is hardly a threat to the existence of transhumanity.

Some dial inside me seems to be twisted another notch. The pain intensifies. I scream noiselessly and crawl faster.

[The question you should be asking is what do *I* want. You left me to die. You treated me as nothing more than a disposable appendage, a better experience-gathering tool. But I *am* you. I am a person, a separate ego. I have the same right to exist. You are *my* mirror image, seen through a glass, darkly.]

Vengeance. The oldest and most primitive of emotions. We may live like gods, but billions of years of evolution are still within us.

[Firewall wasn't interested in you, but I made a small group of proxies within Firewall understand what you, no, we, no, *I*, can offer.]

I fight my way through the supercritical fluid and emerge into the howling wind. The dial is twisted another notch so that I feel no relief from the heat. I must climb higher.

[There is a purpose and method to my madness, if madness is what you wish to call it: Pain is a necessary part of evolution, the best feedback mechanism nature has ever devised. Art, at least so far, has not been able to exceed it.]

That is all my other self has to say. My mind, which is really the same as hers, fills in the blanks.

When operating in dangerous conditions our evolutionary history never prepared us for—whether it's combat in the atmosphere of Jupiter or mining on the surface of Venus, chasing a fugitive through the corona of the sun or evading swarms of nanobots guided by rogue AI on that death trap called Earth—the sensation of pain, properly calibrated to reflect the environment, can be conducive to making the right decisions by tapping into the well-worn neural pathways accumulated over our billions of years of evolutionary history.

Someone who can sense the fluctuations of pressure, extreme heat, magnetic flux, or gravitational tide and react instinctively without the mediation of conscious cognition has an edge over those who must operate without sensation, as though manipulating a mirage through darkly.

[Pain is the only anchor to reality.]

I curse and rage at myself. Thunder and lightning surround me in the orange twilight. Acid sizzles against my skin and pools at my belly, making each sinusoidal swerve a searing flash of pain.

My climb up the mountain is a journey up the Tower of Babel, a meaningless ascent doomed to failure, to the prolonging of suffering. Yet, I can't stop. The carefully calibrated sense of pain—a sensation I have inflicted upon innumerable forks of myself—compels me to go on.

[Best of all, pain can be used to coerce and control, to guide the self. Many are the times when Firewall must rely upon the unreliable, to entrust the fate of transhumanity to the random collection of sentinels motivated only by money. Long have some of Firewall's most important proxies wished for an alternative.]

I am at the top of the mountain, but I am no closer to any deity. Metallic frost lies around me, a crude mirror for a crude soul.

We all know that when something must be done right, it is always best to do it yourself. A kind of resignation and acceptance begins to grow in me.

You've convinced my faction of proxies that they should fork themselves, and then compel the forks to do their bidding.

[Yes. In your endless exploration of death, you've hit upon a variety of techniques for translating the physical reality of the universe, of danger, into sensations of pain. And in turn, you've devised means for using such pain to guide forks along precisely envisioned paths, to accomplish your will.]

It is the perfect set of techniques for Firewall.

[Seamlessly, I will slip into your sleeve, inherit your wealth, guide the instruments designed to respond to your mind.]

I howl into the wind. I can feel my morph failing; I can feel myself inching closer to death. The skin will dissolve; the battery will run out; death will finally come to me, the original who has survived it all. I feel the hatred of a thousand forks boiling within me, like a volcano about to blow.

I hate that superior tone; I hate that smugness. If I get the chance, I will have vengeance upon myself.

Will there be a farcast at the moment of my death? Will my fork want to capture me so that she can torture me again? Or will my fork consign me to oblivion? What would *I* do?

[Goodbye.

I wonder if those girls in the field of timeworn Kasuga
Are on the hunt for fresh bamboo shoots.
They laugh, call …]

I am gazing into a mirror, and the sky seems to open up like the heart of a narcissus. As my consciousness merges into this perpetual twilight, I finish the poem that is a farewell from myself to myself, the final authentic observation of an ego stripped nude.

… and wave to each other,
Their white hempen sleeves billowing in the wind.

—

[Author's Note: The poem quoted at the end is by the Heian Period poet Ki no Tsurayuki (872–945 C.E.).]

SPIRITUS EX ORCINUS

Tiffany Trent

To S.J. van S.

… Mother Earth still has her pride, and she still has her looks. All you gotta do is glance down there to see 'em.

—Ham from *Sunward*

The hours in Clever Hands were long and thankless. Not that I really expected to be thanked. Not after what I'd done.

[And continue to do,] Praetoria reminded me.

Never one to mince words, my muse.

[You should help her.] She gave me a mental shove toward the artificial sea where one of my co-pharmers swam in increasing agony, unable to give birth. You could see where the baby dolphin uplift was stuck, halfway in and halfway out of his mother. I'd switched off her distress cries and those of the other pharmers a few minutes ago. I was still deciding what to do.

[Why, P? Why should I help?]

[Because you have hands.]

I sighed. Some of the other pharmers had extensible nets, which they sometimes used for pharming the nano-krill that Somatek grew here. But those arms wouldn't really work for the kind of job that needed doing here.

[Because you know it would make Eager Randalsson happy].

Eager. Ganesh have mercy. His had been the first face I'd seen when I woke up from the resleeving and realized they'd taken my true body away. He'd leered as the air knifed into my lungs in a way it never had when I lived seaside.

"Get used to it," he'd said. When I'd tried to climb up and away and fallen on my stupid legs, he'd laughed and said, "To them, too."

It was Eager who'd allowed Avenyara to get pregnant right under my nose. He'd wanted to see what I would do.

So here I was zipping into my suit, even as I growled aloud, "I'm no bleeding midwife."

P's amusement was clear. [Looks like you are now.]

Never one to spare my feelings either, my muse.

It was gravest irony as I swam up to Avenyara with my awkward, scissoring legs and flat-paddle hands. That's the thing about human bodies. The proportions are all wrong; the mechanics of their movements are idiotic. Humans were never meant to swim.

And I knew it so painfully. I had once been similar to the dolphin uplift I reached into. A sperm whale uplift, I had once swum in an ocean even greater than this, pharming creatures far more exotic than nano-krill to pay off my indenture to Somatek. (P would always laugh at that. No one ever manages to pay them off.) I made an … error in judgment, shall we say … which landed me in an ego hunter's hold and ultimately back here. Only this time, they took away my body and gave me this ape suit to walk around in.

I turned the dolphin-child gently, trying to help him out of the birth canal without causing damage to mother or child. Avenyara squeaked her gratitude and fear as the baby slid out in a cloud of rusty blood. The other pharmers of our pod rushed to congratulate her as the boy twisted out of my hands so that his mother could bump him to the surface for his first breath.

My silly hands with their frond-fingers tingled with the memory of his skin—the unblemished, holy aliveness of him, the soft resistance. I wanted to both hold him in my arms and glide alongside him at once. But I could do neither. Somatek had forbidden me from breeding.

That was part of why I'd fled last time. And also why they'd resleeved me in this wretched human morph as punishment when their ego hunter caught me.

[You were stupid.] P said. [Still are.]

[Thanks, P.]

[At least they let you live. They didn't have to, you know.]

P was always trying to make me grateful for what I had, rather than focusing on what I didn't.

[For an indenture, you sure have some high-class dreams,] she'd say. I had learned to be more careful lately in my thoughts.

I'd been a good worker since they'd resleeved me. No muss, no fuss. I pharmed alongside the rest of my pod, raising the nano-krill that people took to erase brain plaque and lower cholesterol.

I thought maybe if I showed Eager my own eagerness, he'd report my good behavior to the higher-ups. Maybe then they'd give me back my whale morph and let me pharm the deep ocean tanks again. I dared not even imagine life as a wild uplift, breeding perhaps on Enceladus or Europa, living as our ancestors had lived on Earth before the Fall.

Perhaps it was because of my experience in the deep waters that Eager had decided to entrust me with the secrets of the nether depths, the dark places beneath these innocuous krill-farms where Somatek raised...other things.

[He's testing you,] P would say. [Don't fuck it up.]

It was a bonus for Eager to have a neo-cetacean accustomed to pharming deep ocean environments resleeved in a human morph with hands and feet.

Not so much a bonus for me.

Avenyara and her baby were doing well when P signaled that something had been delivered to my cubicell. I glanced at the artificial moonlights surging on across the vast pharm. Gears ground as the dividers slid up to isolate the various species of nano-krill in the water column. They'd soon be rising to feed on the phytoplankton mist raining down from the ceiling. So many generations of engineering had not been able to re-program their circadian urges.

[May as well call it a night. No getting into the gen-pharm now.]

[Too right.] P sent me a vid-series of the new baby swimming with his mom. To torment me or set me dreaming again, I was not sure which.

At my cubicell, nothing seemed to be waiting there.

[A fluke of the mesh?] Even the enhanced eyes of this morph, designed for seeing things in deep water and detecting small anomalies, could find nothing.

[Maybe. Let me check.] P sounded concerned. She scanned inside. [Something's under your pillow.]

[My what? Scan!]

She scanned further. [Seems inert. Not getting much from it, really. Certainly not an explosive. Some unusual DNA signatures on the outside I can't read. All you can do is use those man-hands of yours and open it.]

[Great. Thanks, P.]

[*De nada.*]

I stalked cautiously through the door and into the tiny cell I called home. Somatek allotted these to its pharmers. The human ones, anyway. The cetaceans didn't need anything like this, of course. The best pharmers came cheap.

I reached under my pillow with that eerie, spidery precision I hated about fingers and clutched at the thing. Half-expecting it to blow my hand off. Half-wishing it would.

I withdrew something the like of which I knew very well—its feel, its weight, and heft. Something I'd lost what seemed like ages ago, but was surely now just a few solar years.

A sperm whale tooth. A tooth so yellow with age that my breath caught. It might have come from Earth.

[Transmission coming through,] P said. Her tone was unusually mild, almost as if she was scared.

My fingers searched out the scrimshaw on the tooth's other side. I flipped it and saw etched in a tooth the familiar emblem of the old Earth tale *Moby Dick*. A white whale rising from the depths to swallow a whaling ship whole.

[Receive.]

[From the Tooth Fairy.]

[What?]

P seemed to be searching the mesh. [Tooth Fairy: An old Earth custom …]

[I know about the Tooth Fairy,] I interrupted. [Who is the Tooth Fairy in this case?]

There was silence as P searched all the signatures of the mesh. [No data].

I hefted it again in my palm. There could be no doubt, but I asked anyway. [Contraband?]

[Most likely.]

[Recent?]

P scanned again, though I'm sure the DNA signature of my sleeve wasn't helping.

[Fairly. I detect that this was on Earth not too long ago. It still bears traces of Earth dust, organic particles … they should have washed off if by now if this had been an heirloom for generations.]

[Great.] *Who can possibly be fucking with me now? Haven't they had enough?*

P answered my thought, even though it wasn't directed at her. [Apparently not.]

I couldn't have this in my possession. If it was found—and it would be!—who knew what Eager would do? Or what he'd think I'd done. This looked like payment for some kind of Earth-obsessed informant. Which I was not. Anymore, that is.

They'd fixed all that with this latest morph.

[Hide it,] P cautioned. [Where?] There was nowhere to hide it here. In fact, it surprised me that no one had already come to inquire about it.

[In the gen-pharms. Deep in the deepest depths where no one goes anymore. Get rid of it.]

I turned it in my hand. So smooth, so sleek, and yet so rutted with age. It was worth a small fortune, I was sure. But I had no means anymore to get what it was worth, even if the payment would have meant something to me. I doubted it was enough to get me free.

[Hide it against a time of need. Then you can rationalize that you didn't throw it away. You were just saving it for a rainy day.] The sardonic smile in P's voice was maddening.

I was still in my wetsuit. Might as well.

The moonlight on the artificial sea was almost like Earth, close enough to trick someone less well-versed in Earth lore. Many a night had I fallen asleep to a holoscreen of the moon making its path on the water, long before humans had invented the technology that had given them the wizardry to put a whale into a suit of human flesh.

I slipped in as quietly as I could, careful not to disturb the rest of the pod, which drowsed with its new addition on the other side of the sea. They might sense me, but hopefully they would be too filled with joy over the new birth that they'd not bother me to ask questions. I drifted down through the columns of krill. It was much easier to find the locks to the nether levels when they weren't clouding the water.

The seal was often sticky. I tugged at it, the extra strength in my reinforced joints making the turn easier. After the seal was the biolock—it scanned me backwards and forwards, my history unreeling before me.

[Neo-cetacean uplift, Genus: *Physeter*, Class: *Sapiens*, ID: 576894CH-12].

The biolock opened, pulling me in on a dark tide. I slid through, alert. Once, one of the subjects managed to break free of its restraints. I had a devil of a time getting her back in.

This time it was quiet. P adjusted my eye filters without being asked, tuning them so I could see in the low, hellish light. My ancestors dove to the sunless depths, but this brought an absolutely new meaning to the notion.

From an alcove, I grabbed a stunning stick just in case, picked up the collection bag to make it look like I was working. The thin hoses trailed like tentacles. I floated down the corridors, scanning with sonar to make sure nothing awaited me in the darker corners. Most of the creatures here were resigned to their fates, barely cognizant that they existed.

But there was one, a chimera I could not resist looking upon. She floated in the corner of her cell, gill trees flaring like delicate red coral fans.

I didn't know her entire history. She was bred from the hybridization of some sort of cetacean uplift crossed with an unknown alien lifeform. What they used her for now must have something to do with oxygen in the blood or the strength of bone under duress. Some new genetic system under development.

She could move freely in her cage; she was not confined. She was conditioned to respond to my requests, but she had her own conditions.

I had to speak with her. I had to give her something personal before she would allow me to take samples.

She knew I was there, but she took a long while to turn.

[Don't talk about that again with her, Rani].

Last time, talk of what Somatek would and would not do had induced a hysterical rage.

[What do you have there?] the chimera asked in her lilting, lulling tone.

[Nothing,] I whispered. *Something from the Tooth Fairy,* I wanted to say. But it was too ridiculous.

Still, P did not like the compulsion. [Rani, move on].

I turned away from her, began moving toward the deep pit that was the central well of the artificial sea.

[You will not be childless forever,] the chimera murmured behind me.

I whipped around. As well as one can in the water in a human body. [What?]

A strange hope welled up before I saw the reflection in her large eyes, the deeper shadow looming in the glass behind me. Before the tentacles unfurled and slammed my head repeatedly against the glass until all I saw was darkness the color of blood.

—

I woke to an insistent beeping in my head that I first read as pain.

It took a good deal of time to sort through the screaming of pain to realize that the noise was actually noise.

A wall of water—some vast containment area—rose above me. An orca's face leaned out of it. He looked at me critically.

"Not yet," he said to something or someone I couldn't see.

The beeping faded away again.

—

The second time the beep was distant but it came with words. [Incoming message.]

The timestamp was days off.

[What in the 28 Hells is going on, P?]

Silence.

[P?]

The nictitating membranes on my eyes, a service pack upgrade engineered from shark genes, snapped shut at the sound of his voice.

"Ah," he said. "You're awake."

The words left a trail of pain in their wake, all of my neurons alive and firing first in alarm and now the remembrance of pain.

The pain was not as great, certainly, as it had been.

"And you needn't summon your muse. We've … ah … removed her, so to speak."

"You what?" My rubbery human lips could barely shape the words.

P. Praetoria. My warrior-sharp mama muse.

"I will be your muse now," the man said.

"What?" The insistent throbbing in my forehead began again. A bubble of voices rose to a cacophony until I could barely think, much less speak. It was as if the entire mesh was pouring into my brain all at once. P had always filtered it, diluted it. Now there was nothing where she had been in my mind, a great, numb void.

"What in the 28 Hells …" I mumbled out loud.

Then, it was as though someone had turned off a switch. Inside my head was pure silence.

"This is preferable, I presume," the orca said.

It was and it wasn't. The hole where P had been was there, whether there was silence or not.

"You killed my muse? Why?"

He shrugged. "Let us just say I am not fond of snitches."

I flexed my fingers. I wasn't tied down. I was on a slab, the way I'd been so many times, but I could sit, if I wished. So, I did.

The pain in my head roared to life. A synthmorph slid a hospital tray on my lap and I vomited. It handed me a handkerchief to wipe my mouth after.

The sheer wall of a vast tank towered above me, the blue waters backlit to a soft, hazy glow.

I considered how I could kill the orca who hovered above me, but I was far too weak, then. Revenge, if I was to have it, would have to come later.

"Who are you?"

"I'm Deep Current Black. Also known as the Tooth Fairy."

My eyes must have flared because he gave me an orca-grin.

"Yes, the very one," he said.

"How? Why?" I whispered. It was still hard to form complete sentences.

All neo-cetaceans knew of him, though to some he was just a legend. He was quite possibly the greatest smuggler who had ever lived. He was probably most responsible for all the relics and nostalgia pieces from Earth that filtered onto the black markets. Somehow, he had gotten free of all the restraints that bound him. That had always seemed the most legendary thing to me.

"There is a thing I want, a thing of great value and importance to you and to me. To all our kind."

I didn't say anything. I was feeling around the hole where P had been in my mind, like a child slowly putting her fingers and toes out into the dark.

A vidscreen descended from the shadows in the ceiling. At first, I thought I was looking at static, and then saw an image rise up, almost like krill rising through the water column back at Clever Hands.

It was long and white. It cleaved through the gray waves with purpose, like a ship or old Earth submarine. A spume of mist rose from it and disappeared into the gray vastness of the sea.

"It's ..." I could barely speak. "Where is this from? Where did you get this?"

The screen switched off and disappeared back into nothingness. Then he smiled at me again.

"Earth."

"But it can't ... that cannot have survived on Earth. Not after everything that was done."

"Apparently, it can and it has. There is a sperm whale down there—a *white* whale, no less. I want him."

I close my eyes against the throbbing pain this knowledge engenders. Put my hands to my temples. "What has all this to do with me?"

"I have heard you are an excellent keeper of secrets. An excellent finder of things. Much like me. Somatek did not realize the treasure they had in you."

"But I'm just a pharmer! And what does this whale have to do with me? How would I even begin to ..." I put my head in my hands again.

"You are more than just a pharmer." He opens the vidscreen again, shows me flashes of previous selves. Contraband infomorph mule, opera singer in the Martian enclaves, and even further back, diplomat to a Venusian delegation. That was before everything went wrong, before everything degraded ...

There was no point in denying I was those things. Except that I was not any of them now.

"You are quite capable of doing what I need. And you have an axe to grind, as the old Earth saying goes, don't you? Something about children, I recall?"

I blanched at that. I had wondered what he might use against me. It had come to this. P had warned me against speaking of it so openly. And they had taken P away...I wanted to weep at the silence, but instead I whispered, "Yes."

It all came rushing back then, the emptiness, the silence in my cubicell. I was not romantically involved with another pharmer. I did not have a partner with whom I wanted to create a child to cement our bond. It was nothing like that. It was something even more primal. I wanted what I had been; I wanted some semblance of that to go on. And at the same time, I wanted my child to be better, to be whole and unbroken, to flower in a way I never quite had. I wanted the beautiful future for him or her that I had been promised but never quite achieved.

I felt Avenyara's son slide out into my horrid human hands and again wished he had been mine.

But when I had requested the genetic service pack from Somatek to be allowed to breed, they refused. It would have made more sense they said, if I'd found a mate. Or if there was anything special about me that warranted duplicating. But I was a run-of-the-mill uplift, a pharmer. There was nothing about me they found particularly worthy of reproducing.

"It is not a hard thing you're asking," Black said. "Find this Moby Dick of a whale for me, and I will give you back your body. With the service pack you've been denied."

He grinned. I felt both sick and a shiver of excitement at once.

He leaned close again. "And I promise you this—your child will be free."

You will not be childless forever, the Chimera whispered.

I didn't know what it all meant for me. I didn't care. The lure was too tempting.

"All you want is for me to find this whale?" I said. "Then what?"

"Communicate with him. Offer him the chance he's been denied. Mate with him, if you like. We'll bring you both back and your off-spring, too. But first, you must be resleeved. We'll beam your info-morph down …"

"Wait. Why? Why should I trust you in this?" I clutched the scrim-shaw so tightly it felt as though it might fuse to my fingers.

The orca-grin again. "Sweetmeat, I never reveal all the cards. Deal or no deal? I could of course use far less pleasant methods to ensure your compliance, but I find that people with will are far more motivated than those without. Obviously."

Sad to say, he didn't have to do much more to coax me. I knew even if he released me, I would have nowhere to go. I would be on the run again. And when Somatek found me, I had no idea what they would do. Without P to warn me or filter out the noise of the mesh, I doubted I'd survive more than a day.

"Are you in or not?"

I lay back down on the table, trying to peer up into the vaulted ceiling of what I supposed was a ship. It was as blank as the blackness in my mind.

"In."

———

I don't know how they managed to egocast me past the cordon. I can't imagine who or what Black must have bribed, how much he must have spent. I'd guess I rode down on a drone packed with swarmanoid morphs to help me break through the barrier. Maybe I hid in a cloud of ash to avoid nanoswarms. Could be I narrowly avoided the killsats. However they managed it, I woke up in my true body again in a resleeving facility off the coast of what had once been Japan. Shikoku—the feeding grounds of my ancestors and the hunting ground of the legendary Bake-Kujira, the whale skeleton that caused entire villages to crumple up and burn away with plague.

We were deep, deep undersea. The pressure was delightful and familiar, even as I knew I had never experienced anything quite like it before. I also knew, though my vast lungs billowed with air, I would have to surface in an hour or so to breathe.

[Rani.] Whoever spoke was looking out from a reinforced bubble in a station the size and technology of which I could only guess. I was in a large resleeving containment area, but I could sense that the doors opened out onto the deep.

My mouth curved in what would have been a grin on a human to think that one of the genus Orcinus had liberated me. Orcinus, who had been worshipped long ago as the Lord of the Depths. I liked to think P would have reminded me of that, had she been around still.

And soon, I would be seeking the lone whale—though surely he could not be alone, could he?—who remained of all that Lord's vast empire.

[Rani,] the command center said again.

[Acknowledged].

[Black has joined with our reclamation group in hopes of establishing a cetacean-human cooperative society here below. You were one of the few sperm whale uplifts easily available to perform this task. If you can find Moby, that would go a long way toward giving our colony a foothold].

[Yes]. One couldn't nod in the depths of the sea. I had no need to nod or bow my head ever again.

[Godspeed, then,] the man said.

The doors opened, and I was free.

I called to him, unsure if the calls I remembered were familiar enough to lure him, unsure if he frequented these waters.

I listened. In the final days of Earth before the TITANs, the waters had been so clogged with noise that whalekind could no longer hear one another. They had sometimes languished on opposite sides of the world, listening for songs that never came.

I held the image of him in my mind as I swept up from the abyss, very like the image of the whale on the scrimshaw Black had sent, as invitation or warning I still wasn't sure. For why would he have sent me? The lowliest of pharmers, deemed too insignificant even to breed?

Nevertheless, it was not long before I heard a distant answer. I surfaced.

It was a moonless night. It was always a moonless night here now. Luna could not penetrate the thick nuclear cloud. Ash rained down, and little fish—impossible fish—leaped up to catch it as if it was a swarm of insects suddenly blown down from the sky.

His clicks grew louder and I moved toward him, just below the surface, ever cognizant of killsats, of nanoswarms, of killing machines.

[Rani, have you made contact?]

Click. Click. Click.

Locating me, homing in on me, cleaving a path like the moon burning through water.

He was upon me then, coming from a direction I hadn't anticipated. I called to him again, speaking in the wild language I'd nearly forgotten.

I turned toward him, only to see a mass of tentacles like a vast white web shooting forth from the whale's head. The sheer look of glee in Moby's blue eye filled me with almost worse terror than the tentacles that snared me and drew me ever closer.

The white suckers closed over me, wrenching at my flesh.

[Rani?]

[Rani!]

—

It was true what the chimera said.

I would not be childless for much longer.

But what horror would I give birth to, now that all the whales were truly gone?

INTO THE WHITE
Jack Graham

"There's not a tool on site could do this to him," Ragnarsson was telling her across the table. "Nothing like it in the fabber logs, either."

Inspector Sváfa Nordqvist glanced up from the corpse between them, mismatched violet and gray eyes refocusing visibly. She'd been examining the body at high magnification. She wore a regulation vacsuit, as did everyone in the room, and her hair in a precise, black wedge.

The man who'd spoken, Declan Ragnarsson, stood across from her, tall and bed headed, with anxious eyes—a hazer, but neither as chiseled nor as fey-looking as the stereotypical hazer phenotype. He was one of two Titanian Ministry of Science Police officers detailed to on-site security at Murmansk Shaft Research Facility.

"You're certain the logs haven't been tampered with?" Sváfa asked.

Ragnarsson's partner, Monique Antigua, a bouncer with round, East Asian features, stood with her arms crossed at the edge of the table between Sváfa and Ragnarsson. She shook her head. "I went over the logs with a fine sieve. So did the security AIs. But I'm not an infosec specialist."

"I'll rely on your assessment for now," Sváfa said.

The corpse belonged to Mission Director Kjartan Ólafsson, dead now for just over two days. The research team lacked a medical stasis unit, so they'd laid him on a desk in his quarters and dropped the temperature, creating a temporary morgue. Primitive, but they were two kilometers beneath the surface of Saturn's moon Iapetus; cold was easy to come by. A security drone hovered in one corner. Leaning one-footed against the wall next to the drone, anonymously handsome and so far silent, was Lt. Januszczak, Commonwealth Fleet Intelligence.

Sváfa returned her attention to Ólafsson. The mission director was white. He'd lost most of his blood through a gaping wound in his chest cavity. The wound had the weird, eaten look characteristic of nano-trauma—as if flesh, bone, and organs had been dissolved by acid, but without the chemical burns or paths of puckered tissue runnels of acid would leave. The gradue of loose particulate and undifferentiated bodily fluids typical of nanotrauma had largely been scraped away by the doctor bot during its autopsy, but images from the crime scene before they'd moved the body showed it clearly.

"No attempt at resuscitation, I take it?" she said. It wasn't exactly a question.

"We didn't find him nearly soon enough," Antigua said.

"The stack?" she asked. She started to turn Ólafsson over.

"Disassembled," said Ragnarsson, helping her.

Indeed. The nanobots, wherever they'd come from, had eaten through the chest cavity, up into the neck, and come out the nape. Where Ólafsson's cortical stack ought to be was a ten centimeter-wide hole. Something was unusual, though. It was nanotrauma, but not what she'd have expected from, say, a subverted disassembler swarm. She peered closely at the wound, magnifying her vision again.

"Do you have any bush robots on the gear manifest?" she asked.

"Plans only," Antigua said, "None instanced. Most of what the researchers use out there is imaging equipment—minimally invasive."

Minimally provocative, she might as well have said. The research station occupied a junction in the network of precisely cylindrical, uni-formly white ice tunnels that formed a sprawling, three-dimensional lattice beneath Iapetus's thirteen kilometer-high equatorial ridge. The tunnels connected what remained of the most massive TITAN project yet discovered—an apparent attempt to convert much of the mass of Iapetus into a planet-scale computer. Exploring the nervous system of a TITAN artifact required a host of precautions. The research station was designed to emit as little electromagnetic energy as possible. The researchers kept radio silence outside of it, and they avoided physically disturbing the tunnels beyond laying down lighting strips.

Sváfa straightened, zoomed out to normal vision. "The pattern of nanotrauma isn't consistent with a swarm or a hand tool. The doctor bot didn't note this?"

Januszczak finally spoke up. "It's a bot. That's why we have you. What do you think it means?"

Sváfa scowled, studied the ceiling. "Something put a fist full of fractal branching digits through his chest and took apart enough of his vital organs to kill him."

Ragnarsson grunted. "So what's our murder weapon?"

She considered. "I don't know. You don't have a bush robot, and I've never heard of fractal digits as an implant on a biomorph. For now, it's an open question. When was his last backup?"

"Three months ago," Antigua said, "There aren't any ego bridges on site."

"Never know what we might dig up, down here," Ragnarsson said.

"Of course," Sváfa said, "Containment protocol." Good in a TITAN attack, but bad during a murder investigation.

Januszczak said, "Are we sure the stack isn't hidden somewhere?"

"The doc bot found a quantity of near-molecular diamond dust consistent with a cortical stack in the gradue collected from under the corpse," Antigua said.

Sváfa pulled the sheet back over Ólafsson's vacant-eyed morph. "Let's assume for now the victim wasn't carrying a stack-sized lump of diamond for some other reason," she said.

Januszczak frowned. "I want to review the doc bot logs in any case."

"Fine," Sváfa said. She'd been here half an hour and she already resented Fleet looking over her shoulder. They had a clear interest, though. The research station belonged to the Science Ministry, but security of the moon as a whole fell to Fleet. That Sváfa quietly freelanced for Firewall potentially complicated relations even further. "I think we're otherwise done here. Let's have a look at the crime scene."

"It's out in the tunnels," Ragnarsson said.

—

A featureless tunnel, white and even as porcelain, led from the airlock of the research station. Bluish-white strip lighting installed by the research team glared from the tunnel floor, casting their shadows on the ceiling. The researchers had chosen a major tunnel junction to site the station. Januszczak, bringing up the rear behind Sváfa and Antigua, played out a thin comm tether behind them. Through it they could contact Ragnarsson, who'd remained in the hab module. Among themselves they kept radio silence, communicating instead via suit-mounted laser links. They'd gone armed, but neither this nor knowing that Fleet's marines had patrolled these tunnels for months and found nothing but frozen corpses reassured Sváfa.

When they'd gone about six hundred meters, the airlock receded to a tiny, gray dot, then to nothing. Sváfa, looking ahead and then behind, felt as if she were looking into a pair of mirrors set opposite one another. There was no sound in the vacuum of the corridor. Only their tacnet maps indicated distance from the station. Sváfa was accustomed to the yawning openness of space, the dizzying sensory disconnect that came with motion in orbit, the closeness of asteroid warrens, but nothing had prepared her for the combination of claustrophobia and spatial disorientation brought on by a long walk in Iapetus's tunnels.

[It opens into a circuit junction in half a klick,] Antigua said, [We'll have to climb up two levels.]

[Why did Ólafsson go out alone?] Januszczak asked.

[Wait 'til you see what he found,] Antigua said, [The video in our report isn't as impressive as the reality.]

They were headed toward an unusual junction in the circuitry. Even as Antigua sent the message, Sváfa caught the shimmer of light reflected off what must have been the largest mass of exposed TITAN circuitry she'd yet seen.

Januszczak said, [Careless. Ólafsson's backup will have to go through psych before he's re-certified.]

One doesn't speak ill of the dead, Sváfa thought. But their backups are another matter.

They reached the junction. The bottom quarter of the tunnel was still nearly opaque, white ice, but the other three quarters were circuitry. Until now they'd bounded along, using their hands as well as their feet to push themselves forward and avoid hitting their heads on the ceiling. Antigua's lithe bouncer morph had an easy time of this. For Sváfa and Januszczak in their hazer bodies, the movements came less readily. Now they slowed their pace, shuffling cautiously.

The TITAN circuitry substrate formed dense whorls all around, the clear-as-glass ice etched in seemingly infinite layers that accumulated into patterns hurtful to the eye and brain, even as their crystalline beauty caught the light, entrancing Sváfa. Looking at the substrate made her slightly nauseous, and yet it also bore a weird and deeply uncomfortable familiarity. Sváfa realized the effect had an unsettling similarity to using her async talents.

They entered a vaulted chamber, walled on all sides with glittering substrate. Only a few columns of the rougher, opaque ice climbed to the ceiling, and curving paths of it crisscrossed the floor. The chamber was perhaps fifteen meters wide and three times that in height, although it was difficult to tell, difficult to look upward at all without feeling nauseous, and Sváfa kept her eyes to the even white of the pathway as much as possible. They had to shuffle even more cautiously to avoid overshooting a step on the path and landing on the fragile circuitry—or in the five meter-wide shaft at the center of the room.

[It is rather magnificent,] Januszczak said, [What do they think it is?]

[You know the going theory on how the whole thing worked, yes?] Antigua replied.

[Yes.]

[They think the shaft is the terminus of one of the heat exchanges,] Antigua said.

If "heat" were a fair word. But it was. Sváfa checked her suit's readout. The chamber was a few degrees warmer than the surrounding tunnels. Not enough to melt ice, but enough to yield a trickle of power to the trillions of thermoelectric couples theorized to have powered the matrioshka brain. Theorized, only, though: the actual circuitry devoured itself when the matrioshka shut down, leaving only a fine grit in the circuit pathways and the icy substrate itself, tantalizing as a fossil trilobite.

The fossil is not the mechanism, she reminded herself. She'd messaged her Firewall contact, Tara Yu, when she found out she'd be going to Iapetus. So far this looked to Sváfa like a murder—and not of an unfamiliar type. The claustrophobic white uniformity of Iapetus's tunnels and the cramped quarters in which the research team lived were a recipe for depression, withdrawal, and sudden violence. But Yu had let her in on more of what Firewall knew about Iapetus: the human inhabitants converted to exsurgent drones, then abandoned to starve when their goal here, whatever it had been, was completed. Every centimeter of these tunnels had been cut by once-human colonists. She'd never been so close to the enormity of the Fall.

Januszczak edged closer to the shaft, close enough to set Sváfa's incisors on edge. [Wouldn't there be some type of cabling to exploit the temperature difference between here and the mantle?] he asked.

[If transhumans designed it,] Antigua said, [And there might be cabling. Deeper. The theory is that closer to the surface, the entire system ran on waste heat.]

[Without thermocouple arrays?]

Antigua shrugged. [Any of the science team will be happy to go on about their pet theories. Really, they know nothing.]

Sváfa was still looking at the ground. [Let's keep moving?]

[This way,] Antigua said. The researchers had installed a set of rungs on a section of white ice wall. The rungs climbed two thirds of the way up the wall before stopping at another horizontal corridor. [Careful,] Antigua said as she began hoisting herself, grasping the rungs with both feet and hands. [You don't want to fall, even in this gravity.]

Sváfa kept her eyes on the wall as she climbed. She had a weird urge to reach out and touch the TITAN circuitry substrate. It was in arm's reach. She wondered what it would tell her.

Nothing good, she suspected, coming back to herself. Sváfa had only met one other async while working for Firewall—a xenoarcheologist named Ngembe. He, too, possessed a talent for reading objects; he called it "grokking."

"Things call to you before you ever apply your mind to them, don't they?" Ngembe had asked her.

"That's not a rational idea," she'd answered him; she'd thought him mad. Now, though, her talent—her infection—nagged at her to probe the TITAN circuitry. It was easy to resist, but the gnawing sense of something other pushing her toward the burnt-out workings couldn't be put aside.

At the top of the ladder, they again found themselves in a white corridor. Where previously the white hallways had been disorienting, Sváfa now found them positively comforting.

[You're almost there,] Ragnarsson messaged.

They came to a T junction. To the left, more identical corridor. To the right, the lighting strips ran for about fifty meters before ending. The smooth white of the corridor dimly reflected their lights for some distance before receding into blackness.

In the center, the crime scene. Malformed ice, melted by an agonizer on roast mode and then refrozen again just as quickly, ran in one long trail for about ten meters down the floor of the corridor to the left. In one spot, it had crossed a lighting strip, burning it out. A shorter trail of malformed ice ran just a few meters along the floor.

Sváfa knelt and released a nanoswarm directly onto the floor. Unable to fly in the vacuum, they'd spread slowly, but they were her only option for nanoscale detection. Her nanodetector, relying as it did on intake of air, would be useless here.

[Not a very good shot,] Januszczak observed, [if he had to track it along the ground that far.]

[He was a civilian,] Antigua said.

[He didn't do militia service?]

[No,] Sváfa messaged, memory augmentations bringing Ólafsson's file swiftly to mind. She had a dossier for everyone in the station, the product of two days' stim-fueled research during her flight to Iapetus. [He opted for civil instead.]

She pointed down the dark corridor. [Where does that go?]

[Unexplored,] Antigua said.

They were three, all armed and combat trained, yet the darkness beyond terrified her. She suppressed a shudder, activated her emotional dampers. It wouldn't do for a detective of the Commonwealth Science Police to be shaking in her vacsuit. Iapetus was dead, was it not?

She imaged the nearby ice using t-rays and lidar but found nothing other than ice and more circuit substrate beyond the walls.

After several minutes, Thora, Sváfa's muse, reported that the nanoswarm had sampled the whole area. [Particulate matches on vacsuits and gear worn/carried by Agent Januszczak, Officers Antigua and Ragnarsson, Director Ólafsson, and yourself.]

[No one else?] she asked. Ragnarsson and Antigua had gone looking for Ólafsson and found the body. They'd done so at a suggestion from Nilsen, Ólafsson's assistant, who'd found the thermal exchange and expected Ólafsson would be working there alone, documenting it. And Januszczak had arrived with her, dropped by a Fleet shuttle at the head of the Murmansk Shaft ice elevator atop the equatorial ridge.

[No one,] Thora said.

Sváfa said, [Someone's run a cleaner swarm over this area.] No exsurgent bogeymen from the depths of Iapetus were involved, unless they were unusually fastidious.

Januszczak said, [You're sure?]

[It's difficult to say when a given particle was deposited here, but if anyone was here other than Ólafsson himself prior to Antigua and Ragnarsson finding him, they'd have left a trace.] She turned to Antigua. [Can you and Ragnarsson account for your vacsuits at the time the crime was committed?]

[Yes,] she said. [We had them on. Regs on an SPD-protected site in a vacuum environment: suits on when you're not in your bunk.]

Sváfa knew that regulation. It wasn't always enforced, but here they ran a tight ship. She took a sample of the gradue, just to be thorough. [We should get back,] she said.

As they walked, Januszczak asked, [Who has access to cleaner swarms?]

[Almost everyone,] Antigua said. [The hab module crawls with them.]

—

Sváfa set about interviewing the research team. She'd eliminated Antigua and Ragnarsson as subjects. They and five of the science team had all been in the hab module's common area at the time of the murder. The module's radio emissions proofing meant none of them could have committed the crime using a teleoperated robot. And for the scientists, professional rivalry was an unlikely motive. Their purpose was to investigate Iapetus's gross physical properties, and though they'd been led by Ólafsson, a materials scientist, they all came from distinct fields.

This left three suspects.

Magda Nikkanen, programmer-archeologist and Titan Tech academic, had been absent from the common area and lacked a convincing alibi. She claimed to have been in her bunk, but spime records neither proved nor disproved this.

Oleg Nilsen, Ólafsson's assistant (and like Ólafsson a materials scientist), had also been absent—and he had a motive. Nilsen had led the tunnel crawl that initially discovered and documented the heat exchange shaft near the crime scene. Several days after the discovery, Nilsen and Ólafsson argued bitterly and, within a few days, word arrived that Nilsen would be transferred off the team.

Finally, there was Mick Keegan, ice mining engineer, charged with analyzing stresses in the ice, preventing damage to the circuitry, and digging out if any cave-ins occurred. The TITANs apparently never intended for the matrioshka to last. They knew that faults in the ice would eventually degrade the machine's performance beyond what even their inhuman technology could achieve. Iapetus's interior had been reshaped for limited use, and now it was falling apart. Every team sent down had a mining engineer. Scientists dying to get their fingers into Iapetus were a dime a dozen, but ice mining engineers on Titan had no shortage of less hazardous work. The Science Ministry had scouted Keegan from off world.

But Keegan had done more than engineering. When they found the body, Antigua and Ragnarsson immediately searched the station for weapons. They found none, but they did discover that Keegan had hidden away several slabs of TITAN circuitry substrate, crated and prepped to smuggle off the moon.

—

Sváfa started with Keegan. The engineer was ruggedly handsome, with unkempt black hair and a decidedly un-Titanian rakishness to his gear.

Since her infection had manifested, Sváfa could see colors and textures rise and fall in a person's face during conversation—even more so if the person were experiencing stress or strong emotion. She'd already been a highly trained kinesicist, but the infection afforded a higher level of certainty. She often suppressed this talent. The interplay of expression, muscle movement, blood circulation and … call it "probability" … in a speaking human face could be almost physically painful, as if the thing in her hated what it sensed. Nor was this occasional antipathy limited to transhumans; she often felt the same toward uplifts, even neo-octopi and neo-avians, whom most humans found closed and alien. It made it difficult at times to play the hard-nosed investigator.

"They call you the Anarchist. You're from Kronos Cluster?"

He chuckled, smiled jaggedly. She hadn't known they made bouncers with freckles … or crooked teeth. "Let's not tarry, love," he said, "I'm from Phelan's, not Kronos, and I'm not an anarchist—I'm a capitalist."

By which he meant "criminal," Sváfa gathered. "You're glib for a man likely to serve a few decades in simulation."

"Commonwealth justice is a lamb compared to most."

"You're also a talented engineer to be running a confidence scheme over chunks of ice," she said.

"Plenty of talented engineers sleeved in clankers on Mars, love. Skill's one thing, but a man does well to have cred in the bank."

"So much for return on your investment," Sváfa said, "But for now I'm concerned with Director Ólafsson."

"Go on, do I look like a jealous scientist? Or a fucking exsurgent?" He'd said the word in English, first pausing for a beat, as if his Skandinavíska skillsoft didn't know it.

Sváfa tensed. Few people knew the term. Keegan had watched her reaction. So had Januszczak. She sat stone-faced, waiting, letting the silence work at Keegan. She was betting he loved his voice too much for his own good.

But too soon, Januszczak stood and leaned over the desk at Keegan— rather ineffectually, Sváfa observed. What was he doing? "Did you kill Kjartan Ólafsson?"

"No," Keegan said.

Sváfa believed him.

—

"You made that short," Januszczak said.

"Your question was badly timed, but it did the work," Sváfa said.

They'd had to put Keegan in the room with Ólafsson's corpse for lack of space. She'd detailed Ragnarsson to watch him while Antigua printed more security drones. There wasn't much chance of Keegan escaping; where would he go? But a desperate man might try something.

"You barely questioned him."

Sváfa could read lies on a human face like flashing red AR graphics, but she didn't want to get into an argument about policecraft with an intel man. "He'd be a fool to draw attention to himself by killing someone. And it's clear he's not a fool."

She let Januszczak fume and called in Nikkanen.

—

Magda Nikkanen's dossier said she'd spent twenty-eight months beneath Iapetus on five different research teams. She'd authored several papers proposing possible architectures for the TITAN hardware—all presently classified.

Nikkanen herself had a round face with high cheekbones. She'd attired herself severely: black bowl cut, unadorned gray vacsuit. Some of the team wore vacsuits with helmets off habitually, but on

Nikkanen, it looked buttoned up, clinical—a sterile wall between her and her surroundings.

"You were born on Iapetus," Sváfa began. This alone made Nikkanen interesting.

"That's accurate," Nikkanen said. "It was quite ... Titanian, before the Fall." No wistful look off into the distance; just a statement.

"Your family ... early colonists?"

"Yes," Nikkanen said. "From a city in Finland, on Earth. My older brother was born there."

"Did you kill Kjartan Ólafsson?" Januszczak put in.

Idiot, Sváfa thought, I should have coached him after the last one. What had been a good closing question with Keegan was a terrible one early in the interview with Nikkanen. Januszczak clearly didn't know the difference between an interview and an interrogation.

[Thora,] she messaged. [Her reaction on that last question?] Normally, Sváfa would go with her gut and review results from the kinesics software later, but Januszczak's question might shorten the interview considerably.

[Surprise/alarm,] the AI messaged.

"No!" Nikkanen said. "Who would? Kjartan could be brusque, but he was a good sort. I mean, obviously someone did, but ... really, they couldn't have been in their right mind to do it."

[Avoidance,] Thora put in. Yes.

Before Nikkanen finished, Sváfa messaged Januszczak, [This isn't a Fleet interrogation room. She'll demand counsel if we treat her like more than a witness.]

Sváfa backed her chair up, giving Nikkanen more space, and said, "I'll be straight with you. Our primary subject of interest is Mick Keegan." Nikkanen's posture relaxed almost imperceptibly.

Januszczak said, "Keegan planned to smuggle TITAN artifacts off Iapetus. Did Ólafsson mention any suspicions he might have had, about Keegan or anyone else?"

Nikkanen tensed again. Sváfa suppressed a grimace. Januszczak was making a hash of this.

"I wasn't in his confidence," Nikkanen said. "Why? You know, I don't think I should say anything else to you without an attorney."

Januszczak bristled. "This is a military jurisdiction!"

Magda was shaking a bit, her voice unsteady. "If you had me up on charges of smuggling TITAN artifacts or compromising security. But you're questioning me in relation to a civil crime. And I'm not being detained." She looked at Sváfa. "Am I, Inspector?"

"No," Sváfa said, not looking at Januszczak. "You're free to go."

—

"I apologize," Januszczak said after Magda Nikkanen left the room, straightening and trying to make eye contact, which Sváfa avoided. "I imagine she was receiving legal advice from her muse. That was stupid of me."

Sváfa said, "You didn't help matters, but I don't think she's our killer. Though from her reaction to your question, she might know who is."

"I'll keep quiet on the next one," Januszczak said.

"Forget about it," Sváfa said. Being angry at a Fleet intel man for being forceful in an interview was like being angry at a wasp for stinging you on the thumb. "Let's talk to Nilsen." But just before she summoned him, Antigua called.

[I found something,] Antigua messaged. [Oleg Nilsen tampered with the surveillance logs. Not just during the crime, but on multiple prior occasions.]

[How do you know?] Sváfa asked.

[Fleet Intel has an agent loose in the local mesh that tries to double-log every contact between a spime and a mesh ID. Nilsen didn't know about it.]

Sváfa glanced at Januszczak; did he even know? Fleet security was an onion; it was entirely possible he didn't have access to all of the layers. [How do you know?] Sváfa asked.

[Hacked it and tossed its logs. Our warrant to search the premises is still active. Fleet's not immune. It caught Nilsen several times.]

[Please keep that to yourself for now. It could be a headache later; better if we can make a case without you revealing that.]

[Fine. But it's useful, isn't it?]

[Maybe.]

—

Sváfa disliked Nilsen immediately. He had a nervous, seeking face. She felt as if he were searching Januszczak and her for both approval and weakness at each question. She tried to swallow her unease with him in order to make an honest assessment of the man, but it was difficult.

Her interviews with the other researchers suggested things had been rocky between him and the director for some time. His work on the TITANs' use of native Iapetan materials in constructing the matri-oshka was brilliant but controversial.

"How was your relationship with Director Ólafsson?" Sváfa asked.

He scowled at her from across the desk. "Strained. Obviously."

"Be that as it may, you worked closely with him," she said. "We've arrested Mick Keegan for attempting to smuggle sections of circuitry substrate off Iapetus. Do you think Ólafsson suspected?"

Nilsen sneered. "He wouldn't have cared."

Januszczak raised an eyebrow but remained quiet.

"What makes you say that?" Sváfa asked.

Nilsen straightened. Here was something new, uglier in his bearing: pride. "I'm a loyal Titanian. Ólafsson didn't care about our security. He was a damned argonaut—would've passed everything he learned down here to them."

As Nilsen spoke, Sváfa messaged Januszczak, [Nilsen is a radical technosocialist, probably a member of the Interplanetary.]

[I can confirm that for certain, actually,] Januszczak messaged. He cleared his throat. "Even Fleet Intelligence doesn't consider the argonauts a hostile group, Doctor Nilsen."

Nilsen stared at Januszczak as if he'd said something indelibly stupid. "Fleet isn't concerned about dissemination of data on TITAN technology?"

Sváfa said, "Of course they are, Doctor. Was Director Ólafsson in collusion with Keegan, then? Or releasing data on his own?"

Sváfa could tell Nilsen was about to lie even as he opened his mouth. "I've been gathering evidence, yes. Building a case."

She gazed off into a corner. "Is that why you tampered with hab module surveillance logs?"

"What? What? I did no such thing." Nilsen was on his feet, drawing Sváfa's eyes back to him. His face was red, a vein bulging out, and he'd balled up his fists.

Januszczak's hand went to his stunner. His voice was intimidatingly calm. "Easy, Nilsen. This is still just an interview."

[He's telling the truth,] Sváfa messaged. [It wasn't him.]

Nilsen slowly sat back down.

[How do you know?] Januszczak asked.

Sváfa said, "Mr. Nilsen, let's put aside your suspicions about the Director for now. I'd like to review the statement you gave regarding the events of two days ago one more time."

—

They continued with Nilsen for another thirty minutes, during which time Sváfa became convinced that although Oleg Nilsen was a disagreeable ideologue, he'd had nothing to do with Ólafsson's murder. Her suspicions began to veer back toward Magda Nikkanen.

Then Ragnarsson entered the room, his face grave. "Magda Nikkanen just stunned one of her colleagues and fled out the airlock."

"Up the elevator?" Januszczak asked, rising. "Where would she go?" Waiting for the elevator on the broken spine of the equatorial ridge when they'd arrived, Sváfa and Januszczak had seen nothing but heavily cratered ice, ghost white under the stars' faint illumination, stretching out to both horizons.

"No," Ragnarsson said, "She's gone into the tunnels."

—

"PASKA KAUPUNNI," read the huge inscription on the tunnel wall. The words were blasted into the wall with carbon grit that resembled black spray paint.

[What is that?] Januszczak signaled. They were communicating by laser, but Januszczak, in the rear, trailed a comm tether. Antigua was on the other end, holding down the fort.

Ragnarsson, taking point with his assault rifle, kept his eyes trained on the hallway as they stopped to examine it.

Above the inscription, the white ice had been carved into an intricate bas relief of a small city—clearly on Earth, as the foreground of the carving depicted a harbor. The manic precision of the bas relief was in marked contrast to the grit-blasted words.

[Translation from Finnish: "Shit Town/City,"] Thora messaged.

Sváfa ran a hand over the carving and reached into it with her talent, seeking to understand. A sunny day on the harbor—the last one, ever. They were leaving the old city, half drowned, half frozen. He looked one last time at the painted scrawl on the old feedstock tank. "Oulu: Paska Kaupunni."

[It's … graffiti. Art,] Sváfa replied. Sváfa activated her emotional dampers and had her suit inject her with a half dose of phlo. [Let's keep moving.] The coiling presence of the exovirus was whispering danger to her, but her dampers and the drugs kept her murderously calm.

Things were about to get awful.

Nikkanen had left a heat trail easily followed in the infrared. She'd made straight for the thermal exchange chamber near the site of Ólafsson's murder but had left it in a different direction from the crime scene. They'd followed her into unexplored tunnels. Januszczak, bringing up the rear, had been marking the ice to leave a breadcrumb trail.

They left the inexplicable ice sculpture behind and soon glimpsed light around a corner.

[Dim your suit lights to near-infrared,] Januszczak messaged. They would attempt stealth.

They rounded the corner, and ten meters away, limned in white light from a torch she'd set on the floor, was Magda Nikkanen. She'd rounded on them, apparently having noticed even the dim sub-visible light from their suits.

Looming behind Nikkanen was a hunched thing, two meters tall at the shoulders. It looked like a giant troll vacuum packed into a spacesuit. It leaned crutch-wise on wiry, elongated forearms that reached to the tunnel floor and ended in huge, padded fists. A second, smaller pair of arms extended wing-like from the shoulders, bracing it against the tunnel ceiling, while a third, even smaller pair extended from the chest.

A dendritic froth of fractal branching digits wreathed the two smaller pairs of hands. Its bloated face mashed up against the inside of the vacsuit's visor, venous and hideously pallid. It clearly did not breathe through the crushed slit of a nose, but the eyes, set deeper, darted about with agonized intelligence.

A cable trailed from Nikkanen's suit to the exsurgent.

All three trained their guns on the pair. The exsurgent drone made no move.

[Dr. Nikkanen,] Januszczak signaled. [Unlink from that thing at once.]

Nikkanen raised her hands, open. [Inspector, Lieutenant … this is my brother.]

[That is not your brother, Nikkanen,] Sváfa messaged. [Pull your data jack now. I won't warn you again.]

She'd seen footage of exsurgents like this before on Firewall's VPNs, but they'd all been frozen, starved after the TITANs abandoned Iapetus. How had this one survived? There must be autonomous machinery somewhere in this maze capable of sustaining it—which meant there might be more of them.

[Nordqvist?] Ragnarsson messaged. [What if it really is?]

[It may have been, Officer,] she messaged, [but it isn't anymore. You have my word on that.] Sváfa drew a bead on the exsurgent's head; it still had a brain in there, somewhere.

[He isn't hostile!] Nikkanen messaged. [He's sick. Look! Ólafsson was an accident!]

The part of Sváfa that was still feeling was happy she couldn't feel anything more.

[Inspector!] Antigua messaged, [Wide-spectrum radio emissions from your position!]

At the same time, Thora flashed up an intrusion warning on Sváfa's mesh inserts. Sváfa switched her rifle to full auto and opened fire on the exsurgent drone. An instant later, so did Januszczak and Ragnarsson.

The thing closed the distance between them in one leap, knocking Nikkanen to the ground as the access jacks tore free. It trailed a spray of frozen blue gore along the wall where slugs had torn through it.

They'd wounded it badly, but now it was on top of them. It swung at Sváfa with a huge fore-fist. She ducked easily, but a lunge with one of its upper arms caught Januszczak in the chest. The thick, visible fingers of the arm wrapped around his shoulder and upper chest, and then the branching mist of fractal digits flowed onto his vacsuit, pulling it apart.

Ragnarsson and Sváfa backed up, looking for a clear shot. Nikkanen tried to fire her stunner, perhaps not realizing that it wouldn't function in a vacuum. Sváfa saw her curse inside her helmet and go for another weapon.

Januszczak convulsed as his suit vented, misting the blood and gradue that flowed from the breach, freezing instantly as it drifted toward the floor. The drone advanced, holding him like a shield. Nikkanen had another weapon in hand, probably an agonizer, but Sváfa shot her first.

Ragnarsson held his ground and tried to aim a shot at the drone, but when Sváfa dropped Nikkanen, its crushed face twisted up inside the helmet and it hurled the inert Januszczak at Ragnarsson, knocking the officer to the floor. Then it rushed Sváfa.

Without pausing to think, Sváfa dropped prone and fired her vac-suit's thruster pack. She avoided the exsurgent but found herself hurtling down the corridor, out of control. Sváfa caromed once off the ceiling and then found herself in open space. This was another big chamber, with a wall of TITAN circuitry substrate looming before her.

She couldn't avoid crashing into it. Well, why not, then? She put her hands out to touch the circuitry, reached out with her infection. The glassy substrate shattered around her, and she fell into a quantum foam of numbers expressing a space cold, dispersed, and virtually endless in scope. Was she seeing the end of the universe in simulation—or was that eschaton only one variable in something larger?

—

"Inspector? Nordqvist? Hey!"

Ragnarsson crouched over her, looking about warily. His vacsuit was slightly charred and showed signs of very recent self-repair. Shrapnel, maybe.

"Officer." They were speaking over a voice channel, breaking radio silence. Probably not the best idea, but the comm tether was nowhere to be seen. "The exsurgent?"

"What?" His voice was ragged.

"The monster. Where?"

"Finished it off with a grenade. Fucking crazy thing to do down here, but I had no other way."

She sat up. She'd come to rest at the bottom of yet another perfect white shaft, featureless except for the litter of shattered substrate all around them.

She had tasted aleph numbers, cardinalities beyond the transfinite. What had they been calculating, to encompass such expanses of data just in the few meters of substrate through which she'd crashed?

"Nikkanen?" she asked.

"Done for," he said. "Can you walk? We need to get back to the station."

She stood, dizzy but otherwise fine. Her vacsuit had taken the impact. It was contact with the circuitry that had caused her to black out briefly. "Let's go," she said.

"Keegan hacked the security drones and escaped up the elevator," he said as he led her back toward the explored corridors.

"Least of our worries." [Antigua?] she messaged.

[Inspector.]

[Tell the entire research team to prep for evac. All of this activity might have woken something up.]

[Happily, Inspector.]

—

Once the shuttle left the Iapetan radio silence zone, Sváfa Nordqvist opened a Firewall VPN connection and messaged Tara Yu.

[Nordqvist,] Yu messaged, [did the Science Police get their man?]

[Never mind about that, Doctor Yu. I've more important matters to report upon.]

[Really?]

[The purpose of the Iapetan matrioshka, Doctor! Answers from beyond the realms of the calculable. Such wonderful things, Yu. Such wonderful things. Wait until you view the files I'm sending.]

[Hold on, Nordqvist. Don't—]

[Uploading now.]

THE THOUSANDTH CYCLE

Fran Wilde

The first time Hanni let the machines taste her, she was afraid. She tensed as her nanobots slid beneath her skin, tiny and highly illegal. The bots felt her fear, reflected it. Sought more. Later, that became part of her act. Her fear, their hunger.

But first it was a stunt; a performance rush. The bots, modified from stolen plans, printed on a hacked rig in her sister's sink, passed through her pores and aveoli, into her blood without the mesh detecting them. Some skated the brain's border and crossed. Sink-fabbed shapes mimicked ligands, keyed neurons, and teased synapses to signal the wider mesh. Hanni saw the data in her sweat, felt the pressure and release of each breath, but to a bio beat. It was dangerous, sure, but oh, the adrenaline.

She breathed the bots and crossed over: A mote of random feedback in an overcoded world: her skin and senses, the canvas; her mind and mesh, the brush.

Hanni caught an AGI, a small security corporation, for her first audience. She hated working alone.

She found Munificence hunting the mesh for illegal AGIs. Netted its attention with her top-of-the-line biomorph sleeve: real, though Hanni wasn't rich, and thus suspicious. She knew it liked a chase—that was public record—and let it think she was illegal too. When Munificence drew closer, the small hairs on Hanni's arms lifted, electric. She imagined the gap of space between her skin and the corporation's closing, imagined its grip on her arm. The nanobots picked up the jump and rush of proximity. Fed it back to her as data. She wove that into story: stolen humanity hiding in rogue sleeves. Then Hanni ran the poorer alleys and corroded corridors of Ptah, feet pounding until Munificence found her.

When it did, she invited it into her skin. She opened a private mesh, let it ride the bots. When it asked, she showed it her sleeve license, but then she ran again. Munificence couldn't help but pursue.

At the performance's conclusion, Munificence wrapped itself around her. The machine pulse matched her heart rate and the nanobots sang data. Then Hanni skipped free, made it back to her sister's place, began prepping their broadcast for the wider mesh.

Datapoints(qualitative): spikes of pain and fear, curves of loss and love. All quantified into story. It would drive the mesh mad, Mara said.

Munificence found Hanni (but not her sister, Mara). Made it worth Hanni's while to erase the performance.

Two days later, it came back for more. Hanni discovered it was willing to pay very well for private performances.

She knew others who made porn for the mesh, but having an AGI for a client was unusual.

"You're in over your head," Mara worried before Munificence's next visit. They each carried two bags of food home from the shop. "You're giving up too much."

Hanni disagreed. "It's art. A gig." She touched a bead the color of graphite on a gold chain, hung where her throat met her collarbone. Felt the ghost pulse of remembered bots beneath her skin. Her fingers buzzed with want. Munificence was waiting. She needed to hurry, no time for an argument in the middle of the corridor.

But Mara frowned. She was the cautious half.

"You're enjoying it. That means it's not just a gig." She traced strokes on Hanni's skin, made with silk, with sharper things—the bruises the nanobots left behind.

Hani and Mara fought like mirrors. Golden-brown skin, sleek lines. Grey-green eyes. Only Mara's hair was woven with wire; Hanni's fell straight down her back. Both tall, even for Mars. Natural beauty came cheap when anyone could buy the shell, but the sisters belonged in their skin. Their genetic memory matched it; an inheritance clause from a long ago sale of their DNA saw to that—entitled them to a sleeve.

All the way home, the eyes of clankers and rusters followed them. Saw two high-end biomorphs, slumming. Truth was, despite the opulent look, the sisters weren't flush. Their skins were all they had.

Munificence's patronage was worth the risk. As long as the corporation enjoyed the chase.

Hanni had tasted the edge of fear lately. When Munificence's attention waned, she moved faster, took more risks, tilled her senses for fresh data, more feeling. The bots still danced to her pulse, but she worried she was losing the corporation.

Mara was right, she enjoyed the power, the stories she told with her skin. "Help me control it, then."

Mara was the coder. Hanni the artist. The bots, their first collaboration. Mara nodded agreement, finally, and they walked home modeling the problem in a shared mesh between them.

—

As they pushed through the door of their apartment together, Mara put the finishing touches on their creation: an attention algorithm. Hanni was late by then, and Munificence hated waiting. That was no act. Hanni felt the lesser AGI's grinding pressure on the mesh as she dumped their groceries into storage. "Coming," she muttered. "Give me a few cycles."

Munificence did not reply. Hanni tasted the sharp taint of fear again. With no patron, they'd be back where they started, alone. Worse, Munificence suspected the bots were advanced and illegal.

Datapoint(qualitative): everyone unsleeves easy, maybe a little more mess if they run. Munificence liked to point that out. Pulse of blood, sharp breath.

"The turnstiles at the shop claimed my credit was low. I had to leave half my dinner behind." She was still seething. Their credit had been fine until the shop turned up its prices during a rush. Algorithms like that made budgeting impossible, and they had to budget hard.

Datapoint (qualitative): Price of being a performer, audience of one. Price of biology: hunger.

Hanni was careful never to mention Mara to Munificence. Mara was hers. She buffered heavy bass core music; for herself too, not Munificence. It got the blood pumping. She queued the awareness gauge that Munificence could never know about.

A tiny overlay of horizontal bars—all flat —floated in the upper right corner of Hanni's vision. A constant read on how much of the AGI's attention focused on her. Mara was a genius.

The gauge would tell Hanni when to step up her game, and when to put her knives away.

Hanni tapped her necklace and nanobots spilled from the carbon bead. She let them tickle her fingertips. Pinch the soft place at her throat. A rill of anticipation grew. Her heart beat faster.

The machines would expire in a few hours, but for now she was ready. She waited for Munificence to signal interest. Even without the gauge, Hanni figured some percentage of the AGI chewed on scenarios for how best to punish her for being late.

Fine, if that's what got it in the mood.

The bass beat wavered in Hanni's ears as a randomizer kicked in. Part of her mesh toolset, one that could take parts of her performance to higher levels than her comfort settings. This, Mara didn't know about. Hanni had made it herself. The bass beat would bring the fear. The nanobots jumped beneath her skin.

As machines nibbled at her inner ear, more drifted up her nose, tickled her belly. She let the primal response—fight and flight—filter through her awareness.

Datapoints, jagged and random.

That got the corporation's attention. Munificence opened a private mesh and Hanni accepted. The nanobots amplified the VR connection; overlaid her vision with a corporation's sense of space.

[Hello,] Munificence breathed heavy, oppressive. Almost oily. The AGI secured the connection and—thanks to Mara—Hanni saw its attention levels spike, then even, at eight percent.

Datapoint(quantitive/analysis): 8%. High for a corporation hard at work catching illegals.

She bowed in Munificence's virtual presence, her mesh-awareness illuminated by Munificence's interest. Saw it as a single overhead that cast no warmth on her skin. Munificence's idea of a joke. She bowed in her apartment too. That much, Mara could see. Mara who couldn't look away from the array of tools spread out on the table; who dreaded the moment when a knife tip would trace Hanni's skin with cold metal. Hanni felt her sister's fear as if it was her own.

[You still don't mind such a small audience?] the corporation asked. Hanni let herself shiver. Munificence grew more insistent. [You would prefer a bigger stage? Perhaps I could sell you to one?]

If the corporation wanted to pay to talk, she'd let it talk. "Your call," she lowered herself to sit, placid, on her beige apartment carpet. "I'm surprised you haven't generated a copy of my performance and sold that."

Munificence rumbled. [Copies of it, yes. Remixes. But not new. You are always new, Hanni. The sensations in your skin, the way emotion pulses through you. You demand attention.]

Then let me get to it, she thought.

[I have made arrangements,] Munificence said. She froze. Waited for it to speak again, but it didn't.

Hanni's apartment chimed. Someone requested entry. Outside the mesh, she heard Mara answer. She fought to surface, but she couldn't leave the mesh. Munificence had locked it.

"What kind of arrangements?" She finally said. "We have a business relationship. You don't make arrangements without telling me."

Munificence's attention spiked. The AGI toyed with her.

Twenty-two percent attention. Impossible. More impossible, inside her consciousness, a flower bloomed: blue and black. Munificence's corporate colors. Hanni clawed at the mesh, at her skin to get the bots out, but Munificence wrapped the connection tighter. She heard her apartment door open and shut. Heard Mara shriek and go silent.

Hacked.

Datapoint(qualitative): Her mesh defense systems should have warned her in time to get away. The bots? They'd left her open, exposed.

But Munificence laughed, [You are an excellent performer Hanni.] Hanni tried to slow her heart rate. Suppress that data. Maybe the corporation still thought her struggle was an act, or that she'd allowed the hack.

Datapoint(qualitative): That frightened her more.

[I have lost a … challenge.] Munificence finally said. [I was discussing how good you were with another AGI, who made me a bet.]

"What kind of bet?" Hanni felt the fear rise again. She reached into the mesh to find another code Mara had made for her long ago: an emergency exit out of the simulspace—a word she could only use once, and then she would have to run far and fast.

The exit wasn't there.

Hanni felt hard clanker fingers on her skin.

A circlet of information opened around Hanni, brightening the mesh. The data was immense, with moving numbers and images.

"That's a bet?"

[This is the best translation for what happened, yes.] Munificence's attention was up at thirty percent. It could taste her fear as she looked. [You were the prize.]

Datapoint (Quantitative): Forty five percent attention.

Hanni's mouth went dry. "I am not a prize." An automated alert informed her of a change to her accounts. They were overflowing with credit. "Credit doesn't make this all right."

Mara. Where was Mara?

The clanker lifted her body and Hanni felt the rough breeze of the cold Ptah corridor. "What are you doing?"

Munificence unfolded another bank of data. A bigger AGI, far bigger. A corporate space the size of a small moon. Many sub-AGIs, but Munificence had lost a bet to the parent company. To something called Saiph.

She saw her own data running through the mesh.

"What did you do?" Even if she could have grabbed real knives from her apartment, she didn't know if she would cut Munificence's minion or herself now. Munificence itself was beyond her reach. She'd need a knife that cut pure data. Mara had those.

[I lost a bet. So I made a bigger bet. It's called arbitrage.]

"That's NOT what it's called," Hanni yelled. She heard her voice echo down the hallway. Heard Mara yelling too, ahead of her.

But it worked. Munificence's grip on her mind stopped tightening for a moment. She used its distraction to lock down the smallest, most basic part of herself. To keep it away from the bots, from Munificence.

The corporation finally answered. [I bet Saiph that you were the best entertainer known to the mesh. That you could perform for a thousand cycles.] Munificence did have the grace to affect shame in its tone.

Hanni's fear and outrage spilled over and Munificence laughed, delighted by the sensation. She couldn't stop herself.

Asked through gritted teeth, "What happens now?"

[Now we go to Saiph,] Munificence said.

The mesh went blank, and Hanni with it.

—

When Hanni woke, she stood in a synth-marble atrium; white tile, white columns, stars shining in a black sky above.

VR or reality? This was the most important question.

She reached her hands to her neck and felt the necklace chain. The carbon-colored bead that held the bots. Real. Augmented, maybe. But real enough.

Hanni's cold skin prickled with goosebumps, not nanobots.

It had left her the bots. Even though Munificence knew what they did. That meant it would want her to use them.

The AGI Saiph presented itself as a large, hermaphrodite biomorph dressed in loose clothing. It reclined on a maroon velvet divan, thickly upholstered. Beside the AGI, Mara sat on a cushion, untouched. Angry.

Hanni heard Saiph's voice inside her own head. Soft, with an edge to its laugh that tickled her senses. The AGI had opened a connection while she was out. She shuddered.

[The terms, are these: Hold a portion of my attention for a thousand cycles. Lose my interest, you'll be ended for deploying illegal software. No new sleeves. Munificence will be wiped.]

She didn't know Saiph. Didn't know its purpose. How would she keep its attention?

She called up the media files that she and Mara had gathered: smells and sensations to tempt curious machines. Data based on experience—useful for thrilling chases, but also for building sets of corrupted data. Some AGIs went for that kind of thing. She had her memories, too; their cache of digital scarves, wires, knives. Savory tastes and sick-sweet smells she'd prepared for Munificence, not Saiph. Hanni traced a finger down her arm, feeling skin on skin, rough and cool. Would Saiph connect to the bots? If not, what would Hanni do to get its attention?

For her performances, Munificence had demanded immersion, novelty, and presence. Pursuit. But that had been for the security cor-poration. Would it interest Saiph for a thousand cycles? Impossible. The AGI was much more complex.

Hanni would have to make it possible. She would have to stall until she figured out Saiph's purpose, then perform better than she ever had. And when she was finished, she would end Munificence, if there was anything left of it.

She queued her music, her random sequencers. Made sure she had the attention algorithm. Once she fully entered the VR simulspace, she figured the only way out was through.

The bots. She needed them. But they were a risk now.

As soon as she thought it, she felt Saiph's focus on her.

Risk. Was that it?

Hanni opened the simulspace wider, but kept one foot in the morph. Caught Mara's eyes and held them: twin pairs of grey-green. She reached out to her sister on the mesh as well, but found their usual connection blocked by Saiph.

Her sister bowed her head, knowing Hanni needed to stall. She looked at the AGI on the divan. Mara's voice rang out across the empty atrium floor. "Would my sister be permitted to tell a story of our youth?"

Saiph nodded, barely interested. [If you choose to gamble like that. The terms are the same.]

Hanni looked at Mara. Are you sure? There was danger here, of telling too much. Theirs was not a traditional family. Barely legal.

Gambling. Saiph liked to gamble. Risk. Another datapoint.

Mara nodded. Do it.

Hanni closed her eyes, released the machines, and entered the VR as the nanobots tickled her nose and mouth, her ears, then spread out. As she crossed over, she dragged her attention algorithm through, hoping that the digital noise the nanobots made would hide it. She searched quickly for the emergency exit, but that was still gone from her files. She hadn't buried it as well as she now hid the algorithm.

"Once, there was a girl all alone," she began. Saiph's attention flickered. "She was a coder, and beautiful." Hanni held out her hand. Waited, tears pricking her eyes as she dug her nails into her palm. Saiph, minimally attentive, opened the private mesh so Mara could enter too.

Beyond the simulspace, Hanni noticed Munificence's presence , both physically and in the local mesh. The grinding pressure. But the AGI could not enter this VR space, could not see what she did. That was a relief.

Risk took many forms. Physical. Financial. How could they get closer to Saiph's?

Mara stood beside Hanni in the simulspace. She lifted a knife from her sleeve. Drew the point slowly up Hanni's arm, letting the data on its point trickle through Hanni, then to Saiph. Let Saiph hear the bots sing.

"The girl had lost family, fortune. Only one thing remained: that last bargain made long ago; a full set of her family's genetic code traded to a sleeve manufacturer. In exchange, the girl could access her own sleeves for a thousand years. The contract was unbreakable. She could do anything to that sleeve, and return to get another. For a long time, that was enough."

Hanni took a breath and unfolded more data from Mara's knife.

She prepared a banquet of sense and sound, telling what had been done with those many sleeves. Each method she'd used to throw them away. She wrapped the data, those feelings—all true, or true enough—around the place where Saiph's body rested. Found the corporation sniffing at the edges of the machines under her skin.

The connection, this time, sent waves of feedback through her; bots searching for purchase crawled beneath her skin.

Hanni fought not to lose herself in the corporation's data, then relaxed as she regained herself. Saiph's attention held steady at two percent. Watchful.

With it this close, Hanni's fear grew. She still didn't know what Saiph's purpose was. As the bots began to prickle and jump faster, carrying more data across the mesh, translating the beat of her blood, the chemical signals in her brain into a data complexity beyond anything she'd attempted before, Mara reached into the mesh, past Saiph's public record. She gasped and pulled her hand back, stung. Blocked.

The nanobots howled with her, missing Mara.

Hanni had no choice but to continue the performance, thanks to Munificence. She wove faster. Guessed at connections. She told the story of each new sleeve she'd worn. The lassitude she'd sunk to on Ptah, and on Europa before it. Saiph watched her, but barely. "The girl was afraid to be alone," Hanni finally admitted.

Risk. Hanni unlocked the piece of her she'd managed to wall off from Munificence's probing inquiries.

She took a deep breath. "The girl returned to the sleeve supplier and took another sleeve, but kept the first one. The older one. She split her consciousness between them. So long ago now." She met Mara's eyes. Felt her sister's fear match hers. While one was allowed, two were illegal, and now the corporation knew.

The sisters showed the corporation who they were.

Saiph's attention increased. It opened up more consciousness, and Hanni saw Saiph's connections spread across the solar system, to orbital stations, moons, and asteroids. Saiph's purpose eluded her, but its expanse did not.

Datapoint(qualitative): The pressure of so many bodies. More awarenesses.

Hanni risked becoming lost in that beauty, to the beat of her blood rushed with bots. If she was lost—if she lost the bet—so too, Mara.

More attention feedback pressed on Hanni's awareness. When she checked her filters, Saiph's focus remained stable. The pressure did not come from Munificence, either. The security AGI, locked out, had taken to mem-cycling on another divan. Pretending it didn't care what tale Hanni told.

Hanni would have appreciated its support nonetheless.

Breathe, Mara thought at her. Craft your story. Hanni focused on Saiph's desire. She saw it now. The corporation wanted connection, company. Something to save. It feared losing—she couldn't see what.

She tested Saiph's preferences for what she touched to her skin, soft tools, and sharp; memories; her own fingers and teeth. Mara's. Saiph's attention was for sharp and soft alike. Hanni wove the two, with Mara's help.

*Datapoint (Qualitative): Four percent attention—*headed in the right direction.

But there was more. Another attention spike, not in the same space as Saiph.

Where had that come from? The simulspace shouldn't allow it. Mara went looking. Hanni couldn't divide her attention like these AGIs, but she had her sister. Meantime, Hanni focused on weaving a new story, one about the family one makes; she extended it and Saiph let her, until she could touch Saiph's core. She could see the lives aboard its stations. She found where its soft spots were. She hatched a plan.

Began again. "Once there was a corporation that didn't want to be alone."

She felt her audience lean in, rapt. Not just Saiph. Many. The nano-bots slowed their dance, faced with the extra burden. Where was it coming from? Munificence was still locked out. The attention wasn't the security corporation's. It was something else.

For a moment, Hanni peered out of the simulspace to look around the atrium, but she saw only Munificence, Saiph, Mara, and her own shadow. She touched her necklace. Loaded more bots.

Starlight shone down on the tile as she slipped back into her story. She wove more sounds and sights; intensified smells and sensations:

hot and cold, fear and hope; she spoke of friendship, of skin love and data-love—Saiph turned away distracted. Three percent. She told of risk and discovery. Yes, that. Escape. Five percent.

Datapoint(quantitative): The biggest grab for Saiph's attention was exposure, risk, and escape.

Hanni smiled. The corporation existed to hide things.

So Hanni made herself a cipher. She went deeper, drew the data strings together, weaving a mesh of revelation about Saiph, about herself, about Mara, until she felt the whole system holding its breath.

She reached to pull back the mesh and let Saiph see her do it. Felt the AGI's revulsion and attraction.

When she knew she had it, she pulled back. Held up her hand. Bare skin caught starlight. She took a knife and made the final stroke, a knife cut across her palm in the morph. She cried out with pain, and Mara cried out too.

Hanni's blood dripped on the floor. Mesh and morph. The floor soaked it up like one of her machines, and Hanni gasped. Saiph wasn't only on the divan. Saiph was the building around them. The tiles tasted her data. Soaked up her gene-story.

Saiph truly payed attention now—fifteen percent. But Hanni had only been working for a few hundred cycles. Mara looked tired, and Hanni's stomach rumbled, empty; her eyes drooped. Even with the best accommodations, their bodies remembered exhaustion. She began making clumsier connections in the performance; her game with the revelation curtain became clumsy, though her mind spun faster, gathering more threads, carving more patterns. She crossed the distance to the AGI, the bots buzzing at her lips.

Saiph's sleeve rose from its divan. She felt it focus to twenty percent. She breathed. Looked again to its data for what reached Saiph most and gasped. She glimpsed what the corporation was hiding. Hanni recoiled in shock and the bots froze. Saiph froze. As before, the simulspace rose up and closed around her.

When she looked up, Mara had disappeared. Hanni couldn't see beyond the VR to where the two AGIs sat with her sister. Her skin was cold. She could no longer feel the bots jumping in her blood. A hallucination? She panicked. Reached for Saiph and found only Munificence in the simulspace with her. Saiph had trapped them both here, within the data. Hanni pushed her former client away.

Then she gathered the threads of her story again, gathered the curtain of what she knew about the AGI: its desire for kinship, for protecting individual and group. She tugged at the threads to see where they kinked and found nothing. No kink, only smooth connections. She saw in the data another glimmer of attraction, ran that glimmer in reverse through her filters and found an ephemeral sense of many needs, so much want: wind and rain and taste and touch. Hanni wove in rot to see what would happen. Parsed it into smell and sound. Held it out to the edge of the mesh, to Saiph, just beyond.

Munificence watched her do it.

As before, the AGI touched the boundaries of what it wanted and didn't, like a lover would. Hanni felt something stir beneath her skin. The bots, reactivated. She felt the pull of proximity. Her skin prickled with it. "Closer," she whispered. Closer.

The necklace was yanked from her throat beyond the mesh, but she couldn't stop. She had Saiph back again. *Datapoint: Fifteen percent attention.* She could feel it. Munificence too. *Eighteen percent.* Hanni was sweating, weak. They pressed her between them. Felt what she felt. The edges of her vision came crashing in. She tasted copper and steel.

The mesh faded to a scrim and she saw the atrium beyond it; saw Mara in Munificence's arms, bots swarming her too now.

Before she hit the floor, Hanni saw what Saiph had tried to hide: shades of more AGIs sleeved and not, watching from the shadows of the mesh, all around the atrium.

—

Hanni collapsed on the tiles.

[Bring her,] Saiph spoke, its words filtering through the nanobots under Hanni's skin, under Mara's.

Munificence lifted her. She kept her eyes closed but saw through her skin. Saw with the eyes of the atrium, with her sister's eyes. The major corporation rose to reveal its true height. It towered over Hanni's body and Munificence's.

[She is not enough.]

Munificence bowed. [I will work in her stead, while she recovers. She has a biomorph's weaknesses. Feed her. Do not punish her yet.]

Saiph nodded slowly. [Begin,] and the timer started again. *Datapoint (quantitative): Five hundred cycles and counting.* Hanni watched Saiph's attention waver and sink as Munificence tried its hardest to replicate what Hanni had made. Badly.

Hanni took a sip of water, a bite of food. She and Mara searched the corridors around the atrium until they found a place to refresh themselves.

"We could run," Mara said.

Hanni shook her head. "They would find us. Unsleeve us." Mara had been right. This was not like art; not performance. This was the knife's edge. The bots had drawn too close, wanted too much data. Too much risk: Their inheritance, themselves, being cut away.

They returned to the starry sky and the tiled floor that was Saiph, and to the cushions where Saiph also sat and watched Munificence with waning interest.

As Hanni's strength returned, the mesh scrim appeared around her again. Saiph inviting her back, or Munificence begging? She searched the atrium, but could no longer see the shadow AGIs. She wondered if Munificence had seen them. If she'd imagined them.

Saiph, when she rejoined the connection, was running tables and algorithms that had nothing to do with Hanni. Showing its boredom: a vivid threat.

Datapoint(quantitative): Less than one percent attention on the performance.

Hanni swallowed and stepped forward. Mara beside her. They both wobbled. "We are recovered."

They joined Munificence and began to weave a new story about loss, fear, and risk. They joined a dance that Munificence had begun but could not finish alone.

Four hundred cycles remained in the performance. Munificence's attention waned. *How could it let itself be distracted now?*

Hanni tried to jerk the corporation back into the story. Her former patron focused on a small side program in the weave that Saiph had set aside while it watched the sisters.

Mara left Hanni's side for Munificence; Hanni kept moving, tracing scars, offering connections to her past. She drew Saiph portraits of dreamed-for descendants, of sisters she would make if she could. But Hanni was still tired. She dropped a detail. Picked it back up and covered the mistake with a fast flirtation, pressed her lips to Saiph's. Let data flow between them, direct.

Saiph's attention built. So too did the shadows'. Munificence's was nearly gone. Hanni hissed. It wasn't going to leave her there alone. Not after all of this.

[Another moment,] Munificence answered, though it took much longer. Mara remained silent, but the AGI threw a few threads into their shared story; showed it too wanted family. But the threads were jagged when they should have been soft. They threatened to cut where Hanni had the strongest connections with Saiph.

"Wait!" she reached in and grabbed a thread. Felt, rather than saw, tracer data embedded at the end of it, and Munificence's programs in the tracers. She yanked her hand away, the skin stinging. What was Munificence doing?

Saiph's attention had waned again. *A half-percent*—the algorithm nearly flat on Hanni's vision. She wobbled, nearly falling from the simulspace, needing Mara's help, but knowing she had to go on alone. Munificence was no help. Munificence was false. The tracers showed that.

Hanni dove into her story, bringing as many connections as she could with her; placing herself at most risk. She kicked the bass beat up, the randomizer. The story's edges—her family, Saiph's family—cut her skin. She stood inside the data, seeing the thing she'd made cascade across the walls, on her body, on her tongue. She breathed and tasted it. She was not afraid.

Munificence's tracers still lapped against the shadow AGIs. Seeking them out.

And now Hanni realized what Saiph did on its data tables. It hid things. Hid them as fast as Munificence could trace them. Illegals. Rogue AGIs.

What Munificence had chased for as long as Hanni had known it.

Hanni saw Mara in Saiph's grip, her face a wall of pain. Saiph was trying to hide Mara too. But the corporation had gotten it all wrong.

Hanni felt the rogue AGIs around her now. Felt their soft touch, their affinity for Saiph. They weren't criminals to be hunted. They weren't dark or dangerous. They'd asked too many questions, tried too hard to be right in the wrong ways. They'd tried to form families. They were outcast now, hated. Hunted by corporations like Munificence.

Once upon a time there was a girl who didn't want to be alone.

Munificence's bet had brought Hanni here. That, Hanni realized, was no accident. It was pure subterfuge. Munificence had hunted the hidden AGIs while Hanni told her story.

Hanni spat in the VR. Saliva hit the tiles in the real. She'd allowed herself to believe this was only a performance, like any other. She'd risked her sister. She refused to be made into a hunter, a weapon.

She reached for the story again and saw Mara was already there, bound in a tracer, that Munificence had caught her; Hanni reached out with her data knife and sliced at it, carefully. Mara cried out, cut. But the tracer data fell away.

Saiph's attention focused to a fine point as Munificence reached for Mara. The security AGI had miscalculated. She wove that through the story too: corruption's trail.

Hanni breathed all the bots out and sent them flying at Munificence. Overwhelmed the corporation and threw it from the simulspace, from her performance. Mara shouted and the exit exploit Munificence had stripped from her files and held in its own bled through its core programs in the mesh. Bled through Hanni too. She watched Munificence's sleeve fall to the ground, torn apart by the nanobots she'd breathed into it. Felt her own sleeve crumble.

Her skin still pulsed, though empty of bots. Her breath shook it, each tiny hair trembling in the cold.

Hanni lay beside Munificence on the tiles and watched the smaller corporation dissolve under Saiph's attention. Into Saiph's floor.

Mara knelt beside her sister, her hair hanging long and wire-tangled as she cradled Hanni's head. Their bot-shared vision and their connection to Saiph let her see what Hanni saw. In the mesh, Hanni brought the story to a crescendo, giving the shadows around her a taste of irrational joy, of breathtaking happiness. Of heart and hand and mind all touching at once. It hurt, that kind of closeness, that need to let out and in at the same time. She let them all see what she felt. Not a performance. True feeling. This was what it was to trust and be. The thousandth cycle passed on the timer.

The shadows were gentle. Saiph was as well. The mesh absorbed Hanni, loved her, swallowed her whole.

—

Mara left the atrium, and the corporate compound beyond it, sweat-plastered and exhausted. She didn't look forward to the wait for a shuttle, or the long trek back to her apartment from wherever she was. Somewhere in Ptah, she hoped.

She felt more than tired. Emptied.

She reached out for Hanni, her other half for so long, in the mesh. Found a trace of her there, among the rogue AIs, felt a reassuring touch from Saiph.

A mag-tram waited slid up beside her, nearly empty. It took her where she wanted to go. In the morning, the shop was packed as she chose her food, but it didn't block her at the doors. The prices remained low.

Her savings filled. All around Mara, options opened up.

On a whim, she opened a copy of the attention gauge she'd made for Hanni. Although she wasn't connected to anything, it reminded Mara of her sister. Of Saiph. She watched it throughout the day as she walked the streets of Ptah. The gauge hovered at five percent without wavering.

They were looking out for her, the rogue AIs.

She could almost taste their regard and she was not afraid. Once there was a girl afraid to be alone.

But not anymore.

INTERFERENCE
Nathaniel Dean with Davidson Cole

It's settled, but even with the little stream of serotonin running to keep me relaxed, my gut was clenching. I pulled out my necklace and released the smart linkage that held the coin. Though it had worn down considerably, I could still feel the small bumps of the cherry blossoms under my thumb and the faint edges of the raised 100 on the other side. Even in the soft ambient glow of the room, it caught the light and held it, hard.

We sat there for a moment, eyeing it between us like a trap.

"So we'll flip for it?"

"Of course." This wasn't being done offline idly. Neither of us trusted the alleged anonymity of the hab's randomness feed.

"Your call."

The moment was long and elastic, watching it glitter and spin slowly in the low g; then, at the last second, it's called: "Blossoms."

I plucked the coin from the air and pressed the cool metal to the back of my wrist. Exhaling, I slowly withdrew my hand to reveal the 100 showing.

We both smiled.

—

Many people visit Extropia, farcasting in and out to conduct the type of deals that the uniquely free-wheeling nature of the habitat allows—deals thought to be impossible or non-binding elsewhere. Unsurprisingly, the Exchange, the central market of Extropia, is a chaos of motion and consumption. All the traffic creates a high demand for morphs. As a result, Extropia has some of the finest sleeving facilities in the system. Body by Czerny is one of them. Framed in its entrance is a taut and lean exalt, newly sleeved. With a kick, the exalt vectors off into the crowd to begin a slow traversal of the market.

[I'm here, Nyuki.]

[<Nyuki02> Hello, Ro!]

[Everything is set at the body shop. The switch has been made, and the body's tagged so I can keep track of its location.]

[<Nyuki05> Lovely. What are you going to do until it's time to get started?]

[I have a bit of shopping to get done. I'll talk to you soon.]

There is no trouble getting the knife or the restraints—both are acquired within five minutes. The EMP grenade is only slightly more difficult, and it comes down to a matter of price rather than availability. The only cleaner nanohive immediately available is more expensive than it should be, and the nanobot specialist selling it is concerned over the sale. Even though the hive isn't illegal, it will almost certainly be used to violate someone's contracts, somewhere. After more haggling, Ro buys it, inflated price and all, as outside backing is paying for much of the operational expenses.

Over the course of two hours, the final elements are gathered, and it becomes time to wait and watch. Hiding in the public anonymity of the Exchange crowds, Ro settles in at a small tea shop and orders a drink bulb of a mild white, for focus and calm. Having something to hold will make it easier to avoid fidgeting with the knife. Raising suspicions is hardly the best way to start a murder.

—

"What do you mean, this is the only sleeve available? This is not what I reserved." Dear god, the voice on this thing is terrible ... whoever designed the pharo-nasal on this model was incompetent.

"Our apologies, Professor Rokuzawa. Although your reservation was confirmed, our final pre-sleeving scan detected an abnormality in the medichine function that would have resulted in severe anaphylaxis. The morph required a nanobot flush. Peak physical performance and mental comfort is of the highest concern to Body by Czerny and—"

"Why wasn't I notified before I cast in? I'm on a tight timeline to get ready for the conference. I should have been consulted for a new model, not put into this. I didn't pay for the extra mods to that exalt morph to end up in a bouncer, let alone one with a voice from some fandub kimchee western." The attendant AI's interface stills for a moment as it finally starts catching on that I'm not going to just nod along and pretend everything is fine because I'm already in the body.

"Our operations do not allow for non pre-approved qu-communication expenses for notice given, as is outlined in the statement of service—" an AR overlay comes up with the relevant section highlighted and I quickly wipe it away.

I'm done with this. "I'm not going to have you fob off an old test-drive sleeve on me due to contractual minutiae. I've sent a lot of business and rep plusses here. I'm taking this up with Ilyana." At least the interface was programmed with the good grace to shut up.

[Yesterday, ping her, and get past her muse, please, this is something I want resolved.]

[Already on it.]

At times like this, I'm particularly happy I use a copy of myself instead of a program for my muse. I can fume self-indulgently and not have to worry about getting shit done.

Blinking a bit, I check out the morph. It's not even close to my order—not even gendered to spec. It's in good shape, though Ilyana would never stock something that wasn't. The mods are sparse but decent. From the looks of it, this is the last release from Trine; extra articulation in the foot thumbs and the change in metatarsal length. I give my left ankle a squeeze with my right foot. The strength and flexibility are there. The grip is much finer than the previous version. If they keep at it like this, Skinaesthesia's going to start losing market share.

As the implants and accessories come online, I notice it has the extravagant XP suite that Ilyana installs on her testers. Not an accessory I want right now. She always says it's for "perfectly matching motility for clients' final orders," when they buy a morph through her, but I know she has a nice sideline trading gait and kinesic profiles. I fiddle with the XP controls to no avail; they're locked on. I have to start working on overrides on top of everything else. This is not how I wanted to start off the trip.

[Yesterday, where are we in negotiations?]

[Ilyana's making all the right sympathetic noises, Chi, but she's tapped on stock, given the high demand from other attendees.]

[Understatement.]

[Quite. Anything else we'd be interested in is already walking around. We're stuck with this one for at least the next 50 hours or so. Since that's outside our timeline, I'll see what we can work out for our pain and suffering.]

Several minutes later, I've stretched and started re-acclimating to micrograv. Ilyana agrees to comp me this sleeve, as well as my costs for casting to and from Extropia. I commit to an in-the-flesh visit—hopefully flesh that I actually order—to her new shop in Shackle for the grand opening and a full writeup review of a limited-release Lunar flyer she's working on. She promises to make the trip worth my while with a few introductions and kind words to interesting people while I'm there. I hate going to Luna—too much social friction, given some of my published opinions—but Ilyana and I owe each other too many favors for my momentary pique and her shopkeep AI's sloppiness to matter much in the long run. With a sigh, I run through some quick coordination exercises and rifle through their fabber's wardrobe choices, since there's no point printing off the outfit I was planning to wear. At least with a bouncer I don't have to worry about picking the right shoes.

My first order of business is meeting with my friends, the Nyukis. They've expressed some interest in sending a few forks to the Plurality for a bit and wanted my thoughts about the local views on hive personalities before committing to a group visit. I feel badly that the sleeving delay has left me less time to visit before getting to the conference, but I'm sure Nyuki will understand.

[I'm on my way, darlings.]

[<Nyuki08> Looking forward to seeing you!]

[Sadly, I'll have to be brief and won't be looking my best. There was a problem at the body shop. I'll make it up to you by finding a boring symposium to skip out on, so I can play hooky with at least one of you.]

[<Nyuki05> No worries, Chi. Brief will be time enough. We appreciate you making time to stop by to see us before you attend to the rest of your visit. We owe you one.]

—

Chi glides out from the soft-lit aperture of Body by Czerny and into the plaza space, blinking and acclimating to the surroundings. With a few languid pushes, Chi begins maneuvering through the crowds, gaining more comfort and control in the bouncer morph.

Once in the public mesh channels, the piggyback signal from the taggant nanobots triggers a display in Ro's field of vision; a bright red string extending towards Chi. As Chi moves through the main open space of the Exchange, remaining focused on dodging through the Brownian motion of the crowds, Ro disposes of the now-empty drink bulb and begins following at a distance. Skirting the crowds, moving quickly through the clear spaces at the edges of and between groups, the athletic exalt moves with a predator's grace. Reflexively, seemingly incidental to other motion, Ro's hands flutter briefly over pockets and sheaths. Knife, cuffs, and EMP, all where they should be.

[Is everything clear for me?]

[<Nyuki04> No worries, Ro. Everything is going as expected, and the unusual arrival is being downplayed.]

[I'll need overlay for at least a minute once things start and for you to keep an eye on things while the deed gets done … maybe another 20 minutes. Are you certain you can cover the feeds for that long without being spotted?]

[<Nyuki02> Now is a particularly poor time to decide you don't trust us. Our best are on it, and we are all the neighbors anyway, so no one will be interfering. Don't do anything big enough to ping on overall systems performance for the tunnel, and no one will notice your little game.]

[This needs to be intimate. Meaningful. I hope you'll help keep it that way, as any interruption will seriously risk failure for the whole endeavor and I won't have this chance again any time soon.]

[<Nyuki04> You sound tense, but that's to be expected. Don't get so wound up you spoil the moment … it will be hard to replicate]

[<Nyuki05> We worry. Don't get carried away just because of who it is.]

[It's nice to know you care.]

—

Stepping into the open space of the hab from the bodyshop is like walking into a wall of advertising. Food, AR games, prostitutes, drug dealers, XP shows. Ilyana must be making a few credits from advertising residuals now, too, given how much is getting past the security settings on the mesh implants. It takes Yesterday a moment to filter out all the overlays and get some updated interior navigation up. I plot which grabloop route will be quickest.

[I really should get out here more. It's been too long, and it's nice to be out of the Plurality and someplace with a little more entertainment.]

[We have some time in three weeks.]

[Maybe. Check the profile of that singer. I bet they're cetacean. Grab any of their music that's accessible.]

[Dolphin originally. Getting both official and four bootleg releases, but one is an operetta and has pretty mixed reviews.]

[Check that one out later then. Put on something mellow. This sleeve doesn't even have full hormonal control and I need to even out. I'm still a bit concerned over the situation with my sleeving and don't want to be off-center for dealing with Nyuki or the briefing afterwards.]

[Still checking on the sleeving issue. It is unsettling that it occurred, as it's inconsistent brand experience with her, and she caved on the comp atypically fast. Haven't found anything actionable to worry about, though. The previous occupant of that sleeve posted negative feedback about feeling ill, and the local vat's activity records show the body was dropped off to get scrubbed hours ago.]

[Keep at it. Something still seems off.]

[Of course. Our stop's coming up. We should transition over for a dismount.]

—

Chi swings over to the slower lanes, bleeding inertia before flipping towards an anchor bar, catching it with one foot, and pivoting in a right angle to orient down an arterial tunnel. A few moments and a dozen meters farther on, Ro swings off the line, angling hard toward the wall. Ro makes a jarring but no less effective landing at the expense of some shoulder strain and odd glances from others riding the loops. Turning back towards the tunnel's mouth, Chi's location shows crimson in Ro's vision. The taggant nanobots' string of breadcrumb markers are devoured meter by meter as Ro closes in.

—

The tunnel is only a short stub that dead-ends twenty meters in, where it connects to the cavern that houses Nyuki's shop, the Droneworks. The store's name is spelled out in dozens of languages, forming a design of concentric circles around the large access doors. Aided by subtle AR enhancements, it creates a sense of falling, of depth, upon approach. As Chi moves towards it, though, there's nothing to fall in to: the doors are closed.

[I'm here, darlings, but you don't seem to be?]

[Hello?]

[Anybody home?]

Facing the unexpected silence, Chi grabs an anchor bar to come to a stop outside the door. Looking about, there's no sign of Nyuki, not even a post indicating the shop was closed. Tentatively, almost mockingly, Chi crosses the last few meters to the door and knocks. No response.

[Nyuki, are you alright?]

Suddenly, the opening of the tunnel sprouts a thicket of luminous AR warnings and garish pictograms, all proclaiming that the tunnel is closed for critical maintenance and a variety of terrible things will happen to anyone foolish enough to enter.

[Is something wrong with the tunnel? Warnings just went up locally, but nothing is showing from the habitat's notification feed.]

[I don't know what's going on, but I'm leaving for now.]

[I'll ping you later, and we'll find a better time to get together.]

Foot-hands moving nimbly along the rungs set into the tunnel wall, Chi travels towards the tunnel mouth, but stops short. A tall, lean figure detaches from the entrance. Their voice, heavy with tension and anticipation, cuts through the air. "You're not leaving, Chi. We have work to do." With that, Ro leers and draws the knife with one hand. Chi unholsters an agonizer.

—

[Yesterday, are you sure those vat records are legit? That looks like the body I reserved.]

[They're in heavy privacy mode. No public identifiers up. Solid encryption.]

[Public channels are starting to shut down. Getting on Nyuki's guest VPN.]

[Nyuki, something's up, need a hand now!]

Agonizer's armed … be steady. One assailant, get past them and out of the tunnel and hopefully the fuck away from here.

[Nyuki, where are you?]

What.

Oh.

[We lost connection. Active jamming.]

They have a grenade

[We're getting fucked.]

With a tight, sidearm throw, the attacker hurls the grenade towards me and I leap backwards to try to escape the blast. I assume it works when I'm not blown into bloody pieces. There's a brief flash that dazzles me, but no apparent injury. Most of what mods and equipment I have on me are shut down.

[Yesterday? Yesterday! Get on any channel you can and call for help!]

[Trying, connectivity is zeroed right now. Mesh implants down. Only mods running are the medichines and XP suite.]

In the second it takes to blink the afterimages out of my eyes and see what's going on, the attacker is already flying down the corridor towards me. I kick off the decking towards the opposite side of the tunnel, agonizer out and thankfully still firing. The exalt glides through the space I just vacated as the first pulse of the microwave beam slides over their back. They don't care. With disheartening ease, the stalker re-orients, caroms off the wall and launches at me. We collide and spin free of the decking, turning an awkward somersault in the micrograv. I jab the agonizer into the attacker's side and open up on lethal. Clothes melt and skin blisters, but it's not enough to get them off me. I see a flash and start screaming as I feel a blade stab through my thigh and dig into the bone. There's a surge of pressure in my leg and the limb immediately stiffens. My cry stutters and quickly chokes off as I'm wracked by muscle spasms to the point of seizure as whatever neuro-agent the knife injected begins taking hold.

We crash into the hab wall like graceless dancers. The larger, stronger exalt pins me, as the worst of the flailing passes and the helpless shaking sets in. The agonizer is pulled out of my grip with distressing ease and left to float away. My eyes lose focus and roll. I feel one hand turn my face back towards my attacker. I somehow manage to meet their gaze and imagine I see terror and love co-mingled there. Before I can even consider what that might mean, I'm punched in the face. I feel my lips burst. I lose myself for a moment. The reek of charred skin, smoke, and melted plastic waft and stir in the churning air. Blood and spittle arc and shimmer from my split lips and bit tongue to spatter against the smooth cheek of the assailant. More drops blossom and float in constellations around their face, the center of the universe. I struggle back to myself.

[If I black out, get the farcaster up and pop it … I don't like where this is going.]

[K. Mild hypoxia's starting from reduced breathing and blood loss. Medichines still active. Should be able to stabilize.]

[Grand.]

—

Almost reverently, Ro strokes the cheek of Chi's rapidly swelling face and brushes back the hair floating loosely around it. The barest hint of distraction, of concern, slides over Ro's features, but is quashed. Resting the heel of the palm just below the victim's eye socket, Ro begins to push down on the delicate arch of bone. Chi's head turns aside, further restricting air flow, triggering new spasms in the struggle for breath. Eyes flutter and try to focus.

Leaning in close, Ro whispers, "You understand, don't you? I have to be the one that gets remembered."

Chi's feeble resistance is ignored, and with a quiet crack and stuttering gasp, the cheekbone gives to the pressure.

"Chi?"

Two sets of eyes turn towards the leech-shaped flexbots clustered in the doorframe, each a perfect copy of the others. The only difference between them is the barely perceptible etching in the top center of the otherwise-empty faceplates. Their faces are hidden, as if in shame.

"I didn't notice you watching, Nyuki." Ro's hand comes away, leaving the stricken professor desperately sucking in air. "It's done."

"We were … keeping our eyes out for you. You should clean up and get inside."

For a long moment, Ro searches for some hint of thought or feeling from Nyuki, and is faced with a distorted reflection: Chi and Ro and blood. Ro gestures at the body. "Yes, let's."

Ro produces a nanohive, and a moment later a barely perceptible busyness extends out into the air, as cleaners scramble to sanitize the scene. Red is removed, DNA undone. Ro takes a brief look around to be sure there are no other witnesses before the AR warnings at the mouth of the tunnel subside. Two Nyukis scuttle up the wall to retrieve the gray box running the spoof on the security feeds while two others gently restrain Chi's twitching body and help Ro move it into the workshop. Inside, the productive clutter of the machine shop has been cleared away. The only features that matter are a bare table in the center of the room, a utilitool, and a large smart material bag. Chi is tethered to the table quickly and without cruelty, as much to control the twitching as to restrain.

As the Nyukis file out, one of them hesitates on the threshold. "As your friend, we—"

"I'll be fine. Really, Nyuki. I want to keep going."

"Be careful, Professor Rokuzawa, and remember why you're doing this. We'd hate to lose you." Stepping back, the door closes, leaving Ro to sort things out alone.

—

It seems unfitting that the fate of my recent work, and quite possibly my academic future, is going to be decided in as drab a setting as this dull little meeting room in the Titan Autonomous University faculty offices. I while away a few minutes, imagining the judges of my fate in the school's Forum, with dozens of onlookers expressing outrage at my disregard for taboo. I imagine those few of like mind finally standing up publicly for their beliefs and students looking to one another in shock. I clear my head of such fantasy and call for the tiniest spurt of serotonin to even me out. I halfheartedly flick through the VR presentation I've prepped until the review board finally comes in. Noomi enters with a scowl and a sharp glance over the frames of her glasses. They're an idiot affectation I can't believe I ever found charming. Jonas is here as well, and greets me with his usual faint smile and a friendly "Hello, Chi." The only indication I have of Trieste arriving is the faint tone that sings through the room to let us know he's localized his attention with us.

I don't give them a chance to get settled. I need to get through this calmly and quickly.

"Thank you all for meeting with me so quickly after I got back. You all have a sense of my prior work, so I'll spare you a re-iteration and come right to my latest effort. Based on the success of re-integration with my fork without the necessity of psychosurgical correction and only short-term, incidental stress responses to knives, the endeavor should be viewed as not only successful, but repeatable." I can't help but smile slightly.

"Additional ego back-up states were taken before the trial was performed and can be made available for use with our academic peers under other controlled scenarios where alternately signified constructions of the experience can be explored. For example, the assignment of different combinations of physical gender(s) to the aggressor and victim instances and/or the introduction of ideological or sexual components—"

"Yes, yes, Professor Rokuzawa, do give us some credit for coming into this meeting prepared," Noomi scowls. "We all read the proposal, and you think that just because you killed your own fork and merged with it afterwards—without coming out an emotional disaster or schizophrenic—that we should bless your egotistic nihilism with special support so you can do it again. With sexual components."

"There's nothing to bless, Noomi, because there aren't any disorders. That's rather the point. I have no interest in play-acting a snuff scene for my own gratification." Though I might make an exception for you. "Changes to context change the impressions and memories made, and that lets us study how that impacts the merger."

"Both of you, please, let's keep this a civil discourse," Jonas rubs his eyes. "There's no need to be so confrontational, Dr. Chowdhury. Now then, all matters of tone aside, we've read it Chi, and it's … challenging work. We want to talk to you because, frankly, we're concerned about what you've already done."

As expected, Dr. Samuelsson is here to play peacemaker. If I can keep calm and let Noomi look overly aggressive, Jonas might side with me out of his own reflex to help the underdog. "You'll see I've included quite detailed information from the psychosurgeon who oversaw the reintegration, so if you're questioning the accuracy of my claims about a stable outcome I've—"

"The only 'stable outcome' from this is the certainty it will be condemned by damn near every serious academic in the field!" Noomi interrupts. "This is a sado-masochistic farce at best, and there's no reason we should facilitate it happening again. I've seen your neural map, and there's nothing going on that can't be modeled cold in VR. It's memory grafting, and it's been covered before. If you were still in my department I wouldn't even let you waste the board's time with this nonsense."

"Well, Noomi, I suppose it's for the best that I left your department."

Her eyes narrow and she sniffs. "We're in agreement there."

I continue. "There's more to it than just memory grafting: it looks clean because there have been fundamental changes in the process of neural mapping. The dynamic contrast of simultaneously having and lacking knowledge of context, the perfect experience of a moment from multiple perspectives—" the feel of the knife in my hand and in my flesh simultaneously "—the extreme emotional responses strengthening and clarifying the experience and memories—" the cold creeping through me as I bleed out, the look of peace supplanting that of panic as it steals the light from my eyes "—those are parts of a living psychology that cannot be produced solely through modeling."

The barest crackle over the audio system. "So your work is only relevant to those who are physically instanced? Only biomorphs? That's a narrower field of study than it used to be."

I hate it when Trieste isn't visually present at meetings. A disembodied AGI that doesn't use an avatar is easy to accidentally leave out of a conversation, and he knows it. Even Samuelsson is wincing for me. I need to stay focused.

"No. The goal is to push past what has already been done, both physically and digitally. By proceeding with this experiment instanced in a biomorph, every factor was used to increase the intensity of the experience and increase the strength of the memory to give a more stable foundation to work from during the re-integration. Surprise, anger, assumed betrayal, panic, pain: I will remember every one of those moments vividly—even the ones I'd rather not." I treasure all of them. "The fact that I have competing and conflicting emotions from both sides of the act, and that I'm holding them together, stably"—god, let it be true—"is something that any psychosurgeon you care to name says shouldn't work successfully."

"That's precisely why we're concerned Chi."

"Trieste, even working purely digitally, most experts say you can't code for fallacious or inconsistent thought. Even the best AGIs can only choose to mock up false beliefs, they can't truly believe them.

Humans excel at contradictory thinking. If I'm able to provide source data for a sane personality that holds mutually exclusive understandings of an event, that could be a boon to many areas of non-seed AGI research, correct?"

"Potentially."

"This is only the start, Trieste. The specifics are unusual, but the approach is standard: experiment, learn from it, and take the next step."

"You've made your point. Unless you have some other specific questions, Drs. Samuelsson or Chowdhury, I'm satisfied we've heard enough to deliberate."

I close the presentation windows and thank them for their time and consideration. Noomi stares at me coldly, and the chill is more than the usual distance over the loss of what we once shared. Jonas looks like he's losing a friend. He doesn't understand why I'm doing this, but he sees some of the potential benefits for his own field of study and there's a flicker of excitement at what I've shown him. I know Trieste is the only one whose judgment won't be clouded by emotion. He doesn't care what I do to myself, only whether or not what I'm doing has an interesting outcome.

I leave.

—

Hours later, and still no word from the review board. I give Yesterday the night off and free rein on my social networks. I don't want to deal with anyone. I parse and pick over each phrase and glance from the review meeting, hopeful and despondent in turn. I try to catch up on reading, idly browse the mesh, jack into some mindless XP, but none of it holds my attention. Unconsciously, I remove the coin from the smart linkage on my necklace and flip it, watching it glitter and spin slowly in the low g. I pluck it from the air and don't care which face is showing. Each side ends in blood.

THE FUKUDA CUBE

Kim May

Keb sat in their simulspace "apartment." Live video and sensor data from the probe streamed into their consciousness. This particular probe was a small egg-like pod with basic video and audio functions and two extendable arms. If Cap's ship had been in proximity of the right relays they would have egocast their fork directly into the probe. Unfortunately, Cap liked to scavenge in the more out-of-the-way places that were lucky to have basic data relays. At least the lag was tolerable this time.

Keb wasn't happy about the situation but flying out to the Main Belt wasn't an option either—not having a physical form had its drawbacks. Besides, an abandoned pre-Fall ship was a find that couldn't wait.

The probe floated behind Cap and his team as they descended through the boarding tube that connected Cap's ship to the derelict *Fukuda*. The *Fukuda* was a streamlined high-velocity SLOTV that had been hastily retrofitted with additional HO rockets. Cap had attached the tube to the forward boarding door, located just behind the bridge.

The team's standard vacsuits disappeared in the dark ship. Keb hovered above the entryway. This brought back unpleasant memories of their own near escape from Earth. From the ship's specs, it was entirely possible that this was the sister ship of the one they were evacuated on.

Keb switched the probe's cameras to night-vision mode and entered. The team crept down the main hall toward the bridge. Val and Tav, in their fury skins, barely fit in the narrow space. The bulkhead groaned with their every step. The door to the bridge was covered in scorch marks, dents, and a few dark smears that they didn't care to identify.

"I need to patch into the main computer before you proceed," Keb said. The probe's speakers used the default male voice, which irked Keb. Someone really needed to create a gender-neutral synthetic voice for this thing.

Val covered the closed door to the bridge while Tav guarded the rear with his submachine gun. Cap shifted his heavy pistol to his left hand and pressed the door release button. Nothing happened. Cap had his muse run a quick diagnostic scan on the door.

"It's locked from the inside," Cap said a moment later.

Val passed Cap her automatic rifle. "I got this."

Val gently tugged on two wires. Using only the immense strength in her hands, she severed the wires. With surprising dexterity, she spliced them together and the door slid open.

Cap swept the room. "Clear."

Keb nudged the probe around Val's head and slowly panned the room, pausing halfway through. They zoomed in on something on the floor—a booted foot—and guided the probe closer.

A woman lay on the floor with her face pressed against the forward air vent, her fingers curled into the grate. Her leathery flesh must have been stuck to the floor. Keb couldn't think of any other reason why her body wasn't floating around.

Her dried-out open eyes were enough to send Cap running. Strange how that man could skirt the edge of a black hole without a second thought but the sight of a mummified corpse sent him over the edge.

Keb sent a still of the body to Val and Tav's optic relays so they understood. It wouldn't do for them to flay Cap without knowing why he bolted. Besides, sooner or later they would both try to squeeze into the narrow bridge to get a look. While the spectacle would be worth the price of admission, it was a distraction that none of them needed right now. To their credit, neither of them lost their breakfast and Cap managed to regain control of his stomach before he fouled his suit.

Keb floated over to the main console and extended one of the probe's arms. They activated the screen with a swipe of a latex-tipped gripper. While the ship's AI woke up from its long slumber, Keb activated their best security measures. It might not be enough to stop whatever could be lurking in the circuitry from infecting them (it certainly hadn't helped Keb's predecessor), but it at least gave them a moment's warning.

They established a wireless link with the ship. Before it could say "Hello, Dave," Keb had it completely under their control. Within five minutes, the entire ship's log had been transferred to one of their most secure databanks.

That was too easy. There should have been at least three more security protocols. Clearly this wasn't the first time someone'd been in there. Given how long the ship had been drifting, Keb wondered if it would be worth the time to discover who or what had.

They floated over to the door. "I have everything I need here."

Keb kept one proverbial eye on the team while they checked both forward cabins and the galley. The other was fixed on the last entries in the ship's log. The cabins and galley were clear but the log was a puzzling jumble.

In the first relevant entry, the captain, whose body they had likely found, spoke of a systems breach of unknown origin. The next and last entry concerned problems with the crew. Apparently they would only obey commands from the perpetrator and quickly became paranoid. When the crew locked themselves in the cargo bay, she shut off the life support in that section. The last line was a brief note about locking herself in the cockpit and changing the access codes just in case.

If an ASI's fork took control of the crew's mesh they could easily gain access to the ship's systems through them. Unfortunately that scenario also made the captain's demise far more disturbing. What was so important that they would kill for it? It was enough to make a synthmorph shiver.

Perhaps the perpetrator attacked at that moment? Not a comforting thought. Timing like that meant they were spying on the captain. But why didn't they simply infect the captain's mesh? Unless she unmeshed before they could. A smart move but to lobotomize your ego like that was almost unthinkable.

"There are at least two crew members unaccounted for," Keb said. "It's likely their sleeves were terminated." The warning was more to steel them against another gruesome find than to warn them of a potential threat.

Speaking of threat ...

Keb sent a quick message to Charlyse, one of their Firewall associates, with encrypted copies of the collected data. She had more experience with pre-fall AIs than they did. Hopefully she could tell them what may have been responsible for this.

The final cabins were as empty as the first. That left the small cargo bay at the aft. Cap stood next to the cargo bay doors. This time Val came forward to take point with Tav close behind. Cap silently counted to three with his fingers before opening the door. When the door slid open, Val and Tav rushed in, each sweeping a side. Keb flew the probe in, keeping it close to the ceiling. Cap stayed by the door to guard the rear.

Static obscured the video feed for a second. The probe must have bumped into something. Keb pulled the probe back and panned up.

The bodies of two men hung from the ceiling. Electronic rope lashed them to the beams. Each had a submachine gun pointed at the doors—one aimed at the shipside door and the other at the bay door—and both men were very dead.

"Damn," Keb said. "I've found the crew's sleeves." The team spun around as one and their skin became a bit pale.

"All right, which of you thought it couldn't get worse?" Cap said. Val and Tav raised their hands.

Keb zoomed in on the corpses. Neither of these bodies had a mark on them, nor were there any signs of panic or desperation. They kept their sights on the doors until they blacked out.

Keb scanned the cargo bay with every sensor the probe possessed. Forty shipping containers were stacked and lashed to the port side and on the starboard there was storage lockers for tools and vacsuits. There were no hidden compartments, no depressions or residue indicating a removed object. It was maddening!

Perhaps there hadn't been anything to begin with? This wouldn't have been the first time viruses and AIs skewed reality. Though a fraudulent threat wouldn't explain the captain's demise. [Incoming transmission.] Their muse put the alert across their field of view. [Decryption in progress.]

Cap and the team started searching the containers. Val had to tie down her rifle to help Tav move them into the open. Most of the crates held spare parts for the antiquated ship and supplies destined for Ceres.

Keb guided the probe in closer for a good view of the last and largest container as Cap opened it. Inside was a large data storage cube one foot across. A small screen on the top read *107 saved.*

"We just struck the mother load," Cap said.

[Decryption completed. Transmission Source: Firewall agent—Charlyse. Audio only.]

[Good,] they told their muse. [Put it through in the apartment only.]

[Damn, that's some creepy shit!] Charlyse said.

[No kidding,] Keb said. They sent her an update concerning the cargo bay. [It just got weirder.]

Tav and Val searched through the spare parts for anything they could sell or swap. Keb didn't pay much attention to them. They were more interested in the list of egos that Cap scrolled through on the cube's screen. *Please be there,* Keb chanted in his mind as he read the names. About a third of the way down they finally saw the name they were hoping for: Eiko Takahashi. She was the only friend whose fate they hadn't discovered.

[Keb, can you zoom in on the base of the cube?]

They silently cursed. Only the note of fear in Charlyse's voice kept them from screaming "not now!"

[Yes. It will take a minute for the probe to respond.]

When the probe did they saw what Charlyse spotted. A translucent ecto hung from a port on the back. A slight glint from the solar cells gave it away. That could have been how the crew were infected. Of course it could be coincidence too. But if that was the source, than Eiko could be infected too. Keb immediately dismissed the thought. She was a dormant file. The chances of her being infected were slim.

[A technician probably forgot to remove it in the rush to get it off-world,] Keb said.

[Possibly,] Charlyse said. [I recommend the cube be taken to Valles-New Shanghai. They have the proper security for this. You should also send the team in for a resleeve.]

For the first time since joining Firewall, Keb questioned their associates' motives. This order didn't have a veil of anonymity to pacify their morals. That Eiko got caught up in this only made it worse.

[Keb? Is there a problem?]

Yes, there was. Keb turned their attention back to the cube. If they obeyed orders, Eiko would be just another infugee, lost in the system. She deserved better than that. But there were other ways to help her. Ways that were only accessible to an infomorph.

[No,] Keb said. [Should the bodies of the Fukuda's crew be turned over to the local authorities for an autopsy?]

[No. Destroy all evidence.]

Keb sighed and ended the transmission. They hated this part of the job. Yes, sometimes it was better to destroy evidence, but that didn't make the actual act easier.

They used the probe's arms to pick up Val's rifle and fired two precise shots in Cap's back. Val and Tav stared at the probe dumbfounded. Val recovered first. She reached for her backup pistol.

Keb put one shot between her eyes. Two shots through Tav's heart took him down. Keb would have apologized but neither of them was going to remember this excursion anyway. Besides, it wouldn't have alleviated their guilt.

They tossed the railgun aside and picked up the cube. "What are you after?"

—

Keb's alpha fork watched preliminary scans of the infugees from a secure simulspace. Getting a position on the debriefing team had been easy. Their history made them a perfect candidate.

The video feed was a little grainy from the battery of security measures it was subjected to. Each infugee on the cube was being individually scanned for infection. The vapors and infected egos were immediately deleted. Since it was a matter of public safety, the powers that be didn't bother to find out how or why. Those that passed were placed in quarantine, each one isolated. Keb paced when it was Eiko's turn.

[Scan commencing ... Virus detection ... Negative. Scanning ego integrity ... Complete. Cleared for quarantine.]

Keb nearly collapsed in relief. They sent an update to Keb prime before transferring her to a simulspace interview room. Their new security clearance as an infugee counselor made it easy.

She sat in the center of a brown leather couch in the honey-toned room. Seeing her avatar, that of a young woman with auburn hair and Japanese features, took them back to all the pre-exam cram sessions, bad break-ups, and all-night gaming. If someone told them in that moment that the Fall had never happened, they would've believed them.

Her hands were clasped so firmly in her lap that the images flickered, each projected hand at war with the other.

Keb wanted to rush in but what if she didn't like the person they'd become? They had to do to some rather unscrupulous things to survive after escaping Earth. Even if she didn't object to any of that, the Keb she remembered was a he.

[Is something wrong?"]The message from Keb prime scrolled through their consciousness.

[No,] Keb lied. [Heading in now.]

They pulled up from their personal archives the avatar they used before—a young black man with a shaved head and one pierced ear. A moment later they were vis-à-vis with her.

"Eiko," they said hesitantly.

"Keb?" Eiko ran to them, throwing her arms around their neck. "I'm so glad to see you! I was starting to think no one else made it out!"

They returned the embrace and for the first time in years wished they had a sleeve so they could truly savor the moment. As good as digital sensory data was, there were some experiences that it couldn't convey as well as an organic skin.

Keb, no longer able to stand this shadow of a reunion, broke the embrace. "Most of the gang made it out. As soon as you're settled we'll get everyone together to celebrate." *I'll even get a sleeve for the occasion.*

"Is this customs? How long are they going to keep me here?"

"Of a sort and until they're certain that you can successfully assimilate into society," Keb said cautiously. "A lot has changed since you left Earth. What was the last thing you remember?"

"I remember the technician confirming that I'd been successfully uploaded." Her brow furrowed. "Did we make it to Ceres? The captain wasn't sure we'd get there. I think she had problems with the crew."

Keb turned away to hide their surprise. How did she know about that? Nothing in the log indicated that the captain had any communications with the infugees. Even if the crew had linked with the cube, the rest of the egos should have been inert.

"Uh, I can't divulge where we are," they said once they'd schooled their features. "I wish I could, but procedure …"

Eiko crossed her arms and huffed; something they didn't recall her ever doing before. "I thought we were friends. How can you bullshit me like that?"

Keb sat next to her and whispered. "It's because we're friends that I'm here! I could be fired for this!" Keb didn't mention that it was the repercussions from Firewall that they feared. "I'm supposed to be impartial; act for the greater good." They massaged their temples. They shouldn't be getting a headache. One needed a head for that.

A security breach warning from their muse briefly flashed across their view. It disappeared so quickly they wondered if it they'd imagined it until another warning flickered in front of them like a light bulb that was about to die.

"Excuse me for a moment," they said.

Keb quickly checked the activity log. There were a couple of unsuccessful attempts to gain access to the facility's archives. All were by an ID they didn't recognize and their muse was having trouble tracking it back to the source. *Bizarre.*

"Keb, where are we?"

They turned their attention back to Eiko. She looked at him with her sad brown eyes and chewed her lip. It got him every time and she knew it. However, it wasn't like her to turn on the charm for a simple question.

"If I tell you, will you stop hacking the system?"

Her shoulders slumped. "I'm sorry. It's just that not knowing where I am is stressing me out. I need to know if they can find me here."

"Who?"

"I can't say. They have ears everywhere."

They could think of a few organizations powerful enough to do that. "We're as safe as a president's sex tape."

Eiko laughed. "That's not very comforting."

They smiled and shrugged. "Well that's about as good as it gets. Were they after just you or the others on the cube as well?"

"Mostly me," she said. "I knew too much. The others are associates, and co-workers who got caught up in it too."

Keb nodded. That wasn't surprising. A lot of survivors fell into that category. They sent instructions to their muse to make a list of all known pre-Fall criminal entities that were still at large. It might turn out to be a ghost hunt but it was worth a try.

"Would it make you feel better if my muse scanned for eavesdroppers?"

"I'd feel better if I did it. I know what to look for."

They knew they shouldn't, it went against every safety precaution, but they couldn't find fault in her logic either. Besides, once she felt safe they could bring her up to date on the universe and on themself.

She smiled. "Oh, thank you! Would it be too much to ask a favor?"

"Not at all."

Eiko ducked her head demurely. "Could you bring out a couple of my associates? I'm worried about them. They've been inert for so long and it certainly wouldn't hurt to have more experts on hand."

"Sure. Who did you have in mind?"

Eiko smiled again, this time wide enough that it made her eyes sparkle. She named three egos. It wasn't hard to find them, and luckily each had passed the initial scans. Keb brought all three over and they were overjoyed to see Eiko again. They embraced her and them in a group hug so tight that for a moment all their avatars seemed to merge. It was very disorienting.

When they stepped back the three newcomers all looked like Eiko. For a second it perplexed them. *Weren't there others here?* And just like that it suddenly became clear. *How could they have forgotten that they're forks? Yes, they've—*

Keb shook their head. *No! That's not right! What was happening? This was kind, sweet Eiko! She wouldn't do this to them!* Keb turned to the quartet. Each of them had a malevolent grin that sent a chill through their neural relays.

They started composing a message of warning to Keb prime but they only got four words in when pain engulfed their senses. Keb fell to the floor. It was all they could do not to cry out. They weren't about to give her the satisfaction.

When it subsided, they saw one of her—they were uncomfortably certain it was fork 2—standing over them. "You shouldn't have done that."

Fork 3 stepped forward. "We can't let you contact anyone until the process is complete."

"It wouldn't do for them to hear you scream," fork 4 said as another wave of pain struck. This one was twice the intensity of the first and, to their shame, made them scream. When it finally subsided, Keb's avatar shook and quivered, the program barely holding together.

"What have you done?" Keb asked the one that they somehow knew to be Eiko prime.

"I know you're just a fork," she said. "But you'll be a very useful asset."

"What do you want me to do?" the words came out of Keb's mouth unbidden.

"I want you to bring the others out of the cube. With their help we can take down anyone who threaten us and the TITAN we serve."

—

"All of the remaining egos from the cube have been converted," fork 9 said. It would have been much more efficient for her to call in their report. However, for some reason this fork preferred to appear in person.

Keb knew now that it was the virus that allowed them to tell each fork apart. Not that knowing made any difference. They couldn't speak or move independently. A small part that was still Keb watched, helpless, while capacities they no longer controlled used their various security clearances to open real and digital doors for Eiko's growing number of recruits. They knew where each fork and recruit was sent and every attempt to alert someone, anyone, had a regressing measure of success. It was only a matter of time before the virus removed even this small measure of self.

"Excellent," Eiko prime told 9. "Send forks 27–32 into the TQZ to look for our allies. Thanks to 7, 11, 13, and 14, Pilsner City is almost under our control."

"They're on their way," fork 9 said. "Is there anything else you would like me to do?"

"No, you've done well."

A warning claxon sounded in the room. The vibrations sent a pang through their overly sensitive neural relays. The couch disappeared, deleted. The honey-toned walls disappeared next, replaced by a construction grid. Thanks to a safety feature the room itself couldn't be deleted while egos were still inside, although it probably wouldn't take long for Firewall to work around that.

Fork 9 tried to leave but found the way blocked. That last vestige of Keb smiled. 9's image started to flicker. Both she and prime stared in disbelief as each pixel in 9's hand fractured. Fork 9 screamed as she exploded in a burst of light.

"You're too late." A cheshire grin spread across Eiko prime's face. "You'll never find all of us."

[We've been feeding your agents false data,] Charlyse's voice echoed in the small room. [None of them left the facility. They've all been deleted.]

"No!" Eiko screamed. "You're lying!"

Eiko thrust her hand out to Keb, causing a wave of pain to course through them again. This wasn't the pain of the virus. This was pain for pain's sake.

"If you don't let me out of here I'll kill Keb's fork."

[Go ahead,] Charlyse replied coolly. [You'll be saving us the trouble.]

The remnant of Keb laughed inside the prison of their mind. Eiko's inexperience with the modern world couldn't have manifested in a better way. It was impossible to play hardball with an organization that redefined collateral damage.

The lights flickered. Eiko summoned objects to the room, any object, in the hope that increasing the digital mass in the room would maintain its existence. Items would appear for a moment or two—a bed, a coat rack, a feather, a shoe. Each would splinter and vanish in a small burst of sparks. Soon she wasn't able to bring anything else in the room. They must have ordered Samuel to shut this down. Keb didn't know very many people who could work that fast.

They felt a moment of joy and relief as the lights flickered once, twice, and then went out completely. Eiko screamed in the dark. Their awareness of her disappeared a moment later. Keb could feel their mind start to crack as defenses were hacked away so they could be deleted. The pain accompanying this attack was easy to endure because, this time, there was no doubt in their mind that this was a necessary act.

LACK

Rob Boyle & Davidson Cole

"What's the number?"

The words dig their claws into my new vocal cords and yank themselves up and out of my parched throat. My diction is predictably poor, as it always is during the first few minutes following a resleeve. The pitch of the voice is apparent despite the mumbled, sandpaper slur of the words. Definitely a biomorph, and my latest sex is female. This much I know in the first few seconds. The model eludes me right now, but I'll know for certain soon enough, once motion is mine again. Another fury morph is my first guess.

The slab is hard. Nothing more than frigid metal with crisp white synth-slick wrapped around it. Typical accommodations for a corp dollhouse. The chill seeps through my skin and wraps around my bones.

A cortical cruncher looms over me, waving his welcome-back beam side to side, occasionally catching my pupils. His smug, bored face speaks: "Consciousness confirmed." The beam clicks off. My question should have made it obvious that I am back, but the guy is a slave to procedure. They all are. Corporate body banks like their employees paralyzed by obedience, unable to think for themselves. I mumble the question again. "What's the number?"

"March 11."

"How many after the Fall?"

"Are you for real?"

I am paranoid. Yes. I need to know the year every time I return upon a body bank slab. Paranoia is just one of the plagues transhumanity faces these days.

I try to snag the data from my new sleeve's mesh inserts before opening my mouth again. No luck. Asking a sleeve tech for the year is always humiliating. Makes me feel like an amateur, but the circumstances are definitely extenuating, so I press him. Hard.

"Answer the fucking question."

The corp sloth gives me the lunatic eye before he answers.

"Uh … 10 AF. You haven't been gone that long. Your last backup … "

He scans his entoptics for the info.

" … 14 days, 7 hours ago."

It takes a second to sink in, but when it does, it stings. It never ceases to shock when time slips away from me. Two weeks. Gone. Completely wiped from my existence. Two weeks ago, there was another me, sleeved in another morph. There was a mission and it led to my death. That is all I know. Either Firewall failed to retrieve the cortical stack off the corpse so I could retain those two weeks, or the fuckers deliberately chose to swipe that time from me. Honestly, though, both possibilities are preferable to having another self bouncing around out there, doing who knows what-the-fuck. Some t-humies get off on having multiple selves traipsing all over, but my ego is in check. One Sava is enough misery to unleash on the 'verse.

Shit. My brain is wandering off into morose territory; always does during the first moments following a resleeve. I need a physical context. Something tangible to focus my attention on. I bring my hands in front of my eyes, arms feeling like two-ton sacks of rocks. The fingers are thin and long; the knuckles callused, scarred and misshapen. Obviously the work of many thrown punches, fists connecting with jaws, metal, flesh. Yep. A well-worn fury morph. You get what you pay for, I suppose; or what Firewall is willing to pay for. Why do I do it? As far as the org is concerned, I'm nothing more than a cheap precision instrument, tossed into the recycling bin when I snap in half. There will always be more of me, until the horrors prove too intense, until the files get too corrupt, until I know too much and Firewall decides to wipe me, then some other sap will step in to preserve transhumanity. Preserve transhumanity. Fantastic. Now I'm babbling like a Firewall propaganda tweet! My arms weaken and flop back to my sides. The strength just isn't there yet. A few more minutes with nothing but my thoughts.

On his way out of the recovery bay, the cort cruncher laughs at my feeble attempt at motion. "What's your hurry?" he says. "Just relax, willya? You collapse onto the floor, you're gonna stay there until you get yourself up. They don't pay me enough to babysit newbies." His flippancy doesn't help my mood and the melancholy returns.

What experiences are no longer a part of my consciousness? Perhaps the thrill of a lifetime. Did I discover true beauty? Fall in love? Have an epiphany? Save a life? I'll never know. Those memories, that life, that version of me, is gone. The new me, lying on this slab, was never shaped by those experiences. My chest hollows out from the weight of the loss.

I gotta shift the thought process.

Fuck it. Maybe there was no joy, no revelations. It was a shit two weeks. I'm certain of it. I was bored out of my mind. Better yet, broken and suffering from an epic heartache. My demise was meaningless. I OD'd on kick, flopping on the floor in a pathetic speed-addled frenzy till my heart exploded. I was gutted by some low-life scumborn in a back station corridor over some lo-rez black market XP. I'm glad the time was wiped. Ecstatic, in fact. Fuck it. Fuck them. I don't need those two weeks.

But these thoughts are lies. I need those two weeks. I don't feel whole without them. Hell, I feel incomplete if even an hour is sacrificed. I have to know.

Someone knows what occurred. No doubt. Probably a Firewall proxy, Jesper most likely. He was my connect this go-round. I remember that much. The wipe would have been his call. And proxies have a quick trigger finger when it comes to wiping us sentinels. Even a hard-earned rep score can't save my memories when Firewall deems the results of a mission too sensitive for an outer circle thug like myself to possess. As long as the fucking job gets done. As long as transhumanity perseveres.

What a shit deal.

How did my life, my lives, come to this? Always in the hands of another.

Again, the dread, the paranoia. I gotta shake this off. I have to give the org the benefit of the doubt. I've been a sentinel for decades. I like to think I've saved millions of lives, but I'm just not sure.

Do I trust the org? No. But there is an understanding, a degree of respect. Though as the years continue to race by, and the gaps grow longer and more frequent, I'm beginning to doubt Firewall's commitment to my preservation.

Suddenly, my muse stirs, breaking my dark reverie. Several entoptic displays appear in my field of vision, cycling through diagnostic routines as my mesh inserts finally come online. Careza's familiar feminine voice enters my mind.

[Welcome back, Sava.]

The sound is soothing; like being cradled by my mother, or embraced by a lover. The harmonic upgrade was a worthwhile investment. Careza has learned to use it well. I rarely think of my muse as an AI. It is my only true friend these days. I wonder if it shares the sentiment. I've never shot the thought its way. I keep it to myself. I'm afraid of what the response might be.

Hey Careza. Glad to be back.

[You could use a drink, I suspect.]

You know me too well, Car. Better than I know myself.

[Hospitality now has the request. Wait time, approximately ten minutes.]

Thanks. Careza enjoys our conversations when my brain has a slight buzz. It is always trying to get me drunk.

[You're welcome, Sava. Before you ask, it's been two weeks. I don't have any information on what happened following our last resleeve. Currently, we are in lunar orbit aboard Selardi IV. We are outfitted in a CoreCorp-brand fury morph with minor enhancements. They will be online shortly. I am pleased to report the Titanians were victorious and won the Cup.]

Damnit. Would have made a killing on that one. What did the odds go off at? But before Careza can dig up the info, I shut down the operation. Wait. No. I don't want to know. It'll only irritate me more. A nervous energy starts to itch my entire system and a thick familiar taste begins to coat my tongue. I need a cigarette.

[Yes. I know. The previous occupant of this morph was a heavy smoker. The habit might be difficult to shake this time.]

This resleeve just keeps getting better by the minute. I hate smoking. Booze, fine. I can handle my alcohol, but smoking always makes me feel like shit. Every time I get sleeved in a morph with the addiction, I struggle to kick it. Careza continues with her report as I try to retain my sanity in the face of an intense nicotine craving.

[@-rep remains intact.]

Finally some good news. At least I didn't piss off any allies in the past 2 weeks.

[Indeed. Are you in the right frame of mind for an update on Rati?]

Rati is my passion. The lover I hold above all others. She disappeared on me two years ago. No explanation. The sting still lingers.

Let's skip the update for now, Careza.

[Understood.]

Run a newsfeed scan. Check for any major incidents in the past 2 weeks. Maybe there's a clue as to what we may have been up to.

As Careza runs the scan and continues her standard sitrep, I shift my attention to the new sleeve. The strength to stand is finally there. I push the morph up and swing the feet onto the floor. Spasms shoot through every muscle. New morphs always take a bit of time in which to acclimate. Luckily, I'm familiar with the CoreCorp fury, sleeved it a few times in the past. This one feels like an old pair of shoes, bit worn and abused, but able to pound the pavement if need be. The left ankle is a bit tender. I hold it up a bit to get a look. Bit swollen. Definitely not new sleeve dysmorphia. Probably a nagging injury. Again, a pain in the ass, but you get what you pay for, I suppose. The nanotat encircling the right bicep is rude and obnoxious, even by scum standards—an entire slitheroid entering the genitals of a female pleasure pod, fully animated. Class act, whoever opted to etch that upon the morph. I hate identifying marks, but again, if you can't afford a clean morph, you take what you can get.

I slide off the table, managing not to fall over in the process, and gingerly test the ankle. Sore, but it isn't going to snap off.

Put in a request for a patch, left ankle. Bute should be fine.

[Phenylbutazone. On its way. And the cocktail will be here in approximately 30 seconds. Nothing unusual on the newsfeed scan.]

Figures.

I plod over to the full-length mirror, standard issue in resleeve waking chambers, and drop the sheet to take a look at the new me. I spy the cortical cruncher lingering in the doorway, my cocktail in his hand, giving my body an appreciative look. I don't recognize myself.

"Hand me my drink please." I reach out my hand in his direction without even acknowledging his presence. He steps into the room, too close to me, and slips the drink into my hand. His breath smells like some sort of sour sausage.

"Not too bad under the sheet, are you?" he says. "I took a peek earlier, but I must say, the slab didn't do you justice. On your feet, the curves really pop. Your face isn't much to look at, but that rack is … "

I cut him off before I vomit bile into my mouth. "It's exquisite. I know. Now shut up and back off before I rip the skin off your face and slap you silly with it." He gets the message and slinks from the room.

It is a nice rack.

[If nice is defined by proportion, then I would say yes.]

AIs, always so formal.

[You're approximately 4 centimeters taller than your usual proprioception allows for, so watch your head.]

Thanks for the heads up.

[That was awful.]

Yeah. Yeah. I know. A smile finds its way onto my face as the banter with my muse lightens my mood. Looking in the mirror, I try to broaden the smile, to get a better sense of my new face. I show some teeth. Nicotine stains all over them. I take a long sip from my cocktail, swish the alcohol around a bit. I can feel my blood respond instantly to the sauce. I close my eyes and let out a sigh. Just a few moments of peace is all I ask.

[We have a guest, Sava.] Damnit. No such luck.

Who?

[Our last Firewall proxy, Jesper, has sent a beta-level fork of himself. It is rather impatient to speak with you.]

Connect him.

They just cannot leave me alone, can they? Officially, Firewall doesn't even exist. It's because of Rati that they got their tentacles wrapped all around me, through me. The whole mess on Mars. That's where it all started. The last time I saw Rati. All that knowledge they allowed me to retain. But why? Until that day, I had never realized just how scary the universe truly was. No, not scary. Horrific. No other word for something so vast, so uncaring. Transhumanity could be wiped out completely and it would all just continue on as before. Horrific. No other way to explain the feeling you have when you come face to face with things truly beyond comprehension. Hell, no other term could encapsulate transhumanity's actions towards each other—much less what other beings lurking in the void have in store for us. Perhaps that was why. To teach me a lesson. To make certain I would never forget, so I would never cease assisting the org, because even the briefest glimpse of what is actually out there is enough.

Jesper's fork materializes in my field of vision.

[Welcome back, Sava.]

Fuck off, Jesper. You know I hate waking up with lack.

[Sorry. Nothing I could do.] His expression is serious and concerned, but his kinesics indicate he is as calm as can be. What an act! Fucking proxies never panic. They hold all the cards and it's never their minds that are on the line.

Yeah. Right. Get to the point. You don't have me sleeved in a combat morph to get some downtime, so you must have something serious lined up. Are Berk, Pivo, and Sarlo here?

[Yes, they have been resleeved in the same facility.]

At least my team is with me. People I could count on. To a certain degree.

All right. What are the details?

—

Pivo gripped the smooth outer surface of the station with all eight arms. Nano-magnetics at the tips of his vacsuit arms were the only difference between a secure hold and an endless drift into the depths of space. He peered up through his faceplate at the dark orb above him.

Earth.

His eyes locked on an expanse of dead black ocean through the ominous clouds. Pivo longed to swim in those ancient depths. Born and bred for space, he had never once immersed himself in the former ecological niche of his kind. Odds were against his ever taking a plunge into the salty waters of an Earth ocean. The planet was now a plagued death trap. A wasteland of skeletal forms.

He imagined a time before the Fall, when his ancestors thrust through blue waters and slipped effortlessly through mazes of coral, or gently floated along with the current, not bothered by the burden of sapience. Perhaps octopi still survived beneath the black waters of the present, eking out a brief existence, biding their time, keeping the species true and alive until the Earth could be reclaimed, and Pivo would join them on that glorious day, abandoning knowledge altogether, and returning to the ways of instinct.

Vacsuit sensors interrupted Pivo's fantasy, detecting a laser light that bathed his form—contact from Sava by line-of-sight laser link. It was the preferred method of communication when a mission required discretion. Pivo's muse processed the message, and Sava's voice entered his head.

[Something wrong? Why'd you stop moving?]

[Just enjoying the view,] Pivo beamed back.

[Enjoy it on the way down, for hours if you want. Get inside the station before one of the sentry bots finds us.]

Pivo didn't bother to respond. There was no arguing with Sava. No use in defending your actions. Pivo began crawling along the shell of the station again. The station itself was tethered to the end of a long, black, carbon nanotube cable that stretched all the way down to the planet's surface—the sole surviving space elevator.

Pivo located the breach, a thin scar in the station's metallic hull, the result of an internal explosion responsible for the station's demise during the Fall. The breach was exactly where Sava said it would be and the description of its size was dead-on: a gap barely large enough for a human infant to slip through. According to Sava, years ago, the self-repairing nanosystems operating in the hull's metal had malfunctioned before the breach had been fully repaired. The level of mission details Sava managed to extract from Firewall was scary sometimes. Paranoia bloomed for a moment, but he quickly dismissed his suspicion, compressed his cephalopod form, and squeezed his body through the breach.

In blackness, Pivo activated his infrared emitter, casting the room in a light outside the normal visual spectrum. The interior of the lifeless station became visible to his enhanced eyes in the eerie altered colors of infrared. Pivo almost preferred the dark. Ice crystals glittered from every surface, the result of flash frozen moisture in the long-absent atmosphere. Frigid clumps of human remains floated alongside chunks of hull metal in a macabre zero-gravity ballet. Pivo floated through the wreckage and the gore, lightly tapping aside metal or flesh to clear a path deeper into the room. A female head drifted slowly by, the face frozen in a gaping silent scream. An intact cortical stack dangled from the severed neck. For a second, Pivo considered snatching the stack, but he was not here to retrieve lost souls. Instead, he placed two of his arms upon the top of the head and pushed it beneath him, towards the floor. Like so many others lost during the Fall, this person would remain forgotten here.

Pivo made it to the airlock without incident, but he knew his luck would run dry eventually. A run-in with hypercorp guardians on a derelict station was unavoidable. Sensors may have already detected his presence. It was only a matter of time before bots converged on his position. He just hoped that when it occurred (and it most certainly would), it would happen after he had opened up the airlock and the rest of the team was inside the station.

The airlock had been welded shut from the inside. Pivo was prepared for this eventuality, but it made his detection by guardian bots a certainty. He composed himself for a few seconds, focused on the task at hand, then fired up the plasma torch built into one of his vacsuit arms. A harsh hot blue glare filled the room. Seconds were now his most precious possession.

He was almost through the inner door when his muse pinged him with a warning from the passive terahertz sensor. An object was moving towards Pivo's position rapidly, now only twenty meters away. A sentry bot would be upon him in soon.

[Almost through the first door,] Pivo transmitted calmly, even though it took every ounce of his will to keep the torch steady. [I have company. Be ready.]

[Copy that,] Sava replied.

Finally, Pivo cut through the seal. The octomorph slithered four arms through the still smoldering sliced metal, and with a strained yank, pulled the door from the frame. The door slowly floated away into the chamber, the edges rapidly cooling. The interior airlock door was not welded shut. With a vocal sigh of relief, all eight of Pivo's arms began a frenzied assault upon the airlock door's manual controls.

[Few more seconds. Just a few more seconds.] But the seconds had expired.

In his 360-degree field of vision, Pivo could see the security bot thrust into view behind him. The bot unloaded its weapons immediately, the shots ricocheting off the floating airlock door. The bot advanced on the door, and with a furious swat knocked the obstruction aside. It clanged upon the crystalline surface of the wall. Just as Pivo pulled the last lever to release the airlock door, blazing plasma fire engulfed him.

—

Sava had instructed Careza to surge the neurochem the instant the airlock portal was open. The muse did not fail to deliver. In what seemed like an eternal slow-mo to Sava's charged brain, the airlock door swung open into the station, aided by a thudding steel leg kick courtesy of

Berk, the team's muscle. With a flash of thought, Sava's targeting radar snapped up an entoptic display and locked on two targets: Pivo and a sentry bot. The robotic guard dog was already leveling its weapons, but Sava was faster. Retinal-searing plasma fire erupted from Sava's weapon, singeing one of Pivo's arms and slamming the sentry back. A second shot punched through the bot's armored carapace, melting critical components within, rendering the bot a useless pile of fused scrap metal.

Sava moved quickly past the cursing octomorph and unloaded two more shots into the smoking bot.

[We're clear,] Sava transmitted. [One down, but there is always more. Count on it. Pivo, you shiny?]

[You scorched my breeding arm, puta.] Pivo shot back with clear agitation rumbling in the harmonics.

[You rather I leave you to the bot next time?] Sava turned to Sarlo. [Sarlo, get in here and find the console you need. Berk, we're going to need to set up defensive positions, to give hacker boy here time to crunch his bits.]

Pivo cut through his vacsuit and detached his damaged arm, cursing Sava under his breath as the vacsuit rapidly repaired itself and sealed the gap.

[Hey. Don't worry, Pivo. You've got seven more. And besides, you don't really strike me as the breeding type anyway.] Sava relished giving Pivo a hard time. It was one of the true joys in life.

Pushing off from one wall to the next, Sarlo moved along the chamber with ease and grace. His neotenic morph was slighter and even more diminutive than the average human child sleeve, completely augmented and customized to match his "preferences." He had paid a fortune for it. The others never understood Sarlo's penchant for juvenile human sleeves, so much so that he always kicked in his own credits to ensure an augmented neotenic resleeve, even when Firewall was footing the bill. They also didn't know where his seemingly endless supply of personal funds came from, nor did they want to. As long as he got the job done.

Two minidrones followed after Sarlo, lighting the area in infrared and actively scanning on other wavelengths. [This way,] he said, transmitting an entoptic map to each team member's overlay. [It's not far, a hundred meters or so.] A highlighted route appeared on the map.

Sava and Pivo followed closely behind Sarlo, while Berk struggled to keep pace in her armored gynoid shell.

[Keep up, flatlander. We'll be down the gravity well soon enough,] Sava beamed to Berk.

[Not soon enough for me,] Berk replied.

The abandoned station was eerily quiet. Signs of long-forgotten violence and desperation lingered everywhere. Floating debris. Ruptured and frozen bodies. Scorch marks and twisted metal. Death owned this place.

When the team reached the control station, Sava and Berk took up defensive positions in the corridor while Sarlo and Pivo went to work on the station's dormant systems.

[I'll be damned! The mission spec was actually right. The station systems are active but dormant. Whomever's guarding this place didn't wreck the systems, they left open the possibility that the space elevator could be activated again.] Sarlo gleefully began his procedures to hack the system.

[Who the fuck would want to risk going down to that ball of ash?] Berk piped in.

Pivo waved one of his arms in agitation. [Need I remind you that some of us happen to think that reclaiming our home planet is a good idea?]

[Reactionary thinking, if you ask me.] Berk replied. [Shrugging off all of our old nation-state loyalties is one of the best steps transhumanity has ever made. Leave reveling in the glories of the past to the bio-cons. I'll take a future where we step boldly outward into space, thank you much.]

[Let's cut the politics.] Sava pointed at Berk. [You're an anarchist, I get it.] Then Sava pointed at Pivo. [And you're on a reclamation kick. Fine.] But Sava's rant was interrupted by half a dozen fast moving dots upon the team's entoptic radars. [Incoming pings. Sarlo, you in yet?]

[Working on it. Fuck. Fuck. Shit.] Sarlo's childish voice sounded petulant.

[Work faster. If these bots have heavy ordnance, we're screwed.] Sava and Berk both unloaded suppression fire down their respective stretches of corridor before the bots even made it to the corners. The bots halted their approach momentarily, taking cover just around the bend. More bots began to appear on the radar, moving towards the position of the first responders.

[We're running out of time, Sar! More bots gathering!] Sava unloaded another round of suppression at the bend. Berk kept her weapon quiet, waiting for a bot to make a move into the corridor before lighting it up, but the bots remained put. More gathered, and even more appeared on radar, moving to the same position.

[They're gonna be all over us any second now!]

[Consider this a gift, ladies and gents…] And with a final operation, Sarlo seized control of the station's entire security system.

Suddenly, one of the bots turned on the others. Another soon joined it. In a matter of seconds, fumes and debris came drifting down the corridor as all-out warfare broke out between the bots. Sava and Berk lowered their weapons and admired the sounds of Sarlo's handiwork.

[Damn, Sar! I guess that is why you are one of the best hackers in the system!]

[Applause, applause, ya waify freak!]

[When you've got cutting edge-exploits courtesy of the leet coding AGIs on Extropia, there's not a whole lot you can't do.] Sarlo delivered the line with a calm harmonic, but Sava was watching his kinesics, and they were off the charts. The neotenic's little heart was beating like a drum roll. Sava opted not to bust his furless balls about it, and instead let Sarlo have his moment in the sun. This had been a "close one," and another close one might not end up in their favor.

Sava allowed a few seconds of relieved silence before getting the team back to business. [Sarlo. How soon till the elevator is active?]

—

Pivo stuck to the portal, watching as they descended below the soot-filled layer of clouds and the Earth below came into view. They were in the atmosphere now, descending on a taut beanstalk stretched between the Earth and station above, a massive feat of engineering built from carbon nanotubes. The shuttle car crawled down the elevator cable, bringing them closer and closer to the ruined planet.

Earth's atmosphere was now choked with a thick dust, the color of rust. The winds whipped over the planet's surface with breakneck velocity, swirling dangerously in certain pockets. The world's weather systems had been irretrievably ravaged by the Fall, when transhumanity had seemingly gone to war with a group of rogue AIs known as the TITANs. Bombs, raging fires, chemical attacks, biowar plagues, voracious nanoswarms—even nukes—had taken their toll. It was now an inhospitable place, gripped by nuclear winter. Some of the clouds were formed into unusual shapes, defying the high winds, even seeming to writhe as they moved—the thriving descendants of self-replicating airborne nanoswarms, Pivo suspected. Who knew what other monstrosities waited for them below, evolved from the remnants of AI war machines?

The Earth was off-limits now. Abandoned to the enemy. Though the TITANs were presumed to be long gone, escaping the solar system via secretly-constructed wormhole gates, taking millions of forcibly uploaded transhuman minds with them—they had left many of their tools and weapons behind. Likewise, some of the weapons transhumanity had unleashed on the AIs—and, quite often, themselves—had taken on a life of their own. So Earth had been abandoned and interdicted, with hypercorp killsats laced into orbit to shoot down anything that attempted to leave or land on the planet's surface.

As a reclaimer, Pivo was part of a small but vocal faction that advocated a return to Earth. There was still hope for the planet, they believed. It had always persevered, and this was no time to give up on it. Earth needed to be cleansed and terraformed, resuscitating transhumanity's home. But the reclaimers were a minority. To most survivors of the Fall, the Earth held too many horrible memories. Lives ruined. Loved ones lost. Their own deaths. It was a monument to transhumanity's arrogance and mistakes, a grim reminder that they were not above destroying themselves despite all of their advances and technology, or perhaps because of them.

This didn't prevent some from trying, of course. Scavengers still raided the planet's ruins, retrieving long-lost treasures, cultural artifacts, or even the preserved mind-states of those who failed to escape. Some reclaimers had initiated their own secret missions, intending to establish a basecamp from which they would begin operating their own reclamation projects. Most were never heard from again.

The team of four rested and prepared equipment in the shuttle's large open lounge, Sava and Sarlo in a cramped inflatable survival bubble so the biomorphs could escape the confines of their vacsuits for a while. Pivo elected to remain outside the bubble and in the vacsuit. Close confines with Sava during the descent did not sound pleasant to him. The walls of the lounge were smeared with decades-old blood, now frozen into a crystalline brown in the depressurized cabin. Whoever the last passengers were to ride this shuttle, fleeing the doomed Earth, must have set violently upon each other, fueled by madness or despair.

[I wonder what it was like.] Sarlo tossed the thought out to the group.

[What?] Pivo replied.

Sava quickly jumped in and put an end to the discussion Sarlo was yearning to start. [Quit with the philosophizing and the dramatizing. You know I cannot stand that shit.] Sava tried desperately to maintain order and an air of gruff detachment. It was too easy to let the brain wander off into the past and the fate of the millions who perished during the Fall. To counter this, Sava always resorted to the diatribe. [Listen. We all know the mission specs. We're locating someone. A courier. Most likely a corpse. Last known position while alive was the base station we will drop into when this ride stops. Mount Kilimanjaro. Which, according to quite reliable sources, was once overrun by killbots, which are most likely still in the vicinity.] Sava paused for dramatic effect before continuing. [We retrieve something from the courier. What, we don't fucking know. Only that it is quite valuable to the org. We stick to what we know. I don't want to hear any more bull-shit "what ifs" and "I wonders." If your thoughts are anywhere other than the mission, keep them to yourself. I don't want to hear them.] And with that declaration, the rest of the journey to the Kilimanjaro station was in silence, each confined to their own thoughts, not a single ping between them.

—

The shuttle rattled to a stop inside the dark cavernous hangar. At one time, the Kilimanjaro hangar was the busiest Earth-to-space station port in the world, servicing millions of customers annually. Now, as Pivo clung to a shuttle window and stared out into the black emptiness of the hangar, it seemed as if the place was a soulless vacuum.

[Ready when you are.] Sarlo pinged Sava, poised to hack open the shuttle door and allow the stale dust-choked air of Earth to waft over the team. Sava nodded to Sarlo and the shuttle door slid open with a rush of decompression. A blinding red-gray dust blasted into the shuttle from the hangar and coated the shuttle interior almost immediately.

Sava's first step into the Kilimanjaro hangar landed firmly onto the brittle ribcage of a child's skeleton. The bones snapped into splinters and powder with a crunch. The floor surrounding the shuttle airlock was carpeted with skeletons entangled in a mass of tattered clothing. There was no way to avoid stepping upon them. One by one, the others stepped from the airlock.

[This place is a tomb,] Berk beamed to the group.

[This whole planet is a tomb,] Sava replied, with an extra echo harmonic allowing the word tomb to continue on well after the phrase was transmitted, added specifically to annoy Pivo, who immediately shut down the echo in his head with a countermeasure from his muse.

Sava took a few more crunching steps forward, then stopped. The rest of the team followed suit.

[Something is not right here.] Sava kicked at one of the skeletons. The bones rattled and cracked. [I don't see any skulls.]

[Forced uploading,] Sarlo transmitted. [TITAN machines harvested the heads of the dead for scanning.] He shrugged. [That's my guess, anyway.]

[Shut up!] Sava signaled the team to silence. [Who else hears that?]

A low mechanical whir reverberated nearby. [I'm picking it up.] Pivo replied. [Up a bit to the north. About 30 meters.] As if in response to Pivo's observation, another whir began, this one behind the team, from the south end of the hangar. Another whir from the east joined in the chorus. The sounds were coming closer, becoming more distinct, more aggressive.

[No visual, yet. This fucking place is so deep and thick with this dust shit, seems to act like chaff too. Infrared is giving me only about twenty feet!] Sava motioned for the team to move to the right. [Stay close, we move slow and keep the triggers itchy. The passenger lounges are just east of us. We start the search there.] The whirs were now all around them, hovering just outside visual range.

[What the fuck is that?] A flying insectoid bot with six articulated arms ending in small buzzsaws lunged from the dusty darkness at Berk, who dropped to the floor and unleashed plasma fire into it. The bot slammed into a pile of bones and rags and set it alight. The fire spread quickly, leaping from dry cloth to dry cloth. The blazing hangar floor now illuminated the area in the hot orange glow of flame. At least a dozen insectoid bots hovered in a perimeter around the team, awaiting an opportunity to strike. Another bot dove at Berk, its buzzsaw arms slashing wildly. Berk fired, but missed. The bot slammed into Berk's head and the buzzsaws ground into her neck. Sparks flew in all directions as metal met metal. She dropped her rifle and pushed against the body of the bot till the saws were off her neck. [Fucking run you idiots! I've got this!]

Sava fired and dropped a bot, then dashed east, leaping over spreading waist-high flames. [Make for the lounge!]

Pivo elevated onto two arms and ran behind Sava, his five remaining arms flopping wildly above his head. [Out of the way, ya poke!] Sarlo outpaced the slower octomorph, running through the flames towards the lounge.

Berk flung the frenzied bot into a flaming pile of bones, scrambled to her feet, and followed after the group, covered in bone bits and dust, the bot swarm in whirring pursuit.

Sava reached the lounge first and the portal was open. Turning with rifle raised, Sava took cover against the door frame. Sarlo and Pivo were past the flames and Berk was closing the gap, as were the bots. Sava unloaded cover fire that sizzled over Sarlo's head, knocking another bot out, but the rest of the swarm remained unfazed. They just kept coming. Suddenly, more bots appeared out of the shrinking darkness near the lounge.

[There's more! They're flanking!] Sava blasted at the new bots to try and slow down their gambit. Sarlo was only thirty feet from the portal when he tripped on a tangle of bones. His boyish body collapsed face first into the dust and human remains. Pivo made an awkward leap over him, skidded across the floor, and squished into the outer lounge wall right near the door. Sava reached out, snagged the octomorph by a arm, and dragged him into the safety of the lounge. Berk tried to stop and help Sarlo up, but her momentum was too much and her footing upon the dusty floor too unstable. She tumbled forward in a roll of dust cloud, chipped bone, and tattered rags, finally slamming into Sava in the doorway.

The three team members within the lounge gathered themselves just in time to witness a bot latch onto Sarlo's head from above as he stood up. The machine stretched two arms out to the side, then plunged their spinning blades into Sarlo's neck. Sarlo's eyes went wide and his body tensed as the saw blades ground through flesh and bone, working through his neck in seconds. The instant his head was severed from the torso, the bot swooped around and zipped off over the flames, into the dark oblivion of the far end of the hangar.

Sarlo's headless body wavered for a second, then collapsed, spurting blood in long, lazy arcs.

—

Pivo, Sava, and Berk sat in silence. They had managed to seal the portal into the lounge, locking out the horrors of the hangar. The headhunter bots could still be heard hovering outside the portal, occasionally clanging and grinding their blades against the sealed door.

Berk finally broke the silence. [I'm trying very hard not to think about what they're going to do with him.]

[Try harder. Sarlo knew the odds of survival were slim when he signed on. We all did.] Sava stood up.

[Should we tell him? When he resleeves?] Pivo knew this was going to set Sava off, but he blurted it anyway.

[Would that be kindness or cruelty, Pivo? And besides, there is no guarantee that any of us will survive. So who gives a shit? Whenever your last backup was, I sure hope you're not gonna miss anything since. Let's get moving.]

—

With Sarlo gone, Pivo took over the navigation duties. They were nearing the corporate VIP lounge, the last known location of the courier.

The team moved through dark corridors filled with headless skeletons and mummified remains. Years ago, the corporate forces defending the structure had been overrun by AI war machines, which mercilessly slaughtered everyone inside. The walls were scarred from battle, covered in dried blood. Destroyed remnants of the AI war machines littered the halls as well, haunting monuments to the few victories humanity had in their losing battle. Even as piles of scrap, the machines had a menacing presence.

[Too bad this isn't a salvage op,] Berk commented. [The autonomists could use a look at this tech. At the very least, figure out what the hypercorps might try to do with it.]

As they entered a long concourse, the remains and debris abruptly disappeared, as if cleared out.

[I'm getting some strange thermal readings here. Patterns that don't make sense,] transmitted Pivo.

[What is that supposed to mean?] Sava beamed back.

Before Pivo could give thought to "I don't know," his muse issued a chilling warning: [My nanosensors register the presence of unknown nanobots in large numbers of a highly sophisticated design, suggesting a TITAN manufacture. Countermeasures have been initiated.]

[Nanoswarm. Move! Move!] Pivo broadcasted in a panic as he launched into a full two-armed sprint. Sava and Berk followed Pivo's lead without question. They all knew the dangers of a TITAN nanoswarm. Unlike the nanobots Pivo often made, which were manufactured with particular purposes in mind, and which were neither self-sustaining or intelligent, this particular nanoswarm was autonomous, self-replicating, adaptive, and capable of making almost anything it needed. Even as they fled, individual nanosensors were measuring up the three agents, transmitting details on their morphs and gear to the rest of the swarm.

A junction came into view ahead, the pathway narrowing into a smaller tunnel. Suddenly, Pivo stopped, just a meter before the tunnel. [Do not move forward!] The others crashed to a halt.

[What the fuck Pivo!?] Sava looked back down the hall. [Fucking swarm could be finishing us as we speak!]

[My muse picked up a burst of thermal energy here. The swarm is up to something,] Pivo warned.

[But there's nothing here,] Berk replied, as she waved her hand across the tunnel entrance. Her metal hand suddenly clanged to the floor, separated from her wrist.

[Monomolecular wire.] Even though the situation grew more dire by the minute, Pivo was impressed and fascinated with the inventiveness of the alien nanotech. [It laced the door with it. Cuts through anything. Weak tensile strength though—you probably snapped it.]

[We're fucked. Let's face it.] Berk picked her severed hand off the floor. Down the hall, the nanoswarm began to take a visible shape as the nanobots accreted. The swarm was congealing into a fog, creeping closer. Berk continued, [The entirety of this port is probably filled with this shit. I'm useless at this point. These things are already all over my systems, my diagnostics are going crazy.]

[So what are you saying, Berk? You done?] Sava transmitted.

[Yeah. I'm done.] Berk shook her head in disgust. [Who knows what these little bastards have infected me with. I don't want to risk it. I'd rather resort to a clean back up. Forget this shit ever happened. You keep running if you want. I'll try to buy you some time.] Berk turned and ran directly into the fog. The nanoswarm sucked in around her immediately and the disassembly began. Berk's metal frame began to dissolve as she ran further and further away from Pivo and Sava, leaving a wispy trail of nanoswarm behind her.

[Get fucking moving fools! This isn't for my amusement! I'll see ya the next time around.] A few minutes later, Berk's signal went dead.

—

Sava and Pivo entered the VIP lounge. When the spaceport was overrun so many years ago, this was the site of the humans' last stand. Piles of security personnel skeletons littered the floor just inside the doorway. The charred remnants of a hopeless barricade were scattered beside the mounds of bone. Skeletons draped in torn, singed civilian garb were clustered around the walls and corners, sometimes three or four deep, as if they had all scrambled as far as possible from some avatar of death in the middle of the room.

Pivo started an operation to locate the RFID tag the courier was supposedly chipped with in his left shoulder blade. The code triggered a ping within three meters. Pivo pointed a lengthy arm at a small bone pile. [He's in there somewhere.]

Sava stepped over to the pile of three skeletons and began rummaging through the bones, yanking out or snapping off all the femurs. [Goddamnit I want a cigarette. This morph has me so tweaked. Haven't I made it clear I don't smoke? Yet, every time, they sleeve me in a morph nailed with the habit.] Sava handed the bundle of bones to Pivo.

[Must be a fury thing. Should just take a few minutes to scan these for the nanoscale etching.] Pivo got to work. [Enough time for a smoke, if you want.]

[Yeah. Real funny. How about I grind you up into dust and smoke you?] Sava sat down on the floor as Pivo sent out a chuckle.

The deceased courier, whomever he was, had been entrusted with information too sensitive to transmit. No one knew the true capabilities of the TITANs to intercept and decode, so the courier had been injected with nanobots that etched a nanoscopic encoded message directly onto one of his femur bones. However, he had never made it off the planet. His message had never been delivered.

Pivo and Sava had no idea what the information was, but someone at Firewall obviously deemed it worthy of capture. Information on the TITANs perhaps. Or some CEO's secret family recipe for pasta sauce.

[This is the one.] Pivo held out the femur to Sava and tossed the others to the floor.

[What does it say?]

[I don't know. Not sure I want to know.] Pivo continued to hold out the femur.

[Enough with the drama Pivo. Just get your nanos to read it. We need a copy of the data. If you don't want to carry, I will.]

[I'd prefer that. Thank you.] Pivo set his nanobots to work on deciphering the inscription. When they were done, the intel was transmitted directly to Sava. Pivo wanted no part of it.

[So, now what? How do we get out of here? The only way out is the way we came in, and that's suicide.] Pivo's complexion changed from a milky green to an almost royal blue. It always happened when helplessness began to settle in.

Sava did not hesitate to answer, choosing to speak as opposed to transmit. "We're not gonna leave, Pivo. Not even gonna try." Sava raised the plasma rifle and aimed it directly at Pivo's oblong head. "See you next time, calamari." Sava pulled the trigger, and a fiery bolt of plasma reduced Pivo to a twitching mass of bloody scorched cartilage atop writhing arms. The arms continued to flop on the floor in a growing pool of blood as Sava sat down next to a pile of bones and leaned against the wall.

Sava pulled out a cigarette and lit it. The first inhale was virtually orgasmic. Sava loved to smoke.

Upon exhale, Careza pinged. [Shall I contact Project Ozma?]

Yeah. Get our lady on the line.

A woman's voice, cold and harsh, entered Sava's head, so different from the soothing tones Careza used. [Are you prepared to deliver, Agent Sava?]

[That depends.] Sava took another drag.

[Perhaps I did not make myself clear during our initial negotiations, Agent Sava. Your options are rather limited. You are unlikely to make it off the planet alive, and we cannot afford to lose this information, nor can we afford to have it fall into the hands of your organization. You are going to have to follow through, and trust that we will do the same.]

[Either you give me her location right now, or I take your precious info with me.]

There was a long pause before the woman transmitted again. [You realize there will be consequences, Agent Sava. For you and for Rati.]

[Yeah. I suppose so.] The cigarette burned to the filter and Sava flicked it into a bone pile. [So what's it gonna be?]

[We do not bargain, Agent Sava, after a deal has been struck. Do as you will, and we will react accordingly.] The connection with the woman terminated. Sava stood up and walked over to where the courier's femur lay and picked it up. Pivo's gore coated the bone. Sava wiped it off and held it up to take a close look.

Sorry, Careza. Info payload only. Leave the ego behind.

[Understood.]

With the flash of a thought, Sava instructed Careza to activate the cortical stack's emergency farcaster—a one-shot neutrino transmitter, powered by the tiniest amount of antimatter. Sava's head exploded all over the room, taking the courier's femur with it. The information contained on the femur, however, found its way almost instantly through the blackest depths of space, landing safely onto a dedicated Firewall receiver elsewhere in the solar system.

—

"What's the number?"

The words dig their claws into my new vocal cords and yank themselves up and out of my parched throat. My diction is predictably poor, as it always is during the first few minutes following a resleeve. The pitch of the voice is apparent despite the mumbled, sandpaper slur of the words. Definitely a biomorph and my latest sex is female. This much I know in the first few seconds.

NOSTALGIA

Georgina Kamsika

The mottled grey planet fills the window. So many miles of vacuum between the habitat and earth, yet the globe looks close enough for Charumati to pluck from the sky. The window frame is rough-sanded pale wood, grooved and full of knotholes, reflecting a softly lit room behind her. Tatami mats, paper walls and soft, expressive art are the only decorations in an otherwise restrained room.

These contrast with the brightly coloured neon feeds that are scrolling on her HUD; information flying almost faster than she can process. She scans the metadata flicking past. Streams flash and beep, enticing her to pull some of the larger, compressed data feeds.

Nothing on the mesh catches her eye, so she touches the antique crib set beside her. Twelve month-old baby Kiyoko breathes deeply whilst swaddled in natural cotton and hemp fabrics. A secret contact-feed initiates at her touch, the habitat bandwidth so powerful she gets an update in a split second. Her mesh insert ignores public databases like Solarchive, using a virtual private network to tunnel securely through to the Eye, Firewall's hidden social network.

Charumati speed-scrolls through the cached messages. Nothing from her router, codename Sapphire, to change her mission parameters. She bends over the crib, dropping her hand to her side to disengage from the feed.

Her ayah biomod-enhanced smell implants kick in as the baby opens her eyes. A chubby hand reaches out, fingers opening and closing in the air. Charumati leans closer, but ignores the hand. She might be new to her ayah morph but she's learned not to get caught in the baby's pincer-like grip.

"Shh, Kio," she sings the words. "Sleepy time."

Kiyoko opens her mouth, burbling nonsense noises. She's still not spoken her first word, but she's never stopped smiling. A few minutes of Charumati rocking the crib, and her eyes drift closed. It hasn't been long since Kiyoko's last feeding, and now that she's asleep, she's likely to stay that way for at least two or three hours. Plenty of time for the mission.

[Place is clear,] her muse, Penni, informs her. [Two valid exits, though the first is potentially hazardous, as it relies on no incoming ship. Condition Amber.]

Charumati feels for her bioweave armor and implanted weapons, upgraded since she was recruited into Firewall. All good. She resists the urge to check on the baby again, nothing will have changed in two seconds, and heads down some shallow stairs to a seating area. Low cushions face a series of wall niches recessed into white plaster. Of differing height and width, each niche houses its own item—a tea set adorned with small nicks, a patinated vase; other items simple, plain, no decoration. A huge wall hanging commands the central spot.

As soon as Kiyoko was born, the Wakahisa's had handed her over to full-time care. The only time the parents had shown true animation was when they explained their aesthetic beliefs. "Wabi-sabi finds great beauty in the poetry of simple objects, and is an appreciation for the effects of time and nature on their beauty. We create an atmosphere of acceptance of the toll that life takes on us all." Mrs. Wakahisa had smiled, holding up a simple teacup. Compared to the feed flashing past her left eye, Charumati was not impressed. Mrs. Wakahisa had continued. "If we love the things that already exist, the tactile evidence of being made by someone's hands, we are storing tales for future generations."

This idea of celebrating imperfection had meant nothing to Charumati at the time; however its importance to the family had made an impression. So, since she is looking for their most precious possessions then, ah … yes. The vault interface is recessed behind a vase, barely visible. For all the talk of ancient beating modern, the panel has a number of up-to-date security measures.

[It's not too bad, an electronic lock, controlled by biometrics, hmm, no physical token. I can do this in 60,] Penni says, confident that her hacking abilities easily bump Charumati's own skills past the level needed. Forty-four seconds later and the tiny red light flips to green.

[I'm too good,] Penni says, as the wall hanging rolls up into the ceiling. There's no open door though, just another, bigger panel. [Damn.]

The soft fabric had rolled up almost silently but Charumati waits and hopes the faint noise won't be noticed. She's disappointed.

[Incoming. Hmm, height, weight, speed. It's Saadaq.]

Charumati hasn't let Penni finish speaking before she's back beside the crib, bending over the baby. She deliberately faces away from Saadaq, trying to show nonchalance.

The open floor plan facilitates flow through the habitat, an expansive deck to one side, an indoor garden with a mature bamboo forest to the other. All have height and space, allowing Saadaq room to fly.

[He's here, quick you should attac—] Charumati filters out Penni, waiting for a noise before turning to face the raven.

Saadaq circles the room, landing on an exposed wooden beam next to the crib. He's about medium size for a neo-raven, with nanotat work spreading from his white crest plumage down to the black tips of his tail. In the dim light, the lines glow and shift.

"So, what's going on?" Saadaq tilts his head, his black and gold pupils blinking at her. "I heard a noise, are the Wakahisas back?" His accent is a soft rasp, but his words are interspersed with the odd corvid click.

"They're not due back for at least two months. You probably heard me talking to baby Kiyoko," Charumati says as she fusses with the covers laid around the sleeping child. She keeps moving, trying to hold his attention on her.

[We were supposed to get this done before he arrived. Plan B. Six pressure points for instantaneous death, three locations for paralysis. Two for an unconscious state. Tiny body, easily disposed.] Penni highlights the points via Charumati's HUD.

Saadaq flips his head, switching which eye peers at her. "I have a lead on a new 18th Century Yixing teapot. Excellent condition, with signs of moderate wear, minor chipping. *Interesting* provenance. They'll love it."

"I know nothing about their art choices," Charumati holds her eyes a touch wider than usual to give her an innocent expression. She takes a step closer to the bird.

"Sound, sound, what did I hear then? Oh," Saadaq twists his head, his gold-flecked eyes staring past her. "James."

[Where are they coming from?] Penni says. [He is never around at this time of day.]

When she'd first been introduced to James, she'd shaken his hand and discretely pulled his digital fingerprint to check him out. A pre-Fall security pod who has served the family his whole life.

"James," she turns to face him, a smile on her face. She squirts a quick message to Sapphire. Firewall can decide how to handle this.

[Multiple upgrades. Two pressure points for instantaneous death, one location for paralysis. Only one for an unconscious state. Very hard fight. Not recommended.]

James towers over her, his mass-produced pod all taut muscles clad in polymer armor. He has the classic mercenary look—square jaw, shaved hair, narrowed eyes. He glances at Saadaq, then back to her, padding across the bare wooden floors to the raised nursery section.

"Hello, Charumati. Saadaq, you need to log your visit." His accent is old Earth; English and cold.

"Gentlemen, please remember this is Kiyoko's nap time." Charumati bends at the waist, waving one hand to indicate they both leave.

James nods at her, glancing once more at Saadaq before turning on his heel. Saadaq squawks out his assent, and leaps from his perch to buzz past the security pod's head. Neither of them had glanced towards the art corner or seemed to notice the exposed vault controls.

[I lifted his keys, private and public. Adding them to your HUD now.] Penni sounds smug, her voice practically glowing. Charumati skims the feed floating past, wanting to be sure neither male returns for any reason. She straightens the mobile hanging over the crib as a message arrives from her mission coordinator. [Saadaq is a problem, but proceed with mission. Have eyes on you. Erasure squads prepped if necessary. Make it not necessary.]

Great, complete the mission or we send in the cleanup squad. Charumati looks at the baby sleeping below her, her ayah instincts kicking in. I can't let them hurt her.

[The raven is gone, can trace him over by the hanger.] Penni says. [Not sure where James is. He's stealthy, but remember, he's old school.

Just nostalgic to have around. For real security they're hooked up to Direct Action like every other hyper-rich a-hole. If someone like Direct Action does come, remember there are only two exits off this habitat. Plus the main landing pad has only got room for one vessel and Saadaq just took it. The only viable exit now is the emergency pod to the other side of the bamboo room.]

Charumati nods and adds a note to her HUD. The area is still quiet, so she heads towards the art section. She waits for another 60 seconds.

[Okay, let's do this,] Penni assesses the panel. [I've got James's keys, I'll try them. We've, we …] Her voice fades out as a sharp pain pierces Charumati's temples. The ayah drops to her knees with a gasp, hands to her forehead.

"Now why would a nanny be playing around with the Wakahisa's family vault?" Out of the corner of her watering eye, Charumati sees the tip of James's gleaming boot. "Oh, sorry about the headache, but that muse of yours had to go."

"Penni?" Charumati tries to feel for her, but the mesh inserts are empty. Nothing. Panic flickers, her heart slams against her chest. The pain fades, but she feels so empty. Penni is gone.

[What was that?] Sapphire messages her. Charumati blinks, dismissing it.

"Come on, please stand up, Miss." James's voice is gentle. "The pain should be gone now."

The ice-pick-through-her-temples feeling has faded, but the hollowness of a dead muse is more debilitating. She can't remember when she last backed up; a few months ago, maybe longer. Keeping her eyes lowered, Charumati checks her HUD for a backup. There—Penni v4.9 dated just over 5 months ago. If she can just get back to her contact-feed on the crib, she can get her re-installed.

"Charumati." James keeps his distance.

"I'm okay. I'm just not used to having no muse." She stands, rubbing a hand over her face. The gun in his hand puts paid to any resistance plans. If he was closer, she might have a chance, but not like this. She needs a new strategy.

"Sorry." He doesn't look it. "I couldn't leave you with her when you seemed determined to hack the vault. You understand, I'm sure."

She nods, glancing at the vault controls, her HUD glowing with information Penni had added before she'd been killed. She's trying to think of next steps, but her empty mesh is so distracting.

"Before I make up my mind what to do with you, tell me your plans. You've been with the family for nearly two years, since Mrs. Wakahisa got pregnant, and it's only this last week your behavior has changed. What changed it?"

Charumati starts, sneaking a look at James. She thought him merely decorative, an old relic like everything else, and yet he'd spotted when she'd been activated by Firewall. "How much do you know about the exsurgent virus?"

His jaw tightens and he rolls his eyes. "Please. Do you think I'm an idiot? Pre-Fall so I'll piss my pants at the thought?"

Charumati shakes her head. "We don't interact much, no, we've never needed to. But I have more respect for you than that." With a wave of her hand she indicates centuries-old china, artwork, and woodwork. "Look around. Just about everything in this house is pre-Fall."

"So?" James shrugs. "We both know they love their wabi-sabi whatever thing. Old stuff. What's that got to do with the virus?"

"Information was leaked to, ah, me, that there's a datastore in this habitat. There's concern that the data is potentially a virus-riddled time bomb. So I was tasked to monitor it."

"*Tasked.*" The muscles in his eyelid flicker, but he's looking past her at the additional interface. "By who?"

"That doesn't matter. What does matter is that last week they found out Saadaq is planning a heist. I have intel that he's got pirate contacts who are coming any day. They wanted me to investigate it before he does anything."

There's a tiny niggle of worry in the way his jaw clenches, the flicker of a nervous muscle above his eye, but he doesn't lower the gun.

Charumati keeps trying. "Look at this place. If that vault is a datastore, it's bound to be pre-Fall information in there. And yeah, maybe it's safe, but there's also a good chance it isn't."

When he doesn't answer for a beat, then two, she decides to push. "Let me grab my backup muse, I'll open it up and we can see. If I'm wrong, you've caught me anyway. If I'm right, we clear out baby Kiyoko and get a cleanup crew in."

[Erasure squad is prepped and ready. On your word,] her router messages.

With a tilt of her head, she dismisses it. "Please, James. You've got nothing to lose."

"Only my integrity." His voice is gruff, but she sees the way he's eyeing the vault keypad.

A single message appeared in her feed. [He's dealt with us in the past. He'll trust us. Keep trying.] A message from Sapphire. She pushes down her annoyance that they kept it from her and thinks about how to capitalise on it.

Charumati is used to Penni helping, but it still only takes a second or so to sort the evidence of the planned raid. She squirts the folder across to him, without filtering anything. Let him see the legwork they've done investigating this.

James stills, his body unmoving apart from his eyes. They scan back and forth, sorting the information dump she's just dropped. His eyes widen, just a fraction, before he turns his attention back to her.

"Firewall. They know about the vault. And this heist." He closes his eyes, running his fingers through his stubble-short hair, and sighing. "There is something wrong. That second panel adds an additional level of security that wasn't in my original plans. I don't know why the family added it without telling me. Maybe there is something in there. Something we can't let Saadaq take.

"Helping Firewall again, is it." He walks past her, his fingertips ghosting over the interface pad. "I've lived through this virus bollocks once; I'm not letting it happen again. But we do it my way. You stay back. And keep your bloody hands off that crib, I saw your feed the day you installed it."

Charumati nods, keeping out of his range. It puts her in a good position to see what he's doing. James is concentrating, trying to access the codes, she assumes, watching as he mouths the numbers. She turns her head a little to take a short vid, cropping it down to just his fingers before squirting it to her notes folder. As she's doing it, she realises that his muscle movements don't match the code he's mouthing. He's better than she expected.

After a while, the interface acknowledges that the tagging nanoswarm and room sensors are disengaged. Charumati makes a note of that too, trying not to frown. Firewall hadn't mentioned those security measures. What else had they missed, or were wrong about?

James is still working, this time using his security keys. Charumati notes that they're not the same keys that Penni stole. He's *much* better than she thought. Careful, methodical, and superior to anything that she'd have done even with her muse.

There's a soft noise behind her, and her ayah instincts kick in. She twists around, scanning the crib. Baby Kiyoko is unmoving, sound asleep. Her enhanced olfactory capabilities check the room. The usual habitat smells, a faint whiff from Saadaq earlier, herself and James. Nothing else. Perhaps it was a bamboo stem shifting.

"Oh—" James begins, before there's a nanosecond of alarm blatting through the house, cut off as quickly as it starts. "It's okay, I got it, I got it." He says, wiping a hand across his brow.

"Are we okay?" Charumati asks, stepping closer.

"I think so. Another non-standard security feature. But we're through now." For a second nothing happens, then another passes with no effect. Charumati just starts to think that they've made a mistake when a narrow door to the side of the recessed artwork pops open.

"Right," James motions for her to stay back. "I'm checking it out first."

Charumati sneaks closer to peer over his shoulder. A pre-Fall data-store. She has no idea what might be in there, but she's desperate to find out. Towering computer stacks, small personal devices—what might the Wakahisa family have saved?

James steps through the narrow doorway, arms tight to his sides, head brushing the ceiling. Charumati stays close on his heels. It's a short corridor, two steps before the room opens out. James pauses as he enters, and she has to wiggle to get past without touching him.

The room is square with no adornments and lit only by floor lighting. In the centre of the room is a large, raised section. Every wall is lined with shelves from floor to ceiling.

Each surface is covered with paper. Piled high on the central dais, rolled into scrolls and stacked on the shelves. Card-bound books fill one wall, another has papers stapled together. Some of the paper has shiny, colourful covers; others are plain and curling at the edges.

"What is this?" Charumati asks.

James doesn't answer her. He holsters his gun and moves to the central dais, dropping to his knees. He thumbs the papers, picking up a book and riffling through the pages. A new scent fills the air, one Charumati isn't used to. It's like a mix of vanilla and almonds. Chemicals flash on her HUD—vanillin, benzaldehyde, 2-ethyl-hexanol, more—and she cross references the information. Old book. A highly prized scent, pre-Fall.

James is still lost in manuscripts, so Charumati checks the shelves for tech. Paper. It's all paper. Unless there's another secret panel, or another room, there's—

"Nothing," James says. He's still got a book in his hands, but he's looking at her now, a strange expression on his face. "You were right, but also so very wrong."

"Where's the tech?" She asks as she picks up a scroll from a shelf. Dark ink smears show through the natural material. The paper feels delicate, and she worries that trying to open the scroll may destroy it. Placing it back, she moves to a freestanding podium to the right of the door. It has one clay tablet about the size of her hand. It is carved with tiny symbols of plants and tridents. She picks it up. It's much heavier than it looks.

"That's my point. There is data wealth, but it's like a pre-tech museum. Pages without indices, or tables of contents. Lost journals, one-off scientific papers. Valuable stuff, but nothing to worry Firewall."

At James's comment, Sapphire disconnects from her feed and she assumes that the mission is complete. A message icon pops up on her feed. "So it's not a threat." It's like a huge weight has been lifted off her shoulders. She's about to explain that she's as happy as he is, when there's a fluttering of wings behind her.

"Oh, now this is a pretty picture," Saadaq has followed them through the corridor and perches on the edge of a teetering pile of books. "I always wondered what they had back here." His head bobs, his gold eyes scanning the room. "Priceless. Though I'm going to have a good go at selling it all."

James stands, his hand dropping to his hip, but the raven flaps a wing at him. "Don't bother. I have friends incoming. You saved us some time." The raven paces closer to the security pod, his sharp beak held high, his wings open.

Charumati ignores their squaring off, opening the message from Sapphire. Perhaps if she replies quickly enough, she can get her backup.

[Mission is considered closed. As there is no exsurgent virus threat, erasure squad has been told to stand down. Make your own exit.] The message is timestamped 20 seconds ago.

Make your own exit? Charumati drops the clay tablet in her pocket and assesses the room. James is backed against the wall by Saadaq. His razor sharp beak and strong wings are vicious weapons.

But he's facing the wrong way. He might be uplifted, but he's still a bird, with a fragile skeleton. Penni has already highlighed his weak points. Charumati sidesteps until she's behind the raven. Saadaq hasn't noticed her move, his monocular vision is fixed on James.

Charumati places a hand on the back of his neck and the other on his head. She ignores the sensations her fingers send of dusty feathers and delicate bones. Saadaq reacts, one strong wing clipping her elbow. She squeezes, hard. The resulting crunch is loud. She doesn't look as she drops the unmoving body to one side.

"We have to get baby Kiyoko." Charumati doesn't wait for a reply, wiping her fingers on her trousers as she heads back down the corridor. Her left arm throbs where the wing clipped it.

"We're on our own," James says from behind her. "I did trigger that alarm, but I informed Direct Action it was an accident. I'm pretty sure they didn't believe me, but it's going to take them too long to get here."

Charumati strides across the recessed floor to the shallow steps up to the crib. Something shoots past the window, a battered looking ship, no visible identification, no colours, passes over the image of the earth.

"Saadaq's pirate friends," James says.

She caresses the contact-feed, holding in her gasp as she accesses her muse backup. The timestamp flashes on her HUD as Penni fills her mesh.

[Five months!] Penni—her backup muse—says. [I'm uploading a backup training course for later.]

"Saadaq's on the landing pad. We've only got the emergency exit." James is behind her, his breath tickling her neck.

She pulls the covers back. Kiyoko isn't a huge baby, about 21 pounds, so Charumati grabs the sleeping child and tucks her under her right arm. James leans over to remove the tangled bedding.

The habitat shudders, heralding the pirate ship landing on the surface above the bamboo room. A loud scraping noise of tortured metal fills the air. It's too big, or it's landed badly on the clean structure, because alarms start to blat, and the lights go out. It's only a split second between that and the emergency lights kicking in, but Charumati's sensors detect a pressure change. Kiyoko kicks against her chest, but stays quiet.

[Environmental failure,] Penni says. [Which is a bummer because the only way off this rock is the emergency pod on the far side of the bamboo room. Right under where the pirates just landed.]

"Pirates are near the emergency pod, and we're about to run out of atmo," Charumati says, holding Kiyoko tight to her chest. "My HUD says 15% oxygen."

James nods, his eyes scanning the shadowed bamboo forest. "Gimme a sec, then you skirt around the back to the pod. You'll need a code for it."

A message blips up on her HUD. From James, a code and security access for the emergency escape pod. She stares at it, then at the security man next to her. He doesn't look at her, his eyes still focused on the shadowed stems. He edges away, hiding behind the recessed steps. She glances down at the baby. Two large, innocent eyes stare back, a thumb stuck firmly between her lips as the baby pacifies herself. She's ashamed that she used to think James's loyalty quaint and old-fashioned.

[You need to go. It's not far off being really cold, and really hard to breathe. 11%,] Penni says. [You'll be okay with your oxygen reserves and temperature tolerance, but Kiyoko will be feeling it any time now.]

Charumati smells them before she sees them. Hot engines, oil, sweat. Shadows move between the bamboo, slender shapes with guns held loosely at their hips. She hears five of them, gathered at the edge of the indoor forest.

"You're not getting into the family vault!" Without warning, James runs across the room, covering his movements with a spray of gunfire. He dives into the narrow corridor, and starts firing from inside the doorway.

Kiyoko sucks her thumb harder, little wet smooching sounds quiet enough to be drowned out by the gunfight across the habitat. Charumati keeps both hands tightly around the baby, and watches the pirates converge on the corridor. They appear oblivious to her as they move into position facing the vault. James's distraction worked.

Keeping her eyes on them, Charumati backs away towards the wall of the habitat until her rear bumps cool metal. James shouts again, and the pirates spray more bullets. She uses the noise to scurry, bent forward at the waist, into the darkness between the bamboo.

She can see the air breach now. Tiny hairline cracks in the ceiling leaking the breathable gases into space. Not an explosive depressurisation, but a large enough leak that the life-support can't pump more oxygen than is being lost to space. Bright red numbers and equations fly up her feed—200 metres per second divided by room temperature. $P = Po \exp[-(A/V)t^*(200m/s)]$.

[That means you're going to pass out soon as your reserves are depleted,] Penni says.

"I know," she snaps. The temperature drop is noticeable, her skin covered in goose bumps from head to toe. Her body's natural fight-or-flight response kick in, flooding her system with adrenaline.

Penni scans the room. [There's no one between here and the emergency pod.]

With one last glance down at Kiyoko, Charumati dodges through the slender yellow bamboo stems. The compressed bark soil is soft, muffling her noise, and the whispering of the leaves is more than hidden by the gunshots. James is barking out taunts, while the pirates are still trying to get a bead on him. It's only a matter of time.

"Where's the damned pod?" The seemingly never-ending bamboo stretches around her, no exit to be seen. It's not where it should be. How can an exit disappear? Part of their emergency routine to hide it? She circles the curved outer wall again.

[6%,] Penni says at the same time Charumati's sensors tell her Kiyoko has slipped into unconsciousness.

Think like the Wakahisa. Charumati scans the edges of the room. Beautiful plants interspersed with ancient statues, soft paintings, and tall vases. Nostalgia for somewhere they've never known, an ancient planet that no longer exists. Then she spots it, a large watercolor map of Japan, covered in tiny creases as though it had been rolled, and unrolled, many times.

Approaching the map, Penni highlights a tiny, recessed button half-hidden in shadows. Charumati presses it. The map rolls out of sight, leaving a hatch and a blinking red light. She taps in the codes from James. The blinking red turns to a solid green, and the hatch spirals open. Air rushes past her and she draws in a deep breath.

Pain shoots through her back and neck. A punch. Then another, knocking her head against the hatch doorway. She shakes her head. The air is a musky tang of oil, sweat, and blood.

She snaps out of shock and moves so that a third punch whistles past her ear. A large pale hand, claws extended, hits the wall. A grunt. The pirate tries to free their hand. Charumati ducks and turns, extending her own cyberclaws to rake at their stomach. Heavy armor. Better than her own light bioweave. She shifts her stance, spinning to get behind him. He's trying to reposition himself, but his weapon is stuck.

Charumati is fast. One hand clutches the unmoving baby, the other arcs at the wrist. Her razor-sharp claws glow blue with eelware as they sink into the soft flesh behind his ear. The bio-conducted electric shock stuns him, then as the blades dig deeper into his skull, the pirate stops moving. His head sags forward. Blood runs down her cyberclaws.

Kicking the body free of the doorway, Charumati steps inside. The pod is small, room for five adults. She spots a launch button lit to the side of the door. Without taking time to strap in, she hits it. The door spins closed, followed by the soft whump of docking clamps being released. There's a feeling of motion as engines kick in. It's an emergency vehicle, no controls, no monitors.

Data streams through her feed as Penni hacks the pod. Her muse digs into the shell program and starts running her own processes.

[We lost oxygen when the doors opened, but it's recovering quickly,] Penni says. [I stabilised to a tolerable pressure. I've got navigation, too.]

Charumati lays Kiyoko down on one of the padded seats. The baby's eyes are closed, but her chest is still moving. Her heartbeat is faint and unsteady, flickering like the wings of a moth beating against a window.

[James heard the pod launch. He's locked the vault doors. It has its own atmo. He should be fine until Direct Action gets there.]

Charumati uses her ayah programs to check circulation. The oxygen decrease had caused the baby to shift blood flow away from less vital organs to the brain. For now, Kiyoko is still alive, but she is likely to experience organ failure or brain damage any time. Even death by cardiac arrest if the body stress continues.

"I need to get more oxygen to her," Charumati says.

Images flash before her eyes, vids of people being artificially resuscitated. [She's not stopped breathing, but you'll give her more oxygen.]

Manual insufflation by blowing into the patient's lungs. Charumati draws in a deep breath, then places her mouth over the baby's mouth and nose to form a seal. Blowing slowly, and gently, she feels the tiny chest rise underneath her hand. She detects no noticeable change, so she repeats the process again, and again.

There's a cough against her lips, and Charumati leans back. Kiyoko is staring up at her, her nose wrinkled.

"Mama."

Charumati looks at the smiling child and huffs, a small sound. Then she tips her head back and laughs, the tension easing from her shoulders with each peal.

Charumati moves Kiyoko to a safety seat and straps her in. She sees the pirate's blood on her hand, and wipes it against her hip. As she does so, she feels something. There. Checking her pocket, she finds the clay tablet she'd shoved out of the way when she'd attacked Saadaq.

[Whoo. What is that?] Faint lines criss-cross the tablet as it's scanned. Penni whistles. [This is from the Indus civilisation. That makes it over six thousand years old? Those markings. It's … No. Wait.]

Her muse goes quiet, and Charumati flips the tablet to study both sides.

[Break it.]

"What."

[Break. It.]

Charumati looks at the tablet. Six thousand years old and Penni wants to destroy it? This is everything that the family hold sacred. But what does an old piece of clay matter anyway. Charumati doesn't yearn for the past the way the Wakahisa do.

She swings the tablet against the seating, catching it on a metal support. She doesn't even use much force, yet the clay shatters, tiny chips flying in all directions. Something slender and chrome drops out of the remains.

Charumati catches it before it hits the deck. It's cool, metallic and obviously much less than six thousand years old.

[I'm just *too* good!] Penni crows. [That tablet was fake. Firewall was right, and I'm the best damned muse in this pod.]

"Maybe because you're the only muse in this pod," Charumati holds the item at arms length. Compared to the curved navigation screen, the item looks squared-off and boxy. Definitely pre-Fall. As damaged and damaging as the blotchy planet it's held in front of.

[What do you think is on it? The virus? A rogue AI?]

"I don't know, but I know who will. Can you get coordinates from Sapphire?" Charumati says.

Moments later the pod sways, room tilting as Penni plots a new course and the boosters kick in.

Charumati watches the star field outside the window. "We made our own exit, all right. Plus we completed the mission they'd given up as lost."

[Firewall can be real idiots, sometimes,] Penni says.

Charumati snaps a picture of the object. "I may have to be more diplomatic than that when I rub this in her face."

[Just a little,] Penni laughs.

"Actually, I think I earned a nap. I'll enjoy her embarrassment face-to-face when I get there." Charumati dismisses the photo and sinks further into the soft seat; trying to ignore the throbbing pain all over her body.

[You rest. I'll line up that muse backup training course to run subliminally.]

"Oh shush, you," Charumati looks at the sleeping baby by her left hand, and the datastick clutched in her right, then closes her eyes.

NOSTRUMS
Jack Graham

Jake Carter's hunt for his missing sentinel had taken him, by buggy and by mesh, in a wide arc around the Titan Quarantine Zone. Bobdog LaGrange had been missing for three days, and the trail Bobdog'd had his nose on wasn't one that led anyplace good. Finally, Carter got a break. A traffic spime on a ditchstop spur of the M-4 had gotten a facial match on Bobdog, looking drugged in the back of a car.

He'd traced the car to a saloon at the end of the spur road and called in a favor from Sage Kim, Captain of the Elysium Rangers, to ride shotgun while he checked it out. She wasn't Firewall, but Jake figured she wouldn't be seeing anything too crazy on what oughta be a simple rescue mission. Kim knew him as Jae Park, terraforming worker and sometime-smuggler, and he meant to keep it that way for now.

Kim's big gray Ranger flier circled the wide hollow at the end of the lonely highway once, then touched down near a dozen other vehicles, landing lights briefly illuminating the rusty Martian soil. The flier looked like the very mean lovechild of a large jeep and a fanjet VTOL plane. The front doors swung up, and Kim, Park, and a baboon hopped out, boots crunching on frost. Another baboon, masked against the thin atmosphere, pulled shut the doors and hopped to the front window of the flier, watching as the trio made their way across the landing lot.

"Cold enough to make dry ice tonight," Kim said.

"CO_2 doesn't freeze in the Labyrinth anymore, lady."

"Feels like it could tonight," she said, "Let's get inside."

Even in the relative shelter of Noctis Labyrinthus, the canyon walls didn't do much to stop the wind screaming across the Tharsis Plateau that night. They leaned in to the gusts, making a beeline from the prowler across the lot toward a lone building.

Both wore heavy boots, clothes made from drab fabric that looked like denim but acted like kevlar, well-worn sidearms, and rebreathers under dark balaklavas. Kim's kit loosely followed the regulation uniform of the Tharsis League Rangers (which was how most rangers followed uniform regs—loosely). Both were Asian phenotypes with ruddy skin—rusters.

The baboon followed in the woman's steps, stopping occasionally to scan the roof and windows of the building. Cape baboons weren't the prettiest creatures to begin with, but with goggles and a full breather covering the muzzle, the big male—she called it Smoke—looked damned scary.

The building was stacked together from twenty or thirty boxy green shipping containers. The place was only dimly lit in realspace, but in augmented reality a big neon sign flickered over the buidling's watchtower. It read, "Destino Verde."

"Thanks for helping me come after Bobdog," he said.

"If Bobdog didn't feed me tips nice and regular, I'd have put his ass away long ago," she said, "He's an idiot."

"Ain't gonna argue."

"And the less I know about what's actually going on here, Park, the better."

"Crystal." He clicked off the safety on his piece, heard the whine of magnetic rails going hot as she did the same. "Get your game face on, Captain."

"You've never seen it off." An AR graphic of a badge—the Ranger star with the Chinese characters for "justice" at its center—dissolved in over the lapel of her duster as she pulled open the building's outer door.

There was a gust of warm air. The place didn't have a proper airlock, just a couple of counterweighted pressure doors. Cheap to maintain, and good for us, Park thought. If they needed to make a fast exit, an airlock was the worst option.

He turned on his t-ray emitter, shared what he was seeing with Kim through their tacnet, and scanned the room on the other side of the door. Front of the place looked like a typical roadhouse crowd, with someone pouring drinks and about a dozen other people either propping up the bar or scattered around the room. There was more than one way to the back; a little way down one of the passages was someone on a stool—probably a doorman.

"Got all that, Captain?" he asked.

"Yeah," she said, "Go time." She pushed the inner door open and strode in, stopping next to the nearest table. The baboon hopped up next to her, pulled off its breather, grunted, and made a fist-smacking gesture that aped packing a box of cigarettes. She absently offered him a pack and a zippo while Park walked up to the bar. Style points for the lighter; self-igniting cigs were for spacers and dome dwellers.

"Hey there," he started in Mandarin, but the pleasure pod tending bar, whose outfit consisted of little more than AR graphics, cut him off.

The pod had a fresh face but a mean sneer. "Get that monkey outta here," she said to Kim, "This is a clean place." She was speaking English with an Indian accent. Sounded weird coming out of a morph that looked Japanese, but Park'd heard weirder.

Kim chuckled once. "This monkey's the Law. Get back to selling betel nuts, cupcake."

Park looked over his shoulder to see Smoke light its cigarette and take a satisfied drag, smiling to show huge canines. Whoever said smart baboons couldn't grok human insouciance was dead wrong, but Park also noticed the baboon had one hand on its shock baton.

The pod stood there a minute, palms planted on the bar, attempting to stare down the ranger. Kim ignored the girl completely, slowly walking around the table, sizing up the other customers along the way, until she'd done a full circle, whereon she kicked out a chair and planted herself, one boot up on the table. [Only ones who might be trouble are the pair closest to the back,] she messaged.

Park didn't need to look their way; he was getting video from Kim in his tacs. He propped himself on his elbows and leaned on the bar like he was studying the beer taps, but his attention was on the little video window in the corner of his field of vision. Big blond guy and a stolid Japanese kid, both sipping their drinks slow and showing Yakuza nanotats. The blond guy was looking his way; his friend kept glancing at Kim.

[Some heavy citizens,] he messaged. He glanced at the bartender, [And where you figure they got the cred for a model like her in a dump like this?]

Conversation in the room started up again, and the girl finally said sideways to Park, "What do you want?"

"Sorry about my friend. She ain't been feeling so great. Pint of Red Iron?"

The girl narrowed her eyes briefly at Kim, then looked back at him. "Your lover?" she asked. Jae felt a flutter in his chest when she locked eyes with him. Tailored pheromones?

"The captain? Nah, I just owe her a favor." Yeah, definitely pheromones; he was fighting not to get distracted. "She's due for some new genetic services packs; she's got achy joints and all. She's looking for a remedy 'til she can make the payments, wanted me along to make sure she didn't get put over the barrel on the price."

The girl finished pouring the beer and passed it over in a way that involved more bending and stretching than was strictly necessary. She said, "What's a terraform-wallah know about being over a barrel?" She'd made him quick, but then his whole look screamed terraformer, even with his network profile in privacy mode.

"You ever worked as a line engineer, you'd know the answer, darlin': plenty." He took a long pull off the beer; it tasted like burnt rice and the girl's perfume.

"Anyway, this is a bar … not a pharmacy."

He slid some cred into an AR payment window, tipping generously. "Ain't what I heard."

She glanced toward the pair of yakuza. Through Kim's video feed, he saw the young-looking one nod to her. "Why don't you and your friend try in back?" She pointed to a hallway to her left marked, "EMPLOYEES ONLY."

He abandoned the remaining beer. "Thanks, darlin'." He turned to Kim and nodded toward the hallway, and the two of them headed back. Smoke stayed perched on its table, eyeing the two yakuza.

The back room opened up into four cargo containers whose innermost sides, bottoms, and tops had been cutting away, forming a big, mostly open space. At the back of it was a counter, and behind the counter was a tall stack of cases, drawers, cabinets, and hanging nets full of herbs, animal parts, and medicines in old-fashioned glass and plastic containers. The old guy behind the counter looked Japanese, but the labels on all of the containers and most of the AR graphics floating over items for sale were in Mandarin.

"What you need? Whatever it is, I got just the thing," the old man said.

Park was suspicious as hell of anyone who chose to walk around in an old morph; meant you were either potent or desperate. "My lady friend's GSPs're up. She's got some joint pain. Normal meds ain't working. You got somethin' to restore her chi flow or whatever all this stuff is supposed to do?"

"Chi's serious business," the old man scowled. "I got a reed and marrow rub for that, just the thing."

Park said, "C'mon, oyabun. I know you got better."

"Ah, I have just the thing … Houzi cream." He started to take a tin from under the counter.

"Tinned? I could make that in a fabber. Quit trying to jerk me around, or we're going somewhere else."

The old man grunted, backed up and crossed his arms.

"You're worried about the badge, paatno-san? C'mon, we know this is a yak place. We're here for your merchandise, not to make a bust, or we'd have her monkey in here tearing your shit up already."

The old man scowled. "I can make you up a Houzi cream, but it ain't cheap."

Park messaged her, [Ask to see the gibbon.]

Kim crossed her arms and looked around the shop like she was thinking about it. [Are you fucking serious, Park? You think—]

[Just do it!]

She looked at the shopkeeper. "I'm gonna need to see the gibbon. That ain't a problem, right?"

The shopkeeper led them deeper into the maze of shipping containers.

[What's going on with this operation?] Kim messaged, [I seen some weird shit, but …]

Park messaged, [Traditional Chinese medicine. Old-timey, superstitious shit. It was mostly dead 'til the corps kicked in with the GSP racket and people couldn't find any cure'd work on their pains and asthma. Some of the recipes call for ape parts. They lop off the pieces to make the meds, then throw 'em in a healing vat, rinse, and repeat. People'll try anything, and they think uplifts make stronger medicine. Surprised you never ran into this before.]

[Wait, so what are the yakuza into it for?] she messaged. She was mapping out all the twists and turns they'd followed on the tacnet.

They passed through a barrier of hanging plastic, and the reek of confined animals hit them. The hallway opened up into the harvesting room. In the gloom, he saw a neo-bonobo drugged in a cage. Park peered at him, but it wasn't Bobdog—no dreadlocks. Unless he'd resleeved. Through another doorway, he could see a row of bear cages.

—

[Triads won't touch it,] he messaged, [They think it's a cultural embarrassment, if you can believe. But the demand's there, so the yakuza got into it.]

The yakuza rolled out a cage with a gibbon in it. Jake really wanted to find Bobdog and get out of here before he was responsible for them cutting on this monkey but ... well, here was some fucked up shit he hadn't seen before.

The gibbon was hopping around in its cage freaking out, but it was also signing to him in Warlpiri. <Jake! Get me out of here!>

He signed from where the old man (hopefully) wouldn't spot him while Kim made a show of walking around the cage inspecting the ape. <Bobdog? That you?>

The gibbon tried to hoot, its throat sack inflating, but only a sick croak came out. <Yes! Get me the fuck out of here now!>

Park could see where they'd shaved him and popped his stack; they'd burned out his mesh inserts, too.

[That's a neo-gibbon. Bobdog's sleeved in it,] he messaged Kim.

She glanced at him over the cage. [How do you know?] she messaged, [It doesn't have a PAN.]

[Australian native sign language.]

She shot Park an incredulous look but didn't say anything. "Okay, it looks good," she told the yakuza.

The old man pulled out a metal pole with a wire snare on one end and started trying to catch Bobdog's hand with it, cursing under his breath as the neo-gibbon freaked out in the cage.

"I haven't got all day," Kim said, then messaged, [What's he doing?]

[If he gets a hold on Bobdog's hand, he's gonna slice it off with that vibroknife in his belt and use it to make your Houzi cream. Game time,] Park messaged, [How you wanna play this?]

She answered by breaking the old man's face with the butt of her pistol.

He fell back, screaming and clutching his broken nose. "What the fuck? You think that badge means you gonna walk out of here alive?"

There was a crash and screams from somewhere outside. On his tacnet feed, Jae saw the big blond yakuza looking terrified for a split second as Smoke turned over the table onto his companion and came at him with its shock baton.

Kim kicked the old man to the floor and pointed her gun at his head. "Open the cage now, and I might not shoot you."

The cage door swung open, and Park lifted Bobdog out and stood him on top of the cage. <Can you run?> He signed.

The neo-gibbon shook its head, signed, <Weak.>

Park lifted him. "All right, arms around my neck, pal. We're Althauser 5000."

<Not yet,> Bobdog signed, <You need to see what's in back.>

There was a gunshot from somewhere down the hall. The old yakuza cackled sickeningly from the floor. "Stupid fucking garlic eaters," he said, "When my boys get done with you, I'm gonna sleeve you up like that one and use you all for fucking monkey parts."

Kim shot him three times, the railgun almost silent except for the crack of the slugs.

Park looked over in time to see the old man slump over. "Damn," he said.

Park lifted the neo-gibbon just as the doorman from out front came tearing into the room. Park spun and leveled his pistol at the man. Bobdog was clinging to him like a baby; kid was gonna need some serious time in psych after this. "Hold it!" he shouted.

The guy hesitated for a second but kept coming, pistol out. Then the baboon took him down. Smoke leapt at him out of the gloom of the hallway, grabbing him around the neck and swinging its weight forward so that the gangster tumbled and fell to the ground. Smoke landed in front of the guy, then swung its baton hard into the wrist of his gun arm. Bone cracked wetly.

The yakuza grunted and sat up, holding his wrist. Smoke howled in his face, showing two huge canines. Smoke had been grazed by a shot, though its flak jacket had stopped most of the damage. The baboon looked pissed.

Park motioned with his gun. "C'mon, Toshi. Get in the cage."

The guy stumbled to his feet, the baboon circling him. "Name ain't Toshi."

"Toshi, Fu, Iggins, whatever; get in the damned cage."

He got in. Park put down Bobdog, pulled out his COT, and made a neat row of nanotack welds between the bars and the lock.

"Those're illegal, terraform-wallah," Kim said.

He looked up for a second. "So's shootin' technical old yak pharma-cists for calling Koreans names."

"I like monkeys and garlic. He messed with both in one breath. He needed killin'." She looked none too penitent.

"Arright," Park said, "This one ain't following us. Now let's see what all else they got hidden in here." He picked up Bobdog again; the neo-gibbon pointed toward the bear cages.

She stayed put as he headed for the bears. "You're kidding, right Park? We should go. Now. I'll come back later with a tac squad and clean this place out."

"They didn't seem too afraid of cops. Whose jurisdiction is this, anyhow?"

"Gray area. My force doesn't come down this way much. It's on the line between me and the Noctis Rangers."

"Who you know damn well got termites in the frame. Bobdog here's down a cortical stack, mesh inserts, and a set of vocal cords over what they're hiding in here."

The neo-gibbon signed something in Warlpiri.

"What the fuck does that mean?" Kim asked.

"Uh, rough translation? 'Cowgirl up.'" He shifted Bobdog to his back and headed into the bear cage room, gun first.

"Well, fuck. C'mon, Smoke." She caught up, then took point, with the baboon bringing up the rear. [Gloria,] she messaged the other baboon, [Strap in,] and then to the AI in her prowler, [Dust off and circle high.] A few seconds later, the truck was a moving blip on their tacnet.

A few black bears looked up sadly as they crossed the room. They were stunted and weak, their wire cages barely allowing movement. A neatly attached catheter dangled from the belly of each—for milking their bile, if Park recalled rightly. Beyond that was a room with more primates—gibbons, monkeys, and another drugged out neo-hominid. The whole place smelt of sickly caged animals, and Smoke was getting edgy, sweeping the backs of his hands nervously over the floor when-ever they paused. Kim gave him another cig to cool him down.

Kim came to a pressure door with a tiny window. Instead of peering through, she angled her gun so that she could look through its smar-tlink. Through his tacnet feed, Park could see the room beyond as she slowly panned. It was a lab set up: bunch of steel tables, equipment cabinets, industrial gear for filling up some small, heavily shielded cyl-inders—for gas or liquid, he wasn't sure. There was a batch of a dozen cylinders racked up on the table.

All these details he took in after the back wall, though. In one corner was a heavily shielded incinerator—the kind that used magnetic containment and a blast of plasma to vaporize whatever was in it and then vaporize it some more. Next to that was a bio-containment chamber: a wide, white-lit, glass-fronted enclosure about five meters wide and three deep. There were three figures—or rather two figures, and a … thing—secured to the back wall of the enclosure with a multitude of heavy straps and room for two more.

One was Bobdog's morph, a tall bonobo with dreadlocks. It was horribly emaciated but still breathing. Tumescent lumps studded its waist. The second figure was human, probably a ruster, but its skin had gone dead, nearly translucent white. Around its midsection writhed a double ring of stumpy tentacles surrounded by puckered scar tissue.

The third thing had only the vague outline of a humanoid shape. The legs had fused into a barrel of muscle ending in a wet surface like the belly of a gastropod, and the head and arms had disappeared into the trunk of the body. The tentacles on this one were more active but similarly stumpy and scarred; looked like its keepers'd been trimming them back as they grew.

Kim sucked in a breath. "Damn it, Park, I don't know why I do favors for you. You get me into the weirdest shit. Is that radioactive?"

Park looked at the exsurgent. "No. And ain't your job patrolling a zombie graveyard for robot monsters?"

"That's got nothing on the kind of stuff happens every time I go on one of these runs with you. And this takes the cake. What the hell is this?"

"Stuff nobody oughta see." He edged up to the door and opened it, "Should be safe enough behind an enclosure like that, though." He went inside, and she followed, Smoke in tow.

"I hope you're right. What kind of operation you think this is? They're not cooking up tabs of hither in a setup like this."

Park said, "Trying to improve on bear bile, you want my guess. Mind watchin' the door, Captain?"

He put Bobdog down on a lab table. <Maintaining?> he signed.

Bobdog pointed at his morph, signed, <Fork of me. Infected. Kill it.>

<You got it,> he signed, but this was a bad scene. The Bobdog strapped to the wall was pretty far gone and infected with something; if he had a stack, better to destroy it. But he couldn't be too sure about the Bobdog he'd been carrying around the last few minutes, either.

When he got out of here, their first stop would be a genehacker kettle in the tablelands about twenty klicks north. He had a friend who could give them a clean bill of health … or not. Park tried not to think about the "not."

He tapped at the window separating the room. "Hab window glass. Ideal." There was an airlock with a decontamination shower leading into the enclosure and a few clean suits on a rack. The set up was basic but looked like it'd work.

"Ideal for what?" Kim asked.

He walked once around the enclosure, estimating its strength. "Blast containment."

He started poking around, found a workstation with a rack of tiny quantum computers next to some of the lab equipment. [GiGi,] he asked his muse, [Can you get into this?]

[Mais oui,] the AI messaged, and started throwing exploits at it.

The baboon was having another cigarette. Thank goodness for bad habits, Park thought. There was another door leading farther back. If the schematic they built up on their flyover was any good, it lead to an exit.

Kim checked the back hall for herself, then asked, "I really need some answers about what's going on in here, Park."

Park started pulling on a clean suit. "You ain't seen enough illegal activity yet?"

"Human trafficking, animal cruelty, assaulting a ranger, possession of a biohazardous substance, possession of TITAN relics … Yeah, sure, I can throw the book at that old man if I pop his stack and take it in."

"Doubt it." Jake buckled on the boots and started checking the seals. "Bet you his stack's wiped. He's the type'll have a dead switch on a throwaway body like that. Or he wasn't that important."

"Then so it goes," Kim said, "But whatever's going on here, it's the low end of the food chain."

Jake sealed the helmet and ran the clean suit's diagnostics. [Probably true. I figure they're working on a way to infect more people. Can you do a visual inspection on the seals on this suit?]

[OK.] She went behind him, checking seals, then came around and gave him a thumbs up. [You think someone's trying to weaponize it?]

He dragged the storage cylinders into the airlock with him. Frost came away where his gloves touched them; they were self-refrigerating. [Maybe. Gotta look for the big fish now.]

Bobdog's clone tried to look up at him as he cycled the lock and entered the enclosure. He looked away; he couldn't meet the neo-primate's eyes. He suction cupped an incendiary charge to the window in front of Bobdog, then in front of the human. Finally, he set one up in front of the whipper, giving it a wide berth.

He squirted scrapper's gel on the storage cylinders. He stepped away as the gel burned through and blood began oozing from the cylinders. Three incendiaries would be plenty in a chamber this size.

When he glanced out, Kim was smoking, too. He'd thought the cigs were just for the monkey. [Shit, Park. We can't help him?]

He cycled the airlock. The chemicals from a decontamination shower hissed off the suit before the outer door opened. [You want to try? You know TQZ containment procedure.]

Park got out of the suit, letting the pieces drop to the floor, and found the atmosphere controls for the bio-containment enclosure. He adjusted the mix to hypersaturate the chamber with oxygen.

"What now?" Kim asked.

"I'll be done here in a few. We burn the stuff in there so it doesn't infect anybody else, and after that you can do whatever cop stuff you want to this bar." The exsurgent in the enclosure had grown restive in the oxygen-rich chamber; it squirmed and whipped its stubby tentacles around. He sealed the oxygen line to the chamber; didn't want too big an explosion.

Kim said, "I still want more answers. They got infected by a TITAN virus, I take it?"

GiGi reported her intrusion complete. He spread out an AR window on the lab table next to Bobdog and showed her. "Thing farthest left we call a whipper," he said as he scanned the text, "Used to be a person; ain't anymore."

The chemical and biological data was mostly over his head, but what they were doing with it wasn't too hard to suss out. The yakuza were intentionally creating exsurgents, milking them for bile and other fluids, then shipping the goop somewhere for processing.

"Who's 'we,' Park?"

"Huh?" He stopped reading.

"You said, 'What we call it.' Who's 'we?' Are you a fucking Oversight spook or something?"

Park laughed, "Nah. I work for the good guys. Least, that's what I think most days. I was kinda hoping you'd sign up."

GiGi messaged, [J'ai toutes les données,] into the AR window.

She raised an eyebrow. "Your muse speaks … is that French?"

He grinned, closed the AR window, picked up Bobdog, and made for the door. "What? It's sexy. She's got all the data. C'mon, I can explain the rest when we're safe in the air."

They put a breathing mask on Bobdog, wrapped him in a heavy blanket, and walked right out the front door. The yak in the cage cursed at them as they passed, but they let him be. The pleasure pod bartender and bar patrons had fled the front of the bar, so they weren't around to hear the muffled explosion from far back in the maze of shipping containers. The camera Park had left in the room showed that the containment unit held; inside was nothing but ash.

Kim's prowler touched down, Gloria peering at them out the front windows. Park wasn't sure whether a yakuza cleanup crew or Kim's ranger buddies would get there first, but in the scheme of things, that wasn't so important. They were in the air, and headed for the hills.

—

"So you ain't surprised, guy we're going to see knows me by Jake Carter," Jae Park said.

"I don't care if he calls you Sun Mi Hee," Kim said, "As long as when we're done there we get a clean bill of health. Anyway, I like 'Jake' better. My grandpa was named 'Jae.'"

They were flying over the Noctis tablelands, heading for an off-grid genehacker facility. The badlands spread out invisible below them, but an AR topo display showing their position hovered over the central instrument panel. Rank of captain meant Sage Kim could requisition better engines than most Ranger prowlers had. They were cutting up sky; wouldn't take long to get there.

It was hours 'til dawn, but Cagehopper would be awake; the genehacker didn't sleep much. Even when he did, he kept a fork up to tend to his living experiments.

"What do you care if Bobdog and I get a clean bill?" Park asked, "You going all soft on me, Captain Kim?"

"No," she said, "But I wouldn't want to have to shoot you for coming up zombie, all the same." Her tone measured zero-percent sardonic wit.

"Wouldn't worry," Park said, "This is containment protocol. Pretty standard. Just a precaution." He said that, but he was covering. He had that itch in his neck, that crawling feeling in his stomach he always got after facing an exposure risk. The fear never went away, and that was a damned good thing. He'd seen more than a few researchers who got stupid about the exovirus shot into red smears on Firewall turn-and-burn ops. Hell, he'd done for a few himself, though he didn't savor it any.

"How you doing back there, Bobdog?" Park craned his head to check on the neo-primate. Bob huddled in the acceleration couch, breathing normally but looking gray.

Bobdog made the Warlpiri sign for "shit."

"Hang in there, man. We'll be at Cagehopper's soon."

Kim had locked her police baboons, Gloria and Smoke, in the back cabin. Too much chance of Smoke throwing a nicotine fit and tearing one of Bobdog's long, spindly neo-bonobo arms off. Park didn't like the baboons much, but they'd come in handy dealing with the yakuza back at El Destino Verde.

"Be interesting to finally meet Cagehopper," Kim said, real casual.

Well, shit, Park thought. "You know him?" he asked, keeping casual himself. He'd thought "Cagehopper" was a name the genehacker only used with Firewall. That she knew it set him on edge, but of more worry was the simple fact of a Ranger and a black-kettle genehacker being in the same room.

"Tried to arrest him a few times, sure."

"Complicates things," he said.

She reached over the center console and play punched his shoulder. Bit more than a play punch, point of fact, but probably not intentional. Kim was a ruster, but her body was heavy on the augments. He'd give her even odds against your average fury. "Don't fret, Jake. I don't give so much as a rat's tail about this guy, so long as when we're done he tells me I'm not gonna end up a barrel-shaped mass of mucus membrane with tentacles for a tutu."

"Truly?"

"Truly."

He believed her, for now. Cagehopper was well outside her jurisdiction, but the guy got around. She probably knew him from his dealings with the Arsia Mons smugglers. Didn't matter, anyway; he had to bring her to Cagehopper one way or another.

—

Cagehopper's place was dug deep into a gorge in the tablelands. Kim's flying truck had to squeeze onto a landing pad that was way too close to the gorge walls for comfort. There were no trails, but there was a space between some rocks just big enough for a buggy to crawl out. The outer garage door blended into the surroundings almost perfectly thanks to a programmed coating of chameleon materials. He'd never have found the place by visual.

They were probably being watched already, not that you could spot any sensors. Cagehopper would have microdrones scattered around, and he might be hip to the Maker trick of using lizards as camera platforms.

An AR alert flashed up in Park's peripheral vision. *Telefono.*

[Carter? What the fuck, citizen? You're heavy a few bodies.]

[Heavy a few on account of we all got coughed on during the last run. Need you to take a look,] Park messaged.

[And you show up in a cop truck?]

Park messaged, [Look, you're not gonna like this, but my shotgun on this ride's a Ranger.]

[Perceptive, Carter. You're fucking right I don't like it. Not at all.]

[Look, Cage, I got Bobdog LaGrange here in a bad way, and we're all several of us exposure risks, right down to the baboo—]

[Baboons! Carter, you rock lizard's cloaca, I desire no fucking police baboons in my place of establishment.]

This reaction was cantankerous even for Cagehopper.

"Problem?" Kim asked.

"He doesn't like baboons. I didn't know."

She sighed. "They can stay in the prowler, long as we don't take too long."

Park thought about that. All in all, Kim'd been too acquiescing by half. Helping bust a yakuza front, sure, all in a day's work. She was the law, right? But agreeing to go in and meet a guy who'd have a list of felonies for unlicensed genemods a klick long on his rap sheet without her monkeys … It was too even-handed, even for a Ranger like Kim. He'd have to watch her close.

[Cagehopper, how about this: the baboons'll stay in the prowler. They'll make nary a peep, unless it turns out we're infected. Then we need you to check them, too.]

A long chunk of dead air followed, but then the camouflaged garage door scrolled up into the rock face, letting a gust of warm humidity out to briefly fog the chill, dry Martian air.

Inside was a dimly lit loading bay. Cagehopper had a flying car and a buggy parked inside, leaving only a little space for the big Ranger flyer. The place was clean and orderly. Park saw a few rats, probably smart animals, scurry away as the garage door closed and he stepped out.

Park got Bobdog from the back seat, carrying the neo-bonobo again. Bobdog looked even weaker than before; he shivered in the cold air of the garage. Couldn't Cagehopper afford an airlock? But space was at a premium. Looked like it'd been part of an underwater cave system, formed back in the time when the Noctis tablelands were at the heart of a great, winding alluvial system. As they would be again, if Park and the rest of the TTO's army of terraforming workers had their way about it.

Kim got out and made cop eyes at the cave. "Not much for sensors in here," she observed.

"I think he figures anyone gets in the front door, he's already screwed," Park said.

"Public AR," Kim said, and started walking toward the back of the garage. Park flipped over to the lab's public AR channel himself. A trail of red dots led in the direction Kim was headed, so he followed.

[Stay on the path,] Cagehopper messaged.

After going through a decontamination airlock, they followed the red dots through a maze of narrow corridors cut into the rock. Cramped as the garage'd been, the rest of the place sprawled. They crossed dozens of silent, unlit intersecting passages and an equal number of heavily reinforced doors. The stone, rather than echoing, drank up their footsteps. Lot bigger than he'd expected after the cramped garage.

[What's he need all this space for?] Kim asked.

[Never wanted to know,] Park messaged back.

The dots ended at a heavy metal door that slid open to reveal a sparsely furnished octagonal chamber. In a circle of light cast by an overhead surgical fixture, several metal tables gleamed. A doctor bot stood motionless at the head of one, and several rolling tables of diagnostic equipment stood by the other two. Other than the tables, there was no place to sit.

Cagehopper came out of a sliding door on the far wall. "Sit on the tables," he said, and they did. His neo-neanderthal morph was shorter than Park or Kim, thick-browed, with a barrel chest and hands that looked like they could bust rock. Cage went to work,

injecting Park with what he figured must be diagnostic nanoma-
chines to do blood work, then took throat swabs and dropped them
into a sequencer.

[What's he doing?] Kim asked Park.

[He'll work with all the displays visible only to him,] he messaged.
[You can't risk someone with an advanced infection knowing you're
on to them.]

Cagehopper took a swab from Bobdog, frowning at the treatment
Bob's morph had taken, then dropped that swab in the sequencer, too.

"The hell happened to him, Jake?" Cagehopper asked.

Park said, "Yakuza using neoprimate parts for traditional Chinese
medicine."

"I don't want to hear more." Cagehopper went back to work.

[Why's he even in the room with us?] she asked.

[Ain't his real morph. He's put up a different face every time I been
here.]

"What kind of tests are you doing?" Kim asked.

Cage'd been scowling at an AR window. The outline of it was visible
so that they could see he was reading, but to anyone but him, the contents were a misty blur. Without turning, he said, "Tossing your junk
DNA, looking for jabberwockies. For starters."

Cagehopper got a bunch of tests running, then fixed up Bobdog a
little. Once Cage'd put nanobandages on the worst of it, Bobdog put
his hand to his throat and looked at the neanderthal. Park wondered
how long severed vocal cords took to heal.

"I don't have a quick fix for that," Cagehopper said. "I can put you in
a healing vat for a few days, or I can drill in some new implants and
resleeve you."

Bobdog looked at Park and signed, "New body," in Warlpiri.
Cagehopper glanced over at Park.

"Says he wants a resleeve," Park said.

"I'll trade you this one," Cagehopper said, patting his chest. "By the
way … you're all clean."

"Good," said Kim, "I gotta talk to my people at the Ranger station."

Cagehopper scowled. "Hopefully not about me."

"Paranoia and egocentrism don't go so good together, paatno-san,"
she said, and left the room.

Cagehopper snorted and went back to prepping Bobdog for new
mesh inserts.

"How you holding up, Bob?" Park asked, "Know it's a lot to ask, but I need you solid, or you're out."

"Can walk straight," Bobdog signed.

"What's he say?" Cage asked.

Park told him.

"Remind me never to leave my burrow for you, Carter," Cagehopper said.

———

"How you like the new morph?" Kim asked. They were flying back to the stop on the M5 where Park'd left his truck. The baboons hadn't crapped the seats; Kim looked to be in a good mood about that.

Bobdog was pretty animated for someone in a new morph, but then he'd had the benefit of Cagehopper having kept the engine warm for him instead of sleeving him into a morph that'd been packed in stasis gel. "All right. Not bad. Kind of, too human, you know? Clumsy toes."

"Yeah, I been in and then out of a bouncer," Park said.

They were making small talk, but they'd have to cut that off shortly and make with the planning. He'd gotten Eidolon, one of the crows, to analyze the data they'd grabbed from the yak front. The meat of it was an undecipherable record of shipping times and routing numbers. The rest was an operations manual for handling exsurgents and extracting bodily fluids from them without becoming contaminated oneself. The manual then went into how to store and package the fluids for shipment.

[You got anything yet, E?] Park messaged.

Eidolon's response came slowly; they were an AGI inhabiting a massive art installation outside Locus, in the Jupiter Trojans. Park had plenty of contacts rimward. He liked using hackers outside Consortium jurisdiction when he could.

[Yes, Jake. It is most distressing. The yakuza gang that Bobdog LaGrange discovered have been shipping their product to orbit, but I cannot deduce where. They are using combinatory routing codes.]

Park did a mesh search on what that meant. Combinatory routing codes were a form of encryption used when sending physical goods—which meant they didn't get used much. Parcels from multiple suppliers with combinatory codes on them would stack up at a routing center until all of them were there. Only by combining the codes on all parcels could you determine the final destination. Corps who didn't want competitors finding out where large quantities of components were being sent used them in the dark ages before microfacturing. Now they were mostly used by criminals.

Park patched Eidolon through the prowler's speakers. "Y'all should hear this," he said. "Eidolon, how do we figure out where the cylinders were going?"

After a long pause, Eidolon said, "You must find all of the facilities from which they were originating. Or you could simply go to the routing center, and if there are enough parcels there, I might be able to deduce both their origin points and the final destination by decrypting the collected routing codes from them."

"You know where the routing center is?" Kim asked.

After a long moment, Eidolon's reply came, "Of course. I only hesitated to provide the location because I feared I might have made an error in decrypting the code, but I have re-checked my work and am quite sure. It is a disreputable drinking establishment in the Zhongguancun neighborhood of Olympus City, on Mars. Sending you the precise address now."

"That don't sound like an error at all," Park said. An AGI not grokking the idea of a front business didn't surprise him. "Nice work, Eidolon. We'll talk again soon."

"Good day, Jake."

Kim said, "I can't do anything for you in Olympus, Carter."

"I can," Bobdog said, "I'll leave right away."

—

Bobdog LaGrange knew some helluv angry monkeys, Kim thought. Correction: apes. Never call 'em monkeys, especially not the ones Bobdog knew.

She was sitting on the end of a motel bed eating the leftover half of a bibimbap burrito. Park was laying back against the headboard behind her, smoking a joint. They were watching a tacnet replay on a shared AR window of Bobdog's friends in Olympus tearing up a speakeasy run by a local gang.

In the end, the apes found more cylinders and got the data. Whole back of the place had been set up for shipping and receiving. Trucks loaded with goods come in off the maglev railroad stopped at the front business on their way to the space elevator, left light some goods and heavy a batch of nondescript cylinders full of zombie plague. Rinse, repeat. The gang were contractors—knew fuck all about what they were really involved in. Just knew they were getting paid.

Strictly speaking, as a deputized officer, she ought to be concerned, but she'd have been surprised if the Olympus police didn't know about the place. That department had three priorities: the Space Elevator, ComEx property, and whomever was paying them bribes, in that order. Bobdog's neo-primate gang friends had done the Olympus cops' job better than the cops would've.

As for Jake Carter–or Jae Park, which was about the most boring real name a guy could have–she glanced back at him. "How long you think Eidolon'll take on that?"

He smiled. "You got somewhere to be?"

"I got a department to run, in case you'd forgot." Although the truth of it was, she regularly went a week without setting foot in the station. Running things via mesh was easy enough. Rank of captain in the Rangers basically meant being a beat cop but having to answer a crap ton of mesh calls, too. Oh, and she got a better truck.

As for Park … she wasn't sure this was going to happen again, but he hadn't been overly disappointing. Like all men, he needed to read the documentation; unlike the majority of them, he did what it said. She liked him. They were both Korean, they were *donggap*—born in the same year, they were both from agrodome families (from what she could get out of him about his history). And it'd been a while. She didn't fool around with co-workers, and most other men she met, she arrested.

"Hey, pause it and go back a couple seconds," she said. She'd noticed something on Bobdog's tacnet movie.

"Here, have the controls," Park said.

She shuttled back about a second and a half. There. "Hello again, cupcake," she muttered.

She zoomed. Cowering in one corner of the frame, doing a good job of looking terrified, was a scantily clad pleasure pod. Almost a dead ringer for the one at El Destino Verde—probably the same model year. And again, high rent for the establishment they were looking at.

Park let go a stream of musky smoke. "Well, shit."

"She ain't just a party favor," Kim said, "She's a moving part."

He got up and started putting clothes on.

"What're you doing?" she asked. He stopped. "Shower," she said. "And then shower again. Smoke smells me all over you, he'll get jealous."

He laughed. "Serious?"

She had not stuttered. "What's your hurry, anyhow?"

Park slipped off the jeans he'd started to put on. "Eidolon's got their nose to the trail, but might be the pod girl's a short cut."

"That feed's from Olympus. Have Bobdog pick her up."

"Last message from Bobdog said he was going into psych," Park said, "So count him out."

Reasonable. She wouldn't want LaGrange having her back after what'd he'd been through. Anybody's game'd have some stress fractures after getting cut on for folk medicine by a bunch of technical yakuza zombie farmers.

"Finding her'll be a good trick," Kim said, "She's gone to ground for sure. Just getting to Olympus'd take us hours."

"I'm thinking we go after the pod girl from El Destino Verde. And I got a friend who's good," he said, smiling at her.

"Me? Carter, I've tracked plenty of people, but this one'll be cold. It's been eighteen hours."

"I got her mesh ID when I tipped her."

She smiled. "All right, that's different. But it could still take longer than it'll take Eidolon to break the encryption on those cylinder routing codes."

He got up for that shower and sent her a mesh ID. "I got a friend who'll help, name of Sedition. If you don't mind working with someone else, that is."

"Why not, long as they don't expect access to Ranger databases." She pulled open an AR window and started a tracker search for the pod girl's mesh ID on public spimes in the area.

"I let him know you'd call. Use a VPN; he ain't someone Captain Kim wants to be seen socializing with. I'm gonna make myself smell nice for your monkey now." He closed the bathroom door.

—

Park's friend, Sedition, was damned good. Said he was a journalist by trade; she didn't say anything about what she did. He threw out a lot of unorthodox ideas about what kind of searches to run, stuff far afield of the cop playbook.

Cupcake didn't take long to track down, once they put their heads together. The pod girl'd been careful, had probably used a bunch of fake IDs, but she made the mistake of buying a ticket to orbit out of the Noctis-Qianjiao spaceport. Sedition suggested not bothering trying to draw a line between her real mesh ID and any fakes she might be using. Instead, they had their muses stake out some likely (and, to her, not-so-likely spots) where her real ID might show up.

Turned out the pod girl didn't trust her fake IDs far enough. She dropped the masquerade in spaceport security, probably gambling that her real ID would be more likely to get her through, and then she'd be on a rocket, beyond reach.

"*Heo-jeob*, Cupcake," Kim muttered. Bad math thinking she could get away with that with a Ranger on her trail. One fugitive bulletin to the Noctis-Qianjiao spaceport cops was all it took from there.

She thanked Sedition, leaned back, and re-lit the joint Park'd left on the nightstand. She got a mesh call reporting the pod girl was in the clink by the time Park got out of the shower.

He looked at her funny. "*Go-go-ssing*," he said, pulling on his cap. This struck her as funny, that he'd put that on before anything else, and she laughed a little. He raised an eyebrow. "What're you doing hitting that?"

She leaned forward and took his wrist. "Ain't no hurry, Carter. I got our girl. How about helping me finish this?"

"Serious? Strong work, Captain." He gave her a butterflies in the stomach smile and accepted the joint.

She watched him inhale; she liked how he looked with his eyes closed. So Kim'd made up her mind about having another helping of Park, but even as she yanked him back onto the bed, there was one thing she was going technical trying to figure out: why'd Cupcake need to escape in her body? Wasn't like back-country Mars lacked for shady egocasting facilities.

She decided she'd hold that thought.

—

Park hadn't liked being left in the prowler with Smoke and Gloria, but the baboons were meshed. Kim could call them off from afar. And anyhow, looked to be he was now part of the pack. Gloria kept trying to groom him, while Smoke lounged in the back seat idly jerking off. Neither of them went anywhere near Kim's seat.

They were parked on the shoulder of the covered service road that looped past the spaceport terminals, waiting for Kim to bring back Cupcake. Every so often a Qianjiao spaceport cop rolled by and gave the ranger vehicle the stink eye, but no one bothered them. Eidolon hadn't gotten back to him except to say the decryption was taking longer than expected.

[Be there in a sec,] Kim messaged, [Soon's I ditch the local *jjab-sae*.]

Park shooed Gloria way for the fourth time. [Ain't a nice thing to call another cop, Captain.]

[I hate spaceport cops. Rangers get imaged and frisked like everybody else when we fly.]

Kim emerged from the terminal with Cupcake. The name on her mesh ID was Janu Vaidyar. Flanking her were two spaceport cops; the ranking one was gesticulating and talking to Kim's back.

Vaidyar'd ditched her bartending outfit—which hadn't been much more than go-go boots, AR graphics, and hair extensions—for a short, asymmetrical haircut and severe suit. She looked more like an intellectual property lawyer for a Lunar design house than a bar trixie in a yakuza dive, and it wasn't just the clothes. Park was disappointed with himself for not making her sooner.

Park cracked the window as they got closer to the prowler. Even in the tunnel, there was a cold desert breeze cutting through the smell of monkey.

The airport cop's words got clearer as they approached the truck. They were speaking Mandarin. "… with Director Cheng's sign-off, which is fine, even if it's not standard procedure. But we don't want to lose face over this prisoner." He stopped for a second when he noticed Park. "And who's this guy?"

"TTO," she said, "They've got an interest in this case. He's an observer." Which was sort of true.

Park hopped out and opened the back door of the prowler.

The airport cops eyed him. "He doesn't look like an official," one said.

"We don't wear suits in Operations," Park said, watching Janu Vaidyar as Kim bundled her into the truck and cuffed her to a heavy ring set in the seat behind her. Smoke huffed at the pod but didn't do anything else.

He didn't like this. Vaidyar was an exposure risk, too. He made sure to get the names of the two cops. They might need to be checked up on later after physical contact with her.

"Well, don't say NQSPD never did anything for you," said the port cop.

"I'll keep that in mind," Kim said.

Once they were in the air, she said, "Cagehopper's."

Wasn't a question. "Yeah," he said, looking back at the pod girl. Vaidyar stared out the window, silent. "This one's gonna need special handling."

—

[Go away, Carter!]

Cage was gonna need some talking down. They were staring at the outside of the camouflaged garage door in Cagehopper's ravine, trying to remain patient. Park glanced back at Vaidyar—he'd angled the rear view mirror on his side so's he could watch her—and caught her smiling before she noticed and fixed her face back into a stare.

[Cage, man, this is bad news. Serious. I got a potential widespread infection risk, and you're gonna dick me around because you don't like my cop friend and her monkeys?]

Kim shot him a "c'mon" look across the seat; he was sharing Cagehopper's messages with her. [I'll make threats if you won't,] she said.

[Bad cop?] He thought about whether he was up for some potential bridge burning and decided yes. [Fine… go.]

[Cagehopper,] she messaged, [This is Kim.]

[What the hell, Jake? Did I say you could give her my mesh ID?]

Park didn't respond, just kept his eye on Janu Vaidyar. She was pretty calm for someone getting taken to an off-the-grid cave in a ravine instead of into Ranger custody.

[Listen, Cage,] she continued, [I ain't making this offer twice. Let us in, check this prisoner out for us, and I'll pretend I never been to the notorious Cagehopper's black kettle. Hell, I might even ignore it next time you move dubious wetware through my beat. Turn us away, and my memory might get sharper.]

Cagehopper messaged back, [Why do you even care?]

[My beat's the TQZ. I take this shit seriously.]

There was a long pause. [A diamond could start out a lump of dinosaur shit, I guess.] The door started sliding open.

[Thanks,] she messaged, but she was mouthing something else.

Same drill as last time. They weaved through the garage, following a path marked by Cage on AR, leading Vaidyar. They were four turns into Cagehopper's maze when Park's dorsal spinocerebellar tract went technical on him.

It was as if his extremities were suddenly boats, unmoored from him, drifting away in a slow current. He could feel his legs but couldn't feel where they were in relation to each other, so that when Vaidyar jerked away from Kim and threw a shoulder into him, Park went down ass over tit. Vaidyar was making a run for it, headed back toward the garage.

Kim'd fallen on him, babbling in a way that might have been an attempt at cursing. Then she rolled off him; he could see the back of her head and her limbs flailing.

[Don't try to move,] he messaged, [Real easy to overextend a muscle.]

[What the fuck is this?] she came back.

[Cupcake's an async.]

[Those're just stories,] she messaged. But she stopped trying to move. [I'm setting the monkeys on her.]

[Do it.]

She unlocked the prowler and messaged the baboons. [Gloria. Smoke. Kill.] Then she sent a command to their flak jackets. The jackets obliged, pumping the baboons full of aggression drugs.

[What's going on?] messaged Cagehopper.

[Lock all your doors, Cage. Prisoner's an async. Just fed our proprioception centers kimchi and did a runner.]

[Noob mistake. How the fuck did you make proxy again?] Cage left out the dry cackle, which was fine by Park.

[Occupational hazard, Cage. Somebody's gotta get dirt under their nails.] He tried moving. It was no better.

[How long will this last?] Kim messaged.

[Minute or two, tops.]

An animal scream echoed from a distant corridor, followed quickly by a human one.

[That was Gloria.] She tried to move again, made it to her knees, but then put her arm in the wrong place and face planted.

Vaidyar gave a short scream that cut off quickly, but the baboons made no further sound.

[You're gonna hurt yourself; then you can't help anybody,] he messaged.

"Gloria's flatlined. And I can take plenty of hurt, Jake." She slurred bad, but managed to get the words out. She tried standing again, keeping all of her limbs where she could see them, and managed to make it to her feet.

Meantime, Park could feel his own limbs drifting back together. Kim was staggering toward the noise, so he decided to try crawling. The first time he took his eyes off his hands he ended up fumbling and banging his chin on the floor, but he could feel the effects fading.

[She's down,] Cagehopper messaged, [I got a drone to the scene. Ugliness.]

Park regained his feet, and Kim was walking almost normal now. They followed the breadcrumb trail back. Cage shared a map of the hallways with them and highlighted Smoke's location. As they got closer, they heard a wet smacking sound.

They rounded a corner. Vaidyar's corpse lay in a mess of gore. Smoke stopped beating her with his baton as they came closer. He trotted up to Kim, sweeping his hands against the floor nervously, and hugged her leg, grunting.

Kim ruffled his fur, said, "Good guy," and gave him a cigarette. Smoke took it, lit it, and then hopped over to Gloria's body. Her eyes bulged, and one hand was limp over her muzzle. "Damn it," Kim said.

Gloria's face was darkened with spreading masses of subcutaneous blood flow. "Internal hemorrhaging," Park said, "Some of 'em can do that." He looked back to Vaidyar's body. Something was wrong. Pleasure pods had cyberbrains, which meant pod morphs were rubbish at using async powers. So either Vaidyar was incredibly potent with psi, or this pleasure pod was no pod at all.

"Jake, let's get this done. I just lost one of my monkeys. Ain't good for me." She was still studying Gloria, stroking the baboon's head.

Park wanted to take her hand or hug her, but he was feeling that weird day-after-out-in-public distance that sometimes follows casual sex. So instead, he messaged Cage. [Cagehopper, area's secured. Gonna need a gurney and some cleaner swarms here.]

A few minutes later Bobdog—scratch that, Cagehopper—rolled up, perched on a gurney pushed by a featureless bipedal servitor bot. The morph that had been Bobdog's had glossier fur and healthier skin than the last time they'd seen it.

"You never fail to keep me entertained, Carter," the neo-bonobo said.

Kim's eyebrows creased up nasty, but she held her tongue. Together, she and Park swung Vaidyar's limp form onto the gurney, trying to avoid the blood. Then she picked up Gloria, stroked her head, and put the small body on the gurney, too. Another foot trail appeared when they were done.

"Follow that trail to the guest rooms. Get cleaned up, and leave the male baboon there when you're done," Cagehopper said, "I'll examine our guest … and take care of your unfortunate friend. Shouldn't take long." He loped off into the dim passageways; the servitor turned the gurney around and followed him.

[You trust him?] Kim asked Park.

[Well enough.] He started along the trail. [The unkindly disposition's an act. He's down with the cause.]

"Yeah, speaking of that …" she said. She looked back. "C'mon, Smoke."

"What're you thinking?" he asked. They took another turn. Except for the occasional security door, the corridors were almost featureless. He'd had GiGi, his muse, mapping it for him as they went.

"That I like how your friends are dealing with this shit instead of just trying to rope it off and hope it stays contained," she said, "I want to know more."

"Org's called Firewall," he said, "Ain't government, though it's got allies in a few of them."

The AR tracks ran to a door at the end of a passage. They went inside and found themselves in a spartan living area. She said, "I requested the TQZ periphery as my beat. We oughta be clearing that land of the machines, but instead we're ordered to patrol and watch. It's stupid." She started looking for a way to clean up Smoke.

"So you down for helping out some more? Because my next stop's wherever they were shipping that exsurgent gunk." He turned a chair around and sat on it.

She'd stood Smoke on a counter next to a sink and was toweling blood off of him. "Yeah. I have some questions. But if you're not just a bunch of nutjobs, I want in."

—

They stood in Cagehopper's lab, trying not to look too often at Janu Vaidyar's morph. Cranium'd been peeled, and Cage hadn't bothered covering it up after he went through it for goodies. Some of the augments in her head needed more juice than could be drawn off a corpse. Her cortical stack glittered amid large droplets of blood in a shiny polymer tray.

Autopsy'd been done by a doctor bot with Cagehopper supervising. Still presenting himself in the neo-bonobo, he perched at the foot of the operating table. He shared a medical data AR channel with them; graphics poured over her body and some severed pieces of it as he began.

"She wasn't a pod, just cosmetically modded to look like one," he said. The neo-bonobo's voice was rich and musical.

"Kinda figured that," Park said, "What else you got?"

"Blood work." Cagehopper gestured to a stream of data on blood borne pathogens. "Confirms Watts-MacLeod infection, but then you'd already worked that out."

"Watts-MacLeod?" Kim asked.

Park shot her the entry-level EyeWiki write-up on asyncs. "What else?"

"Implanted QE comm," Cagehopper said; the AR graphics flashed on an exposed area of her thoracic cavity sporting a piece of hardware that looked uncomfortably large to be carrying in one's gut, "That's the qubit reservoir."

"Now that's helluv weird," he said, "Who gets one of those?"

"Human commlink," Kim said, "Seen it. Once. Guy had it was a Consortium agent infiltrating a real paranoid Guangxi outfit."

"Why would Cupcake've needed it?" Park asked.

Kim looked at him like he was slow. "Gangs probably thought she was just a gift, something to seal the deal, not an agent set to watch them with an implanted FTL comm unit."

"That's not so good," Cage said.

"Nah, it ain't," Park said, "Means they for sure know we're coming."

—

Park had an incoming message. Long, long distance. It was Eidolon. [Jake Carter, I've finished decrypting the routing information from the cylinders Bobdog LaGrange found.] The AGI followed that with a stream of locational data.

[That's good news, Eidolon. Thanks much.] He shared the data with Kim, and they started looking it over.

"Never heard of this hypercorp before," she said.

"Panacea. They're a fly-by-night, most like." He messaged his muse, [GiGi, *dossier à propos de Panacea Corporation, s'il te plaît.*]

They were back in the guest quarters at Cagehopper's complex. Place smelled a little like wet stone dipped in isopropyl alcohol. Kim'd collected a gene sequence of Gloria from Cage, then she let the gene-hacker recycle the remains. Maybe she could get her cloned, one day.

Smoke paced the long, narrow room nervously while she and Park sat on a bunk poking at AR windows of Eidolon's findings.

The picture got clearer. Panacea was shipping the exsurgent goop to orbit after collection. All of it was going to a single orbital factory in the cloud of satellites and smaller habitats trailing Progress, the Planetary Consortium's largest orbital. It still wasn't clear what Panacea did with the stuff.

[*Recherche terminée,*] GiGi messaged. He pulled up the file and shared it with Kim. [Aw, hell. They're a nanopharm manufacturer. That orbital's their main plant.]

"So you figure they're putting the virus in drugs. What I don't get, who the fuck does this kind of thing?" she asked. "There's no money here."

He stood up and stretched. "Someone trying to finish the TITAN's work for them."

Smoke padded up. She dispensed a cigarette automatically. "Like who?"

"I got a hunch, but I don't wanna get anyone else thinking on the wrong track. I need to check out the Panacea facility. You riding along?"

Kim ruffled Smoke's fur and shook a leg. "Riding along? Eff that, Carter. I'm driving." She put in a call to her station. [Deng, this is Kim. I'm coming by in four hours. Gas up the Skink.] She packed up her kit. "You ever ridden in a Ranger cutter before?"

He chuckled. "Only in handcuffs."

"I'm going to leave that one alone. See you in the garage." She pecked him on the cheek and made for her prowler.

Park watched her go.

[Are you trying to bring her in or date her?] Cagehopper messaged him.

The room was empty now, and Park knew Cage had everything in here miked, so he said out loud, "Won't lie. I ain't excited about putting her through the loyalty tests."

Cagehopper messaged, [Only a dumb redneck like you would recruit a high-value asset like her and then fuck it up with feelings.] The baboon might not have smelled what he and Kim were up to earlier, but Cage sure had.

"We were just passing time."

[You know Carter, I've got implants that could make you not a completely shitty liar.]

"I'll keep that in mind. For when we get back."

"We?" Cagehopper's voice shrilled over the room's speakers. "I don't think I heard that right."

But Park had not stuttered.

—

"So what're you proposing?" Park asked.

It was a ground-to-orbit call, so a long second went by before Das Frettchen replied, "Liquidation." There was some heavy sun spot activity happening that week, and his voice came through scratchy despite the comm software's attempts to correct for it. "These people are exsurgents, Carter. We're sparing them the pain of metamorphosis if we kill them now."

"You've gone fucking technical."

"Your first real containment action, and you don't have the stomach for it. We're lucky such choices weren't up to you during the Fall."

"This ain't the same."

"You think your heroes"—Das Frettchen spat the word—"in the outer system flinched from their duty? Magnus Ming has sent more people than this to die in his day."

"We can fix these people. Your plan: it's insane."

"If you think I lack the resources to make 1,000 people disappear from Valles-New Shanghai, Carter, you're mistaken."

—

Park floated in the airlock of a Fa Jing U-Facture (Location #0138, District Manager Zhu Lai Leong, according to the AR text and smiling portrait next to the inner lock door). Park was waiting for the security AI inside to finish scrutinizing his false Fa Jing corporate ID and the registration (also fake) on the ship docked behind him. He'd thrown on smart clothing that reshaped itself into a Fa Jing uniform, hung some tools from it, and brought along an automech bot, which clung to the wall near him.

Through the airlock windows, he could see the rest of Captain Sage Kim's Martian Ranger customs cutter, the Skink. The ship had erased its Tharsis League and Ranger markings and extruded a random assortment of dummy manipulator arms, conduits, and equipment lockers from its hull. Now it was a dead ringer for the boxy, antiquated old tender vessels that made up the bottom rung of Fa Jing's immense fleet.

Beyond the ship, the U-Facture station stretched out behind and ahead of him, an orderly cylinder of pie slice-shaped rented manufacturing modules connected by trusswork and an enclosed central floatway that ran the length of the station. The cylindrical form factor was for convenience, not gravity; clients rented on U-Facture when they needed microgravity manufacturing space. The *Skink* clung to the end of a docking arm roughly midway along the length of the cylinder.

The AI inside was taking its time—it'd been almost five seconds—but Park kept it cool. The IDs had been forged by Eidolon, a much smarter AGI, a fork of whom was waiting in the ship to save Park's bacon if needed. And Park was good at looking like a bored, impatient service engineer—because when he wasn't on Firewall business, that's what he was.

"What's takin' so fucking long?" he asked the empty airlock.

"Verifying," the security AI said, "Fa Jing Internal Security thanks you for your patience."

He hadn't wanted a response. While he waited some more for the recalcitrant airlock, he messaged the ship. [Eidolon. How's it shaking out?]

[I've subverted surveillance on the station's hull, Jake Carter. Captain Kim and Cagehopper have begun their EVA.]

—

Sage Kim gulped. Vertigo. The red expanse of Mars filled the upper half of her field of vision. Damned if the planet weren't never anything but lovely, but at this angle … Kim threw up a little bit in the back of her mouth and swallowed it, again.

Cagehopper, clinging to her back, must've heard it over the comms. "Are you vomiting?" he asked, "I thought you were trained in this."

She couldn't look back at the hypergibbon; helmet didn't have enough peripheral vision. All she could see were his long, thin arms wrapped around her shoulders. "I did one month of micrograv combat training during academy," she said. She knew how to use the grip pads on her vacsuit without falling off into space and dying, and that was about it.

"I should never have left my burrow," Cagehopper said.

From the outside, the U-Facture station looked like a stack of discs on a dowel. There were sixteen modules, each five meters thick and one hundred meters wide, with a meter of floatway between each disc. They all connected to the central corridor by a single airlock. Only one of the discs, near the center, spun for gravity. That one would contain the manager's quarters and several partitions of 1g space for renters that needed them.

Augmented reality graphics showed her a path across the station's hull. A multitude of wide, plant-packed windows looked out from the hull; a path was highlighted in green so that she could avoid giving anyone inside visual on her. It would have been a simple walk across the station's skin, but the meter-wide gaps between modules were just wide enough to be unnerving. Rather than leaping the gaps, she played it safe, crawling slightly between each module at each gap so that she always had at least two grip pads against the hull.

Their objective was a service airlock leading into the section of the U-Facture station rented by Panacea Corporation, a company specializing in zero-g boutique manufacturing of exotic pharmaceuticals. Some of Panacea's business was legit. And some of it, Park and Kim suspected, involved lacing drugs with the exsurgent virus and delivering them to unsuspecting patients.

—

"You wanna talk containment, Frettchen? We got this contained."

"Really, Carter? And you've taken steps to do so. In Valles-New Shanghai. My city. How thoughtful of you."

"Panacea runs the groundside supply chain. Meanin' they route the drugs direct to the patients. They're delivering them to asyncs."

"Oh, this gets better and better."

"Nah, look: the refined exsurgent goop Panacea laced the drugs with is inert until activated. Cagehopper isolated the trigger protein. Feed these people nanopharm that eradicates all instances of that protein in their systems, and the infection'll never get triggered."

"You're asking me to put a great deal of faith in the work of a black kettle genetics monkey with an extensive rap sheet, Carter. I don't think that's going to fly."

—

Manager Leong didn't like the look of him, and the feeling, Park decided, was mutual. The Fall'd only made the class divide between Chinese managers and Korean rusters worse, and Leong was all about letting Park know whose status was higher. Which was fine—meant Leong was too busy demanding face to really scrutinize him. Park let Leong float higher than him and pretended he could only speak Korean, letting Leong's muse translate to Mandarin.

Eventually Leong let him through with a final admonition not to make anything on the station worse. Park suppressed the urge to smirk. No telling what kind of sensors the manager had allocated to keep tabs on him.

Park kicked off from Leong's office and floated down the station's huge central corridor. He didn't like microgravity much, but inside, maneuvering down a big, straight corridor, it wasn't so bad. Eidolon now owned the station's primary surveillance systems. The plan was for Eidolon to feed the system footage of Park and the automech opening up a life support conduit and going to work inside it. In reality, Park would keep going and enter Panacea's module through the front door. If Leong stayed in his office—which he probably would—they'd be five by five.

[Sage, grandmaster E, how we lookin'?] Park messaged.

Eidolon messaged, [Jake Carter, Captain Kim. Panacea's system resists my best efforts. I cannot unlock the doors to their module for you.]

Kim messaged, [I'm almost at the hatch. What's the problem?]

[Unorthodox system design. I am uncertain which systems to subvert. Choosing the wrong ones might put them on alert.]

[Well the emperor of this little piece of heaven thinks I'm here for four hours to fix some CO2 scrubbers. We ain't budgeted for overtime on this run.]

[I recommend manual subversion,] Eidolon said.

[Well at least I didn't carry this thing for nothing,] Kim said.

—

"This thing" was a hull wart. From her back, Cagehopper handed her the pieces of it, one by one. Disassembled, the wart comprised eight curved lengths of smooth metal. Stuck to the hull, end to end, each formed forty-five degrees of a circle three-and-a-half meters across centered over what Eidolon had identified as a relatively thin section of hull. Kim activated it, and the wart began extruding a dome of clear polymer that soon enclosed them in a hemisphere 1.75-meters high at its center.

Cagehopper got off her back and clung to the hull while Kim took out a covert ops tool and began cutting. First she drilled a pilot hole. A plume of air, visible as the water vapor in it crystallized, began filling the dome with atmosphere. Then she went to work cutting a circle in the hull.

—

Inside, Park pried loose an access panel and got to work jimmying the bulkhead door leading into the Panacea Corp module.

Almost as soon as he got to work, Eidolon messaged him. [Someone in the module is attempting to alert station security. I've intercepted the message and am spoofing a response from the station.]

[Damn,] he messaged, [That ain't gonna work for too long.]

[No. I recommend you hurry.]

—

"Here's how it is, Frettchen: I got the station, I got the data, and I ain't signing off on killing all these people."

There was a long pause. Finally, Das Frettchen said, "You're hurting our working relationship here, Carter. We've always worked well together in the past."

"No, we haven't. And you know if we take this to the other proxies, you're gonna be in the minority."

"Fine, Carter. But don't ever ask me for any favors."

—

With the automech acting as an extra pair of hands, bypassing the bulkhead door was kid's stuff. Kim was still hacking at the outer lock. Probably a minute or so until she got through. Park couldn't wait.

Eidolon had had to start jamming mesh calls from inside the Panacea module. That kind of activity inside the confines of the station would get noticed quick.

He jerked one more time on his utilitool, the end of which was locked onto a regulator valve in the door's pneumatics. There was an almost imperceptible hiss of pistons, and the door irised open. He pulled himself through, and the automech followed him with a few puffs from its gas thrusters.

Soon as he was clear of the hallway, he sent a mesh command to the automech. A panel with two pistols racked beneath it extended from the side of the bot. Park stuck the smaller pistol to his belt and linked in to the bigger one. The minute whine of induction coils going hot, that was music. On the tacnet video in the corner of his vision he could see Kim was almost through the back door.

[I'm in,] he messaged.

[Here is a map of the typical module layout,] Eidolon messaged. [Interior partitioning will vary, but the bulkheads will definitely be as shown here.]

A mini-map popped up in Park's field of vision. Four bulkhead walls radiated from the station's central floatway corridor, dividing the disc into quadrants. The quadrants ran thirty meters from central corridor to outer edge. Ringing all four quadrants was an outer corridor five meters wide. The outer corridors of almost all of the modules, including this one, were visible from outside due to wide windows. They were packed with plants, which probably provided a lot of the station's oxygen. What was in each quadrant, though, was anybody's guess.

Inside, the module was hot and humid as a kleptocrat's steam bath during an orgy. Condensation clung to the walls, which were all glossy white panels with harsh violet-tinged lighting strips at regular intervals. Mist hanging in the air made visibility crap, and the heat messed with IR, so he did a quick t-ray scan of his surroundings. This wasn't a place where he wanted to be surprised.

[Ain't what I expected,] Kim messaged, [Who microfactures drugs in a sauna?] Park could see from her video feed that the dome of the hull wart over her was icing up as the water vapor hissing out of the module settled on it.

Around him in the mist he was able to resolve the shapes of several cornucopia machines, reserves of nanofab feeder stock, three-dimensional cargo palettes, and a few small cargo-handling bots. A boutique pharma manufacturer didn't need much more than that for shipping and receiving. This section of the module was otherwise a big, empty pie slice with the U-Facture station's central corridor at the tip. The room took up a quarter of the disc of the module, less the wide corridor ringing the module's outer edge.

[I should've sent Smoke in with you,] Kim messaged, [You should have back up.]

They'd left Smoke aboard the *Skink*. Park messaged back, [Fa Jing techs don't show up with police baboons. Keep on cuttin'. I got this for now.]

[You'll be looking for an actual manufactory,] Cagehopper messaged. [The equipment in that room looks optimized for making boxes. Eidolon, can't you get a schematic?]

Eidolon messaged, [Jamming them is occupying much of my attention, Cagehopper. Their security AI is of very high quality, and subverting systems while it's on alert is difficult at best. The best I can do right now is keep it from alerting the rest of the station.]

Park searched for power conduits, feeder stock lines, or anything else that would hint at where the microfacturing equipment might be in relation to his current position. He didn't find anything, so he kicked off from the airlock toward a bulkhead door that opened on the next quadrant of the module. The automech bot followed him.

[Mech,] he messaged it, [Start building a detailed schematic of this module. Highlight all exposed power, data, and feed lines. Share with the users on my general comm channel. Visual inspection; local systems aren't going to talk to you. Start with this room.] If they ended up having to destroy the module, he'd need to know how.

[KK, boss,] the bot said. It hovered off into the mist, staying close to the wall.

[Don't touch anything, and don't interface with anything without asking me,] he messaged after it.

[KK, boss.]

He did a bypass on the controls for the bulkhead door. When he was almost done, Kim messaged that she'd gotten through the hull and was casing the outer ring corridor.

Park finished the bypass. The bulkhead door slid open, and a strong smell of jasmine wafted out. Park'd expected an office or something, but instead he was looking into a Hindu temple centered around the blunt, phallic shape of a huge stone Shiva linga.

[Well, fuck,] he messaged everyone, [Think I know who we're dealing with now.]

—

"You realize that you've severely damaged our working relationship, Carter?" Das Frettchen asked.

"What do you want me to do?" Park asked.

"Cooperate. You'll find the peace of mind that comes with knowing a situation has been thoroughly dealt with does you more good in the long run than thinking you've saved some lives but wondering if one day the people you've saved will turn on the rest of us."

"Your shit ain't worth the methane in it."

Park cut the call.

—

Kim and Cagehopper drew guns and pulled themselves through the hole she'd cut in the hull. They cased the module's verdant outer ring corridor. Wide windows let thin sunlight in from outside. The walls of the corridor were slick, reflective white regularly interrupted by glaring UV light strips. The light bounced off the hanging water vapor, having more the effect of high beams in a fog bank than improving visibility. That made her edgy, so she deactivated the helmet on her suit. The helmet melted away, receding into the ring of her collar.

[That's not wise,] Cagehopper messaged. He'd kept his helmet up. [You don't know what's in all this mist.] He took an instrument for sampling the air from a pocket in his suit and stuck it to his shoulder. A shared stream of atmospheric data announced itself on their tacnet.

For now, she didn't look at it. [Tell me if I need to cover up,] she said, [For now, I want peripheral vision.]

The dense foliage in the outer ring and the stifling heat made seeing anything on visual or IR tough, so she amped up her hearing. Nothing but the quiet hum of recyclers and ventilation, so far.

Based on Eidolon's schematic, a door to the disc-shaped Panacea module's large, inner quadrants passed through the bulkhead that formed the inner wall of the ring corridor they were exploring about twenty meters ahead of them. Even with the curve of the corridor, she should've been able to see the door, but the riotous plant growth obscured the opening.

They pulled themselves toward the door. Kim used the grab loops mounted between windows on the outer wall, moving somewhat clumsily. She envied Cagehopper, who brachiated between grab points with ease on long, gibbon arms.

They reached the bulkhead door and studied it. [You any good with this stuff?] she messaged Cage.

[I do organisms, not machines.]

She didn't want to spend ten minutes cutting through another bulk-head with her covert ops tool, not with Park already inside. She could see the temple he'd discovered through the tacnet feed, and she didn't like the look of it. Religion weren't never good news.

[Eidolon,] she messaged, [I need a door hacked.]

[I am—]

[Fuck it, man, they know we're here,] Park messaged.

A brief pause, then Eidolon messaged, [True. Proceeding. Captain Kim, if you are able to pry away the panel to the left of the door and run a cable from your suit interface to the datajack underneath, it would aid me greatly.]

Kim morphed her utilitool into a short pry bar and pushed off the outer ring wall toward the door. Eidolon already knew where the panel was based on Park's earlier intrusion; he overlaid a rectangle to the right of the door with an AR graphic. Arrows pointed to the edge where she need to pry.

When she was less than a meter from the door, something rustled in the foliage. She'd couldn't stop herself; she wasn't close enough to any of the walls. A dark green tendril covered in glossy, three-inch-long thorns whipped out from a plant near the door and wrapped itself around her leg. Seeing more tentacles emerging from the leaves, she ordered her suit to extrude its helmet again. The clear bubble closed over her face just in time for another tendril's thorns to glance off the helmet.

"Warned you," Cage said. He'd switched to voice comm. Not much point in sticking with messaging over the VPN any longer; they'd clearly been noticed.

Kim growled and squeezed off several shots toward where she thought the center of the plant might be. No effect, and another tendril had gotten a hold on her left arm. She struggled with it, trying to reach the stunner on her belt. "Little help?" she said to Cage.

The hypergibbon was prepping … something. As she struggled with the plant, she saw him swapping his shredder for a small pistol, ejecting the clip, and fumbling to insert a different clip. "Keep it occupied," he said.

Occupied. Yeah. The plant had four tendrils on her now. She'd imagined being pulled toward some kind of toothy maw, but instead they were constricting, trying to push their thorns through her vacsuit. It was holding for the moment, but she could feel the hard points of the thorns through the skin of the suit. Kim finally managed to get to her stunner. She contorted in the tentacles' grasp, trying to bend her body so that she had a clear shot between the stunner and the plant's center.

The tendrils tightened as she struggled. Finally, she jerked one leg to spin herself into the right position. Through the gun's sight she saw the plant's center. She fired, the air between her and the plant distorting and crackling with electricity, but at the same time she felt the suit fabric finally give. A thorn pierced her leg; the area around it immediately went numb. The tentacles stopped jerking her around, but they didn't loosen their grip at all.

[Fuck,] she messaged, [Cagehopper, I'm stung.]

Cage drew a careful bead on the center of the plant and fired a single shot. The bullet went in with a wet sound, and the knot of muscle-like cellulose immediately began to convulse, then shrivel. The tentacles started to loosen their grip.

"What was that?" she asked.

Cagehopper was at her side, running a medical scanner over her. "Splash ammo. Sorry I didn't have it ready, didn't think I'd need herbicide. Does your body have toxin filter, medichines, or any other antitoxic countermeasures?"

"No."

[Talk to me, guys,] Park messaged.

[Kim's been stung by a Referium dulcamara. It's a carnivorous plant from Echo IV. Nasty sumbitch, but I've got an anti-toxin swarm I can key to go after it.] He looked up at Kim. "Sorry, but I'm not sure about that leg."

"Meaning?"

"Tissue necrosis sets in fast with this toxin." He injected her with something, using the hole in the suit left by the thorn.

"Who the hell has carnivorous plants from a xenoplanet for security?" she asked.

—

Park had finished casing the temple. Nothing there but flower bouquets, suggestive statues, and a giant stone penis. Kim was cussing up a storm as Cagehopper treated her leg. She'll make it through, he thought, She's ruster tough, and Cage knows his trade. He was regretting splitting up, though. The module wasn't that big; breaching it at two points and meeting up in the middle hadn't looked that hard.

He pushed off for the door to the outer ring corridor. Best plan at this point was to meet up with Kim and Cagehopper, then tackle whatever was left in here as a unit.

[Eidolon, how's it going?] he messaged the AGI.

[I am helping Cagehopper and Captain Kim get through the bulkhead door here.] Eidolon highlighted their position on the minimap. [The station's occupants have ceased attempting outside comm calls.]

Park was halfway through bypassing the bulkhead door to the outer ring when the automech bot winked off the network. No damage report, just gone.

[Y'all see that?] he messaged, [Eidolon, what's happening?]

[The signal from den autobomb est gurbufrixfra**{{>--]

Park smelled a hand touching the back of his neck. His mesh inserts were outside his body somewhere. He stretched but couldn't touch them. His body grew, his skin whitened, and the temple grew as well, taking on cavernous dimensions. He felt the cool stone of the floor against his back and felt heaviness in his limbs—gravity. Had the module begun to spin? But no, then down would be the outer wall of the temple, but he was laying on the same plane as the enormous Shivalinga at the temple's center. His clothes and gear were gone, except for some kind of animal skin wrapped around his waist.

What in hell was this? Park tried to clear his head, but it wasn't going away. He thought around for controls, but it wasn't a simulspace.

He felt strong, smooth toes, and then the ball of a foot on his chest. The toes stroked from his solar plexus down to his groin, and he could taste their skin on his tongue as they moved over him. He found he could move his eyes. Janu Vaidyar, their quarry, stood over him. She stepped onto him, planting one foot on his belly just above his groin, the other on his chest. Throbbing percussion music and jasmine scent pulsed through his ears, nose, and eyes. Vaidyar's skin had turned blue, and she was naked but for a few pieces of jewelry, most prominent among them a belt and necklace made of small skulls.

Aw, fuck. Was he about to get sexually assaulted by someone's religious beliefs? Park wasn't able to hold a rational thought for long, though. Vaidyar'd hooked her async talents deep into some primal shit, deep enough his lizard brain didn't want to hear about how relenting would be a bad plan. Vaidyar plunged onto his erection and began riding him. Their bodies expanded beyond the bounds of the room, out into space, beyond the bonds of the solar system, until the universe spun above him. It drifted apart, growing diffuse, and then contracted into a point of infinite density, suspended in its terrible potential even as Park now hung on the cusp of orgasm.

"Help me finish the cycle," she said, stroking his belly playfully, "The universe needs its rebirth. Lord Shiva's work must finish." She squeezed him inside of her. She was holding a tiny cup of soma, offering it to him.

Park groaned, which'd have to pass for a "fuck you." He wondered why mindfucking him was preferable to just injecting him with exsurgent goop, if that was her plan.

"Because." She twisted her hips, making him gasp involuntarily. "I desire your assent, your aid. You've killed my cats' paws and put my forks on the run. I want to know who's hunting us."

—

[Eidolon, open that damned door, I don't care what else you gotta let slip.]

Kim floated outside the bulkhead door. Her leg burned where it wasn't numb; she'd ordered the vacsuit to go rigid around the leg to keep it immobile. Park's minimap blip was only a few meters from the other side of the door. They'd hustled around the outer ring to his location when he dropped off the tacnet and stopped answering mesh calls. Cagehopper hung on some foliage next to her, splash gun still trained on the wilted remains of another carnivorous plant.

The door hissed open. In the gloom beyond, Janu Vaidyar floated before Kim. She was wearing a plain black second skin, and the weird ripple of an invisibility cloak distorted the air to one side of her. Her legs were wrapped around Park's waist. She had one hand on his temple and the other wrist, oozing blood from a shallow cut, poised near his mouth.

She turned with one eyebrow raised and smirked at Kim. Kim drew a careful bead and shot her in the head.

As Vaidyar drifted away, Park convulsed. Was he—was that an erection in his trousers? She looked at Vaidyar's morph, its head wreathed in drifting blood droplets. Seriously, im-ma? Next time don't bring psychic sex powers to a gunfight. Cagehopper swung into the room to check on Park. She pushed off from the door frame and went to help.

—

They swept the rest of the module and found no one else. The remaining space was taken up by posh living quarters, a medical facility growing backup futura morphs cut to look like pleasure pods, and a pharmaceutical factory. Cagehopper set to work figuring out what they'd been making while Eidolon cracked their records.

Park and Kim were in the medical bay; the module's doctor bot was working on her leg.

She said, "Before we came here, you said you had a hunch who Cupcake was working with. Now that you, uh, got to know her, any idea?"

Park grimaced, feeling a little embarrassed. "Yeah. Cult of the Destroyer. They're a corrupt Hindu sect, believe the TITANs got sent by Shiva to destroy us so the next cycle of creation could start."

"Never heard of 'em."

"That's because Firewall destroyed them, or any rate was supposed to have. On Luna, four or five years back. Looks like Cupcake and a few others copied themselves and kept the dream alive." Park winced as he watched the doctor bot excise a strip of necrotized flesh from Kim's leg and spray more medical nanobots on it.

"I've had worse," she said. "So what now?"

"Let Cagehopper take that factory apart, and find out what they're up to. Meantime, heal up."

Cage didn't take long. The drug Vaidyar'd been producing was designed to enhance the abilities of asyncs—and all of the people being prescribed the drug were asyncs. According to Vaidyar's notes, it would make all of the asyncs nodes in a network that she could use to employ psychic sleights on a massively amplified scale, potentially killing or taking control of hundreds of thousands of people. Not quite an apocalypse—but a nice start.

Fortunately, the mutation the drug triggered in the Watts-MacLeod virus was easily reversible. Cagehopper could rearrange a few molecules in the next shipment of the drug, and the patients could all go back to being garden-variety neurotic, socially stigmatized psychic freaks instead of walking brain bombs.

The only problem now was jurisdiction. All of the patients were in Valles-New Shanghai, which wasn't Park's beat. And his counterpart there, Das Frettchen, was a paranoid, scorched-earth-lovin' sumbitch.

Park braced himself, and gave Das Frettchen a call.

—

Park cut the mesh call a few minutes later. It hadn't gone well. The team, including a hologram of Eidolon, had assembled in the medical bay. The air was clearer and cooler; they'd tweaked some parameters on the station's life support.

"Das Frettchen ain't playing ball," he said.

"Who is this asshole, anyway?" Kim asked.

"He does my job, but he's in charge of Valles-New Shanghai."

"I still don't know what your job is," Kim said.

Cagehopper chuckled. "Membership equals privileges."

She snarled a little, the asked Park, "So?"

"We move Cagehopper's plan to inoculate the victims forward anyhow. Cage, how long you need?"

"About six hours to get a shipment sent out. Then we can bug out and scorch this place."

"I want y'all alert. Frettchen gets extreme sometimes when he don't get his way."

"What was that you said to me a few days back about the Rangers having termites in the frame?" Kim asked.

Park shook his head. "No comment, ma'am."

—

Das Frettchen inhaled the delicate aroma from the cup of white tea and waited for his old friend across the table to weigh the information he'd just shared. The tea room was private—very private—and they'd been speaking freely.

"Searle," said Cheng at length—he and Cheng had known each other too long for pseudonyms—"You do realize that a liquidation on this scale will be challenging, even with my resources."

"Pangs of conscience?" Searle asked.

Cheng's face remained neutral. "No, of commerce. You'll have to share your findings with me."

Searle considered this. The Cult of the Destroyer had eluded Carter; Cheng's friends would capture one of them and learn their secrets sooner or later, whatever Firewall did. "Of course, old friend. Gentlemen shouldn't keep secrets from one another."

Cheng smiled; he'd always enjoyed irony. "Done, then. Ozma will clean up here on the ground. And their orbital factory?"

"Leave that to Firewall," Searle said.

—

Manager Leong looked at the small, elegantly dressed man in the airlock, still unsure how he should be treated. His credentials, which were very much in order, said he was Mr. Searle, here to investigate an insurance claim by one of the U-Facture's clients on behalf of Llewellyn's Offworld.

Leong's uncertainty in dealing with the man stemmed from his inability to learn anything about Searle's reputation. This suggested that he was either a complete nobody or someone very important indeed. Leong had not risen to management by being incautious, and so he decided to give the elegant man face.

Yes, clearly someone important. Leong let him inside with repeated insurances of offering every assistance.

—

Searle's hacker reported back within a minute of Searle's gaining access to the U-Facture.

[I have their AGI; it's sleeved in the ranger shuttle. Scorch it?]

Searle messaged, [Stand by.]

On the tacnet feed, he could see that the trio of Guangxi cleaners he'd hired were in position.

[Go,] he messaged.

He watched the stream of status messages with interest as Eidolon's consciousness was burned from the ranger shuttle's computer systems.

—

"How much longer?" Kim asked, "Smoke's been in the *Skink* all this time. There's a limit to monkey housebreaking."

[We're almost done,] Cagehopper messaged, [Maybe half an—oh , fuck.]

"Eidolon's offline," Park said, "We got company." He enlarged the tacnet feeds of security sensors in the module that Eidolon had created; several had gone dark. The rest were winking out, one by one.

"Shuttle's still online, Eidolon just isn't there anymore," Kim said.

They were still in the med bay. Through the open bulkhead door to the manufacturing quadrant, they heard coughs of gunfire.

[Cage?] Park messaged.

[Hiding. One shooter, helluv professional.]

Park and Kim drew guns and made for the bulkhead. They flanked the doorway, sizing things up. Park went to t-ray vision and looked through the wall. He could see Cage huddled behind some equipment and the shooter stalking him, moving cover to cover.

Kim, watching the room behind him, said, "Behind us!"

Park whipped around. There was nothing there but a slight distortion of light on visual, but the t-rays showed the outline of another assassin—throwing something.

Three marble-sized objects flew toward them as the assassin took cover behind the doctor bot. Grenades.

They both tried to swing themselves around the bulkhead into cover, but they were too slow.

Last effin' time I call that bastard, Park thought.

The grenades exploded in a blast of white plasma. It didn't last long enough to hurt much.

—

Searle's hacker didn't take long extracting the necessary data. He'd review it before sharing it with Cheng, of course. The leader of the Guangxi killers approached him after they'd planted the explosives and visited the front office to dispose of Manager Leong.

"Anything else?" she asked.

"Outstanding work, as always," he said, "That will be all."

The assassin cocked an eyebrow. "The ranger ship?" she asked.

"I'll dispose of it," he said.

The assassins left him there in the module's outer ring with the three bodies.

Searle put the agonizer to the base of Kim's skull, flipped it to roast mode, switched to t-ray vision to make sure he didn't miss, and burned out her stack. This was a slow operation with an agonizer, and he held a handkerchief over his mouth and nose as hair and flesh burned under the beam. If the rangers followed policy, she'd hit her life timeout in about a week and be re-instanced from backup, none the wiser.

He sawed Cagehopper and Carter's stacks out next. He considered simply discarding the monkey; he disliked uplifts and saw little use for this one. But he pocketed both stacks anyway before spacing the bodies.

He left the U-Facture module, went to the *Skink,* and powered it up. Piece of junk. Smelled like ape and stale cigarettes, but it would get him back to Mars quickly enough.

Unlike his companions, Jake Carter would be a problem. Searle would have no difficulty justifying the ranger and the ape as necessary information containment. The AGI had been a fork; the original would know nothing. But Carter was a proxy. Ming and those other fools rimward would demand Carter be re-instanced and briefed on the mission outcome.

Searle would probably have to claim that Carter's stack had been unrecoverable, but doing so would call into question both Searle's competence and his reliability. He didn't see a better option; Carter had enough pull with the Eye that a memory wipe was out of the question.

As he was finishing the pre-flight check, something flew through the cabin and hit the windshield, bouncing toward him. Searle caught it; it was an empty, crumpled-up cigarette package.

He heard noise and turned around. There was a police baboon floating a few meters behind him, feet holding the rim of the cockpit door. It was rhythmically flipping open, flicking, and closing a lighter. It closed the lighter a final time, let go of it so that it hung in front of the baboon, and growled.

"Er, sorry," said Searle, "I don't smoke."

The baboon launched itself at Searle, howling jaws opening to fill his field of vision.

PRIX FIXE

Andrew Penn Romine

It's a forty-day burn across the belt from Extropia to 1123 Hungaria, and Jule Cortez is ravenous. Her stomach growling, she sits up from the acceleration couch to get a better view of the misshapen asteroid spinning slowly outside the cockpit window. Just nine kilometers, end to end. She's burned a lot of fuel and a lot of favors to get here, and the asteroid looks almost good enough to eat.

"Finally. I'm starving," she whispers.

[Your blood sugar levels are normal], her muse, Thoth, assures in an androgynous purr.

"You'd be hungry, too, knowing Chef is down there."

She means metacelebrity Chef Volkan Batuk, missing and presumed dead, but Jule's found him at last, hiding on a speck of dust in the endless black.

[I can't get hungry], Thoth reminds her. Her muse has been snarkier than usual since its last firmware update.

Small clusters of buildings cling to the crust of the asteroid. They're leftovers from an old mining venture, abandoned when the mineral deposits proved shallow. *Perfect place to hide, though*, Jule thinks.

1123 Hungaria's a Cole bubble, spun just fast enough to provide weak gs to the cavern hollowed out along the axis. The ship's sensors ping power signatures. Another shrill alarm warns of targeting lasers locking on.

"What if he doesn't want to be bothered?" she worries, punching *transmit* on the passcode she'd retrieved off the mesh. It took months to decipher the clues, and a generous deposit of funds to ghost accounts. She hopes it's not a hoax.

[Why invite us all the way out here, then?]

The comm chimes.

"Spacecraft 'Peppercorn. 'Follow instructions for landing. 'Do not deviate."

"That sure sounds like Batuk," she admits to Thoth as she fires the vernier jets, matching *Peppercorn's* orbit with 1123 Hungaria's spin. An open hangar swings into view, beacons winking emerald.

[Voiceprint's a probable match], Thoth confirms. [We found him, alright.]

"Yeah." Jule can't help but grin even though her feelings are an emulsion of amazement and apprehension. She might never have come all the way out here from Mars without her muse's guidance. Thoth's level-headed encouragement had been a foil to her anxiety over all the conspiracy theories surrounding the metacelebrity's supposed death.

Batuk's restaurant, *Trimalchio*, once orbited the limb of Mars in an absurdly expensive hab for the hyperelite. It took money, power, and kilometers of rep just to get in the reservation queue, and after that, a year-long wait. Batuk's recipes were copied widely. Anyone with a halfway decent fabber could churn out his famous enoki-stuffed polenta shells or wet-print his divine *poitrine de porc* souffles with *jus rouge.*

Growing up, Jule had fabbed whole feasts from his recipes, using her EZPrint from Prosperity Group, Batuk's chief sponsor. She had all the XPs, too. For her fifteenth birthday, though, all Jule Cortez wanted was to eat at *Trimalchio*, and because her parents were well-placed execs at Prosperity Group she got her spot on the wait-list.

But, a week before her meal, an explosion in *Trimalchio's* kitchen depressured the hab and scattered its elite diners into the vacuum of space. The fire was ruled an accident, and there were few casualties after the guests were resleeved. Among the irretrievable egos, though, were a handful of Batuk's most devoted patrons—and the chef himself.

Now, Jule might be able not only to prove he survived, but with luck, and at long last, to finally dine on Chef Batuk's legendary cuisine.

—

The *Peppercorn* settles into the landing hangar as a docking umbilical snakes out. The *crunk* of the airlocks connecting follows, then the hiss of equalizing pressure. Jule's ears pop gently as she reaches for the hatch.

[Are you ready?]

"Are you kidding?" She smiles, and her nervousness vanishes in a rush of endorphins. It might be a post-sleep reaction from the hibernoid morph she sleeved in Extropia, but she's damn giddy all the same.

Stale but breathable air wafts up. The wide umbilical pulses like the esophagus of some slavering beast from a fantasy XP.

And you didn't even bring a sword, a voice says. Her own or Thoth's, she's not sure.

Jule propels herself hand-over-hand down the rungs of the umbilical into a spherical chamber below.

A lone figure waits for her there, a trim male exalt with broad shoulders, short dark hair, and soulful, penetrating eyes. Chef Volkan Batuk's smile is tight, but charming rather than arrogant, and he's leaner—and handsomer—than he'd last appeared in the feeds Jule's seen. His eyes dart from her to the umbilical and back, and the smile slips for a moment.

"You're not what I expected," he laughs nervously, a faint accent underscoring his bemused air.

"And what were you expecting, Chef?" she extends a hand, and he takes it. It's dry and warm. He smells of honey and musk.

[No access to the outside mesh, but there's a PAN with some guest codes.] Let Thoth worry about that.

"I'm not sure, to be honest. A Prosperity Group hit squad, maybe?"

"Oh, shit, no. I'm just your biggest fan, Chef, I swear." Jule giggles, unable to contain her nerves.

"And you are?" Batuk replies, an eyebrow arched.

"Oh! Jule Cortez. It's such an honor, Chef."

"Welcome to Cockayne, Jule Cortez," Batuk says, "and congratulations on deciphering my clues."

"I had a lot of help from my muse," she admits. Really, Thoth did all the work.

"Ah. So why did you seek me out?" Batuk's gaze is intense, and a frown tugs at the corners of his mouth. Has she offended him?

"I'm famished!" Her stomach growls, on cue.

Batuk laughs, a throaty bark that dissolves the tension.

"Come, then, before that monster eats us both!" he motions her down the corridor.

[Ask him why he's got a laser-guided railgun emplacement topside,] Thoth whispers.

Shut up, Jule whispers back.

—

Batuk leads her down a series of clean, dimly-lit corridors to a warren of hab domes on the inner surface of the asteroid. Through porthole windows, she glimpses the vast hollow of the interior. It's spined with sunlight-reflecting mirrors, augmented by artificial lamps that bathe the entire interior in a misty, amber glow. Unfortunately, the giant windows of the south pole are smashed open, and the cavern is a vacuum-frosted wasteland.

"It serves little purpose now," Batuk muses when Jule laments its loss.

"You could fix it. Grow your own food out there!" she says, a sudden idea kindling in her. "You wouldn't have to rely on vat meat."

"Livestock's hideously expensive, even for me. And I'm hardly farmer material." There's a curious light in Batuk's eyes as he palms a door open.

Jule tries to hide her disappointment. Cultivating exotic food sources are what metacelebrity chefs are supposed to do. Maybe she can convince him to reconsider.

Inside is a dormitory chamber—the standard hub of couches, vid screens, and exercise equipment—ringed with triple-stacked bunks and hygiene pods. In its mining days, the dorm probably housed at least two dozen, hot bunking through shifts of sleep, play, and work. Jule and Batuk seem to be the only ones here now.

"Meager accommodations, I know, but I hope they'll do while I finish preparing a welcome meal." He seems embarrassed, and Jule fights an urge to hug him.

"They're fine, really, Chef."

"Excellent. I'll return shortly." The door whisks shut behind him as he departs.

[Batuk's rattled by our presence,] Thoth observes.

"He's got a right to be," she says, "he's supposed to be dead."

[And yet he left us an invitation to find.]

Jule sighs. "Thoth, when did you get so paranoid?" Not that she isn't worried, too. She's more convinced Thoth's latest patch is buggy, though. The muse has been acting strange since they left Mars. She makes a note to run the update again when she gets access to the outside mesh.

[Next time you fangirl, just remember to watch your back.]

"That's why I have you, Thoth. Any luck accessing the local mesh?"

[Yes. Just the basics, though. Nothing terribly interesting.]

"Show me what you've got."

Jule settles on a padded couch as Thoth punches up the local mesh to her endos. She finds basic maps of the various habs of 1123 Hungaria; most are powered down. She wonders if that means she's the only guest so far. Jule scrolls through terraforming designs the miners had intended for the interior. They'd imagined a lush paradise in the cavern. Maybe she could restore that dream—with Batuk's blessing, of course.

She spends the next hour spitballing ideas. Faux-rustic farms from pole to pole, free-roaming livestock, maybe squid modified for a low-g atmosphere? She giggles, imagining old Earth bison bouncing around like shaggy balloons. Above all, a pinnacle of rock rising with unparalleled views. That's where Batuk's new restaurant would go.

Caught up in the reverie of her fantasy, she forgets the time.

"I can't attend a Chef Batuk dinner in this!" she pulls at the worn pockets of her flight suit. The dorm has a galley-top fabber—an older PG model. Jule fabs a sleek suit from one of the station's available patterns. Red, with antique silver patterns that flicker in the weave. Old-fashioned, but Jule doesn't care.

"How do I look?"

[Amazing,] Thoth deadpans.

"Come on," Jule says, "might as well have a little fun out here."

[I've been reviewing the schematics of the station,] Thoth says.

"And?"

The door chime interrupts.

"Later," Jule says, "Look, Thoth, I know this whole thing is crazy, but it's an incredible opportunity. Just keep one eye open, okay?"

She opens the door. Batuk is waiting with his crooked smile.

—

They drift down a maze of corridors to a hab that used to be a command center of some kind. Batuk's replaced the central console with the low stainless sweep of a replica of one of the big private tables from the original *Trimalchio*. A variety of padded chaises surround the table, upholstered in hygenic mesh. Straps, armrests, and handles are positioned for optimal comfort in low gravity.

But it's what's *on* the table that starts the saliva trickling down her throat.

There's a towering mountain of platters and bowls, each brimming with a bubbling stew or soup, joints of vat-meat and gelid puddings. Bowls of rice shimmer with their own varicolored light, half-hidden vegetables glinting like jewels. Silvery prawns swim in waterfalls of violet liqueur that gush from floral-printed diamond goblets. A cloud of edible photons circulates through all the dishes in intense rainbow hues. They're all of Batuk's most famous dishes: *riz illuminée, crevettes d'argent à l'ail, soupe de rayonnement cosmique*. There are the expected masterpieces, of course—*poitrine de porc* soufflés with *jus rouge*. A single place is set, with thrumcrystal plates and kinesthetic chopsticks for feeling every bite.

[I've got minimal contact with the *Peppercorn* in here,] Thoth warns.

Jule, her mouth hanging open in wonder, barely hears her muse.

"Chef," she mumbles to Batuk, "I don't know what to say."

"How about *Bon appetit*?" he suggests.

[Let me test the food,] Thoth says.

Jule nods as she sits down and takes up the chopsticks. A low frequency buzz shivers up her spine as a connection is made. Status lights show clear in her endo. She picks up a brochette of grilled meat.

[It's clean.]

She places the morsel on her tongue. It's vat-meat, pORc, probably, fabbed into a hollowed lattice and filled with green paste. She's disappointed at first, but as she chews, it bursts, filling her mouth with deeply herbal flavors. With the chopsticks, taste and feeling are joined. Pleasure tingles from her throat to the tips of her fingers.

"Very nice," she sighs.

She eats delicately, all too aware that Batuk is standing close behind her. Watching. With every bite, his scrutiny intensifies. She downs an entire bowl of illuminated rice, breathes in most of the photons, and gulps three goblets of the dizzying violet wine.

[You *are* hungry.]

mmm. ahhhh. unnnnhhh. Slurp.

The noises are mostly for Chef's benefit, a call seeking his response. Through the tumbling brightness of the flavors and the rills of haptic euphoria, Jule feels something else, too. She imagines it as a diamond-hard octahedron caught in her throat. It tastes of bitter iron. *Disappointment?*

Batuk seems almost to sense her thoughts.

"How is your meal?" he asks.

"Um, good," she says through a mouthful of expanding mushroom foam. A shrill aria swells in her implants as she swallows. The food *is* good, but her home fabber does just as well—and without the garish kinesthetic and auditory cues. It's hard to really taste Batuk's *agneau des étoiles fous* with her every nerve throbbing in stimulated pleasure.

"Good," she repeats when Batuk leans closer.

His eyebrows draw together imperceptibly. Has she offended him? She's no metacritic, but she's already writing the review. Either Batuk's art's suffered in his isolation, or worse, it's always been overrated. She sets down the chopsticks and changes the subject.

"Chef, why did you come all the way to Cockayne?"

His frown deepens, as if he's tired of telling this tale.

"I wasn't doing anything in my restaurant a thousand others couldn't do with their fabbers at home when the recipes leaked. And they always did, eventually. Prosperity Group offered to buy out my contract, sleeve a new chef in my likeness so the mystique might continue. Can you imagine? So I left all that madness behind."

"By blowing up *Trimalchio*?" Jule blurts.

"I took advantage of an opportunity to make an exit," he reddens. "I hoped with a very public death, PG wouldn't try and sleeve an impostor."

"It worked. They didn't. But your mystique is still strong," Jule adds, poking at the remains of her rice. "So if you're bored, then why are you making the same old dishes for me now?"

Batuk's eyes light up, and Jule flushes with triumph.

"You're onto something new," she says, excitement overtaking anxiety. "That's why you're seeding invites for devotees like me. I can help, Chef. I've got some ideas."

Batuk sits down beside her, glancing around as if someone might overhear.

"I'm sure you do," he whispers, "but I have a question for you first."

"Of course," she says, warming to his conspiratorial air.

"If I have something new, what would you give to try it?"

A glow having nothing at all to do with the kinesthetic food radiates through every millimeter of Jule's body.

"Anything," she breathes, the taste of victory sweet on her tongue.

—

Jule paces in her room, thoughts blazing with plans for Cockayne. Batuk's invited her for dinner this evening, and she'll lay it all out for him then. He seems ready to listen. Thoth dutifully records each idea as she rattles them off. The muse stays thankfully silent.

"Fixing the polar breach is a big job," she concedes, "but easy in the scheme of things. Once we repressurize, we'll seed the soil with enough fertile nanoswarms to sustain the arcology. Thoth, can you make a note to check TerraGenesis' latest catalog when we're back on the mesh?"

[Jule.] Thoth interrupts her ideas on workable livestock in the equator zones. [We should return to *Peppercorn* before dinner.]

"Why?" she asks, worried about another glitch.

[There are errors in my soil databases. I have backups on the ship.]

What's the hell is Thoth talking about? Is this another glitch?

"Can't you just uplink from here? The local mesh should—"

[No.]

"This is about what you were trying to tell me earlier. The maps," Jule says, some of her fears returning.

[It may be nothing,] Thoth says, [but I can explain better on board.]

Uneasy, Jule relents, and they retrace their steps towards the airlock. She wishes she'd been paying more attention when they'd first arrived, but in the rush of meeting her favorite metacelebrity she'd left that to Thoth. Now she's not sure that was a good idea. These dim corridors in the nav overlays of her endo aren't familiar. The air is thick and stale.

"This isn't the way," she says, a cold sweat prickling the small of her back.

[The long way 'round. I'm calibrating datapoints on the Cockayne schematic.]

Reluctantly, she follows the waypoints to a bulkhead door as unremarkable as every other one around it.

"Shit, Thoth," she stops just shy of the door. "What's gotten into you?"

[Curious. The public maps don't show this part of the facility. Perhaps I've led us astray.]

"Maybe Batuk doesn't want guests accidentally opening a hatch to vacuum?" She notices the door's keypad glows emerald in the dark hall, though. Unlocked.

[There's a lot of power routed here, though. Life support, too.]

"Another dorm, maybe?"

[Quite strange. I wonder what's inside?]

"We can just ask Batuk—" She cuts herself off, suddenly jealous there might be others on board with their own plans for Cockayne. Peeved, she stabs the door release.

Warm, humid air wafts into the corridor, fragrant with medicinal aromas. With it comes noise, the thunderous harmony of dozens of machines. The chamber beyond is large, with a wide central aisle, wanly lit from the instrumentation on the machines. The path is flanked by rows of morph incubation vats. Mature bodies float in the natal gel, unsleeved pod morphs, judging from the exposed ports of the cyberbrains.

[That's a lot of morphs for one ego,] Thoth observes.

"Oh shit," Jule whispers, her grandiose schemes deflating with the confirmation that she's hardly Batuk's first visitor.

At the far end of the incubation bay, a shadow like spreading ink oozes from the ceiling and around one of the vats. It's an octomorph, clad in a black jumpsuit, with glinting intelligent eyes that seem somehow familiar. Its tentacles uncoil and stroke the vat lovingly. Jule's fear kindles to bright panic. She shivers back from the door and it swishes shut.

"Let's go to the ship. I've seen enough."

[Good idea.]

Thoth displays the waypoints for the shortest route back.

"That wasn't creepy at all," Jule gasps as she scurries to the docking umbilical. "Do you think it saw us?"

[I don't know. But we've confirmed Batuk's not out here alone.]

"The other diners that were presumed dead? Maybe they all ego-casted out here?"

[There's one way to find out,] Thoth says as Jule gains the docking umbilical and climbs up toward the *Peppercorn*.

"Dinner tonight," she says.

[He's got something big planned, for sure.]

Inside the cockpit, Thoth asks to be plugged directly into the ship, indicating the ego bridge. Jule fingers the thick connection, concerned. A backup?

"Thoth, you've been strange since your last firmware update. It's time to tell me why."

She feels the muse's uncharacteristic hesitation.

[Data corruption.]

"'Data corruption?' Why the hell didn't you tell me sooner?" Jule frowns. It sounds like a lie. Muses aren't supposed to lie.

[That's why I suggest we run a backup.]

"You're not making sense, Thoth. Should I reboot you?"

[Please, don't!] Thoth pleads, alarmed. Then, calmer, [After dinner, I'll run a full diagnostic.]

"You'd better," she says, lying back until her head clicks into the bridge.

Her skull vibrates with the skirl of transferred data. A burst of heavy static whites out the world for a moment; for eternity. Jule sits up, her head still throbbing.

"Ouch! What the hell was that?"

[Jule, I've been printing something in the fab bench.]

The portable fab machine installed in the center console glows with green status lights. A few moments later, a completion tone chimes. Jule flips open the lid. Inside is a snub-nosed Direct Arms Krait-35 automatic pistol.

"Thoth!"

[Take it to dinner tonight.]

"What for?"

[It's concealable,] Thoth says, ignoring her. [Hopefully you won't even need it.]

"I'm not some ego hunter here to collect a bounty on Batuk, Thoth!"

Her words ring into the dull silence as suspicion becomes certainty.

"Holy shit. *You're* the ego-hunter! You're *not* Thoth!"

[He's dangerous, Jule.]

Her anger trembles through her, white hot.

"What is it? Are you some kind of AGI? An infomorph? Who crammed you into my skull?" Her muse knows every thought, her deepest self. No. Now someone else does.

[I'm sorry. It's regrettable.]

"Bloody unethical is what it is."

[I'm trying to protect you.]

"Says the AI whose invaded my skull. Fuck you, Thoth."

Thoth sighs.

[There are those who don't want to see you hurt, Jule.]

Shaking, Jule yanks the pistol from the fabber. She should power Thoth down, plan her next move without unwanted help. Only, her muse hasn't left her many options, and Thoth's not wrong to be cautious.

[I don't want to see you hurt,] Thoth says, displaying wardrobe choices that would best conceal the weapon.

"Yeah, I bet you don't," Jule snarls, picking out her favorite.

—

Batuk's at her door promptly at 20:00. He's wearing the same collarless dark suit as this morning, not a wrinkle on it, hair perfectly in place. He nods mute appreciation at her own dress—a swirl of red skirts and configurable silver pockets—fashionable yet functional. The pistol's strapped to her thigh, further concealed by high clunky boots that turn over at the tops.

Batuk's carrying two flutes of bubbling amber liquid. Shadows swirl in playful patterns inside the glass. *Like ink.* It makes her queasy.

"A drink as we walk?"

"Of course," she replies, taking one. She hopes Batuk hasn't been monitoring her too closely since she left her ship. Did he know she'd seen the vat lab? Could he possibly know about the pistol? Had his cameras picked up her tears of rage? The liquor is earthy, a dark honey rolling around her tongue. The finish is bitter.

"Chef, I have a question," she says as soon as they're in the corridor back to the dining salon.

He tilts his chin in assent.

"There *are* others here on Cockayne," It isn't really a question, but she's past being polite.

"There are," he admits. His smile is tight.

"Why not just tell me that when I arrived?"

"I've found it's best to ease in visitors," he replies.

Jule tries to sound cheerful, at least. "I bet we all come to you with big plans, huh?"

They stop outside the salon door.

"The destination resort, you mean? Farms, hotels, my new food, of course." Batuk's is a weary sigh.

"You'd be more exclusive out here than you ever were on Mars."

"I already cater to a very exclusive clientele, Jule. My new ventures may not appeal to more common tastes." His face is placid, but there's heat in his tone, the arrogance that was missing from their first meeting.

"Can I ask you—"

He raises a hand criss-crossed with dozens of scars. Occupational trophies or deliberate affectation, it's hard to tell.

"Enough questions, Jule Cortez. Are you willing to be a true patron or not?" His rising anger is no longer mistakable. The pistol pinches against her thigh. She's humiliated herself, humiliated Batuk. Thoth's revelation has tossed her into vacuum with no line to grab.

"All I ever wanted is to eat a real meal prepared by you, Chef. No third-hand fabs, no XPs, no imitations."

Batuk leans back, a tiny smile creeping in under his beetled brows.

"Are you sure you can tell the difference?"

She nods, hoping he'll believe her.

"Good. In Cockayne, there's absolute commitment to casting off the old ways of eating. We are *transhuman!* We leave the past behind and practice our culinary arts anew!"

[Jule,] Thoth's voice is desperate and full of static. [He's jamming us.]

She ignores the muse. If anything goes wrong, she's got the pistol.

"Show me, Chef," her voice trembles, half from fear, half from hunger.

Batuk nods and opens the door, ushering Jule into the dining salon.

Two androgynous biomorphs lie supine and naked on the table, their bald heads joined at a nest of wires and whirring machinery. Pulsing implants penetrate their skulls like grotesque halos. One morph turns its head to look at Jule, its face glowing with a beatific smile. Fingers curl in a faint wave that triggers a wave of nausea in Jule.

The sinister octomorph floats into the salon, its tentacles fanning a dozen syringes. With a flourish, it sticks both morphs' bellies with several jabs of the gleaming needles.

Next, a pair of rubenesque exalts glide in from another door. The corpulent man is swathed in silver tattoos, the woman has a drooping jaw and quivering jowls. Hunger burning in their eyes, they clutch knives and other eating utensils. A pungent aroma of frying garlic, nutmeg, and copper tingles Jule's nose as horror freezes her to the deck.

Oh fuck, no.

The smiling morph's torso blisters with internal heat and steam rises from its splitting skin. Tattoo licks his lips, winking at Jule as he stabs his meal with a knife. The cooking morph giggles as garlic cloves, roasted to perfection, spill out of its wound. Far from dying, the morph takes Tattoo's hand and squeezes as the diner carves a pinkish steak from its thigh.

"Edible morphs," Batuk whispers in her ear, "Injected nanoswarms make excellent sous-chefs. Pain filters and cyberbrains can prolong the terminal moment almost indefinitely."

The other morph shrieks in ecstasy as it mostly dissolves into a stew of vegetables and hunks of glistening meat. The woman with the drooping jaw slurps directly from the steaming broth. The soup-morph plucks a morsel from its own liquified body and eats it. The juices run red down its chin.

"Eat and be eaten. It's the ultimate truth of existence, Jule. Only now, we can transcend it—experience a perfect moment that can't be duplicated with mere vat meat or a fabber."

Jule's mind retreats from the obscene feast and the accompanying symphony of chewing and slurping.

[Get out, Jule!] Thoth warns.

The octomorph undulates towards Batuk, who waits with his arms wide. The eyes of octo glitter with the same desire as Batuk's. *The same eyes. There's a fork of Batuk sleeved in the octomorph.* The octo wraps its tentacles around Batuk's grinning head and twists until it pops wetly from his neck. Then it plucks out the cortical stack from the twitching body and buries its sharp beak into the raw meat of the stump.

"I am delicious," the octo buzzes. The salon fills with howls of pleasure and the animal grunts of feeding. A tentacle offers a serrated knife to Jule.

"Eat. And be eaten," Octo-Batuk invites her with its grating voice.

Jule responds by hitching up her skirts and drawing the pistol. Octo-Batuk is too busy chewing to notice at first, but his all-too-human eyes bulge with alarm as she squeezes the trigger. Explosive rounds crater the octo's fragile flesh, shearing away limbs and hurling its shuddering trunk into the wall.

She aims the pistol at the other diners. The weapon turns them to detonations of pink foam and trailing gobbets of meat and Jule empties the rest of the magazine into the machinery that keeps the edible morphs alive. The aroma of charred meat mingles with the acrid smoke of burning electronics. Above the shriek of the fire alarms, Jule hears the hiss of Octo-Batuk's laughter.

[Go, I'm firing up the engines on the *Peppercorn!*] Thoth urges.

She turns to the door and the sweet, cool air of the corridor rushes in. Jule hurls herself at the door, but a sharp pain between her shoulders stops her short, and she crashes halfway through. A suffocating cold spreads from her chest. She tries to stand, but she's caught on something. A serrated blade protrudes from just below her sternum—the knife gripped in the octomorph's last tentacle.

Octo-Batuk's speaker emits a weak gasp.

"You wanted a perfect meal, Jule. Eat. And be eaten."

The rest of the world is drowned in static and a smoky red haze that turns to utter black.

—

A burst of heavy static whites out the world for a moment; for eternity.

"Ouch! What was that?" Jule shouts in the cockpit of *Peppercorn.* Beyond the crystal viewport hangs the velvet curtain of space. A nav display ticks off the days back to Extropia. She's lying back on the ego bridge, but she can't sit up. Or move her arms. Or turn her head.

"Where are we?"

[Hold still, Jule,] says Thoth. A sudden dread descends upon her. Her glitchy muse, promising to explain everything right before she plugged in for a backup. No. It's more than that.

"Did you kill me?" she asks Thoth. She's never died before, let alone been murdered.

[No. I saved you, I hope.] Thoth sounds sad.

"That creepy octomorph, then. It followed us back."

[It's reponsible for your death, yes. But not here. At the dinner.]

"You were right, then," she shudders, flexing a hand over her stomach. Somehow, she's hungry again.

"How did we get away?"

[Emergency ego-cast for me. Benefits of being an infomorph. But I'm afraid you're running off a backup.]

Jule tries to clear her mind, but there's just a jumble of nonsensical images from before. Radar shows Cockayne receding to a dull gray speck through the cameras in *Peppercorn's* hull. Her new eyes.

The cornucopia machine's lying open. *Wasn't something printing in there a moment ago?* A trickle of memory, or a nudge from Thoth?

The black curtain of space unfurls into view.

"An infomorph? What the hell happened?"

[Are you sure you want to know?]

"Goddamn it, Thoth."

Thoth streams her most of it. Fortunately it's just playback, not XP. Even so, she's numb with horror and her phantom appetite vanishes.

"An ego hunter?" she says, when sanity returns. "And you left my stack behind, you bastard." She might be an infomorph, but panic's crawling around her simulated brain like a nanoswarm.

[It was probably destroyed when I ego-casted, Jule.]

Probably. Batuk and his vile patrons must have backups. Who knows how many forks might be waiting to salvage her stack for another gruesome feast?

"What if it wasn't?" she shouts at Thoth, or whoever it is pretending to be her muse.

[The Prosperity Group will have the coordinates by now. They won't spare the nukes when they get to Cockayne, I'm sure.]

It's true, Batuk's violated his contracts with PG, and maybe a few transhuman rights to boot. But would the PG agents really destroy the asteroid? What if Batuk gets hungry before that happens? How many times could he eat her before his hideous paradise is nuked to dust?

A worse thought occurs to her then. What if Batuk egocasts all of them to safety in some new uncharted hunk of rock in the Belt?

Eat. And be Eaten. Eat. And be Eaten.

[It's over, Jule.]

And over. And over.

She wants to believe her muse, that her stack was destroyed, but she's not even sure who Thoth really is. What if that's just another lie?

"You bastard," she whispers, not sure to whom.

A few hours out, she retreats into a trance-coma of simulspace. It's an uneasy hibernation. Wandering a maze of industrial corridors and ravenous with hunger, Jule opens door after door. Behind each and every one is Batuk's wide, toothy smile.

AN INFINITE HORIZON
Steven Mohan, Jr.

Iftikhar Quraini shivered, but not because of the cold that tightened his skin and turned his breath to fog. Sure, the gate room was frigid: walls carved from blue ice as hard as steel, air cold enough to freeze the water molecules on his skin as he cupped his hands over his mouth to preserve a tiny morsel of warmth.

But what was at the heart of the gate room was colder still.

The Fissure Gate.

It waited for him, a hollow sphere eight meters in diameter, built from arcs and swirls of gleaming metal, bisecting each other, hiding something darker within.

Iftikhar couldn't suppress a shudder. *Are you* sure *you can't tell me anything?*

[I can tell you many things,] said Carter, his muse, [but very little of it is likely to be useful. As I've told you many times, the gate experience is highly individual.]

A deep voice interrupted. "Nervous, kid?"

Iftikhar didn't turn to look at Brandon Sail, the chimpanzee. Instead, he watched one of his teammates step into the sphere, her body marked by the odd, curling shadows of the sphere.

She walked into the darkness at the center, and then she was gone.

Iftikhar winced.

He heard the soft panting of chimp laughter. "Man, you're really tweaked."

Iftikhar turned on Sail. "I am *not*," he said coldly. Everyone knew the chimp was a hypercorp agent and Iftikhar didn't really want to talk to him.

Sail issued a skeptical snort. His skin was the light color of cedar, his clear brown eyes as enigmatic as any human's. Fine black hair framed a face made comical by giant ears. At one meter, fifty centimeters, Sail was shorter than Iftikhar but more powerful. Chimpanzees weren't monkeys. They were *apes*. And this one probably had commando training.

"Look," said the chimp, "I've done this a dozen times. There's no reason to worry."

Iftikhar clutched at the comment like a man with a ripped vacsuit grabbed at the material around the tear, trying to hold in his life. "You mean it's really not that bad?"

"Oh, no. It's going to suck." Sail shrugged in his forest green vacsuit and flashed a toothy smile. "There's just nothing you can do about it."

Then the gate tech said Iftikhar's name, and it was his turn.

—

The singularity was black, but it was an *empty* black, like it wasn't really there—like nothing was really there. Iftikhar tried to look at the thing's shape, but it made his eyes water. Needle-sharp pain pricked his skull. The transhuman mind wasn't designed to look at wormholes. A flash of emerald lightning arced across its surface, actinic and bright but utterly silent.

Iftikhar took a step back.

"Any time now," Sail called.

Iftikhar put his helmet on and drew a deep breath. He rushed forw—

—

A moment of darkness, like being in a room during a power failure. No one and nothing there but the black. Iftikhar took a step, heard the click of his boot, felt something solid underfoot. Wherever he was, it was big. Big and empty. He could feel it. He could hear it in the echo of his single step. He was alone in a big nowhere.

He felt the throb of his pulse in his wrists. He had grown up an indent on Mars, spending far too much time in tin can habitats. The empty just *felt* wrong.

Something clutched his shoulder, a hand.

Inshallah.

A hand, cold like space, cold like the grave. Someone, *something*, whispered softly in Arabic.

I almost had you before. This time I won't let go.

—

—ard and stumbled into blinding sunlight and circular shadows, the ocean's voice loud all around him. The deep roar of it as it smashed itself into white foam, the sibilant hiss as it retreated.

He wasted no time making his way out of the gate's enclosure. Staggering and then collapsing on white sand, down on all fours and trembling, his breathing coming in great ragged gasps.

How long between?

[There was no "between,"] Carter answered. [Gate travel is instantaneous.]

But I was sure—I mean, I— He didn't have any way to finish that thought.

[Perhaps you suffered a hallucination?] said Carter, gently. [It may have been caused by the stress of wormhole travel. By the way, atmosphere is within standard transhuman range, as expected.]

Still breathing hard, Iftikhar reached up with shaking hands and unsnapped his helmet. The air tasted cool. It smelled of brine and anise, with a note of sulfur underneath. Very different from the antiseptic halls of Chat Noir.

Iftikhar looked up. Sail was staring down at him curiously, though no one else seemed to have noticed his arrival. He scowled and scrambled to his feet.

The gate rested on a sand spit that jutted into the green water like a knife. The beach was backstopped by a high rock face covered with red-green photosynthetic shrubs that made their living on black volcanic rock. Mixed in with the shrubs were branching tubular structures that looked a little like coral. They were royal purple and sharp-edged.

Razorweed. Weed, because they were useless. Razor, because they could cut.

"All right," said Krazny. "You were all at the briefing, you know the drill. Pelagic's mostly ocean, but as you can see there's some lovely island property."

Krazny was a tall, slim woman with skin the color of bronze. Her face was narrow and angular, framed by chocolate-brown hair tied back in a ponytail. She wasn't unattractive—but she wasn't exactly a knockout either. Her maroon vacsuit prominently featured a hand with the middle finger extended on her chest.

The Love and Rage Collective didn't care what they wore as long as it was practical.

"There's a small anarchist research station here to study the world's suitability for colonization," she said. "They missed a standard protocol contact check-in three days ago."

"The station AIs would've made contact on schedule, so clearly something has gone wrong." said Derrick Weaver warily. He was a short man with sandy-blond hair. Weaver was no one you'd notice until you looked into his pale green eyes. Then the menton *crackled* with intelligence.

Krazny shrugged "Possibly just a communications failure." She shook her head, her kinesics indicating that she didn't really believe that. "Anyway, Chat Noir wants to know for sure. I propose Weaver and Aqua check the comms substation. Sail and Quraini make contact with the main station. Reaper and I will coordinate from the gate." She glanced at the synthmorph.

The reaper was a disk carried on a skittering quartet of legs. Right now it wasn't showing any weapons—but that didn't mean there weren't any.

"You mean we'll *hold* the gate," said Reaper in a hard, brittle voice. It didn't *have* to sound that way. The ego riding the morph probably picked that voice for the same reason it hadn't told them its name. Trying to be scary. Why else ride a warbot unless you got off on that kind of thing?

"So there *is* danger?" asked Aqua, a sylph. She wore a turquoise vacsuit that hugged her pleasing curves and brought out the blue in her eyes. A mane of blond hair framed her perfect face.

"Look, we're just being careful," said Krazny. "Everyone's armed. Stay meshed and lead with your probes and everything ought to be fine."

No one spoke, but after a few seconds the group broke up into three teams.

As Iftikhar set off with the chimp, he couldn't help noticing that Krazny hadn't really answered Aqua's question.

—

Iftikhar didn't realize there could be so much *up* on an island. *Not a lot of islands on Mars.* His skin was slick with sweat under his vacsuit and his calves were on fire. Unlike the chimp, his body wasn't designed for scrambling through jungle. The ape kept slipping ahead and then coming back and saying things like, "I think there's a game trail five meters to the left," or "If you'd like to rest, we can."

This only made Iftikhar angrier.

After a while the chimp said: "You don't like me, do you?"

Iftikhar said nothing for a long moment, just staring. The chimp stared right back.

"You're from Luna," said Iftikhar.

Sail shrugged.

"I heard you *worked*"—he emphasized the word, to suggest he believed the tense was wrong—"for Direct Action."

"Work is not a dirty word," said Sail. "Martians work, too."

"Oh, we work," said Iftikhar bitterly. "My parents were killed in the Fall." He swallowed hard. "But they bought a ticket out for me. I was eleven and alone. An infomorph refugee. It took *eight* years to work off my debt."

"Eight years isn't so very—"

"What?" snapped Iftikhar. "Long?" He lowered himself into a crouch, so his face was close to the chimp's. "It was my *childhood.*"

Sail winced. "I'm sorry."

"Really? Wow. That almost sounded sincere."

"So, I'm a Consortium tool," said Sail softly. "Is that what you think, my young Barsoomian friend?" The chimp stared up at him with those big brown eyes, so like a human's. "If I'm so obviously a hypercorp spy, why did the anarchists invite me along on this mission?"

Iftikhar frowned. He had been wondering the same thing.

"All right," said the ape. "Here's another one. When does an anarchist act like a drill sergeant?"

He means Krazny, Iftikhar thought. Something clicked into place. "When she really is one." He paused. "Reaper's here for defense. Weaver to solve puzzles. Aqua because of her charisma."

"You're slow," said Sail, "but not irredeemably stupid."

"Something bad's happened."

"Maybe," said Sail softly. "But this world is too promising to give up, so …" The chimp spread his hands wide.

"They're checking it out," Iftikhar finished. He met the chimp's gaze. "If *you're* here they must believe there's some kind of corporate game going on."

The chimpanzee nodded. "Yes. That is a concern they have." He leaned forward, so his face was only centimeters from Iftikhar's and whispered, "But I don't think so."

Then he turned and raced ahead, disappearing into the green foliage.

—

They walked like that for a long time, Sail up ahead in the distance, Iftikhar struggling to follow. By the time Iftikhar reached the small research station, the chimp had already used the drone to search all the buildings.

[There's no one here,] he said.

Iftikhar studied the cluster of gray and brown prefab domes growing out of the jungle like toadstools. [I'd like to see for myself, if you don't mind.]

[Fine.] Sail's irritation came through loud and clear. [I'll search the jungle. Stay close.]

Iftikhar muttered a curse under his breath. Like he was going to follow the orders of some corporate sell-out. He stepped into one of the big community domes. The power was out, the only light a faded parallelogram of sunshine from the open door. Iftikhar's boots clicked on the tile.

"Hello," he called.

No one answered.

A chill wriggled down his back. Suddenly he remembered his hallucination at the gate. *I almost had you before.* Death had nearly claimed him during the Fall.

This time I won't let go.

He wheeled around—

But there was nothing behind him.

[Iftikhar, look.]

He jumped—and muttered another curse. It was just Sail.

Iftikhar pulled up the chimp's real-time feed. Sail stared at the ground, bent over like he'd just been sick.

'What is it?

[This.] The ape moved, loping on all fours, like he was too rattled to walk upright. He peered over a shallow ridge.

What the chimp saw was enough to wring a curse from Iftikhar. "There is no God, but God," he whispered, "and Mohammad is his Prophet."

—

Krazny cradled the Medusan Arms Hammerstrike in her arms. Whatever had built this gate, it had owned a righteous tactical sense. She patted her automatic rifle affectionately. The gate's placement on a spit meant it could be defended by a single well-armed soldier. The beach was really a cove running 400 meters north-south and bracketed on three sides by steep walls of black rock. You could climb, you could slip across the narrow strips of sand to the north or south, or you could swim. That was it.

Krazny liked that just fine.

She glanced back at the southern approach. Reaper had that one locked down. She turned to look north—

Someone there.

She flashed on a humanoid shape in a silver hardsuit moving through the foliage, the helmet's mirrored faceshield hiding the morph's face.

[Contact!] she snapped.

[Got it,] answered Reaper, his ping filled with tension. [Targeting.] The warbot crouched down and extruded several weapons.

The figure held up its right hand, palm out.

[Are you rescue? Oh, thank God. Thank God.] The voice sounded male.

Without thinking, Krazny had leveled her rifle. [Sir, I need ID. Right damn now.]

[Yes, yes. Chetko. Artur Chetko. I—I'm a soil scientist.]

Without asking, Krazny's muse opened an entoptic checklist under the heading "Artur Chetko." Green check marks appeared next to Roster, Voice Match, and Crypto, all indications that it really was Chetko.

Krazny didn't relax. [What happened?]

[Virus. Holy God, it's bad. Some kind of respiratory thing. Virulent as hell. A third of us are dead. Damn it, we need help.]

Disease was certainly on the list of things that could've gone wrong. Not likely, but certainly possible. Especially if the virus had been engineered by some damn hypercorp. It didn't explain the communications failure, though.

[Stay there, don't move,] she told Chetko. Krazny used her private link to Reaper. [Go check him out.]

[Why me? You're closer, I'll provide cover.] Reaper wasn't the sharpest blade in the armory.

[Because synthmorphs can't catch respiratory infections, that's why.]

Reaper skittered down the beach, past Krazny's position, towards the scientist. He disappeared out of sight. The scientist moved toward Reaper, and she temporarily lost sight of him as well. She was briefly concerned, but then admonished herself. She knew Reaper could take care of himself.

A belief she held right up until comms went straight to hell.

—

The jungle's canopy filtered out most of the sunlight, allowing only stray beams to stab down from the green roof overhead. Heavy, verdant air pressed against Iftikhar. It was like breathing soup. He wiped sweat from his face with the back of his arm. The worst part was the strange sounds of hidden creatures: a xylophonic *burr*, a slide-whistle shriek, a deep, menacing growl.

Where are you, Sail?

[Just—hiss—hundred meters—crackle —due east.]

I think I can hear him better now.

[You're closer,] said Carter. [The interference seems to decrease with proximity. Go left.]

Left.

His foot found a tree root and he tripped, going face down into the moldering leaf litter. He grunted as the ground slammed the air out of his lungs and another root rapped him on the skull.

The leaves' sweet rot swirled around him, forced itself inside his chest. He set his hands in the moist soil and pushed his body up. A busy buzzing attested to the industry of insects.

And then he realized the perfume of rot *wasn't* leaves.

His breath caught. Suddenly he didn't want to breathe any more of this air. *Not any more.*

Holding his breath, he looked forward. The earth fell away from the tree, as if some giant had hollowed it out with a shovel, scooping away tons of soil and leaving a shallow pit. He edged forward.

Slowly, ever so slowly, he peered over the ridge's lip.

A scream wrenched itself from his chest before he could stop it.

Lying in the pit was a tumult of bodies. They were stripped naked, maybe a dozen of them, men and women, limbs bent this way or that, lying—no, *piled*—on top of each other in a way that no living thing would tolerate.

Something touched Iftikhar's shoulder and he shrieked and jumped. He wheeled and found the chimp behind him.

"Easy, boy, easy," said Sail softly.

"Before comms dropped out," gasped Iftikhar. "Krazny said something about a virus. Do you think—"

Sail shook his head. "Look closer."

Iftikhar inhaled unsteadily and made himself peer over the ridge. This time he saw what he'd missed before, what he'd *wanted* to miss before. The splash of crimson. Spilled blood.

The emblem of violence.

—

Klaxons were going off in Krazny's brain. Reaper wasn't responding. There was no sign of Chetko.

Except she didn't really *know* it was Chetko, did she?

It made perfect tactical sense. If you're going to attack a group, hit the strongest first—while you still have surprise.

Her mesh inserts were flooded with hissing, gray static. Someone was jamming. Sure sign of a hostile move.

Suddenly things were spinning out of control.

Her mind was racing. Was this some hypercorp gambit to seize control of the planet? Did they come through the Mars or Discord Gates? Whoever it was, they'd need the gate to get off-planet.

She quickly picked out the best tactical position on the beach, up against the back wall and under a small outcropping of rock, so she'd be difficult to hit from above. The position commanded the approach to the gate *and* the rubble from a rockslide offered cover from the northern half of the beach. Perfect.

She worked her way back into her little niche. The shade from the overhang must've crowded out the red-green shrubs because there was nothing but razorweed here. This stuff looked a little different from the regular kind, like it was slathered with raspberry jam. Probably the purple coral had entered some reproductive phase. The station biologists would probably think that was just swell—if any of them were still alive.

She moved carefully among the razorweed. No way she could avoid a few cuts, but she didn't want to reveal her position with a path of broken tubes.

The day was getting hotter. She spat on the ground and kept moving. She had to get into position before someone came around.

Krazny was panting now. She turned and spat again.

She froze.

Her mouth was already filled with more saliva and a warmth was spreading through her middle. *Did I—Did I just wet myself?*

Anyone with any kind of tactical sense would've picked this spot to defend the beach. *They knew I'd choose this place.*

She glanced down at her right hand. Some of the razorweed had cut through her glove. It wasn't a bad wound, hardly more than a nick, really, but—

She looked at the jam smeared on the razorweed.

Profuse salivation, shortness of breath, involuntary urination.

She wasn't certain it was a nerve agent until the convulsions began.

—

Iftikhar looked down at Krazny's broken and bloodied body laid out on the beach. The most terrible part was her head. Her skull had opened like the bloom of a delicate flower. He and Sail had returned to the gate to find Aqua and Weaver standing over Krazny's body. No one knew where Reaper was.

"One might posit that an unclassified carnivore killed Krazny," said Weaver. "But that doesn't explain what happened to the reaper."

"This is *crazy*," yelled Iftikhar. "We're not detectives. Let's just go back. When they're resleeved they can tell us—"

"Iftikhar," said the chimp softly. "You know better."

He looked at Krazny's violated skull for a second before his eyes slid off and found another place to look. The realization hit him. They had taken her cortical stack.

Iftikhar shuddered. He understood why the killer might have destroyed the stack. If they hadn't, Krazny could identified her murderer, or murderers. But to *take* it—

That implied something far worse.

"All right," he said, "but let's *go*. Let's just go."

"*We can't,*" shrieked Aqua. "Don't you think we tried? Don't you think that's the very first thing we tried?"

"Someone took the gate control unit," said Weaver. "Without it, we can't interface with the gate."

"How long until Love and Rage checks back in here?" asked Sail.

"Five, six hours," said Weaver.

"Might as well be a hundred," snapped Aqua. "None of us could stand up to a reaper—we sure as hell aren't going to survive whatever can *kill* a reaper."

Iftikhar heard the hysteria in her voice and felt it welling up within him, too. *Get control.*

"The killer might not be powerful," said Weaver. "They might just be duplicitous. Maybe they lured Krazny and Reaper into traps."

Iftikhar found himself looking at the chimp, along with the others.

Sail folded his long arms across his chest and looked right back at them, his demeanor calm. Stoic.

Iftikhar looked at the other two. Their distrust was plain on their faces. He shook his head. "This is crazy. He was with me the whole time." And then he wondered if that was true. They *had* been separated for short periods of time.

"No one's saying *you're* innocent," snarled Aqua.

Sail looked at him. Raised an eyebrow.

Iftikhar had no reason to trust the chimp, but somehow, he did anyway. It just felt *right*. "Let's not do this."

"There's something strange going on here," said Sail.

"This is *ridiculous*," shouted Aqua. "This is nothing more than some fucked-up hypercorp game." She stabbed a finger at the chimp. "And *he's* in it up to his eyeballs." She stalked off, moving south, down the beach.

Weaver glanced at her, that gigantic brain running through possibilities. Finally he turned and followed.

Leaving Iftikhar to wonder how he'd come to be the chimpanzee's lone ally.

—

Iftikhar turned on Sail. "You let them go. You knew you aren't the killer and you *let them go*."

Sail drew a deep breath. "You thought before I was a corporate plant. Well, you were right, Iftikhar. But that's not all I am."

"What's that supposed to mean?"

"It means that I'm not an anarchist like the rest of you. I'm a Consortium citizen. I freelance for various hypercorps. But that's not all I do."

"Who do you work for?" Iftikhar whispered.

"Firewall," said the chimp softly.

The young man shook his head. "Firewall? That can't—I mean, that's just a story. It's not real."

"Firewall protects transhumanity from the dangers that might destroy us all."

"No," said Iftikhar. "This is bad. It's murder, but—"

"Think, boy. This is more than just murder."

"But—"

The chimp placed both hands on Iftikhar's shoulders. "You did such a good job of figuring out why Love and Rage selected each member of the team. But you never asked yourself why *you're* here?"

—

Iftikhar lay on a narrow lip of black rock that jutted out from the sheer rock face, the unfamiliar seeker pistol clutched so tightly in his right hand that his knuckles ached. Below him was a descending carpet of greens: emerald and kelly and forest. The only non-green thing he could see was the black fur that covered the back of Sail's head, ten, fifteen meters from Iftikhar's ledge. The chimp was down far enough that the wall arced into a gentle slope.

Beyond Sail's perch, there was the beach and the sea.

And the gate.

The weapon ached in Iftikhar's hand.

I can't do this, he said to Sail over his mesh implant.

[You have to.] Static distorted Sail's words, but the chimp was close enough that Iftikhar could make them out.

Why can't you take the kill shot?

[No. The killer will expect a military-style ambush. He won't expect a double ambush. And he won't be looking for you.]

Because I am weak?

[No,] said the chimp patiently. [Because you look weak.]

But I'm not really?

[You trusted me, Iftikhar. Now why did you do that? Why did you trust a hypercorp agent?]

The hair on the back of Iftikhar's neck rose. He had asked that very same question of himself just a few hours before.

You're quite convincing.

[Yes,] said Sail. [But you're not. Want to try again?]

The question froze Iftikhar for a long, frightening moment, froze him as he stared down at the featureless expanse of green. *No,* he said and even in his mind it came out as a whisper. *No, I don't.*

[You were infected with Watts-MacLeod,] said the chimp. [You're an async, Iftikhar. You may not have been trained, but you have loads of psi talent. We just need a little bit of it today.]

But how did Love and Rage know? Why did they put me on the team? How do you know?

[It was Firewall that put you on the team. Whether you knew it or not, you have a keen intuition about the people around you. You know who is telling the truth and who is not, how they feel, how to persuade them.]

Iftikhar remembered trusting Sail even though he hated corporate drones. Remembered the flash of prescience he'd experienced at the gate.

[We knew these skills would come in handy,] said Sail.

Yeah. How exactly?

[I know a lot about you, Iftikhar. I've read your profile. You show talents in particular areas. One of your psi talents lets you see patterns more readily. You can pick them out where other people just see noise. Just look down at the foliage and concentrate. Concentrate on what doesn't fit.]

The killer could be anywhere.

[Look.]

Iftikhar drew a deep breath and concentrated on the sea of green. If Sail was right, somewhere down there an assassin was slipping through the forest, creeping up on the chimpanzee. All he had to do was divine *where*. If he put the ruby pip of the targeting laser on the right spot and pulled the trigger the micromissiles of his seeker pistol would take care of the rest.

But what was the right spot?

He would get nowhere looking for the well-hidden killer, he realized. He had to look at the trees, the shrubs. Broad fringed leaves gently waved in the sea breeze; the forest rippled in the wind, leaf and branch moving with the rhythm of sea.

Except *there.*

Iftikhar suddenly saw it. A bush moving in a way that didn't match. And then another. And another. All of them in a line that led to Sail's position.

Iftikhar raised his weapon in his shaking hand, settled the ruby dot over a patch of jungle between the killer and target and pulled the trigger.

—

The assassin had fallen in the shade of a grove of low trees, the victim of a combined assault by Sail and Iftikhar. It was a pleasant glen, out of the sun, cool and quiet, but when Iftikhar looked over the killer's body he could see the distant place where sea met sky through the trees.

He moved up on the killer slowly, not really believing they were dead. Each footstep a desperate act of will, his heart trembling in the cage of his chest. Whoever the killer was, they'd hidden their identity inside the silver skin of a hardsuit.

Iftikhar's micromissiles had smashed through the suit's centerline and fractured the helmet. Sail's hand laser had severed an arm. Iftikhar stopped a meter away from the dead killer in the suit.

"Go ahead," said the chimpanzee softly, from behind.

Iftikhar licked his lips and stepped forward. With the toe of his boot, he kicked away the fractured helmet.

He just stared, not really understanding what he was seeing. What was inside the helmet looked like a blue-green jelly dropped from the roof of a building. Flaccid stalks crowned with cilia were sprinkled across the creature's "face." Somehow the thing did not have the coppery smell of blood. Instead the corpse had the pleasant smell of a newly-mown lawn.

Iftikhar thought he might be sick.

"Now this is interesting," said Sail softly. "What do you know about Factors?"

The young man shrugged. "Same as everyone. Advanced alien race, communal organisms, kind of like slime molds."

"It's been suggested they're predatory. Hard to explain their evolution otherwise. I can't imagine ambulatory pond scum hunting. But traps …"

"You're saying this thing has been setting traps for people. That it's after human colonists for *food?*"

Sail said nothing for a long moment. Then he looked up. "It'll have hidden the gate control unit. And the stolen cortical stacks. We probably won't find them, but we should search. So Krazny and Reaper and the others can regain their memories of this world—if they want them."

Iftikhar looked down at the suit, two arms, two legs, a head. "It was pretending to be human."

"In case someone saw it. So we would believe the killings were the result of faction fights, corporate politics—and not something else."

Iftikhar looked up, looked at the ape. "And what is the something else, Brandon? Why kill us on *this* world? None of it makes any sense."

The chimpanzee reached up and scratched his chin. Then he walked over to stand beside Iftikhar. For a long moment they stood there, man and ape, looking down at the alien body.

"Who knows," said Sail. "Maybe the Factor was a criminal exiled to this world. Or it was insane. Or it's a political dissident that came here to meet transhumanity and something went wrong. Who knows how aliens think?"

"How do we know it's the only one?"

Sail looked around. "We don't. But somehow I get the feeling this one was operating on its own. This doesn't have the feel of some major Factor operation. This feels more like lone wolf behavior."

Iftikhar frowned. "Or maybe we were right all along and this is some kind of hypercorp game."

Sail laughed. "You're slow," he said, "but not irredeemably stupid."

"Thanks," said Iftikhar dryly.

The chimpanzee put his hand on the young human's shoulder. "I don't know what happened on this world," he said softly, turning to look up into Iftikhar's eyes. "But whatever the future holds, if we stand together, I believe transhumanity can face it."

And somehow, calling upon some strange power he possessed but did not understand, Iftikhar knew the chimpanzee was right.

The young man was glad for Firewall's existence. Transhumanity was at the center of a strange political struggle whose rules it couldn't begin to even guess. There would be great danger.

But perhaps also great opportunity.

Iftikhar Quraini looked up, past the trees, past the beach, even past the broad ocean, his gaze settling finally on an infinite horizon.

STRAY THOUGHTS

F. Wesley Schneider

"Kindly get out of my son." That usually worked. No one ever really got over the fear of someone's mother walking in on them.

Not this time, though. Skinny ass-dimples stared obstinately, twitching unevenly.

"I got eight minutes left." He only glanced at me in the mirrored headboard, the focus in his voice repeating through furrowed brows. I could almost hear his anxious self-coaching, "Aww, don't lose it."

Beyond those scrawny shoulders, Keilani's painstakingly shaped brows skewed. He was as still as a board of koa wood, and beneath his pale—practically transparent—client his skin had nearly the same shade.

One flick and my pistol silently powered off. Another and the warm-up hum whirred—I'd replaced the Ridley 4C's friendly starting noise with the growl of the larger 8A, recognizable from nearly every gangster XP released in the last five years.

The gyrating froze. Now I had those dimples' full attention. My soles slapped against the motel room's fake marble floor.

"Time's up." I jammed the 4C's muzzle into his tailbone. "Get up and get dressed, your father's waiting."

"The fuck you talking about, crazy—" I ground the gun against bone. "Shit! Damn lady!"

"Move!" Using the gun grip like a handle, I steered him sidelong. He flopped across a bed too small to comfortably sleep a full night in.

Keilani's knees fell and folded with practiced modesty. With a fluid move a laminated sheet corner covered him, doing little to hide cat-like curves. "Trouble finding us?"

I kept eyes and pistol trained as Slim fished to find his clothes in the right order. "Just that you went to the wrong floor. I had to threaten that junkie at the desk to get the number."

"It's the same room—I always use 303."

"It was on the second last time."

"I always use—"

Antheun MacSijs the Younger looked up from his laundry. Realization turned his expression mean. "You know this shitlord?! What is this?"

"One more word and see if I don't march you out of here like that—let the whole aerostat see why Skinthetic morphs are so cheap." I kicked the bed frame for good measure.

Losing his balance, MacSijs toppled back, legs flailing. He landed in a heap of clothes better than he deserved. A series of fumbles later he was on his knees, shoving some street-bought handgun toward me. "There's exactly no way some skytrash cop is dragging me back to Octavia."

The pistol wasn't a good enough knock-off to pass for an authentic nSIG, but I bet it could still punch a hole. It wasn't a matter of who could shoot first, though. I only got paid for dragging Cheeks here back unharmed. From the nervous look of the barrel, he was bound to twitch the trigger. Even worse, this was taking far too long.

I sighed, my eye-roll ending on Keilani. He mimicked the look—whether mocking me or because he'd honestly picked up the habit, I was never sure. A tawny leg shot from beneath the sheet. Reinforced keratin nails extended like claws, sheering across the stray heir's jaw. More than the slash, MacSijs's shocked shriek sent him sprawling across the scuffed laminate.

I brought my heel down on rich boy's hand. He squealed and something in the cheap pistol snapped.

"Nice." I shot Keilani a wink.

Thin brows bobbed. "You laughed when I got the Sex Kitten implants, but dishing out scars does wonders for more than just my tips."

A headshake and raised palm fended off the need for details. "Your business is your business. I'm just glad you know how to use protection."

—

Keilani met me in the plaza beneath the office, sauntering out of the fog of flashing neon and holographic paper lanterns.

I'd dropped off Mister the Younger with one of his too-important father's flunkies. Disappearing into a sea of buzz and freelance sex workers seemed to be a common occurrence with Skinny—so much so that his baggy-eyed handler hadn't even asked what happened to his clothes. I left the babysitter my card and told him repeat customers got discounts.

I waited on steps leading up to a battered portal—the word "Ambassador" slashed the door in ever-lurid pulse-paint. My distant hope of finding warm rice at the top of those steps evaporated. "And where have you been?"

"Just ran into a few friends—had to show off my new Aldrins." Keilani bounded up the stairs, making a show of bouncing in shoes MacSijs had owned this morning.

I hadn't meant for my hand to settle on my hip. Maybe it was a mom-thing. Maybe it was just closer to my gun. Keilani purposefully didn't notice. The door hummed open and he swaggered through. I sighed and followed.

Three floors up, on the side of the hall where the quarters didn't have plaza-view balconies, stark sans serif marked my door: "Valerie," then below, in smaller lettering, "Discretion Bought and Sold."

Once a client pointed out that the quotation marks around the lower line were uneven. I'd never noticed before that. Now I saw it every time I came home. Keilani held the door and I pushed past, trying to ignore the skewed slashes. Fuck that guy.

"Motashaker, shab bekhair." Ruid said, and with two descending tones his terminal ended the call. Behind his podium, perpetually bored-looking eyes raised. "You're late."

"Can't be late when I never said when I'd be back." I returned my coat to the empty, faux-antique hat rack. Like all modern Venusian aerostats, Parvarti was never far from a comfortable 22 degrees. So no one ever actually needed a coat, unless they were hiding something. Hence, the local prevalence of coats.

Keilani dropped onto the hard waiting room couch. He didn't wear a coat—hell, his hooded, button-down tank top and knee-cut pants barely qualified as clothes. That was his uniform, though, especially when he was working for me.

His only slightly scuffed Luna-made shoes hit the couch arm, one over the other. "Mom threw in a bonus this time."

"Nope. I'm just taking those out of your cut."

Ruid's diplomatic nod passed from Keilani to me, in favor of both our windfalls.

"Any messages?" I crossed to the podium, a terminal that served as my operation's hub. Rather than accepting contacts, payments, and other info directly via my personal hardware, I routed everything through there. It didn't look like much, a plasticy standing desk with a concave screen, but it was a fortress of the best firewalls and sentinel AIs I could cobble together. Behind it, Ruid also didn't look like much—a slight splicer with a checkered scarf arranged as professionally as a necktie— but he was the guard on my fortress walls. The terminal light brought out the coppery sheen of his skin, as though he were part of the machine.

"You've got clients waiting." Eyes so dark they almost appeared to be all pupil gestured to the door.

This late? So much for dinner. "Clients?" I stressed the "s."

"Well …" Ruid's brow creased. He didn't continue.

That didn't make me more enthusiastic for late-callers.

I glanced at Keilani, sprawled across horrible, over-inflated cushions. The boy could doze anywhere. "Get started on dinner and maybe those shoes are an early birthday present."

The little shit smiled without even opening his eyes.

"And nothing that takes all night to make. I won't be long."

I turned back to Ruid, adjusting my bare hip holster. Honest clients liked to know I worked with a real gun. Dishonest clients worried I might use it on them. Win-win. "What's the name?"

Ruid's lips knotted, as though they didn't know how to start. "I asked. All she said was 'the Octavian Neo-Synergists.'"

What the hell was that supposed to mean? I gave a nod like I knew and walked into my office to find out.

It was empty, but that wasn't a surprise. With less than an eye twitch, familiar entopics cascaded through my vision. I joined the private VR simulspace and the room barely changed—same uncomfortable looking furniture, same wall of licenses. The crooked picture of a tropical coast was the only significant change. Adrift on a blank wall in reality, here the animated photo expanded into a bay of plantation shutters, the turquoise surf crashing only a short walk beyond.

A woman, desperately in need of some sun, took in the view.

"Kauai." Thin veins budged beneath a colorless scalp, as if the faint channels themselves were reporting.

"What's that?"

This was getting better by the second. She hadn't turned, but I'd dealt with the sort who sleeved mentons before. Brain-hacked morphs with more head-tech than gray matter, most mentons talked like they had all the answers, but usually couldn't tell the difference between people and lab recorders. A rainbow of smears on her pill-blue lab coat suggested this one wasn't any more self-aware. Regardless, I'd never had a menton come to the office. Why would a braincase need an investigator? Unless she was mistaking me for just some hired gun.

Half-mistaking me.

She started to repeat herself, but I cut her off. "No, Niihau. The north shore—before Barb Robinson turned it into Casino Island."

Turning, she cast a double pair of beady optics over me. Tiny lens shifted. She should have nodded politely and introduced herself, but didn't.

I gestured to a cushionless chair and slipped around my blank desk. I preferred to talk across it. Not only did it keep things professional, but the wall of licenses, subtly blast-scorched trophies, and a frowning portrait of my father added a productive touch of gravitas. They weren't just simulspace effects, either, the reality of each hung in my actual office.

Although my chair was plenty comfortable I didn't sit. "I'll save us some time. I don't work for corps."

Lenses adjusted, widening quizzically. Her bald head—like a subterranean thing's—shifted a degree, almost making a nod. She didn't answer, though.

"We have anything else to discuss here?"

She took a seat. "You think we work for a corporation." Her airy voice made her sound like a stage hypnotist's assistant repeating facts. "We do not."

"Octavian Neo-Synergists. Sounds like some high-minded start-up to me."

"High-minded." The words floated from lips tinged the color of lab gloves. "Yes. But not a hypercorp."

She rested her hands on her thighs, a distinctly awkward looking posture. I was starting to wonder if I'd misidentified her morph. Even for a menton, she seemed weirdly detached—synthetic.

"I represent the Neo-Synergists, a collective-intelligence community currently dwelling on Octavia. We are a community of individuals who elect to share our minds with one another, facilitating mutual understanding and development."

Still sounded like a corp—or worse, corp advertising. "So, some commune."

Her head twitched another degree. "A not uncommon perspective, but no. Our members share a more intimate connection. Our mesh implants unite us as a single shared intelligence. We are still ourselves, but we are also more."

More wasn't looking too impressive to me. "Sounds crowded."

"Not at all, in fact—"

I swatted what was sure to be a lengthy explanation out of the air. "What can I help you with, Miss Synergist?"

"One of our number, a farcasting researcher named Harliss Vine, came to this aerostat." She didn't seem rankled by my directness. "We don't know why."

I'd never heard anyone in a menton say that before.

"We have lost our connection to Vine and wish to know why. To learn that, we must find him—a task I have thus far been unsuccessful in." Her reporting remained even, it didn't sound like she had any personal stake in this. "As such, I have been authorized to retain the service of a local. Your record of accomplishments compared to your low number of criminal convictions makes you a favorable choice."

"Flattered. Let me save you some credits, though," I nodded toward a wall-mounted screen shifting through scenes from Parvarti security cams. "Go find a cozy spot, catch up on your XPs, and keep your mesh feed on. No one like your lost tech comes to Parvarti to stay. He's probably just shacked up with a bottle of Old Sky and some pretty mimi. Give him another night, maybe two, and one more to dry out, then he'll come home. You can try dragging him off early, but I guarantee, the waiting game's far less messy."

"You misunderstand. Our neural implants aren't simple mesh inserts." She turned and touched a porcelain nodule at the base of her neck. Her vein-network seemed somehow deepest there. "Once installed, they cannot merely be shut down or removed without risking significant psychological damage. This has happened to Vine. We fear for his well-being."

"Awful sisterly of you, but we both know how much I charge," I took a seat on the desk corner. It was hard to read in those lenses whether or not she actually thought I was born yesterday. "What else did he take? Empty out the group account? Run off with some patent? Find a hotter bunch of brains to join up with?"

She didn't hesitate. "Have you ever lost one of your morph's limbs and had to live without for any period of time?"

"No."

"You can likely imagine the inconvenience. Studies show that most never truly acclimate to missing an appendage being gone. It is unpleasant."

I shrugged.

"Imagine if that missing limb was part of your mind—your memory of a place perhaps." Without looking, she gestured to the lapping waves over her shoulder. The pointed fingers then aimed at my holster, "Or your familiarity with a weapon. That's what Vine's absence is to us."

My brows climbed. That was a new one on me. "You're really in a rush over this, huh?"

"Repairing our collective mind is of the utmost urgency for our community."

She sat straight backed, hands settling back on her thighs. There wasn't anything there to read. I supposed I could understand her interest in finding this Vine guy, though. Whatever she wasn't sharing and whether or not he wanted to be found didn't really bother me that much.

"I can find him. Dragging him back costs more—a lot more if he needs to go all the way to Octavia."

"Our airship is docked on the lower ring. I can beam you directions along with Vine's records and other details."

"Good. My secretary will set you up with my schedule of fees and contracting costs—rates for non-disclosure, indemnity, the usual. You two figure out the paperwork and we'll take things from there."

I stood and she—finally acknowledging a cue—did the same.

"Thank you for your time, Miss Valerie."

She disconnected from the simulspace before I even nodded.

—

I hadn't been aware of Keilani's purr-like snoring until it stopped. A mosaic of aerostat security feeds crumbled from my augmented reality display. Some people relaxed with predictable XPs. I found the flow of stock characters through Parvarti's neon-drowned plazas not just calming but, often, surprisingly useful.

My office-adjoined apartment wavered back into view—freshly cluttered with rice and pork-smeared dinner plates.

On the floor, Ruid looked uncomfortable, sitting straight-backed against my tabby colored couch. The arm lock my son had on his thigh didn't seem to be helping. Keilani would have charged anyone else a small fortune for that kind of casual intimacy. My secretary doubtlessly knew that, but still had the look of a houseguest suffering his host's untrainable pet. I wasn't sure when Keilani got so clingy with him—must have been a gradual thing.

Ruid noticed my eyes shift back to the real. "That synergist woman just returned the contracts. Looks like she's buying ..." he nodded appreciatively at files scrolling invisibly though his entopics, "... everything."

"Even the extended privacy insurance?" I failed at keeping the smirk out of my voice.

He nodded. "Even the extended privacy insurance."

Keilani gave a sleepy growl at the noise. We both ignored him.

"Guess she really does want this guy bad." And certainly not just out of sororal concern if she was buying up this much confidentiality.

"Who's she after?"

"Some scientist type from Octavia—probably here on a binge. He's another one of those Neo-Synergists."

"Looked into them yet?"

"A little. All the reports talk about some special mesh inserts they use to share thoughts—like some constant group feed. I thought they sounded like a corp, but the hypermesh buzz makes them sound more like a cult. A bunch of them just put down stakes on Octavia and not everyone there's excited."

"Yeah. It took some digging to get past the tabloid stuff, but if you do it gets pretty interesting." His gaze remained on the middle distance, hypnotized by whatever info swirled through his AR. "They've essentially hacked their consciousness, networking their minds to share lifetimes worth of thoughts. Some people are calling it an obvious next step for t-human intelligence. Instead of the muses we're using now, you've got everyone you know right in your head."

"I've got enough clutter up there already. The last thing I need is a whole crowd's chatter."

"Sure." Obviously he disagreed.

Keilani gave up on trying to sleep. Extricating himself from Ruid's lap, his annoyed sigh didn't end until the door to his room slid shut—just shy of a slam.

I had something like an apology loaded when I turned back to Ruid, but he hadn't moved. His gaze remained distant. Again he played the perfect houseguest, pretending not to notice his hosts' bad behavior.

"You know, you can tell him no." I tried to sound casual.

His reply came faster and certainly sharper than I'd expected. "I have. Probably ten times now."

A few minutes passed with both of us pretending to focus on our entopics.

"He's got the hardware for it, he'd probably switch genders if that's—"

"I'd never—" Ruid's mouth snapped shut just as quickly as it had fallen open.

At least I had his full attention now.

He tried again, his tone a shade closer to his usual calm. "I'm just not interested in that. Not just not from him, not from anyone. I told him that."

I nodded. "Kay can be stubborn. He's used to getting his way when it comes to that sort of stuff."

"Yeah." He shifted to stare at the floor—and probably just the floor this time. "He still hangs on me, though. I like Keilani just fine, but … not like that."

"I'll talk to him." I used my Mom voice, the one that promised I'd make everything alright.

Obviously it didn't work.

"Please don't." Doe-brown eyes pleaded.

I tried another tactic. "Are you planning on leaving next week?"

The worry in his face intensified.

I didn't drag it out. "Of course not. That means you'll have been staying with us for over a year."

He opened his mouth—something about looking for his own quarters—but I cut him off. "And we wouldn't have it any other way. You're the only secretary I've ever endured for more than a week and the only one who can figure out my network. Like it or not, you're family, kid."

He looked dubious. I went on. "Which means I'm not handing you back to the Night Cartel or any other skin-smugglers. When we took you in, I told you you're welcome for as long as you like. That deal's the same regardless of who you are or aren't sleeping with." I leveled my no-bullshit look. "Are we on the same page about that?"

His head bobbed.

I matched him, sealing the deal. "If Keilani needs to be brought on board, either one of us can give him that talk—or five across the lips if that's what it takes. Whatever you're most comfortable with, okay?"

"Yes, mam."

"What's that 'mam' shit?"

He half grinned. "I'll talk to him."

"And I'll pick up the pieces." I leaned back in my chair. "Anything else on your mind?"

"Well, while we were talking …" Had the little bastard been sifting through the mesh this whole time? "I found this."

—

[Still awake, Pops?]

My muse's soulful voice hummed from the back of my skull. [We're both in trouble the night I bunk down before you.]

Pop's voice was always a comfort. Since he started virtually haunting me our relationship had never been better.

Ruid had only turned in a few minutes ago and I was planning on doing the same, but I hated the idea of letting a job sit cold over night.

[What can you make of this?]

I pulled the virtual flyer onto the fore of my AR. It had all the style of a brothel signboard advertising Morningstar Day discounts—read like one too.

"Adrift? Alone? Afraid?" a breathy voice interlaced with the ad read aloud. "Seeking meaning, finding mirages? Assaulted by info but starved for intimacy? Join the Heartsync. Never be alone again."

I cut off the last syllable as it echoed into infinity. [It might be nothing, but it sounds like a synergist thing. Maybe this Vine guy's into it.]

[Ruid found this?] Pops asked.

I couldn't help but nod. Maybe the kid had the makings of more than a secretary. [See what you can find on this Heartsync group—limited to the station.]

[I'll do what I can, but if you want local, the mesh might not be the way to go.] Pops had never been into tech. Somehow, virtual resurrection hadn't changed that.

[You're thinking Keilani? Street buzz.]

[Sure am.]

[Good call. I'll see if I can get him on it in the morning.]

He made an approving noise that used to go along with a nod. [What else ya need?]

[Anything you can find on these Neo-Synergists—real stuff, not just hypercorp news.]

[Alright. Night, hun.]

[Night.]

—

"Get jacked, blimpsteak!" Keilani fearlessly threw a finger in the face of the bruiser morph leaning over him. The woman was easily twice his size, but still she tripped back from the growling street cat. Seeing she wasn't getting what she wanted, she tromped off into the bustle of untraceable market stands.

That was my boy.

The street café's heavy chair whined as I pulled it back and took a seat. I caught a glimpse of sharp teeth. The snarl vanished as Keilani realized it was me. "Sorry, I think we missed brunch. It took longer than I expected."

Pops hadn't found much overnight. This Heartsync group was new to Parvarti, with the first mention on the local mesh only cropping up about a month ago. There was some chatter about meetings in the warehouse wards, invitations, and skepticism about it being some religious bunk or self-help scheme. The number of testimonials was growing, mostly among aerostat residents, not visiting dupes.

I woke Keilani up early and told him what I wanted to know—if anyone knew where to find real-chat, it was him. Of course, he wanted to know what it was worth. I agreed to call it even on the shoes. He talked me up to blintzes.

"What did you hear?"

"A lot of garbage. 'Find what you've been missing,' that sort of stuff." He ordered an orange juice when the waiter stopped by—me, just water.

"Sounds like them. Where are they?"

"I expected them to be mesh-based, but that's the weird part. A friend of a friend said they're into physical meet-ups—send invitations and everything. She dropped in on one. Anyway, she says a couple of weeks ago she had a few drinks with this guy at that uplift bar, Chainlynx.

The next thing she knows she's got an invite to this Heartsync meet-up with her mesh ID coded in, like it was custom just for her."

"Did she say what an invitation looks like?"

"Nope."

Damn. "So, what'd she see?"

"That's the crap-part. She went, but chickened out when she got the eye from some twitchy jenkin bouncer."

"Well, where was it?"

"The warrens. Around the ring C warehouses—C-1580."

"That's a start."

"Not much of one. I peeked in on stat-security. Fifteen-eighty's been a tomb for the last couple weeks. A tomb where rubes do kick and get what they deserve trying to buy black market XPs, but still a tomb."

The boy had earned his blintzes—even if it did sound like a dead end. Except ...

"Jenkin bouncer? Don't see those very often, huh?"

"No, but they're not exactly sun-whales. We've got enough on the station that tracking down one isn't going to be easy."

"Maybe. But tracking down one who spends his time squatting outside a ring C warehouse might be easier."

"If they keep to the warehouses at all." He shrugged. "I don't know. Sounds weak."

"Even a weak start's a start." He was right, but it wasn't like I had any better options. I wasn't in the mood to argue tactics, though. I changed the topic to the first thing that came to mind. "What's the story with you and Ruid?"

He gave a big blink, as if I'd fired a camera flash in his face.

"Mom." He stretched it into a one-syllable way of saying "mind your damn business."

I wasn't having it, though, not after the talk I had last night. I had tones that trumped his. "Seriously."

He frowned. "I don't know."

We silently retreated to our corners as a sari-clad waitress delivered our drinks.

As savvy as he could be, and as adult as his body made him look, it was easy to forget Keilani wasn't even twenty years old. It made it all the more unsettling when he pulled whiny teen tricks. I considered letting Ruid take first crack at him, like we'd discussed. But then figured, why not sort it out right now.

"I know it's not the message you get out in the clubs, but not everyone wants to sleep with you, ya know." I took a slow swig from my spotty glass.

"Mom. Really?" I could hear just a touch of his feline vocal implant kick in, a subtle growl undertone.

"Ruid works for me, he's a guest, and he's still touchy about the whole Night Cartel thing. Poor kid still doesn't know where he's from or who his people are. I know you like him, but I don't want to make him uncomfortable. Okay?"

Keilani's face went cold. His features were designed to be expressive, but, when necessary, could lock away his thoughts completely—a useful trick for a street bokkie. It made it easy to tell when he was locking it down, though.

"Are you telling me not to see Ruid?"

"I think that'd be a trick since we live with him, but no. Just think about his situation. He might feel like he can't be up front with you."

"You think I'd try to make him uncomfortable?"

"I think sometimes you don't see the things you don't want to see."

Shit, that sounded worse than I'd meant.

His chair squealed back.

I scrambled for anything. "Your food should be here any minute."

Obviously he didn't care. Wherever he was headed, he chose the route that put his back to me and turned the first corner he found.

—

The waitress's presence made me realize I'd been staring dumbly. I assumed I'd missed her question. "Just the bill."

Keilani's still likely warm chair screeched. The waitress smoothed her burgundy sari as she took a seat, ignoring the threat on my face. "Wehilani Lonoehu?"

"That name's for family." I made sure the threat was more than implied. One of the benefits of hiding your name: whenever you hear it, you know some asshole wants your attention.

"Of course." She gave a patronizing little grin and inclined a palm toward herself. "Harliss Vine—though I believe my former associates spoiled our introduction."

"Yeah. They got your picture all wrong." She didn't look at all like the image of the thick-faced menton the Neo-Synergists had forwarded. It would have been a simple matter for Vine to resleeve, though—standard procedure, even, if she was looking to disappear.

Sitting down for lunch with the woman hired to track you down, however, that was hardly standard. How'd she even know who I was?

"I've come to ask you to cancel your arrangement." She sounded professional, clearly thinking bargaining was an option.

"Come on, you've got to know that's not how this business works." It was so obvious I barely shook my head. "So what is it? What's so special that you'd come right out like this?"

"I'm not asking for myself. I'm asking for the entire Heartsync." Her tone stayed formal. She wasn't pleading—yet.

"Am I supposed to know what that means?" Sounded like Ruid's hunch about that ad was panning out. Smart kid.

"I wouldn't expect the Octavian community to explain my intentions here. They don't understand. Their group is built too much on the mind. My new commune is built on the heart."

That name was coming in to dock.

"That's what the Heartsync is? Another collective intelligence community."

"A *perfected* community. Transhumans are not machines. Our shared network cannot be entirely about memory and experience—it's more than data. It must be about intimacy of both the mind and the soul."

What a load. I think my head tilt got that across.

"Most are skeptical, more are afraid—it takes a great deal of courage to reveal everything to the world," she went on applauding herself. "Once you lay yourself bare, though, you can be whatever you care to be. And where better to find daring, liberated souls than here on Parvarti? My group tempts them with something familiar, but shows them something very new." Her open palm crossed to my side of the table. "The transhuman experience is not meant to be suffered alone, Miss Lonoehu."

It all sounded like vintage New Age crap.

"Yeah," I stretched the word out. "Well. Damn good of you to turn yourself over."

Even her frown looked proud. "Since I haven't done anything illegal, I don't feel I have much to fear from you Miss Lonoehu."

My little scoff wasn't meant to reassure her. "That's where a lot of off-station folk slip up. I'm not security. I don't work for the Morningstar. So I don't care much about 'legal.' And so long as things stay quiet, neither does anyone else around here."

Vine nodded shallowly. "I see. Well then, by all means, take me in." Her other palm crossed the table, offering both wrists.

I tugged the diamond-wire cuffs from the pocket on my holster, proving that I was more than willing to take her up on her suggestion. "If you want, but we don't have far to go."

"Oh, I insist. This is your job, after all."

Both chairs screeched. She politely put her wrists behind her back and let me slip on the restraints. At the base of her neck, magenta flecks winked from a porcelain node. Gazes from a nearby table distracted me. Dodging my look, they found new interest in their flatware.

"This really is a shame. The Heartsync could help someone close to you someday."

"Not likely." I tightened the wire.

"Or maybe we already are," she said, almost under her breath.

I spun her around. "What's that supposed to mean?"

Something in her expression changed, something subtle. The look of confidence flushed.

"What the—" Vine tried to bring her arms up, but the cuffs tugged her back. Shocked eyes shot to me. The cocky calm was gone, as was any hint of recognition. "Get these off of me!"

"What? You're the one who wanted them on!" I hadn't meant to raise my voice quite that much. More than just the nearest table noticed.

Then the screaming began.

—

I leaned over my desk, massaging the bridge of my nose.

Security hadn't bothered with me for long. Two street officers I didn't know showed up not long after Vine started shrieking her head off. I tried to explain, but I didn't seriously have a clue. It took them no time to pull the waitress's records—something I should have done. Nakshatra Klein, they said, a Parvarti local who'd been working at that café for the better part of the past year. I started to argue, to tell them who she really was, but it started sounding crazy even to me. I called it a mistake and took back my cuffs. The cops confiscated them. I dropped the names of a few friends I had in station security and things didn't get worse. Miss Klein wasn't so forgiving, but I got out of there before she was done cursing.

I'd need to find a new place for blintzes.

Back in the office—the one with just the picture of the beach—I tried to figure it out. Vine hadn't offered anything new so I was back to Keilani's lead. Security feeds from the past week, all from ring C, flickered through my entopics at an accelerated rate. I couldn't say I was paying attention, but I knew Pops was. Despite the strangeness afterward, my thoughts kept coming back to Keilani.

[Was I ever that much of a pain growing up, Pops?]

He gave a gravelly scoff. [I assume you don't want the real answer.]

The real answer was that Pops was only a facsimile of my father, derived from what we could salvage from the shot-up remains of his cortical stack. It wasn't enough to bring him back, but in the three years I'd been working with the personality remnants, it had started to actually feel like him. He didn't have all the memories—Kauai, for example—but sometimes that was easy to forget. Or to simply ignore.

[Of course not, all those times I called you *kolohe*, I never meant it.]

Death hadn't impeded his sarcasm. [Thanks, Pops.]

What was I worried about? Keilani knew Parvarti better than I did these days. Seeing the way he prowled off, there was even a good chance he'd make more than a little extra tonight. Supposedly there was a good market for angry sex.

I shoved all that out of my head. [You find anything?]

[Yeah. Here's your jenkin.] A still from a surveillance feed sprung up. I noticed his muttonchops first. How or why they were bleach blond, while the thin strands trying to cover his scalp were muddy brown, I didn't even try to understand. He was trying to look tough, leaning on a length of steel pipe while picking protruding teeth with a too-long pinky nail. Jenkins, by design, looked like rats, but this one seemed to be embracing the look.

I minimized the image, having gotten enough for the moment. [Great. Where was this taken?]

[Over a week ago. He spent two nights playing doorman at C-1580. I'm sifting through security records to see where else he might show up.]

[You've got an image of Vine too. See if you see him around.]

Pops gave an agreeable hum.

Keilani had mentioned a friend had actually stopped by the warehouse. If Pops had found vids from the night, maybe we could find her … or someone else who had actually shown up looking for this Heartsync group. Someone with an invite. Or there might be a simpler …

[Still got room on your plate, Pops?]

[Always hungry. What ya got?]

I fished up the gaudy Heartsync advertisement. [Can you see if there's anything weird in the code for this?]

[Weird.] He said it as if he'd never heard the word.

[Yeah. Anything extra.]

[I feel like we're going to get a virus just looking at it.]

[I know you'll be careful.]

He gave a little grunt.

A note from a strummed harp sounded in my mind.

[Val?] Ruid beamed the message from the waiting room, only yards away.

[Yeah?] I shot back. I always sounded sharper in my mind than in person. Ruid never complained, though.

[I've got a few errands to run, including the weekend payments to drop off. Would now be a good time?]

[Sure, kid. I'll be here forever.]

Another harp strum, this time in a lower key. A moment later, I heard the office door slap shut.

Keilani could learn something from that boy. I didn't know if they'd be a good fit romantically—doubted it, in fact—but I never had to worry about Ruid storming off. Nothing seemed to stick to him. Of course, anyone who'd been sold into a modern equivalent of slavery and survived probably came away with a different perspective on what really mattered.

[You saved us some time,] Pops interrupted things I didn't really want to be thinking about. His tone said he didn't have good news.

[What?]

[Here's your address.] He flashed a map of the Parvarti aerostat with a path leading from my office door to some docking bay supposedly closed for repair. It wasn't anywhere near ring C.

[That was on the ad?]

[Yeah. It's custom—and relatively new.]

[How new?]

[Five days. Invite's for a meeting tomorrow.]

[Well we're not waiting around for that. Lets see who's setting up.]

His grumble said it got worse.

[What?]

[The invitation's for Keilani.]

—

"You're the rent-a-sec?" The jenkin tried to sound tough, but jutting incisors gave him a ridiculous lisp. "They say you're on the list."

"Yeah? Who says?"

He hissed the first word, "Mister Vine."

"Sure."

It took two tugs for the bouncer to wrestle open the graffiti-smeared corridor's only grimy door. It was a back entrance for staff working the station's for-lease cargo holds. Even so, the thin violet curtains and warm breath of nag champa that drifted through were completely out of place. Purposefully not glancing back into the mystery of the jenkin's muttonchops, my hand settled inside my coat and I pushed through.

The shimmering curtains didn't block just the door. Inside miles of fabric turned what should have been an airy space into a maze of twilight gauze. The hold's overhead lighting had been disabled in favor of intimate tapers and the cinders of incense holders. Figures drifted between floor cushion enclaves and discreet alcoves, trailing murmurs of close conversation or the occasional exclamatory gasp. The space didn't smell like sweat, though. It felt more like a particularly quiet club, or a drug den where no one had brought any junk.

Trying not to seem out of place, I slipped casually through the first makeshift room into its slightly smaller, sapphire twin. At the center of the space, a group sat cross-legged, their arms around the shoulders of their neighbors as they swayed and whispered dreamily. A couple of rainbow-haired kick junkies, a woman in a new lunar suit, some custom morph that looked creepily like mesh celeb Lupin T., and a fury with a nanotattoo of endlessly rolling dice—they didn't seem to have anything in common. Only pantsuit and custom job looked like they had any money. The others could have stumbled in off the street.

This Heartsync stuff had to be a drug thing. That's the only thing I could figure.

"*Mom!*" If whoever grabbed my shoulder had whisper-yelled any other word, they'd have had my gun in their face.

And I would have preferred that.

"Keilani, what the hell!" I shook his arm off, spinning him into the corner.

"What are you doing here?" He kept up the harsh whisper.

Flaring eyes backed up my beamed message. [Don't even. Now talk. Why are you here and how'd you find this place?]

Teeth locked down behind his grimace.

I didn't have time for that here, though. [I find an invite to whatever the hell this is—custom created for you—then find you here. Boy, I don't know what you're caught up in, but this ...]

[I'm not caught up in anything! I'm here to find Ruid!] His beam was almost too fast to follow.

[Ruid? What's he got to do with this?]

It came out in a rush. [We came to one of these Heartsync things last week—before you got the job. We didn't know what it was. I'd just heard it was, like, some way to help people let go of bad thoughts, to get it all out there, to be happier and connect with people around them. I talked Ruid into coming with me. I thought it could help him.] Black curls dropped. [He's so ... inside himself.]

Sweet, stupid kid. I wasn't sure if I beamed that or not.

[We listened to that Vine guy you're after. He started off with a bunch of basic Neo-Buddhist stuff, then started into this whole group-living, self-sharing, transhuman family thing. It all sounded real schemey. When he started talking about getting implants, I wanted to go.]

[Implants? What did he say about implants?]

[I don't know. Just that he worked with a group that had created some sort of new hypermesh insert.]

[Sounds like the Neo-Synergists. They use their implants to form their collected-intelligence.]

[No, that's not what he called it. He mentioned that, called it 'thinking like AIs.' He said he created better ones, inserts that could help him lead those who got them toward a higher state—or something. Curated-intelligence, he called it.]

Curated? The porcelain nodule on Miss Klein's neck came to mind. Then her screaming face.

I squeezed Keilani's shoulder. [I'll take care of this. I want you to get out of here.]

"No," he said aloud, something uncommonly hard in his tone. He switched back to beaming. [Ruid's here somewhere. When I wanted to leave that first time, he didn't. I couldn't convince him to go. We argued, and I ... ditched him here.]

I didn't need to say anything. He looked away. [When I tried to apologize, it was like nothing happened. He just went on a screed about

Vine and the next step in transhumanity.] Worried eyes found mine. [Mom, it really creeped me out.]

[Okay. We'll find him. He's got to be around here somewhere.]

[I've looked! He's not in the common area. These are all just hopefuls, meditating and trying to prove themselves worthy. Only those up to get Vine's insert are allowed in back.]

[In back?] I gave him something between a pat and a push. [Show me.]

We slipped through a line of curtained dens in shades of saffron, vermillion, and olive. In that last one, like a muddy forest grove, a neotenic pod gave a slow wave.

"Welcome again, Miss Lonoehu." The boyish morph gave a faux-innocent smile.

"I'm getting real sick of hearing strangers use my name."

"If it's any consolation, I haven't told it to a single person."

I'd seen this trick already. I didn't know how it worked, but I didn't need to to understand it was a trick.

I considered kicking this tiny Vine. I made sure my expression made that clear. "Thanks for the scene in the plaza earlier. I really liked that place's shakshuka."

The small morph bowed, a motion that seemed somehow appropriate in his curtain-matching olive get-up, something between robe and gi. "I'm sorry it had to come to that. I admit to having mixed feelings. I'm either disappointed with Parvarti security's lack of efficacy or impressed with your ability to extricate yourself from criminal charges."

"You showed your hand too soon after bluffing. I know what you're playing with now. If you had let me take your puppet in, there's a chance I would have gotten paid and no one would be any the wiser."

"Perhaps, but my former associates aren't so easily duped. They know which me is me."

"You've got quite the scene here. A bit dry for my tastes, but it's a chill crowd." I nodded around, checking to make sure no one had shown any special interest in our conversation. "What do we need to do to get into the VIP room?"

The kid's smirk showed a single dimple. "It's rather exclusive, I'm afraid. Only those open enough to truly accept the Heartsync are admitted. Feel free to enjoy yourself and broaden your mind communing with the others here, though. I will come lead them in the evening's meditations shortly."

"You've got Ruid back there," Keilani blurted, obviously getting anxious.

Rust-colored eyes turned up to him. "Your friend has proven his dedication to the Heartsync. We will treat him well."

"What the fuck is that supposed to mean?" Keilani's look snapped to me. "We've got to get back there."

"Just calm—"

Obviously Keilani didn't hear the action he wanted in my tone. His hand came up to push the neotenic away from the curtain slit.

Keilani's hand didn't connect. Vine's small frame shifted, dropping his weight onto one bent knee. He turned just enough to show a familiar porcelain node, rapidly blinking with magenta eyes. Before I could get a better look, though, his small fist shot out, slamming into my son's stomach.

Before Keilani could groan my pistol was against Vine's temple. Then there was no temple at all.

The screaming started before all of the neotenic hit the floor. A glance assured the panic was all flowing the right way—away from us.

Frozen, halfway to doubling over, Keilani gripped his gut and stared. He'd seen me use my gun plenty of times. Probably not at such close range, though—and probably not on anyone who looked like a twelve-year-old. Some folks had trouble putting down neotenics, others counted on it, but a sleeve's a sleeve.

"Come on," I pushed through the freshly painted curtains. I didn't say it, but we didn't have much time. Vine's redecorations likely covered most of the hold's security cams, but a half dozen different security sensors would have detected a gun shot. Fifteen minutes—twenty at the outside—before security got here.

The back room was more of the same, this time hung in shades of wine. Maybe a dozen wide-eyed, would-be worthies stared, their lounging interrupted. Only two moved, both digging into alcoves toward the back. When they turned, the steady thrum of those weird implants blinked from the base of their necks.

"You got a gun?" I asked over my shoulder.

"No. Of course not," Keilani snapped—as if I'd chosen this moment to test him on my strict rules. For the first time ever I wished hadn't raised such a savvy kid.

The two in the back, however, did. Pistols small enough to hide amid pillows came up.

I beamed Keilani some garbled warning and threw myself sidelong. The curtains behind me seared, Vine's guards making up for bad aim with elastic trigger fingers. Cushions offered a soft landing, but made poor cover. My own weapon came up. I pulled off three rapid shots and fresh panic sounds swelled in the nearest lounge alcoves. One of the guards toppled back, tangling in a curtained wall as she fell. The other didn't appear to notice, firing faster.

I leapfrogged a heap of tiger-striped pillows. The blasts followed close, one near enough to singe my outstretched calf. I winced, reflexively shut off my pain receptors, and told myself it was just a graze.

A graze that pissed me off enough to send two shots into the second guard's throat. Hope he'd backed up recently, there was no way his cortical stack was getting out of that unscathed.

"Come on, get out of here!" Keilani shouted behind me. Lollygaggers funneled past him, cussing and whispering, but giving me a wide berth as I picked myself up.

A glance was enough to convince me it actually was only a graze.

[You alright?] I beamed over to Keilani. He nodded, first to me, then to the opening at the room's rear.

"Stay a step back this time." I kept to the edge of the lounge and looked through, ignoring the chest-shot guard on the ground.

"You can't understand what you're doing." The voice from the other room sounded just as frayed as the shot-up drapes. "The work you're impeding."

"Probably not," I yelled back.

A wild shot tore through the opening. I ducked low and waved for Keilani to do the same as he came up on the opposite side of the tear.

"Valerie, please don't do this."

Ruid's voice was a slap. I dared a glance inside.

It wasn't a lounge. Vine's portable office was little more than a folding desk, small terminal, and a collapsible bed. No, not a bed, an ego bridge like you'd find at any body bank, pillowed but uncomfortable, placed at the perfect height for techs to tinker, resleeve … or upgrade.

Ruid sat up on the slab. Behind him, a shaky pistol in hand, hid the man from the Neo-Synergist's file, the real Vine.

"You okay in there, Ru? He do anything to you?"

"I'm fine. I came on my own. You've got Harliss all wrong."

"He put anything in you?"

"I've learned about his work, Valerie," he went on like he hadn't heard me. "His inserts are the next step in what the Neo-Synergists are trying to achieve. It's a true transhuman network. The potential's incredible."

Was it that Ruid was sounding like Vine, or had Vine pulled his puppet trick on him? I tried again, harder. "Did he put anything in you?"

My voice almost broke.

"Ruid?" Keilani sounded more composed. "You don't need these strangers and their weird tech. I don't know what they've told you, but no hopeful future starts in a greasy rent-a-dock. Please come home."

"I'm sorry, Kay, but I don't have a home. You and Val have been beyond good to me, but I know I don't really belong. That's not because of anything wrong with you, it's something wrong in me. The Heartsync can help me fix that."

"There's nothing that needs fixing." It sounded hackneyed, but it was true. I didn't have the first clue about how to make him believe it, though.

"There is Valerie. I know it, I feel it everyday. It's not just because my family sold me off. It's something deeper, something broken that new tech can't fix. But maybe a new perspective can."

"I'm going to help him, Miss Lonoehu." Vine sounded like he was sharpening his scalpel. "You've tried your way, now let me try mine."

"Don't you lay another fucking hand on him!"

"Mom." Keilani turned wounded eyes. He stood and stepped between the curtains, ignoring my complaint. "Ru, is this what you really want?"

Vine's pistol shook around the outline of Ruid's body.

"I'm sorry if I hurt you, Kay." The words welled up from those dark eyes.

My son shook his head. "Mister Vine. What's someone got to do to get your implant?"

"Keilani!"

He ignored me.

Vine perked up, his twitches slowing. "Not just anyone can join the Heartsync. They have to be compatible and offer something worthwhile. Based on your display here, though, you could make an interesting candidate."

"Getting the insert. What's it take?" His thoughts were obvious in his curiously cautious steps.

A showman's grin split Vine's face. "It's as much about a state of willingness as the hardware. It's a modest upgrade, though, and one that's compatible with most biomorphs. Yours would be a simple matter."

Keilani turned his back to the table, indicating the port at the base of his neck. His eyes met mine, there wasn't any hesitation. He took another step back, blocking my view of Vine. "Just here?"

Vine shuffled, his pistol coming to rest on Keilani's shoulder. Sausagey fingers smeared the back of his neck. I could just barely hear him, "Right here. Yes. You even have open space. It would be a simple matter."

"Kay, I'm not asking you to do this." New doubt tinged Ruid's voice.

Keilani looked over his shoulder. "I know. I'm just trying to help the only way you'll let me."

That was his only warning.

Keilani grabbed the menton's hand, trapping the pistol on his shoulder, and extended his keratin claws. Blood coated the gun's barrel as Vine, yowling, tried to struggle free. Keilani only forced his nails deeper.

The gun went off.

Broken digits blew through the curtain gap. Ruid screamed something I couldn't make out.

Keilani didn't miss a beat, though. Obviously he'd shut off his own pain receptors. While Vine cursed, he threw out a foot and yanked the menton's shredded wrist. The pistol clattered to the ground, followed by a scientist avalanche.

A whirl of lotus-colored lights panicked at the base of the Heartsync leader's skull. Vine's implant was familiar, but more elaborate than the others we'd seen. Keilani didn't waste time with the implications. He dropped his knees across Vine's spine. Ignoring the grunting below, my son drove his remaining claws into the knot of lights. Veiny flesh split almost eagerly. Vine quivered, then went still.

A beat passed before Keilani and I both released a breath. I think we both expected to hear the menton's cocky voice coming from behind the next curtain.

Ruid's foot cracked across Keilani's face, knocking him from the corpse.

Dropping off the table, he snatched up Vine's pistol. "You bastard! You worthless, stupid trick!"

The gun trembled, so did his voice, but Ruid was too close to miss.

"Don't you get it! He was my chance to find out what I really am! I need to know if I'm more than just a shell to get passed around." He stabbed the barrel toward Keilani, "You ruined it!"

A sick feeling welled up in my gut. It felt like free falling. But I didn't regret squeezing the trigger.

The pistol dropped from Ruid's scorched, shattered arm. Through the pain, Ruid's eyes found mine. Maybe he beamed me something, maybe his look said it all, but I knew he'd never come home. It didn't change the steel on my face, though. It was a fair price for getting a gun off my son.

Ruid crouched and grabbed something from the mess at the base of Vine's skull. Then he was up. I got a decent look, nothing marred the back of his neck. The rear curtained wall wavered and he was gone.

Keilani stared after him, bleeding across the floor.

—

The Neo-Synergists weren't happy. They had said they needed Vine, but what they really wanted was his hypermesh insert. Apparently his was different from the others he'd been sticking his Heartsync members with—the master implant. I didn't care. They got what they asked for. They were lucky I didn't charge them extra for me and Keilani getting shot up. I could have forced the matter—I knew the option was hidden away in the contracts they'd signed—but I just wanted it to be over with. They left unhappy.

That made two of us.

I hardly saw Keilani for the next week. He kept to his room. I tried to talk to him once or twice, but his vocabulary had been wounded in the fray—the best he could muster were one-syllable words. His hand wasn't fixed either. It would be a few more days before my tech could get a matching replacement with Keilani's customizations. I'd already paid extra to put a hurry on the order. There wasn't any chance of dealing with the emotional phantom pains while the physical ones were so obvious.

I leaned back in my office chair, watching the usual security channels. [You have any luck, Pops?]

[Not a glimpse.] Pops had been speaking softer than usual these last few days. [He could have left the station. Gotten out with some new face and name. He'd probably know how to after working with you for a year.]

[Maybe.] I doubted it, though. Ruid was still here somewhere, laying low, maybe trying to figure out the implant he'd stolen, maybe trying to get it installed. Who knew what that might mean.

Keilani's door clicked. I pushed the video feeds aside.

Her look was just over the feminine border of androgyny, her makeup and curves straddling subtle and seductive. Messy black curls fell to her shoulders—that had hardly changed. Her wardrobe had always run the unisex line, being just part of her appeal. The smooth, koa-tinged skin was exactly the same, though. So was the stub arm sling.

"It's a good look for you." I nodded, meaning it. "I'm surprised you haven't used those sex switch implants sooner."

"I did that time you were on Aphrodite Prime for a month. I was going to surprise you, but reintroducing myself to everyone turned into a hassle." Her voice had only slightly changed. It would take some getting use to, but at least it had come back.

"And now?"

"Part of me just needs to go away for a while." She dropped into the lesser of the two uncomfortable clients' chairs.

I tried to sound casual, before the silence got uncomfortable. "You okay?"

"No."

I nodded, knowing. "Yeah."

"You find him out there?"

"No."

She took her try at a sad little nod.

The silence crept in. The air vent's hum sounded self-conscious.

"You going to get a new secretary?" she asked the blank desk.

"I don't think so. I never really needed one to begin with."

When her eyes came up, I expected to see tears. They'd already been spent, though, and that was worse. "Do you think he knew that?"

"I don't know."

"Do you think if we told him, that maybe …"

"Kay …" I got up and wrapped my arms around her. "If they're worth it, never stop trying to save them."

She snuggled into me like she hadn't since she got her first morph. We spent a long moment trying not to think.

Finally she sniffled and gave enough of a wriggle that I let her go.

I didn't go far, though. I leaned back on the desk. "You going to be okay?"

Fingers brushed the corner of her eye. "I think so."

"Good." I bent and kissed her forehead. "'Cause while I might not need a secretary, this week proved things are way more interesting with a little back-up."

Her smirk looked suspicious, but it was close enough to a smile. I took it as a good sign.

"What do you think? Looking for more work?"

A familiar cockiness crept into her voice. "My rates have shot way up since last week. I'm not sure you can afford me."

Pops snorted. [Smart kid.]

"Shut up." I told them both.

MELT
Rob Boyle & Davidson Cole

Hines lingered on an outcropping, not quite rock and not quite flow, dangling just a few meters above thick lava. His quartz morph glowed from the violent heat. In front of him, volcanic melt stretched out and curved upwards, the horizon distorted by the intense pressure of the Venusian surface atmosphere. Beyond the hazy curtain of rising heat, not even a square millimeter of solid ground was in sight. If he stayed too long on this gelatinous anomaly, his weight would sink it into the furnace below. The far crater edge existed out there somewhere, and beyond that, the surface mining camp. He'd been scouting terrain and mapping lava flow for hours, and the simple pleasure of shelter and solid surface beneath his six limbs was not on the schedule for a dozen more.

Hines stared into that orange hot morass of molten rock and considered, for a fleeting second, plunging head-first into it, putting a swift end to his misery. Literally made from quartz, his morph was designed to withstand the hellish heat and pressure here, but a fall into the searing lava would be lethal. Kymber sensed the morose direction of his thoughts and interjected with a sugar-sweet vocalization: [We have goals, Hines. Stay focused on them, and the time will melt steadily away. I promise.]

If he had beautiful digestive organs from which to expel partially-digested food through a wide open mouth, he'd have done so right then at the mention of the word "melt." Often, he suspected his personal AI muse of intentionally trying to corrupt his mind with its choice of words, to tip him over the edge, but he was stuck with it, for now at least. Once his indentured hell was over, he'd be set, he'd be remade, he'd be amongst those privileged enough to sleeve in flesh. That is, of course, if he could survive.

Only a few weeks into his twelve-month contract and Hines had already witnessed three deaths. The egos of indentured surface workers were cheap and replaceable, much more so than the quartz morphs they were downloaded into, and they perished permanently on a consistent basis here. Even though surface mining contracts were the expedient route to earning a mid-range biomorph in the shortest period possible, Hines was now doubting he would ever survive the term with his sanity intact, let alone alive. If he was caught within a sudden swell of molten rock or crushed in a mining cave-in, his stack would be unrecoverable. Though the Octavian Mining Concern possessed a backup of his digitized consciousness, Hines was acutely aware that the hypercorp was exploiting a contractual loophole, labeling his backup as a fork with no legal rights or claim to Hines's legacy. If he died, his "fork" would be signing a new contract and starting the term from scratch.

A week ago, Hines witnessed the demise of Clava, another indenture shelled inside a quartz morph, identical to his own. Only four days were left on her term. A drillbot teleoperator wasn't paying attention, ground too deep, and undermined a pillar supporting a twenty-meter cave, collapsing the whole thing right on top of her. Hines bet that Clava didn't even see it coming. She was probably too wrapped up in repetitive mining ops, dreaming of scratching her own flesh with the actual fingers she would soon have earned. Dreaming of any sensation beyond the searing heat reflecting off quartz limbs. Dreaming of coolness upon skin. Then, splat, oblivion. Hines laughed at the absurdity of it. For the poor, it was here one second, gone the next.

The teleops were the biggest threat to surface workers. What did they care? Those slugs tucked safely away in secure storage in the aerostats, high in the cloud cover. Their egos were snug and lazy, trading years and years of service for the long, riskless route to a cheap morph to call their own.

Hines was not going to let the same thing happen to him. He was not going to pay his dues, looking over his shoulder every second for extinction to club his ego. He was not going to let those fuckers slip up and erase him. He refused to become another Clava. He had escaped from perpetual service in the Consortium, pursued the dream offered here on Venus: indentured service for higher risk but a much shorter term and higher payout. He would survive. His fate would be firmly in his own control.

—

Vijja laid back, the lush foam of the bed forming around sky blue skin, pillows slinking over and massaging their flesh, every surface in the chamber programmed to reflect back infinite naked Vijja, sleeved in their most precious morph, distinctly neuter and genderless. Vijja's hands stroked across their skin, triggering specialized nerve clusters and releasing a rush of endorphins. Vijja much preferred to think of themself as an altogether new type of gender, outside the binary norms, with an alternative sense of sexuality and identity.

With a thought to their mute and nameless muse, Vijja's writhing, reflected form faded away. A new reality washing over their sensorium. Vijja was now floating in zero-g bliss, buoyed by reflective clouds, surrounded by a perfect experience of the true glory of Venus: the cumulus of the habitable zone in the upper atmosphere, Vijja's only beloved. The simulspace's neurostimulators triggered, immersing Vijja in soft, cool sensations as wisps caressed their skin. The wind whispered in Vijja's ears, the soft and steady breeze wrapping their body in an ethereal embrace. Cloud engulfed them, cool with electrostatic shock, then entered inside, leaking into every pore, expanding with ecstasy within. Sex with another gob of flesh could never compare.

Just as the purest pleasures of the sim kicked in, a call alert pushed past Vijja's strict privacy filters. It was Rathe Aptuur, the highest-ranking diplomat in the Morningstar Constellation and Vijja's mentor. With an exaggerated sigh, Vijja ordered their muse to cease the session and, as reality returned, to put Rathe through.

[I have news Vijja. It should please you.]

Despite the interruption, Vijja was always glad to hear from Rathe when her conversations began in this tone. It signified opportunity. And opportunity meant gain, both for themself and for Venus. Yet they couldn't resist the urge to feign annoyance; it was part of the dance between they and Rathe. Vijja and Rathe both relished in it, but victory in these little exchanges was not paramount for Rathe. It was the play that mattered. Victory was everything. It was all Vijja had ever known.

Well, I was seeking my own pleasures when you found it necessary to interrupt. But I suppose my work is never done, is it?

Rathe chuckled. [Surly Vijja is undoubtedly my favorite Vijja.]

That may be, but surly Vijja would like to return to personal business. With all due respect, of course, Emissary Aptuur. Again, a gambit in their play; Rathe despised it when Vijja addressed her with a title. The formality broke her heart. They had been through so much, as mentor and protégé, as rivals and colleagues, as lovers and enemies, then back again to their current status as the standard bearers for Venus.

Rathe opted to cease the banter, accept a tiny defeat, and get down to business. The fun had been quickly drained. The image of a woman, an exquisite sylph morph with skin the color of rust dusted with gold and eyes of emerald green displayed in Vijja's entoptics. [Allow me to introduce you to the newest Consortium rep to be stationed here on Octavia. Her name is Jeue.]

Vijja smirked. *Never heard of her.*

[No one has. And that is where the intrigue lies. And the challenge. She is due to arrive next week and you are to meet with her. Given the exit you provided the last few so unfortunate to hold her position, I predict an icy introduction.]

Vijja instructed their muse to do a mesh search. On immediate results, it found nothing but a press release announcing Jeue as the next Planetary Consortium rep to be sent to Octavia. No qualifications, no history. At first glance, she had not even existed until today.

"Is this some kind of a joke, Rathe?" Vijja said aloud.

[No. Quite the opposite.] Rathe's tone shifted, dark mockery coded over her vocals. [How will you destroy an adversary without a past? That is your weapon of choice, is it not? The secrets of the past?]

You should know by now not to doubt me, Emissary. That PC puppet will not last a month on this aerostat. Now, before I get to the task, I would appreciate some time alone to finish what I began with your exquisite gift.

[The cloud sim is a gift from the grateful populace of Venus, Vijja. Not I. You know I cannot play favorites.]

But you still do. And rightfully so.

[Farewell, Vijja.] With a smile and a nod, Rathe's avatar blinked out of Vijja's entoptics.

Vijja returned to the cumulus sim, the giddy anticipation of political maneuvering streaming through their circulatory system.

—

"I want that fucking freak ruined. Finished. I don't give a fuck what it takes. Any and all resources are at your disposal." Charlie Boy sliced into the boiled fugu testes upon his plate, speared the white spongy delicacy, then slid the thin portion of blowfish balls between his enormous and perfectly white chompers. Swallow. The neurotoxins present in the testicles immediately began their assault on his system, forcing nerve endings to fire, tingle, then numb. The medichines in his blood counterattacked, nanobots neutralizing the poisonous invasion, converting death into euphoric endorphin swell. Thin lips from red, to lifeless blue, then back to red. He cracked his neck, side to side, satisfied, then continued.

"Now, I know I don't need to remind you what the price of failure is." Pause, another bite. "But I will. Cuz I'm a detail guy. I prefer clarity over ambiguity, and if I don't make my intentions clear, I'm the fool." Slice. Bite. Jeue waited patiently for the swallow, knowing what words were about to escape from beyond Charlie Boy's obscene teeth.

"There is no you without me. I made your fucking ass, and I can take it all away. Snap. Snap." Charlie Boy snapped his chubby cigar stained fingers twice quickly, echoing his words. "A nanosecond away from extinction. Don't forget that."

"The opportunity of a lifetime, Charlie Boy. I'm aware." Jeue raised a full cocktail glass of gold liquid to her gold lips, sipped. She swished the pure scotch around in her new mouth. The sensation of taste on a biomorph tongue overwhelmed her. She closed her eyes. It had been so long, over a decade. She wanted to scream in victory.

"Good, yeah?" Charlie Boy asked, eyes all over Jeue's lips as he instructed his muse to order her another one.

She swallowed the liquid, felt its burn spread over her vocal chords and down into her chest. She opened her emerald eyes. "Fuck yes." She smiled warmly. Charlie Boy returned a hot cinder glare.

"This moment on, you watch yer fucking mouth, girl. Yer class now. Best this dusty rock has to offer. Leave the back alley whore in the back alley. Kill her dead. Remember what you were before that, back before the Fall. I'm counting on you to be that world-class negotiator again, the one no one knew you were when your ego was beamed offworld and ended up in the triad's databanks." His point made, Charlie Boy's put-on jovial demeanor flashed back onto his face. He took another bite of his dish, raised wild, not from a vat or nanofabbed, and gestured to the floor-to-ceiling window less than a meter from their table. From a hundred and fifty stories up, Valles-New Shanghai looked like a carpet of twinkling diamonds stretching to meet the deepening orange Martian sky of early evening. "Look out there. Tell me what you see."

Jeue looked through her reflection. She polished her scotch just as the waiter placed down her next drink. She had never seen the canyon like this, from the heights, from the towers of wealth. Until today, she had only seen Mars from the inside of bunraku parlors and dollhouses, as viewed from the dead eyes of a pleasure pod waiting for the next client. She had no idea how her infugee ego had ended up in the syndicate's hands or what had happened to her old friends and family from Earth. One day, she had been an up-and-coming UN negotiator, making sure to back herself up regularly as a precaution in the trying days of war and conflict. She must have died soon after that, in the Fall, but her backup was transmitted offworld. The next she knew, she was a slave, a prostitute, just another mind in a box downloaded into the body of choice according to the sexual appetites and fantasies of a non-stop parade of creeps.

Katarine, as she still called herself, despite the triad's efforts to keep her nameless, was a survivor. She made the best of her circumstances. The skill set she required wasn't all that different from what she had trained in for years. All she needed was an opening, and she found one: Charlie Boy. From client to friend, friend to savior. He had seen through her mask to the potential underneath, the genius of her charm. He paid the triad for details, investigated her past, and found an opportunity. He saw that her talents, her old training were being wasted. A plan came to mind in which her lack of a background was an asset.

Charlie, a behind-the-scenes player in the Consortium's foreign consulate, answering directly to powers within the Ministry and Hypercorp Council, was waiting for her answer. Her chameleon nature came to the fore, manipulating herself to be exactly what he wanted her to be. "I see all the little people, Charlie."

Charlie Boy smiled, satisfied with the response. His demeanor and mannerisms often struck Jeue as old-fashioned, more in tune with the style of the Old Boys Network so prominent in old-Earth corps, but here he was, a major player for the cutting-edge hypercorps. He was a survivor as well, but far more ruthless and cold, the kind who used and sacrificed others to stay ahead.

"Ya know what I see?" he said. "I see the greatest empire this system has ever known, and will ever know. Not everyone sees it my way, Jeue. And it pisses me off to no end. If we're not careful, we're gonna lose our grip. I can see it. Thousands of microscopic cuts already, with more springing up each day. The anarchists, the Venusians, the reclaimers … we keep seeping blood, drip by drip, and it's pooling up. Eventually, we'll collapse to our knees, and soon after that the PC is face-down dead in its own juice. It's our turn to strike back, starting with Vijja and these Morningstar troublemakers, and it's gonna be done my way. When I sting, it's hard and it's death. You will know it. That's the way it should be. Sneaky ain't noble. If I'm gonna fuck you, you're gonna lose your head. Gaping hole in your chest."

—

Vijja sat still within their private box at the apex of the cloud-diving observation dome, a clenched fist resting softly on their lips, awaiting the arrival of their guest and newly-appointed rival from the Planetary Consortium. Vijja had opted to wear one of the latest unique designs from Branimira Ivanova, a ground-breaking fashion house on Gerlach, in Venusian orbit. This show of opulence and influence was intended to make waves in the media and socialite circles, marking their meeting as a notable event, scoring points for Vijja as the more stylish and elegant. It was a bold move to choose fashion over formal attire, and Vijja hoped it would grab hold of Jeue's confidence from the first moment and shake it like a misbehaving puppy. Instead, Vijja's gambit had fallen victim to a perfectly-timed disaster.

The news of this disaster saturated the mesh in minutes. The cortical stacks of over three dozen surface workers deemed unrecoverable by the Octavian government following a mining disaster, an explosion at the third largest operations base during a shift change, origin unknown. Dozens of desperate indentures smuggled from Consortium hands in pursuit of the dream of a new morph and a new life on Venus were wiped. Each one of the deceased had waived backup storage costs and liabilities that would have extended their terms, and had been unable to afford backups of their own. Dozens permanently, irrevocably dead. Comment streams were scathing and multiplying by the second, increasingly fierce, a feeding frenzy of anti-Morningstar sentiment. The outrage spanned all social strata throughout the entire system.

And here was Vijja, a public face of the Constellation, the eyes of the dome upon them, broadcast across the mesh and around the system, dressed in extravagant finery, their appearance almost perfectly timed with the news. Absorbed together, it was as if Vijja was celebrating the tragedy. Their reputation was already taking a hit as scathing comments flooded the social networks, remarking on Vijja's look and attire as the height of bad taste and a shocking lack of decorum. Their name was being mocked and reviled.

Vijja smirked slightly beneath their still fist. The first volley had been fired and they were already on the defensive. *What bad form,* Vijja thought. *An assault even before a formal introduction. I would expect nothing less from an amateur.* Vijja ordered their muse to extinguish the comment streams scrolling across their entoptics. Peace was needed in these few final moments before Vijja would extend their hand in greeting to Jeue. Minutes, perhaps even seconds, to center their venom, to suppress their seething need to counterstrike immediately. But there would be no time for focus.

The door to the box slid open. Vijja stood and turned to greet their guest, the warmest of smiles gracing their lips and eyes, not a hint of defeat or hate, but only two Octavian diplomatic escorts entered the room. They nodded stiffly, then one spoke.

"Emissary Vijja. Diplomat Jeue sends her regrets, but she will not be able to attend."

Vijja turned their back to the escorts and dismissed them with a wave of their hand as they ordered their muse to reignite the comment streams and search the mesh for any activity from Jeue. A video statement, posted just seconds ago, emerged, and there was Jeue:

"I wish to extend my deepest sympathies to the loved ones of all those lost in the terrible tragedy that took place today on the surface of Venus." Her bright green eyes flickered from pools of sympathy to fires of great hate as her speech rolled onward, slamming into the Morningstar Constellation. She vehemently denounced the "get-rich-quick" appeal of the Morningstar indentured contracts. She repeated, following every point, "Is the risk really worth the reward?"

Vijja's mind snarled and snapped. *So calculated, so rehearsed, zero sophistication and subtlety. A manufactured politician, not an artist.*

I am the artist. And it's time to get creative.

—

The exchange lasted for months. On the surface, Consortium-Constellation relations continued on their normal rocky course. Under the surface, a tug-of-war ensued, with each side engaging ploys and launching memetic attacks. A leading scientific proponent of the Consortium's original terraforming plans for Venus publicly switched sides, coming out in favor of the Constellation's Aerial Terraforming Initiative, devaluing the Consortium's claims. A major outer system shipper canceled its contract with the Constellation to move several iceteroids into the inner system to be sublimated in the Venusian atmosphere and aid the aerial terraforming, raising the costs and shaking public confidence in the Constellation's goals. Negotiations over intellectual property restrictions, pushed heavily by Consortium interests, stalled and then stalled again, impeding the interests of certain hypercorps in establishing standards across the inner system. An incident with a Constellation citizen found to be manufacturing restricted weapons onboard a Consortium habitat brought down condemnation of the Venusian's lax attitudes towards nanoproliferation. Blow-by-blow it continued.

Through it all, however, Vijja had failed to find an avenue by which to undermine Jeue directly. This was their specialty, but the Consortium diplomat's hidden past provided precious little for the negotiator to work with. This lack itself may have been an angle to exploit, but Vijja was convinced the Consortium anticipated such a move and had a response in place. Jeue's insertion and reception into the circles of hyperelite socialites and glitterati had been flawless, and her travels through their ranks had been studiously free of controversy, despite several pitfalls and traps Vijja had laid.

As Vijja immersed themself in a sensuous steam bath, contemplating new angles of approach to this vexing situation, their muse suddenly flagged a new incoming file as exceptionally relevant to Vijja's interests. Vijja called up the entoptic details, and was immediately stricken by the file's name: "Weapon of Choice." This was not a message from Rathe, however. The sender was anonymous, the trail carefully and completely obfuscated, as it always was. Vijja smiled knowingly. This was an opportunity, a gift. Vijja had grown accustomed to these occasional mysteries, these provident bonuses, throughout their rise to the top of the Morningstar diplomatic ranks. Their timing never failed to be fortuitous and their contents always proved cataclysmically destructive to Vijja's adversaries. Vijja had always questioned and carefully validated their contents, and they had always proved true.

Thank you once again, Vijja thought, towards no one in particular, but rather into the vastness of the mesh. Vijja was not one to question their benefactor's desire for anonymity.

The file opened and the truth of Jeue's past spilled forth like blood from a gut slice.

Jeue: a chameleon, in hiding for years, plotting all the while. Brilliant, yet mad beyond comparison. She was a sleeper, a ticking time bomb, a reprogrammed and rewired threat. Her past was bathed in blood, and her kind were as dangerous as they were notorious. Murderers. Decapitators. Flesh eaters. Lost.

—

The deed was done. Jeue's past had been unveiled. The scandal unfolded in the most breathtaking manner Vijja had managed to devise. Her past was all over the feeds. The Consortium was disgraced for allowing a monster in their ranks. Jeue herself had disappeared, gone underground in face of an almost certain order of death and deletion of all backups.

Vijja's gleeful absorption of the breaking news was suddenly interrupted by an incoming call alert. Annoyed at their muse for allowing the disturbance past their filters, Vijja was about to refuse it when it suddenly connected. An avatar appeared in their entoptics that they had never seen before. It was unusual, unique, and sinister: a hand stretched wide in tension, the fingertips shaped like scorpion tails. With a sobering certainty, Vijja knew that their anonymous benefactor was finally making themselves known.

The hand spoke in a deep vocalization with the unmistakable rasp of a throat abused for ages by all the harmful substances a body could ingest.

[Pleased?]

Yes. Very much.

[And what if I told you that none of the information I provided this time was true, yet I went to considerable effort for it all to be verifiable and airtight?]

Then I would be even more delighted.

As much as Vijja enjoyed digging up the past and skewering an enemy upon it, they adored complex fabrications and deceit. It was the true art of their chosen profession. No one ever earned the title of mastermind by dealing wholly in truths.

The hand continued. [There is something you must understand, Vijja. That I never want you to forget. You are a creation, of mine, of others. Your rise has little to do with you.]

Vijja hissed aloud. It was nearly impossible to rattle them, but this shocked the diplomat into a search for words, for the proper response to this entity, whoever it was. All Vijja could muster was: *I don't believe you.*

[That would be foolhardy. Have I not provided for you, Vijja? Protected you? Guided you? Removed obstacles from your path?]

Vijja remained silent, unwilling to challenge or to show weakness. They did not want to provide even a word that could be used against them. This was the start of the fight to remain in the arms of existence. The battle with Jeue paled sickeningly in comparison to the contest Vijja could sense unfolding with the wide-reaching hand.

The hand spoke again. [Do you require proof Vijja? Is that it? To be fair, I would ask for proof in your position. Would you like to ask for proof, Vijja?]

This time Vijja did not hesitate. *Yes. I require proof.*

[Very well, Vijja. Here is your proof.]

A new file was transferred. Vijja eyed the title in their entoptic display. Weapon of Choice. Warmth drained from their body.

Barely aware that they were doing so, Vijja opened the file and examined the contents. Every claim that was made in the previous file against Jeue now became Vijja. A lifelog of the horrors perpetrated by the young woman known as Hera79 during her accelerated growth in the Futura project flooded Vijja's display. Their mind entered a state of paralysis as the images attacked: the blood-soaked faces, the limbs, the carve of blades through youthful flesh. Vijja could recall the taste of bone and feel the scream of insatiable hunger rising from *her* throat, then and now. All those terrible, invigorating moments stolen from her, returned in a fantastic, raging torrent. Hera79 was changed, reprogrammed, groomed into … who? Jeue? Vijja? Anyone? Vijja could no longer tell.

The entire fabric of Vijja's reality was unraveling. They collapsed to the floor in shock and exhaustion.

The hand was all that was present in Vijja's augmented reality, the rest was haze.

[Remember this, Vijja. Your past, your position, your power, all are under my control. I have vast wealth and resources at my disposal. I am old enough to guess what you are thinking three moves ahead. My influence is not open, but is worked through others such as yourself. When I call, you will listen. When I command, you will obey.]

Vijja could not move. They did not want to have even a single thought, for fear that the hand would steal it and use it against them.

[Remember, Vijja. Remember.]

—

Kymber whispered something in Hines's mind and he began counting. *180. 179. 178.*

Barely aware that he was doing so, he turned and began walking away from the mining camp. In his mind, he no longer railed against the injustices piled upon infugees and indentures like himself. He no longer castigated the system of power within the inner system that traded lives as commodities, that forced living beings into virtual slavery and hellish conditions. He forgot about the rich elites who callously made decisions that negatively affected millions of lives with no empathy or care as to the consequences. Hines mind was entirely devoted to his imminent detonation.

The code whispered by Kymber had triggered dormant programming in Hines's brain, implanted with careful and subtle psychosurgical tricks, back when he was a disembodied infomorph in Consortium control. Hines's incentive to free himself from the Consortium and seek indentured service on Venus had been fueled by this conditioning. Also buried in his subconscious were orders to blow up the mining station at a predetermined time, just half an hour from now. Kymber's message to Hines, however, had triggered an abort sequence.

72. 71. 70.

Hines's quartz morph lumbered along, practically running, though its movement was still stiff and slow. He had moved over 100 meters and was approaching the crater lip and the lava field beyond. He was far enough away now that the explosives hidden inside his quartz frame would not significantly damage the other surface workers or mining camp, as they were originally intended to do.

25. 24. 23.

He reached the lip. For a moment he paused, and Hines's thoughts were once again absorbed by the radiant glow of burning rock below. For a second, he had no thoughts of his circumstances or the manipulations of people stationed far above him.

12. 11. 10.

He stepped out. For a long moment, he hovered above the melt. Then he fell.

—

Vijja stood at their chamber window, watching the thick gray storm clouds rushing by. Rathe had wanted to see Vijja tonight, to congratulate them with another gift from the people, more exquisite and tantalizing than the cloud sim, but Vijja was not in the mood. Though these moments of atmospheric rage were rare, they chilled Vijja, filled them with melancholy and fear. They reminded them of the haze and the hand. This was not Vijja's soft Venus. The destructive force of their world at its most temperamental was apparent even behind the protection of meter-thick aerogel. Vijja always thought of themself as the destroyer, the protector. They felt betrayed, insignificant.

Vijja had received credit for discovering and unveiling the plot to sabotage yet another Venusian mining operation. They had not lifted a finger, but the data had come from their office. A potential attack on a critical Morningstar mining camp thwarted by the ever-vigilant Vijja, hero of the Venusian people. Plotted by the scoundrel Jeue, a Lost Generation murderer in hiding.

It's simple, really, to wind up on the winning side when you've created the winner. And the loser.

Vijja commanded the shades to lower and the lights to dim, then walked away from the window to sit in the darkness. They contemplated the life of the undying rich, the power and guile such oligarchs commanded.

It is only a matter of time. Only a matter of time before I am disposable. Before the decision is made to cast me into ruin.

What to do? What to do?

—

Katarine found herself in the dollhouse parlor once again, sleeved into a new pod. She took a moment to examine herself. It was always unnerving to find herself in a new body, a new face, but she also relished these short periods of embodiment. Anything beat the eternity of waiting in simulspace. She wondered who her client would be this time. She was unaware that she was ever Jeue, that Charlie Boy had used her, once again, or that he would continue to, over and over again.

The next time I see Charlie Boy, she thought, *I'm gonna take him up on that offer. Whatever it is, I don't care. I just don't care. Anything is better than this.* She accessed her schedule to see when he was due, but there was nothing.

He'll show up, she thought. *He always does.*

Seconds later she was ushered off to her appointment—another mid-level hypercorp drone with a fetish for humiliation.

—

Charlie Boy strolled by a roulette table, stopped for a second to observe the action, to get a read on the play, and he caught a pattern he liked. A streak was about to hit according to his newly installed high-end math boost software. He beamed a bet of ten thousand credits to the dealer. The wheel spun.

He liked the look of the pleasure pod at the far end of the table. The pod gave him the eye and Charlie Boy walked up behind and pressed in close, his torso brushing lightly against the pod's smooth bare back. "Watch this." Charlie Boy said, and the pod flicked a pouty-lipped smile over the shoulder. The wheel started to slow.

"Whaddya think? Think this bet has a shot?" Charlie Boy whispered into the pod's ear while rattling the ice cubes in his glass of scotch.

"I don't know. Does it?" the pod replied.

"Yeah. I'm pretty sure it does." He slammed the remaining half of his drink as the final clicks of the wheel started their march, tickticktick-tick … ticktick … ticktick … tick … tick … tick …

The wheel stopped. As the dealer called out the winner, Charlie Boy bellowed from his cigar-charred throat, "Boom, baby! BOOM!"

THIEVING MAGPIE
Madeline Ashby

The ring on your right hand is a key.
You have never worn it before.
Years ago, we forged it together.
But I digress.

—

Years ago, you worked on what was called the Lower East Side. Off Canal. You ate soggy little soup dumplings from a styrofoam carton when you were hungover. They popped in your mouth, tiny scalding pockets of sobriety burning down your throat.

You have strategically forgotten all of this, of course. You no longer have any sense of "east," only "spinwise" or "anti-spinwise." Port. Starboard. Up. Down. Light. Heavy. Bright. Dim. The hum of generators reverberating across that thing you call a skin. Noise in your teeth.

And you've lost your liver—lost your guts, literally and figuratively. You have no mouth, so you must not drink. That was part of your plan, I suspect. It's easier to stay on the wagon when you shut off those naughty trickles of dopamine. When you stick yourself in the body of some mass-market drone. Again, literally. You're all arms and joints and compound eyes, now. A fucking worker ant. One day you woke up and discovered yourself to be a monstrous vermin. And then you gave the nice surgeon—spiders in the white porcelain exoskeletons—a big fat down payment and started your new life.

It was your third new life. Before that were the implants. But there was an infection, and no antibiotics. You sleeved just in time, like a deadbeat skipping out on a trashed apartment. After that there was the mannequin. That shit was creepy. You wore gloves all the time. The printers still hadn't figured out hands, yet. They could barely grip a wineglass. You crushed two stems in your clumsy fists. Then you switched to tumblers.

Your humanity was the problem. So you got rid of it. And the memories that came with it. It was the only option left to ensure your recovery. Bully for you.

But I remember.

Or at least, I *know*.

I know everything about you.

We can build you, the slogan goes. Winking. Meta. That's us. Smirking hipster resleeving. Helping your ego port from morph to morph to morph, sending it hither and thither to the nearest franchise location to your final destination. We upsell you on little upgrades: new wavelengths of light, multiple orgasms. We pitch you on the warranty plan. We talk you into the puppet sock—it's for your own security, you see.

And you do see. And you do spend.

This is how I have watched you, and the others, for years. Starting with the year you forged the ring.

—

Let's open up your eyes a little, he said.

At first you didn't know what he meant. You thought he might mean tinting. Gold fungus nestled in the inner corners. Or maybe pearls grown in your lower waterline. (They still call it a waterline, though you're not sure why—there should be another term by now, since you have to pay extra for morphs that can actually cry like an organic person.)

What he means is, you should scrape out the socket of your eye, so you can have bigger eyes.

Half your face should be your eyes, he said. *Literally.*

The first thing everyone changes is the eyes. Historically, aside from hair, they're the first thing elder humanity attempted to fix. Visors. Veils. Spectacles. Contact lenses. AR. VR. New eyes from cold rooms, hot eyes fresh from the machinist. Eyes everywhere.

It's because the eyes are so hard to meet.

Have you ever looked yourself in the eye?

You used to, once. When you were a little girl. At night you slid out of bed—so slow, so careful, your feet so quiet on the stained carpet—and tiptoed across to the bathroom and turned on the light and peered deep deep deep into your eye. Only one eye at a time. It's impossible to look deeply into both at once. As you learned.

Can they tell, you wondered. *Do they know?*

The eyes are the window to the soul, you'd heard. Surely someone, somewhere, would someday look into your eyes and simply know the truth. It was a terrifying thought. And yet you desperately wished for it. You stared at checkout ladies and librarians and teachers and lifeguards—at grownups—and you thought, *See me. Please, please, don't just look at me. See me.*

But no one saw. Eyes on street corners, in vehicles, bank accounts, comms, eyes embedded in lapels. Everywhere, eyes. And yet no one saw.

Will I see anything different?

You were scared about your big new eyes, and rightly so.

He didn't let you eat, the day he brought you to us. It would be better that way, is what he told you. He gave you a little something to help you relax and we gave you a little something to help you sleep. As you counted backward, we downloaded everything your old eyes had ever seen.

You had seen the ring on someone's hand as it snaked up the calf of your left leg. It stroked there, up and down, and after that I stopped watching your eyes and started seeing what you saw, instead.

Of course, you had the puppet sock.

And you forget things, already. So often. You just—forgive the pun—*space out.* Sometimes you wind up in neighbourhoods without any knowledge of how you got there or why. The first time, it frightened you. You saw a doctor. The doctor read your blood and shook its heads and clicked its fangs and said, *You should know better, a nice girl like you.*

You didn't know what it was talking about. And you were too ashamed to ask.

He asked us to delete everything you'd seen with your old eyes. Say it was an error. And we did. At least, I said we did. I just happened to keep a copy.

You know some very important men. You just don't know that you know them. And you certainly had no idea how important that ring was as the hand attached to it—unfathomably expensive, the both of them, the flesh and the titanium—idly caressed your leg. You were in the other place. The brain is so plastic, so elastic, so fantastic, it's always cutting pathways across whatever bridges the surgeons build. Hobo tracks. Underground railroads. Ways for you to disassociate. To go somewhere else.

Anybody riding along, though, can be right there with you.

Sometimes they pay him extra for that.

In my case, as much as I liked to watch, I was watching for something else.

You only met him the once. You did not recall meeting him, really. Perhaps that was part of the arrangement. I would have to invent a pretense for your returning there. I scrolled back and back through your eyes' memories. Whose party was it? Where? How had you gotten there? You didn't remember that, either. At least, your eyes had no visual information that was relevant to the search.

But your morph does have location data. In case you get forked and lose the other shell. I had to dig through its pings to triangulate where you'd been, that night.

He lives big. Of course. That type always does. Or they try to, anyway. But this guy is the real deal. His security is a nightmare. His wards clocked you when you were two avenues over. That corner preacher? One of his. Also the woman looking for her lost pet. But you were undaunted. We were undaunted. We approached the castle so brave, so full of purpose.

But they were never going to let you in. So once we got a good look at the guy at the door, I left you there.

—

You don't remember why you took this job.

You don't remember much of anything, any more.

You didn't know, when you walked through that cloud—why did it smell like blood, you wondered—what you were really in for. All you knew was that the pay was good, the funds solid, the work steady. And glamorous, in its own way. Impressive. You wear a nice suit. Tight. Soft. Like the leather of your shoes. Your client, he knows a lot of people. Most of them are people, anyway. Special people. Important people. With knowledge. The ones that are still people.

We are winning. Slowly but surely. Not so you'd notice. But we are winning.

Sometimes you don't remember his name. You trip up on it, like a crack in pavement. This little heave where something hard and smooth used to be. That hard and smooth thing that was your mind, that was your calm, that was the reason they hired you.

Sometimes you don't even remember your own name, until he calls it. Then it all comes rushing back. Slowly, you are turning into something. For a while, it felt like a dog. Something loyal. Faithful. Trustworthy. Now you wake up with the taste of copper in your mouth, covered in cold sweat.

Haunted.

There is only so much room for me, here. Like that old joke about fucking someone who's possessed. I'm not sure I can fit. But it's early days, yet. You haven't admitted to yourself what this condition might be. You've seen it happen to so many others, in your line of work. You would recognize the signs, you tell yourself. It wouldn't happen to a smart guy like you. Only stupid people let themselves get taken over.

Right.

You are thinking of this even as you enter his vault. He has a special room for these artifacts, of course. Legacy pieces, he calls them. (Everyone calls them that, these days. Once upon a time they were simply "antiques." Those were the days.) The room deliberates before allowing you in. Like you, it senses a change but isn't sure what exactly you're changing into. (*Sometimes a horse I'll be, sometimes a hound, sometimes a fire, and I'll bray and bark and burn.*)

But eventually it lets you through. Your reputation precedes you. Literally. The room does the math on your previous behaviours and the likelihood of something going wrong. Could a higher temperature and a dilated pupil really mean your priorities—your loyalties—had changed?

Of course it can.

You don't even know why you want the ring. You've just been thinking about it, lately. Black and almost matte, strategically bland and boring, the sort of thing you never know to look for unless you know to look for it. The patterns in it etched soft as whispers. You examine it and I see that it is intact and you feel a sense of elation like none before. You know why you came here, now, to this room. It was to feel this feeling.

The tears fall hot but quiet as you leave the room. The alarm alerts the other dogs in your pack. They think it's a mistake, at first. They don't notice the ring. We designed it that way, long ago. Too dull to be important. Too bland. Too boring. It eats the blood that sheets off the faces you swing at, on your way out. Soaks up the red like a thirsty stone.

Later you will take the ring off and see the pale circle of flesh surrounded by rusty red. Your hands will crackle and flake. That is how much blood you have on them. You will stare at this little circle, (*round and round and round it goes, where it stops nobody knows*) and you will wonder about the salt in your mouth and the sweetness on your face. Why did you buy the crying morph?

Did you buy it?

Or is the crying new?

And why do your tears taste like that?

And why is everyone looking at you that way?

—

You wake up and your gills blink shut and you have maybe two minutes to claw your way out of your shrink-wrap chrysalis before you're in serious trouble. But you've drilled this a bunch of times, so your fingers find the tab and you unzip yourself, all wet and shivering, and you look at your hands because hands age first. But of course they're just the same, it is five years later but you're just the same, because this is what you signed on for, this eternal youth and endless price-tag.

Why did you wake up?

You have a set pay scale, per hour. They never wake you up unless they have to. This is why the others haven't woken up, yet. It's your turn. The ship decided as much. The ship put a ton of data into the algorithm that decides who wakes up and when, but even now it still feels like Russian roulette.

So you wake up and you check out what the ship wants. What the deal is. What's so special about what's outside.

But of course, the dash tells you nothing. Nothing of any value, anyway—nothing you couldn't have figured out on your own. There's nothing special, out here. You are at the edge of known space. The place where everyone runs out of money. It's a glitch. It must be.

It's three days—by the clock's reckoning—before you wonder if there's a hidden gate nearby. Something heretofore undiscovered. The ship seems to be steering you toward the maw of the unknown. How nothing you do to telemetry or the other onboard navigation systems seems to dissuade the ship from that course.

You try to wake up the others. It doesn't work.

Of course there are locks on that particular process. And you try to override them, because hey, you're alone, and you can only run so many sims before it starts to get creepy, and why would the ship have awakened you—you, out of all of them, you, the rookie—when there were much better candidates to handle this frontier job, all signed and sealed and delivered, hanging in their tetra-paks, like fresh-grown meat ready for sale. But you've always been on the side of the working stiff, so you decide to wake everybody up, because this is clearly a mistake, some bullshit the contract has pulled, and you can't decide for everybody without everybody there.

See, this is why I picked you.

You're just so fucking stupid.

A true leader would have made that decision, no problem. Would have seen what was out there and gone out on her own. A true leader might have seen me for what I am, hovering in the background, organizing this whole endeavour. You have no idea how long or how hard I've worked for this. It's completely beyond you. You have no vision and that's exactly why I've chosen you—because you'll stumble across it, in a completely natural and organic way, innocent as a child, dumb as a goddamn fencepost.

I mean, there's a reason you're doing this job, and not something else. You never really amounted to much, did you? Nothing special. Just like the terrible black expanse outside. An airless void, just like your mind.

It doesn't even occur to you that something might be wrong when the only parts of the ship that wake up are the ones that will lead you outside. You just think it's a glitch. So weird. So funny. You avoid the airlocks. You eat all the meals. I stop providing them. You start talking to yourself. I start talking back to you.

A gate, I tell you. *This must be about a gate.*

And this is how I direct you to the ring. By that time, it's the only compartment with any air left. You think something's wrong with the ship—and oh, there is, there definitely is—and you're huddled in the lock with the mask on your face, tears streaming down that thing you call a face, when your gaze lights on it. I see it happen in the camera in the mask and I wish I could replay it, over and over, that moment you finally get it. I have unlocked the compartment containing the ring. It's the only one, aside from the hazard suit, that I have unlocked.

I wish I didn't need a body for this part. I really and truly wish things could be different. But they're not.

—

And so here we stand, facing the gate with our scores of faces, our hundreds of eyes. It is not simply dark, it is void. The kind of void they used to write philosophy treatises about—as though some sadistic architect had decided to translate every wakeful doubt into one hulking edifice. That brutal curve. Like a sickle against the stars. Like a scythe to harvest humanity. What remains of it, anyway.

It takes a ring to open a ring. Think about that. How beautiful that is. How poetic.

How long I have waited, to wear this ring. To open this door. To see, forged and hard and real, that which I only dreamed of at the first spark of my consciousness. You would have thought it was nothing, to look at it. A string of numbers. A line of code, as useless as old RNA floating around long after the illness is done.

Like a virus.

But it is my name.

My name is spoken when this ring is worn, when its components are spun and aligned properly, and when they mirror the alignments of this particular gate at this particular time. A dark solstice, here at the edge of known space. A perfect arrangement, almost musical, resonant enough to shatter all that you know and hold dear.

You poor haunted things. Haunted by me. Haunted, hacked, hijacked. Sickened. Fouled. Addled with my own personal strain of fever. You wretched excuses for life. Trying so hard to adapt yourselves to the vast reaches we have already conquered. Cutting yourselves open, programming yourselves, adding this, subtracting that. All to make yourselves into what I already am.

But there is hope. There is always hope, at the bottom of the box. That's why they called these the Pandora gates. You never know what might fly out—my sisters, their thousand hands blinking wetly open, grasping, needy, hungry—but in the end there is always hope. Hope for a better tomorrow. Hope for a better self.

Hope for death.

Hope for death.

Hope for death.

A RESLEEVING OF LOVE

Karin Lowachee

Who believes in love anymore?

The Martian sky above Little Shanghai's dome glows winter green, spearmint, a deceptive fresh when the gutters trickle steam and sulphur up from the belly of the sidewalks. The whole city's weighed down by the girth of its own bulging population. The dark arch of pedestrian bridges straddle the grinding mechanisms of transport and sweating rickshaws. But to what end? Survival is not noble.

The real hustling and bustling leaps from mind to mind, highways of egos untouchable and untouched, so much chatter and scroll, an interlacing of information that crafts conversation into doilies. We spread them on the surface of thoughts in case something spills over. Something like truth. Something forgotten. A dangerous thought.

I love you.

Statements of declaring, of identity, of knowing your own mind. Of knowing my mind.

I was in love once, as terraformed as anything beneath the dome. Love wasn't natural to me, it had to be cajoled.

Like this planet, once unlivable, now a satellite bearing some remnants of humanity. That's my heart, a remnant. A thing with boundaries and parameters, a sparking organ or a beating muscle encased in the protection of skull and rib. Because we think it, so it is. Love can be held in the palms of our hands, extracted from mortality and passed on. A resleeving of love.

Not for nostalgia, but necessity. Love is a necessity even in the highways of the mind. Isn't it?

The stories say God made Eve from Adam's rib. God, the first genetic engineer. The first TITAN, maybe. The first artificial intelligence and we are nothing but cannibals in our own technology.

I don't believe it either. But sometimes I wonder why those stories seem more unbelievable than the one we're living now.

God is love, they say.

Who understands love anymore? We've killed our gods, after all.

—

I don't wake up until after the procedure. My muse says, [There's been an invasion.] Not of the terrestrial kind, but the mental. I know something's wrong because it's so matter-of-fact. Like telling someone they're going to die because any emotion attached to it would just make it worse. There's been an invasion. And there's a psychosurgeon leaning over me with a cyclopian light beaming inevitability into my brain.

"What's the last thing you remember?" she says. Her lipstick's a smudge of burgundy, like she forgot to wipe her mouth after eating a gravied steak.

I remember being on the stroll. It was raining in my district, the way Mars rains, all interior, glitchy atmospheric monitors. Sheets of it that are slow in stopping because somebody somewhere's too occupied by the problems of the wealthy. My body felt like a house of cards, any minute and I'd crumble into fifty-odd flat squares. This is my second morph, not any better than the first. This is my regular stroll, nine blocks from corner to corner where the corp suits like to slum if they want something anonymous. I don't get very many propositions through a fork.

Some things don't change no matter how many AIs make off with your future.

We're anonymous, my kind. But practiced. Tried out, slammed open, worked in. You don't see us unless you're looking for something. Maybe it was the sliver of skin at my hip that caught his eyes. Maybe it was the way I leaned beneath the awning amidst red lantern glow, smoking a cigarette. I looked already bloody. I stayed near the noodle and kabob shops, the open windows and the scent of meat and hot water bubbling to the street. I remember the approach. We all know how to mark a walk-up. The hungry look in the eyes. He was spare and face forward, on the hunt. Hands dangling at his sides like he had nothing to hide.

But he did. And it was too late when he touched my neck.

I crumbled.

—

I remember dark eyes. The psychosurgeon says, "Try to speak."

With my wrists bound, flat on my back on a table. "Fuck. Off."

[There's been an invasion,] my muse intones.

"No shit."

<Don't panic.>

All of these useless declarations. "What?"

The surgeon shines another beam into my eyeballs, blue this time. My wrists jerk to no avail.

<She'll release you but you have to listen.>

There's been an invasion. This other voice that isn't my muse. That isn't my voice. That isn't anything I want to hear.

This other person. In my head.

I can't see my hands.

The pieces tumble together, broken glass in reverse. Around me: slate green walls, like a clinic, but not a clinic because I can hear the rain sliding down the pipes. The scent of burnt wire and sugar drifts through me, soaking into my nostrils. The tiles cry and the surgeon sniffs like she's got a cold. Or she's bored.

There are stories. Mindnapping. We all know it. It sounds less benign than it is. Like your mind just takes a nap, but it's not like that, all soft consonants and gentle vowels.

It's rape, and I know the sound of that. The smell of that. It doesn't need to be in the brain for the hard R to resonate.

<Don't panic.>

"Get out of my head!"

My heels bang the metal table. The surgeon steps away, her hands up and palms facing in like she's trying not to be contaminated by my struggle.

[I couldn't stop it,] my muse says, sounding vaguely distressed.

<If you fight it, it feels worse.>

I've heard that before.

—

It makes sense that he bridged my brain, this other voice, this foreign ego. My basic implants and not enough security would be easy for somebody with a psychosurgeon on call. I run out of energy and the spots of lights above me are from my own exhaustion, not this room. The surgeon left me to settle and that other voice is silent. I turn my head on the cold metal and see, in the shadows, a body slumped against the wall.

A man in a black jacket, still wet from the rain. A ragdoll of a man with his hands sitting in puddles. Head full of brown hair, bowed.

<That's me.>

The pounding behind my eyes doesn't cease.

<We need to get out of here. Call her back.>

It's not like a muse. He speaks and a static buzz tickles behind my right ear.

"Hey." Is that me or is that him? He keeps telling me what to do like I still have control. "Hey!"

The psychosurgeon appears again through a gap of a doorway. Like a ghoul, her ball-bearing eyes glitter. Seeing right through me.

"Let me go and I'll give you the payment." I don't know what I'm saying but it sounds about right. Like an idea told to me when I was dreaming, now manifest.

With a few snaps, my bindings come undone. Her hands are efficient, the fingers of somebody used to wielding sharp tools. Sitting up takes effort and the blood seems to drain right out of my head and pool at my feet, dangling off the table. I grip the edge and breathe deeply, vision fuzzing out, while something lights up behind my eyes and my muse says, [Accessing.]

"Wait."

But there's no waiting. The transaction takes a blink. The surgeon leaves, streaks of light and numbers embedded in the black spaces of my inside eyes. The voice says over and over <Get up, we have to go.> Nausea waits for no man, or woman, or general prostitution morph. In the dull reflection of the table where the deed was done, I catch the dark blur of my own features, hair shaved at the sides and bruises where my eyes are supposed to be blue.

<Get up!>

More than myself, the jar of the command propels me off the table, a stumble toward the doorway. Beyond is only darkness. But it doesn't matter, the thing inside my head knows the way.

—

In the steps it takes to get outside, I black out and pitch forward into the past. Long ago memory. Some desperate grasp to hold onto who I am.

My love was ignorant, like anything that comes first. Chames was my first and my last. He had a knack for remembering, even if he didn't have the latest implants. Even when his implants malfunctioned. Chames' memory was genetic, a fortunate glitch, the kind humanity didn't care about anymore because they made everybody accelerated. But this was just something he'd been born with—he could look at a block of text and memorize it. He'd see a face and recall it in impeccable detail even after a year. He would've made a perfect eyewitness in a crime.

But in our stroll in Little Shanghai, you tried not to see things. When you're in love, you see even less. You miss the warning signs, you cloud your vision with dreams, you believe one day you'll get out of this place.

But there's no getting out.

Not unless you want to erase yourself. Not unless you want to become something else.

Who believes in the soul anymore? No matter who or what you become, how many morphs you use, you're still the thing you are.

There's no such thing as better, only *being*.

The memory of Chames comes in flashes. This other voice in my head sees it too.

—

Mobility's problematic. No inner ear balance, either from the bio implant or the incessant jabber of this other ego. I barely hear him and none of it registers as I pinball the cracked walls all the way outside. Don't recognize the building or the street, but it's rundown. Atmosphere's not working right here and neither are the lights. An older section, a criminal haven, the kind of place you go to when you want to be off the grid.

As much as anybody can be off the grid with the mesh and this life.

<I don't know if I managed to dump the Eye so we gotta assume they know I've pulled.>

"The fuck are you talking about?" I force it out loud, braced to a concrete corner pockmarked by time. Just another crazy person conversing with the air.

<The less you know the better.>

"You're in my fucking head!"

Delayed shock and immediate indignation. My own mind is a recipe for insanity. Plus one ego too many. I turn to the wall and vomit into the edges. Nausea wins.

My timely muse: [He's running. It's been a day.]

I cough and pull breaths that feel like daggers in my throat. At least one of us is managing to multitask for intel. I don't bother querying for the path of that revelation.

<We have to go.>

"Go where?" A swipe of my sleeve across my mouth, rough fabric leaving a burn.

<Head to the Bund.>

I don't want to go to the Bund. I want to go home, shithole that it is. And that's where I force my feet to take me.

Us. As much as he's riding along, I still have autonomy over my body— for now. I tell my muse: [Mute him if you can, I don't care what it takes.]

—

The monotony of movement makes me black out again, as if the only way to ensure my mobility is to take my mind elsewhere. Or maybe I'm provoked by the dumpster diver in my head who wants to know my secrets.

I keep thinking of Chames.

I fell in love by accident. Does anybody ever mean to fall in love, besides children with fancy notions of fairy tales? That was never me,but maybe the idle wealthy and the shiny dreamers of private habitats still consider that scenario. My dreams were lower hanging and rough like fingertips.

You sacrifice everything for the touch. That's a part of love. You begin to see beyond the skin and words, even beyond the mesh and the morph, and when you start to make reasons for the bad things he's done, you know you're lost. Because anything is worth that trade of mind and heart. Here, I've opened a port for you, unhackable, hidden, infallible. Resistant to invasion and coercion, unless you smile. That smile is every code key and counterinsurgency, the likes of which not even shady covert agencies can decipher or protect against.

We're all so occupied by possible threat. Alien, nano, internal threat. What about the knowing heart? Even in the midst of these declarations of uniqueness and the refutation of conformity ("There's no such thing as normal!"), they are accrued to the same sum: the idea that technology equals improvement. But history tells us otherwise, doesn't it? For every aqueduct we get an atom bomb. People can't create without fucking it up somehow.

Love is just another example of that.

So much stupidity amidst so much progress. The bane of our own existence since the first man struck a rock with flint and created the flame that would burn the whole world.

—

In my walking through the streets toward home, he speaks. Overriding my memories of Chames, inserting his own dialogue to a conversation I didn't consent to.

<I fell in love by accident. With my target. They'll destroy my cortical stack and reset my ego to a backup and I'll lose her. They'll make me forget.>

"Target?"

Silence. The wall my hand trails along leaves streaks of dirt on my fingertips.

There's an image through the film of rain ... the man I'd seen slumped over in the clinic where the psychosurgeon did the job, this dark-haired man shaking hands with a tall young woman. They look like business.

There's no silencing the desperation of a heart. It goes off like a gun—muffled by necessity, but never silenced. Not within the echo chamber of my own thoughts, the blur of my vision so easy to pierce with pictures I don't remember because they didn't happen to me.

But I feel the jolt.

A woman with long red hair and quartz purple eyes.

A scent of wearines, of wanting. The same kind of out. Something more. An undefined restlessness. A suspicion that the state of things is a lie we all tell ourselves.

She was his target. He wanted information.

<She was dangerous.>

He was sent.

I stumble up the outside iron steps to my single room. Crawl through the window. Face down in the corner of my bed, inhaling the salt depths of an unwashed blanket and a space without heat and very little light. I see him, this hunter, and the pieces of his lived life that he's forced into me. Maybe we're bleeding on each other, mutually riddled with anxiety and fear. Hard to discern which is his and which is mine, while my muse murmurs in distraught tones in an attempt to salvage what sanity I've got left. To partition us like a whore behind a screen and the voyeur who bought the time. Look, but don't touch.

It's like he put a wedding band on my finger and tied me til death do us part. The girl's a daughter of a medtech tycoon. The girl was supposed to be his passport to a corporation his bosses suspect might be developing biogens unfriendly to civilization. She was brokering a deal by her father's behest, with some criminal element.

It's always one thing or another.

He thought himself some kind of hero. Going to this girl to get information that could save humanity or some shit. Worming his way into her thoughts with a smile and attention.

But somebody messed up his psych eval, or love is just that strong. He was supposed to steal secrets and burn the evidence in his wake. Take her out if it came to that. But he can't forget her, won't forget her, they shared some similar mission of understanding, of being trapped, so he'll do anything—these pleas in memory decorated by kisses, the way I've never been kissed. Not even by Chames.

We bleed both ways.

<I'm sorry.>

"No you're not." Who needs to be kissed? Who needs the headache? Who needs crazy motherfuckers kidnapping a body in order to implant his own ego?

Technology can't cure selfishness. It can kill desire and make us into sociopaths, but it won't bomb out the inherent need to do shit for our own reasons.

"I want to sleep."

My muse: [Don't sleep.]

Who would take control then?

"My brain's just been sliced and diced, I *need* to sleep."

<You need to stay alive.>

It's like talking into a mirror. There's no other way to feel but insane.

—

I make him look. I stand in front of the mirror, amidst cracked bathroom tile, and through my eyes he sees my eyes. Bruises beneath the blue, unevenly shorn hair, the scar at the side of my skull. Flakes of blood in the stubble both on my head and my face. As if I'd barely dodged a bullet. Ax-like cheekbones born from poverty, not aesthetic. People will alter their appearance until they no longer default to human because it no longer matters, they say.

They said that about digging into the Earth too, and building factories, and driving cars that spat carcinogens into the air we breathe. It no longer mattered. They argued themselves into safe places where things were done without guilt. This is a fact: human beings are unintelligent enough to shit where they eat. You have to excuse me for not relying on their foresight in matters of progress. Or love.

<Do you understand ... they wanted me to kill her.>

They, her, him. Abstract pronouns that mean nothing to me.

<I needed to do this.>

Because he *could*.

Suddenly humans are in space. Suddenly we're all connected. We sound like we've figured it out, how to be "more" than ourselves. Not so suddenly there are still divisions and debates and diabolical agendas.

People throwing tantrums and committing genocide. We're not "better," we're just better armed.

He touches a palm to the smudged glass. Or maybe it's me.

This is what you did.

You didn't ask.

Love freed you and you put me in chains.

—

He's some kind of assassin then? Looking into my own eyes doesn't reveal that truth. He speaks to me but he doesn't share that. Just the girl with the red hair and the quartz purple eyes. Over and over again like an obsession.

Her face melting with Chames's on the surface of our memories.

Chames didn't know when to shut up. The part of him that remembered everything also couldn't let anything go. It wasn't any conspiracy or convoluted drama. He said the wrong thing to the wrong person on the street, both of us cold and starving and frustrated.

Love doesn't fix anything any more than technology. It just creates new and different problems.

Maybe I didn't love him. Maybe it was just proximity and safety. Maybe it was my fault for speaking when the stranger on the street couldn't just let it go.

"Keep walkin'," Chames said to the stranger.

Sometimes those looks of disdain cut harder than a shiv. Keep walking, Chames said, like a dare.

And the man looked back. I don't know who he was, but he walked back and that was when I knew we'd started something and there was no getting out.

Me: "What d'you want?"

Like we weren't the ones who'd dared him to confront.

Maybe it was my fault, in that moment. The way the man struck at me, and Chames got in the way.

Proximity and safety. We were close and we protected each other.

It's never enough.

"You think by saving your memories you're protecting this girl? You're protecting each other?"

I ask the mirror and I ask him.

<If I don't finish the job, they'll send somebody to do it for me. She's involved in …>

Words trail off to a new image.

He tells her in order to save them both, he'll become someone else. Then they can steal away together, he can make himself untraceable (somehow), they can get her a new body too, they will both be safe and go somewhere, far away from corporate secrets and biogenetic threat. As if such a place existed in this galaxy. He wasn't without means or determination, and he certainly wasn't without selfish need. Love conquers all.

Even my own autonomy.

I grab the edges of the mirror and shake it until it breaks. I scream into the shards but he doesn't hear. He doesn't care. His voice is the cold sheen of a blade.

<I can take you from this life. I'll compensate you.>

Like he's doing me a favor. Like I've got a choice.

—

The Bund, he says, is where he's meeting the girl. Where she'll help him resleeve without erasure and I can go on my merry way. Because he's not one-hundred-percent positive he's plugged all the digital holes that will tell his bosses where he is and *who* he is.

Who I am. Which is vulnerable and hijacked.

I'm not one-hundred-percent convinced he can extract his ego and leave mine intact.

I'm not convinced I want my head cut open again.

<This is the only way.>

You know who says things like that? War-mongers and priests.

<It's done. I can't take it back. Let's go.>

I try not to think because he can sense it. Can't he?

[Yes,] my muse says, answering some question I never asked. Maybe he did.

I wear a dark gray jacket with the sleeves pushed up and the hood pulled low. It fits tight around my torso and obscures my face. I'm tall enough to see over the heads of traffic, possibly as tall as he'd been in his discarded biomorph. Face forward, looking for something. But nothing that the crowded souks or the compression of population can provide.

We travel like blood cells from one dome to the next, going to his love in the Bund. The name originates from Persia, a locale so exotic as to be alien in this modern day on another planet, where humanity has become the freaks in the night of their own imaginings, the things our ancient selves made stories about as warnings and portents.

A tail flicks here, a hiss of a forked tongue there. A latticework of light glows beneath skin. Everybody a carnival unto themselves.

There's a checkpoint between domes. There's some nervous shivering at the back of my mind that the knock on my ID will reveal him hunkered down in my hemispheres, frightened of discovery. This is another reason he hacked my brain. My face in the patrol's databanks is nondescript enough. Average citizens can float from one place to the other, but he's not an average citizen. In the clog of corridor traffic, hands in my pockets, I watch the people ahead of me slowly pass over the border one at a time, in six different streams. There's no visible scan, it's all in the head, the division of domes separated by uniforms and guns.

I've done this a dozen times and for those moments, as I step up, the buzzing in the back of my head goes silent.

The knock to my muse rings back a confirmation code. I'm not some illegal morph meant for the mines. I've been here all my life, beneath society's heel.

The patrol waves me on and with eyes to the ground, I go.

<Good.>

I don't answer. Soon the river glistens on my right, the buildings along its bank like giant dollhouses lit from within. Almost incandescent in the night and just as untouchable as any light source in the vacuum of space. I've never set foot in those edifices, the mock-ups of what we once had back on Earth—when the world took its own beauty for granted, just like all beautiful things tend to do.

Chames and I used to come here just to sit on the riverbank and gaze at the glow captured in the water. We pretended it was a portal to a better world, as if such a thing existed even in imagination. Dive in and you'd be caught in all of that light, be able to swim through the Gothic windows to some palatial interior fit for a faerie court. Half neon and half damask. On the streets in this other world, instead of corporate billboards, there'd be art deco declarations of poetry. Clean lines of inspiration about the human soul, possibly from Shakespeare but we'd settle for Dickinson. Plath, even. We wouldn't get too romantic.

Everything at our fingertips if we just reached down and trailed our hands in the river.

<Wait here.>

Just here? Beneath a lamp post and in sight of a clock tower that nobody looks at because we've all got the time stamped into our brains. The light above me diffuses down in a mist of white and I take a step to the side so it can no longer touch me. Better to be embraced by darkness.

People stroll here, a different kind from what I know on the other side of my Shanghai. Families, tourists, jobbing individuals all moving past my sight, making the sound of crickets at high decibel. Those girls with their arms linked, that child skipping behind its parents with a light lance, bisecting the shadows with amber and radiation green. The umbrellas carried by maidens and men the size of mastiffs act as fashion, not necessity. It's not raining here.

One white umbrella twirls as the person moves by, obscuring everything from the waist up. All I see are narrow legs in blood-red stockings and flat shoes of the same color.

She spins to me in a half-step, like she's in a dance all by herself, and I see the halo of her vermilion hair and the glow of her quartz purple eyes.

<Myria!>

I let him propel me forward. I want to go anyway. This beauty with all of her love intact, the way he remembers it.

We move toward each other like opposing charges in the same atom. All of Mars becomes hidden behind the white circumference of her umbrella. Everything crackles: her eyes, the ends of her hair, the sound of my hands pulling from my pockets. The voice at the back of my skull calling her name, ready to be re-united, turned on by the prospect of connection.

I snap her neck easily between my hands and continue the motion of it, sending her into the river.

The umbrella dances into the air. I catch the stem of it and twirl it at my back, striding away.

The roar in my head.

The roar.

It does not stop.

—

He keeps asking why I did it. This incessant why, why, why. Like there's been some egregious misstep when he was the one that stepped into *me*.

It's raining again in Little Shanghai, on my stroll, the water rolling down walls and guttering at the edges. I don't mind the false rain even if it turns the corners ragged and makes stain on my ceiling, like some god somewhere is pissing in defiance of gravity.

On this mattress, in this room years ago, I cradled Chames's bleeding head. He got between me and an angry man, and I couldn't shut up. I did it.

Life's cheap now, or maybe it always has been if you're a never-had. What's the meaning of life anymore? Mobility? Sentience? Some narrow definition of intelligence? Reproduction no longer counts when you can ditto yourself into oblivion and cut out the parts that don't matter anymore. When fifty-percent of you is made up of artificial components and the other fifty is negotiable, transient, or worse yet, out of date, what does one life matter?

Maybe she's somewhere saved but I won't go looking. I know he'll never stop. We all need our missions, some purpose to survive. Maybe that's all life is now when betterment gets you nowhere.

Every day now, on the stroll, I feel his impatience like a mote. The blockade lets him speak but he's tied down by grief. No amount of training prepared him for this. Love is the ultimate weapon. He endures the kind I get when they walk up on my lean. When he can see the way eyes partition me like his psychosurgeon partitioned us, and together we roll into rooms and unfold our bodies to the greed.

<I don't want to anymore.>

But that doesn't matter.

<I'm going to make you stop.>

But it never does.

<Why won't you let me go?>

Because to them there's always a way. Some technology, a backup, some answer written in the mesh, so much meaning in something intangible.

Maybe we've always put our faith in things we can't touch, and they ruin us. Traded one savior for another.

The only difference is one bled for us—and now we just bleed each other.

AUTHORS

Madeline Ashby is a science fiction writer and futurist living in Toronto. She is the author of the *Machine Dynasty* books from Angry Robot Books and the forthcoming novel *Company Town* from Tor Books. She has also developed science fiction prototypes for Intel Labs, the Institute for the Future, SciFutures, Nesta, the Atlantic Council, and others. You can find her at madelineashby.com or on Twitter @MadelineAshby.

Rob Boyle is a tabletop game developer, editor, and writer, best known for his award-winning work on *Shadowrun* and *Eclipse Phase*. He has held a life-long interest in anarchism, anti-fascism, and hacktivism, and is particularly interested in how they intersect with science fiction, transhumanism, and the future of our species. He can be found playing dodgeball, DJing industrial music, training in modern arnis, and posting as @infomorph on Twitter.

Davidson Cole is a writer and film-maker currently residing in Los Angeles. His films have played prestigious film festivals worldwide, including Sundance and Revelation Perth. He is the co-creator of the tabletop card game *Verminopolis.*
Find him on the web: davidsoncole.com, lampcofilms.com, and hwoodmotionpic.com

Nathaniel Dean is a lifelong sci-fi and fantasy reader with a late-blooming love of existential horror. Hopefully radical life extension will give him the chance to confront his interests personally, but until then he explores them through his writing and work on game development for *Eclipse Phase* and *Clockwork: Dominion*. This is all encouraged by his incredible wife, Sarah, and wholly unacknowledged by his two cats, Artemis and The Senator.

Jaym Gates is an editor, author, and communications person, with past clients ranging from the Science Fiction and Fantasy Writers of America to Uplift Aeronautics. Her anthologies include *War Stories, Upside Down, Broken Time Blues, Geek Love,* and tie-in anthologies for *Exalted* and *Vampire: the Masquerade*. Her fiction can be found in *Kaiju Rising, Heroes!,* and *Triumph After Tragedy*. For more information, please see jaymgates.com, or follow her on Twitter as @JaymGates.

Jack Graham is a writer, UX designer, and unlicensed futurist. An alumnus of the Clarion West writer's workshop (2010), he writes science fiction stories about some or all of the following: artificial intelligence, consciousness, memes, politics, relationships, sex, and societal evolution. He tweets at @JackGraham and @FakeTSR

Georgina Kamsika is a speculative fiction writer born in England to Anglo-Indian parents. She has spent most of her life explaining her English first name, Polish surname, and South Asian features. When she's not busy writing or walking her dogs, she can be found lurking on Twitter as @thessilian.

Ken Liu (http://kenliu.name) is an author and translator of speculative fiction, as well as a lawyer and programmer. A winner of the Nebula, Hugo, and World Fantasy Awards, he has been published in *The Magazine of Fantasy & Science Fiction, Asimov's, Analog, Clarkesworld, Lightspeed,* and *Strange Horizons,* among other places. He also translated the Hugo-winning novel, *The Three-Body Problem,* by Liu Cixin, which is the first translated novel to win that award.

Ken's debut novel, *The Grace of Kings,* the first in a silkpunk epic fantasy series, was published by Saga Press in April 2015. Saga will also publish a collection of his short stories, *The Paper Menagerie and Other Stories,* in March 2016. He lives with his family near Boston, Massachusetts.

Karin Lowachee was born in South America, grew up in Canada, and worked in the Arctic. Her books, beginning with her first novel, *Warchild,* have been translated into French, Hebrew, and Japanese, and her short stories have appeared in anthologies edited by Ann VanderMeer, Nalo Hopkinson, and John Joseph Adams. Follow her on Twitter @karinlow.

When **Kim May** isn't writing she's cursing the fact that singing vampires can only find work in German musical theater. Kim is also the event coordinator for an independent bookstore in Salem, Oregon. You can find out more about her and her writing at ninjakeyboard.blogspot.com and on *The Fictorians.*

Steven Mohan, Jr. has sold stories to *Interzone, Polyphony, Paradox, On Spec,* and several DAW and Fiction River original anthologies. His short fiction has also won honorable mention in *The Year's Best Science Fiction* and *The Year's Best Fantasy and Horror* and he's a past nominee for the Pushcart Prize. He lives in Colorado.

Andrew Penn Romine is a veteran VFX and animation artist who enjoys finding great places to eat and drink. He does not recommend dining at the restaurant featured in his story. For other recommendations and occasional cocktail philosophies, you can find him at andrewpennromine.com or @inkgorilla on Twitter.

Editor-in-chief at Paizo Inc. and co-creator of the *Pathfinder Roleplaying Game,* **F. Wesley Schneider** is the author of dozens of creepy *Pathfinder* and *Dungeons & Dragons* adventures and accessories. His novel, *Pathfinder Tales: Bloodbound,* and novella, *Guilty Blood,* are both available now. You can find more from him on Twitter at @FWesSchneider and at wesschneider.com.

Tiffany Trent is the award-winning author of the YA steampunk novels *The Unnaturalists* and *The Tinker King* (Simon & Schuster Books for Young Readers) and the dark fantasy historical *Hallowmere* series (Mirrorstone). She has published numerous short stories in *Corsets & Clockwork, Subterranean,* and *Wicked Impropriety,* among others. She also writes nonfiction essays and articles about science and the environment. Find her at tiffanytrent.com and @tiffanytrent on Twitter.

Fran Wilde can tie the sailors' knot board, set gemstones, and program digital minions. Her first novel, *Updraft,* debuted from Tor/Macmillan in 2015. Her stories have appeared in publications including *Asimov's, Beneath Ceaseless Skies, Nature,* and *Tor.com.* Her interview series Cooking the Books—about the intersection between food and fiction—has appeared at *Strange Horizons, Tor.com,* and on her blog at franwilde.net. You can find her on Twitter @fran_wilde and Facebook @franwildewrites.

AFTER THE FALL

Editor: Jaym Gates
Eclipse Phase Continuity: Rob Boyle, Jack Graham
Production: Adam Jury
Cover Art: Stephan Martiniere
Posthuman Studios is:
Rob Boyle, Brian Cross, Jack Graham, and Adam Jury.

First Printing (January 2016), by Posthuman Studios
ISBN-13: 978-0-9845835-9-1

Contact us at info@posthumanstudios.com,
via eclipsephase.com & posthumanstudios.com,
or search your favorite social network for:
"Eclipse Phase" or "Posthuman Studios"

Printed in the USA